Herald
of the Flame

Sylvia Engdahl

✳ *Ad* ✳
Stellae

Eugene, Oregon

Book design and layout by Sylvia Engdahl
Cover art © by 1971yes / Dreamstime

ISBN-13:   979-8-9858532-1-6

FROM THE REVIEWS OF
THE CAPTAIN OF *ESTEL* TRILOGY

Book One: *Defender of the Flame*

"This book reaches back to the brio and speculation of Engdahl's classic books of the Seventies... The reader will be taken on an exciting and suspenseful ride... With an admirable protagonist and many interesting and well-drawn characters major and minor, *Defender* is satisfying on multiple levels... I expected to like this book; I was startled that I loved it. A must read."
—Nicholas Birns, author of *Understanding Anthony Powell*

Book Two: *Herald of the Flame*

"A futuristic ride that has many parallels in today's society. This is a 'thinking man's' science fiction book—the type we need more of today!"
—*The Feathered Quill*

"These novels are not so much genre 'Romance' or even just 'Science Fiction' as they are Literature. These are novels about life."
—Jacqueline Lichtenberg, *Alien Romances Reviews 14*

Book Three: *Envoy of the Flame*

"This engrossing book explores the powers of mind (psi), alien contact, and a little romance, all with an optimistic view of humanity's future. A very good read!"
—Amazon Vine Voice reviewer

BOOKS BY SYLVIA ENGDAHL

NOVELS FOR TEENS
Enchantress from the Stars
The Far Side of Evil
Journey Between Worlds

CHILDREN OF THE STAR TRILOGY
(FOR TEENS AND ADULTS)
This Star Shall Abide
(UK title *Heritage of the Star*)
Beyond the Tomorrow Mountains
The Doors of the Universe

THE FOUNDERS OF MACLAIRN DUOLOGY
(FOR ADULTS)
Stewards of the Flame
Promise of the Flame

THE CAPTAIN OF ESTEL TRILOGY
(FOR ADULTS)
Defender of the Flame
Herald of the Flame
Envoy of the Flame

NONFICTION
*The Planet-Girded Suns: The Long History
of Belief in Exoplanets*

COLLECTED ESSAYS
*Reflections on Enchantress from the Stars
and Other Essays*
From This Green Earth: Essays on Looking Outward
The Future of Being Human and Other Essays

Contents

Preface

This is one of five novels—the Founders of Maclairn duology and the Captain of *Estel* trilogy—that are tied together by the concept of a flame as the symbol of the evolving "paranormal" powers of the mind and by their setting in an imaginary future in which those powers are devel-oped first by a small group of people, and later by their successors' influence on human civilization. It is the second book of the trilogy and is complete in itself, although the first, *Defender of the Flame,* should be read before this one for fuller understanding of the hero's past experiences.

Though the duology is set two centuries earlier than the trilogy it is not necessary to start with it, and they are quite different in many respects. The trilogy does not deal with the controversial dystopian view of healthcare on which the first "Flame" novel, *Stewards of the Flame,*is focused. This is a faster-moving story about a starship captain destined to play a significant role in human history, and for that reason some science fiction readers find it more to their taste. It is also of special interest to adults and older teens who have enjoyed my Young Adult novels *Enchantress from the Stars* and *The Far Side of Evil* because it involves the interstellar Anthropological Service that appears in those books.

Each of the "Flame" novels can stand alone. When I wrote them, one at a time, I had no intention of writing another; the idea for the succeeding story didn't come to me until months, or years, later. They can be read in any order, except that each includes enough backstory to affect the suspense of the preceding one. Please note that unlike my earlier books these are adult novels and contain some material inappropriate for readers below high school age.

Sylvia Engdahl, June 2021

A major way of dealing with the fear of Psi is to deny that Psi exists. After all, if there is no Psi, there is nothing to be afraid of, so one has no fear to acknowledge. . . . The vehement denial of the existence of Psi, as in the case of some pseudo-critics whose behavior suggests they are protecting their 'faith' against heresy, strongly suggests that fear of Psi is quite strong in them at an unconscious level.

—Charles T. Tart, "Acknowledging and
Dealing with the Fear of Psi," 1984

Real psychic effects lurking in the dark boundaries between mind and matter are so frightening and disorienting that defense mechanisms immediately snap into place to protect our psyches from these disturbing thoughts. We become blind to personal psychic episodes and to the supportive scientific evidence, we conveniently forget mind-shattering synchronicities, and if the intensity of the mysterium tremendum becomes too hot, we angrily deny any interest in the topic while backing away and vigorously making the sign of the cross. Within science this sort of behavior is understandable; science doesn't like what it can't explain because it makes scientists feel stupid. But the same resistance is also endemic in comparative religion scholarship, which is supposed to be the discipline that studies the sacred.

—Dean Radin, *Supernormal*, 2013

Prologue

WHEN THE ELDERS' small lander disappeared into the perpetually gray sky of sunless Ciencia, Terry Steward, né Terry Radnor, turned toward the deserted forest he was about to cross for the second and last time. Before, abandoned here years ago, he had been numb with despair. Now he was numb with shock. It had all happened so fast: the unexpected removal from Ciencia's prison, intended by his guard to last mere hours; the joy of getting back into space; the miraculous opportunity not just to pilot a starship again but to reach the world to which he'd been told he could never return—and then the discovery that his passengers were terrorists. That he could not reach Maclairn after all, but must crash his ship elsewhere to prevent them from destroying the secret colony on that world.

He had nearly died in the crash. He was barely convinced that he hadn't, for the events since then still seemed unreal. Much more had been restored to him than the life he'd been resigned to losing. He had gained permanent release not merely from prison but from Ciencia itself, after twelve long years of exile here. And incredibly, the once-imaginary starship *Estel,* in which he'd led Ciencian dissidents to believe, now existed, and it was his. He was free to take it anywhere—almost anywhere—he chose to go.

The ship was waiting for him in high orbit, guarded by the Elders, the aliens of whose presence in the galaxy he alone knew. They had rescued him from the crash site and restored him to life. Not quite the life they'd previously taken from him—not the world he thought of as home, or the wife with whom there could be no reunion, or the son he had never seen. Not his once-promising career as a Fleet officer. But his youthful dream of exploring the stars would come true. He had *Estel*. And soon, he hoped, he would have Alison.

Only for Alison had he come back to Ciencia, a world he had hated with good reason. Now, striding through the frigid snow-covered forest toward the planet's single city, he thought again of how blind he had been not to recognize his love for her. He had lived in the spare room of her apartment for more than half the span of his exile, unaware that he wanted more than her friendship. He had gone on mourning the forced separation from his wife Kathryn, although he knew underneath that Kathryn, believing herself a widow, would have moved on. Not until he was dying had he allowed himself to feel what he might otherwise have felt for Alison long before. She had loved him; he had grasped that the day they parted, having repressed it till then despite his telepathic ability. She would still be grieving for him, and would be stunned by his appearing suddenly, in disguise, when she thought he'd been locked up forever. Would she want to leave her world to spend the rest of her life as a nomad?

Terry was not sure. He knew only that it was worth the risk of returning, escaped convict though he was under Ciencian law, to find out.

It took nearly two days of trudging through the dim frozen wilderness to reach the city, guided only by the GPS of his phone. Having done it before, Terry knew what to expect—tall closely-planted evergreens, snow, and glacial cold he could not have endured were it not for the mind training that gave him voluntary control of his body temperature. There were no seasons on Ciencia, just permanent unbroken cloud cover. The trees survived without sun only because they were genetically engineered; they were grown for lumber. No one would come into the forest until it was time to harvest them, which was why the Elders, whose ship couldn't be shielded from sight when near the ground, had been able to land there; they could not risk being seen.

It would be harmful to humankind for the alien observers' existence to become known—they had convinced him of that, though at first he had believed it only because to deny it would be to say that his involuntary confinement to the isolated colony world Ciencia was pointless. Now he was trusted to keep their secret, on condition that he stay away from Maclairn's emissaries and anyone else who'd been connected to him before his exile.

He had resolved to put the past behind him. For the first time in twelve years he could look forward instead of back, Terry thought as he spread his sleeping bag to make camp. During all the time he had served as an underground leader, hacking the Net to insert smuggled literature the citizens of science-obsessed Ciencia were forbidden to read, he'd had no expectation of any happiness. He had thought only of his wish to escape from this planet, insofar as he'd allowed himself to think of anything besides the work. Now he was emerging from numbness into excitement he hadn't felt since youth.

He had a mission now, a commitment to become to others what his supporters on Ciencia believed the elusive Captain of *Estel* to be. "Estel" meant hope, and he had kindled hope on this world, hope of ending the repression of knowledge under which its inhabitants lived. He'd been told that the name had become a slogan, even the name of a political party—that people had demonstrated outside the prison to demand his release. Sometimes, through the psi capability with which he was gifted, he had seen them. It occurred to him that while here he would have to hide from his followers as well as from the authorities, for they'd begun to idolize him, all the more because they now knew him to be the healer who, as a partner in Alison Willard's neurofeedback clinic, had often relieved clients' pain. That was a status he had never wanted, but—in addition to its value as a cover for his subversive activities—the use of his psi gifts and mind training to help others had been, and still was, a responsibility he could not reject.

It wasn't his chief responsibility, however. Above all, he was committed to spreading public acceptance of the potential powers of the human mind: psi powers and the others in which he had been trained that led to voluntary control of the body's response to stress. This had been Maclairn's goal since its founding over two hundred years ago, though actively pursued—with extreme secrecy by emissaries on Earth called mentors—only since the colony's relatively recent discovery by representatives of the League. The Maclairnans were aware that acquisition of these powers was an essential step in human evolution. Only Terry knew its full significance.

He knew because the Elders had told him when, mistakenly, they had allowed him to catch sight of their starship. They had not meant him any harm, but once he'd learned of their existence they were forced to ensure that he could not reveal it. Humankind was destined to join their Federation, they said—but only after psi powers had been independently gained, or at least desired, by a significant percentage of Earth's population. Until then, knowledge that more advanced species exist would quench humans' will to reach that level on their own. They would remain unable to meet those species as equals. Yet Earth's civilization was dying, and the colonies were too small to preserve it; if advanced mind-powers weren't developed soon the human race might never become mature enough for Federation membership. It might even revert past hope of an eventual renaissance.

Knowing that Maclairn alone was capable of spearheading the widespread acceptance of such powers, the

Elders secretly guarded it insofar as that was possible; but the main responsibility for its safety fell on the League's security force, the Unified Colonial Fleet. For Maclairn had enemies and, Terry thought grimly, the two terrorists he had killed would not be the last of them. No longer a Fleet officer, he couldn't play a direct part in its defense. All he could do was convince as many people as possible that new faculties of the mind should be sought rather than feared and suppressed. He had done so on Ciencia instinctively, having nothing but his hacking activity to keep him sane. Elsewhere he would do it with enthusiasm—assuming, of course, that he succeeded in escaping from this world again.

Part One: Ciencia

~ 1 ~

THERE WAS NO way of telling time by sight on Ciencia, where neither the sun or the stars ever appeared, and Terry hadn't bothered to check the clock on the phone he'd been given. He made camp only when it got too dark to see his way. It had been less than six hours since he'd landed and he wasn't yet tired or hungry, though he forced himself to eat some energy bars. He scarcely noticed his dislike of them; his mind was too full of his plan for future action.

It was a perilous plan. Was it right to ask Alison to take part in it? She wouldn't hesitate; if she wanted to come with him, danger wouldn't hold her back. She was a reserved, dignified woman, a psychotherapist admired for her quiet poise—hardly someone who seemed likely to defy the law. Yet she had risked arrest daily once involved in the dissemination of illicit texts. Though the choice to leave Ciencia would be hers, he couldn't pretend that he wouldn't be responsible for putting her at greater risk.

Yet he'd also be responsible for the sorrow she would feel if he went away. So there was really no decision for him to make. He was here, and in one more day he would see her, and that thought was so energizing that he had little desire for sleep.

Aware that fatigue would hinder him in the morning he did sleep, however, dropping off at will through the use of his mind training. As always when stressed, he dreamed of Maclairn—not with the desperate longing of the past years, but with a nostalgia marked more by inspiration than by pain. Maclairn was a memory he would always cherish, but it was behind him now, a foundation for his vision of the future.

Dreaming, he experienced again the psi ritual through which he had become a Steward of the Flame, pledged forever to the support of Maclairn's ideals and aims; unhesitatingly he reached out to the torch, thrusting his hand into fire, and was not burned. It had been the high point of his life, and it no longer mattered that it had been followed almost immediately by the lowest point. The elation it had produced was back, unsullied by the passage of years.

As he woke in the murky Ciencian dawn, he fingered the small copper pin, flame-shaped, that from now on he'd be able to wear at least in private. Insignia of the Stewards, it symbolized the future widespread empowerment of the human mind. It had been given to him during the Ritual; he had swallowed it when the Elders took his clothes from him. They had retrieved it while he was unconscious during the physical alteration of his identity. When they rescued him after the crash they had given it back, saying he had proved himself still a Steward; and he had chosen that as his adopted surname, a choice that could be explained only to a trusted few.

As quickly as possible Terry heated snow for water to fill his canteen, grateful for the battery-powered pot with which he'd been provided, and ate more energy bars. He had no intention of stopping again until he reached the city; though it would be dark before he got there, its skyglow—produced by the lavish use of electricity that enabled its inhabitants to survive the climate—would light his way. It was important that he visit Alison tonight, for the weekend was beginning and if they were to escape together, it must be on a day she wasn't expected to appear at the clinic.

Once inside the city limits, he waited until nearly midnight to proceed. He didn't think he would be recognized, disguised as he was with temporarily darkened skin and hair. But it would be disastrous if a stranger were seen entering her apartment. She might well be watched, considering her past association with him, now that his involvement in underground activity was known to the police.

Would *she* recognize him? Terry wondered. The Elder, Laesara, had said she would recognize his mind-touch even though she wasn't consciously telepathic. That might not happen immediately, but surely she would let him in if he identified himself as a member of the Estelan movement.

Walking through the nearly-deserted streets past Ciencia's tall buildings with their transparent glass-like walls, he thought of the last time he had looked upon them—the day of his trial. The sham trial in which he had been condemned to life in prison, never to see the sky again. He had known the sentence in advance, of course. He had committed the ultimate sin of rendezvous with an orbiting starship, and for that, the government racketeers would not forgive him; their profits from surreptitious offworld trade depended on the public's belief that no contact with starships ever occurred. So he had not doubted that he was seeing the last of the city, which, since he had always despised it, would not have saddened him if the alternative hadn't been worse.

He turned off the main boulevard onto the side street leading to Alison's building. Her front window was dark, but he knew she wouldn't be in bed yet; she had usually read in her room until later than this. He himself had often worked in his own room until dawn.

He entered the familiar vestibule, closing the outer door behind him against the cold, and taking deep breaths, he punched in the code for her comm without activating the vid pickup.

After a long pause, her soft voice came over the speaker, thrilling him with the reality of what he had not quite dared to count on. "Who is it? Why aren't you showing me your face?"

"I'm a friend of the Captain of *Estel*," Terry said. "It's urgent that I see you tonight."

"The Captain of *Estel* has a lot of friends, and also enemies. How do I know which you are?"

She was asking for a password, he realized, and he had no idea what system was in use now; originally the conspiracy had consisted of small cells and passwords hadn't been needed for identification. He, however, had maintained the master file of those used for access to the reading material in the cloud. He remembered hers; he had given her one from illegally-acquired classic mythology. "Only a friend would know where to find the goddess Athena," he replied.

Telepathically, he felt her astonishment and projected reassurance he hoped she would sense. The door opened a crack. "No one knows I have that name," she protested. "No one has ever known, except—" Staring at him, she asked, "Are you really his friend—did you see him in prison? Are you bringing a message from him?"

"Alison. You've no need to look at me, just think of him, and hear my voice."

She stepped back, stunned, letting him push through the door. After a long silence she whispered, "Terry? It's impossible, I'm imagining something that can't be true—"

"Do you want it to be true?"

"Too much not to fear that I'm deceiving myself. How could you have escaped and changed even your skin?"

"It's a long story. For now, just let me in, if you're willing to hide me."

"Of course, if it's safe for you." She was trembling. "But won't they search here?"

"Not right away—only one guard knew I escaped, and he won't admit it. But the sooner I'm away from Ciencia, the better."

"Away from this planet? You mean you've got some way to reach a starship again?"

"I've been aboard a starship the past few days," he said, knowing that no brief elaboration would make such a thing easy for her to believe.

"Then in God's name, why did you come back?"

"I came for you," he told her, smiling.

"Oh, Terry." The next thing he knew she was in his arms, her lips meeting his, and for a while neither of them said anything more.

Finally, reluctantly, Alison broke away from the embrace. "We mustn't do this," she protested. "You're in danger here, and I've got to stay strong enough to make you leave. How could I live with myself if you were caught because of me?"

Terry stroked her smooth hair, now released from its usual chignon to flow over her shoulders; she had evidently been getting ready for bed. "I'm not going to be caught tonight," he said. "But it's true that we've got to make plans. And could you heat up some soup or something? I've been out in the cold for two days, and I haven't eaten since dawn."

He sat down at the kitchen table where they'd shared meals for so long, and Alison brought him hearty chicken soup and some fresh bread. He had not tasted anything like it since the night he left her; both prison food and the Elders' concentrated rations had been unpalatable.

"I've kept your room just as it was," she told him. "I couldn't bear to give your things away."

"Do you want me to sleep in it?"

"No," she said. "Not unless you'd rather."

"I wouldn't, not anymore," he said with feeling. "I had

a long time to think about what a fool I was. I've always loved you, Alison, but I didn't let myself know it until I believed it was too late for us."

"Because of Kathryn."

"That and . . . other things. I'll tell you someday. Right now, though, getting away from this world has priority."

She nodded. "You've got to go—but I thought I'd never see you again, and now, to be together for only a little while—"

Terry drew breath. "I want you to come with me, Alison."

"Offworld? Is that possible?"

"Yes, if you don't mind leaving Ciencia for good."

"You know I don't. I've hated it here since I first read about worlds that are better, and even if they weren't—" She broke off, embarrassed, and asked quickly, "Have you a way to get back to the starship you were on?"

"I'm hoping Jon Darrow will take us."

"He will if he can. He agonizes over your having lost your freedom by protecting his."

"You've seen him, then."

"Yes, quite often. He's an active Estelan—he says that after what you did for him, he owes you that, though I'm sure it's not his only reason for risking himself."

"Do you know if he's onworld now?" This was what Terry had worried most about; Darrow was an asteroid miner and spent much of his time in space.

"Today he was, though he's planning to go out again soon."

"Thank God—I've been afraid there might be a long wait. Call him, Alison—ask him to come over here the first thing in the morning. But don't say why."

"If I did he'd think I'd lost my mind. I'll just say it's an Estelan thing, an emergency."

An emergency it surely was, Terry thought. He had not been aware until he formed his plan just how much it would depend on Darrow.

~ *2* ~

WHILE ALISON MADE the call Terry got out of his heavy camping clothes, took a hot shower, and put on the casual pants he found in the closet that had once been his. On second thought, he added a shirt; she would be puzzled by his uniformly darkened skin. It was actually somewhat closer to its original color than the pale near-albino shade to which the Elders had changed it when they first sent him here; Ciencians not genetically dark-skinned were whiter than people on other worlds because they were never exposed to sunlight. His temporary deep tan coloring would fade, but it would be hard to explain how he'd acquired it; so for now, best to show it only in darkness.

He shivered with eager anticipation mixed with apprehension. It had been more than twelve years since he'd been with Kathryn, and faithfulness was not the only reason he'd had no relationships since. Nor was it just the paralyzing depression he'd felt over his loss of everything that had mattered to him. His early experiences with sex had been unsatisfying—not for any physical reason, but because his sense of something lacking in mere intercourse was deeply frustrating. Then, during the training that had released his psi capabilities, he'd been informed that this was because he was too psi-gifted to be content with anything less than the merging of minds that occurred during sex between telepaths.

He had not fully understood this until he'd met Kathryn. After their first union, after feeling what it was like to merge totally, the thought of sex with a non-telepath had been repugnant to him, as it was, he'd been told, to everyone who'd once had a telepathic partner. And Alison was only latently telepathic. . . .

He loved her, desired her, but was too honest with himself not to know that he had realized this only after he believed he would never see her again. He had held back out of fear, the fear that it would be like his previous frustrating experiences. That it could never be for him what it had been with Kathryn, and that Alison would sense this and be hurt. He could not bear the thought of their not sharing each other's consciousness while their bodies were joined.

Yet according to his mind-training instructors, sex sometimes awakened latent telepathic ability. Could it do so in a person who'd had no mind training? He'd decided, while dying, that he'd been foolish to doubt that it could. Sex enhanced psi by altering consciousness; like stress, it inhibited rational thinking and let other modes emerge. Both he and Kathryn had been empowered by it in a way that carried over to their separate lives. Surely Alison would be, too. Surely their love for each other would break down all barriers to full bonding. . . .

When he came out of his bedroom the door to hers was open, and the warm robe she'd been wearing lay at the foot of the bed. His heart began to pound. As he moved toward her he knew, suddenly, that he must warn her before they went any further, before she was too overwhelmed by feelings to decide freely about her future.

"We've got to talk," he said. "Before you set your heart on coming with me there's something you need to know."

"Not now," she said, turning back the bed covers. "Whatever it is, we can talk about it tomorrow."

"And we will, but it's only fair to inform you before you're in too deep to back away. What I'll be doing from now on will be risky. We may often be on the run."

"From the authorities? I thought they couldn't legally go beyond high orbit."

"They can't—not the Ciencian authorities. But I'm involved in League affairs you don't know about."

"Well, that's no surprise, Terry—you'd have to be, to have contacts that can get you away from here. And I've always known there's some sort of mystery about your past."

"Yes, and that's another problem. There are things I can never tell you, Alison. I'll explain everything relevant to what's ahead of us, but there are secrets I'm bound not to reveal." Not just the existence of the Elders, he thought, but what went on during the Ritual; he'd sworn to keep it from everyone who hadn't been through it. He and Kathryn had shared that experience. It would be hard to stay silent, even telepathically, about events that had affected him profoundly.

Especially since Alison, as a psychotherapist, was used to having people confide in her. "There are pledges I have to honor," he persisted, "and I need you to promise that you won't press me."

"Of course, if it's a matter of what you've promised others—not just fearing that I wouldn't understand some sort of trouble you've been in."

"You *would* understand, and that's what makes it hard. But I can't break my word, no matter how much I trust you not to tell anyone else."

"I won't ask you to." Smiling, to lighten his mood, she added, "What woman wouldn't want to be carried off by a handsome man with a mysterious hidden identity like the superheroes in the fantasy fiction we hid on the Net?" Then, as he recoiled, she said, "I'm sorry, Terry—I know you don't like having people think you're a superman when they find you can relieve their pain."

"I've got paranormal abilities besides healing," he confessed, "and I will tell you about those. You—you may develop some of them, though there won't be a chance for you to get the special training I've had."

Would she really become consciously telepathic? Terry wondered as he undressed. What if their minds did merge and she perceived his knowledge of the Elders? It wouldn't matter; she wouldn't take thoughts about aliens seriously. Unlike the mentors, who were highly trained and accustomed to grasping people's inner thoughts, she would dismiss them as fantasy inspired by science fiction—as would others on every world, even if psi-gifted. Laesara had never told him to avoid contact with anyone but mentors, apart from Kathryn, who was in close touch with mentors; after all, there must be latent telepaths on Ciencia and in other colonies as well as on Earth. If a few did perceive the truth of what he knew, they in turn would be disbelieved.

"Come to bed," Alison said, turning off the light. She had slipped out of her nightclothes and her body was warm and welcoming. He caressed it gently, aware that since she would not share his arousal telepathically as Kathryn had, she would expect foreplay. He was not exactly sure what she would expect. With chagrin, he realized that he did not know how to please a woman whose sensations he couldn't feel.

"Alison," he murmured, "it's been a long time for me—"

"For me, too," she whispered. "There's been no one since I got to know you. I didn't want anyone else." Sensing his hesitancy but misunderstanding its cause, she added, "Don't worry if things don't—go right at first. Just being with you is enough."

He pressed close to her, at first tentatively and then with passion. Suddenly, the pent-up passion of years blazed through him and he lost all consciousness of doubt. He did not stop to wonder whether it was telepathy that told him her yearning matched his; he simply moved as instinct led him to move, driven by mounting ecstasy. They coupled joyously, not caring what was past or what was to come.

Afterward, as she slept in his arms, he was aware that their minds had indeed been joined. Though neither their thoughts nor their bodily sensations had been indistinguishable from each other's, at the height of arousal there had been a connection that was more than physical. And he knew it existed because their emotions were intense and their love was firmly founded. This was what had been missing in his long-ago youthful encounters, not his partners' lack of psi capability. Everyone was latently telepathic, as he had been told many times. He had not fully grasped what that meant.

Psi wasn't something that set those who were trained or exceptionally gifted apart from those who weren't. It was a continuum. The goal to which he was pledged concerned not just humankind's future, but the recognition of every living person's existing capability. He had known this was true in the political sense; since it implied that people couldn't be ruled by authority, it was why Ciencia banned unscientific ideas and Maclairn's enemies in the League government feared the spread of new mind faculties. Now he saw its wider significance.

It would not be enough to offer hope for enhanced human mind-powers in a time to come. He must make people believe that time had already arrived.

~ *3* ~

TERRY WAS AWAKENED by Jonathan Darrow's voice at the door. Alison was already up and hurried to let him in. "This better be important," Terry heard Jon say. "I'd planned to go out again today, and I'm meeting a cargo courier at noon—" He broke off, scowling, as Terry emerged from the bedroom. "What's this? God, Alison, you know better than to set up a face-to-face meeting with a newbie."

"I'm not exactly a newbie, Darrow," Terry said. "Or rather, Jon—it's time we stopped calling each other by surnames like mining crews do, considering that we were close friends for years." It had been an unlikely friendship; Jon Darrow, a hardened miner and smuggler, was older than Terry by at least fifteen years, which meant he was now in his early fifties with hair beginning to gray. Their only similarities lay in the fact that they both loved space flight, were both loners by nature, and were both deeply opposed to the repressive isolationist policies of Ciencia's government.

"I had only one close friend," Jon declared. "Whoever you are, I don't remember you, and if you've lied to Alison to get to me, you'll regret it."

Jon had to be careful, Terry realized, not only because of his involvement in the Estelan conspiracy but because his smuggling activity, though encouraged by the government racketeers who had forced him into it, would land him in prison if exposed. "You remember my voice," he said quietly, "and you remember what I told you about having once been in Fleet."

Stunned, Jon burst out, "He never told anyone else that, at least he said he hadn't, and he didn't mention it at the trial . . . oh, my God. Rivera? Terry? They let you go?"

"Not officially. And I'm not supposed to be on Ciencia, which is why I'm disguised. By the way, Rivera was never my real name. I was born Terry Radnor, but even that's not mine anymore. According to the League files linked to my new ID chip I'm Terry Steward, the Captain of *Estel*."

"I don't know why I'm surprised," Jon said, taking off his flight jacket and the black skullcap he always wore outdoors. "You were a mystery to me even before you told me incredible things about your past—bolder and brighter than anyone I'd ever worked with, in spite of never seeming quite connected to real life. And then when you spoke out at your trial, there was something almost supernatural about it, about the way people took it in, and started agitating for the things you said they should. Most of them still believe the fantasy you made up about a ship called *Estel* you claimed to be captain of. You're sticking to that story?"

"It's not fantasy anymore," Terry declared. He had told Alison this during the night, but had saved the details for what was bound to be a long and difficult explanation that both of them needed to hear. "I've come into possession of a starship, and I've named it *Estel*, naturally. It's waiting for me in high orbit."

Jon stared at him. "Now you're further out of touch with reality than ever. What did they give you in that prison—drugs?"

"None that could damage my mind. The ship's real, and I own it legally. I'll tell you how it happened, but it's complicated, and we haven't much time if you're set to take off today. We've got to act fast—that is, if you're willing to get involved."

Slowly, Jon said, "You don't have to ask. I've not forgotten how you invited arrest to keep me out of prison, and anything I can do for you, I will. If there's a ship in orbit waiting for you, I suppose you need transport to it, and it goes without saying that I'll take you in *Bonanza*."

"I want more than that from you," Terry told him. "I want you to come along as copilot."

"Of a starship?" Jon gaped in astonishment. "There's nothing I'd like better, as I'm sure you know. But I'm not qualified to pilot a hyperdrive ship. I've never been further out than the asteroids, just like everyone else born on this world."

"You can fly the shuttle, and you can learn to fly *Estel* in normal space easily enough. I'll handle the jumps, of course, but since I'm not willing to leave my ship unguarded, Alison and I can't ever visit a planet's surface without someone to stay aboard."

"Alison's coming, too?"

"I am," she told him. "Terry and I are—together. For good."

"Well, I always did suspect you were more to each other than business partners."

"We weren't, then, except for feelings we didn't let show," Terry said. "We are now; she's the reason I left *Estel* to come back here. But I'm not coming again. If you join us you won't be able to return, though I don't expect you'll see that as a disadvantage."

"God, no! All my life I've wanted to escape this hellhole, and since you told me how different things are everywhere else, I've felt more trapped than ever—not to mention how I hate being a slave of the racketeers who keep me just one step away from life imprisonment."

"That's what I figured. But you've got to understand—both of you—that there'll be risk, not just in getting away but for the rest of our lives."

"I thought you said you own the ship legally."

"I do. And so," Terry announced, "I'm going into the smuggling business to earn the money to keep it operating. Which is the other thing I need you for, Jon—your experience in negotiating with interstellar smugglers. I propose a fifty-fifty split of the proceeds after expenses."

"That's more than generous," Jon said, settling himself at the table beside Alison. "I heard from the captain of *Freerunner* that when you sold him the stash of rare metals I'd held back from the government, you were a pretty good negotiator yourself."

"I'm new at it, though, and I don't know anything about acquiring cargo." Terry pulled up another chair and sat facing them, adding, "When I was a courier for you, I didn't ask for details about what I was carrying."

Alison said, "I'm not against smuggling, but isn't it illegal everywhere, not just here where the government bans contact with starships?"

"Yes," Terry admitted. "We'll be outlaws, subject to arrest by Fleet, among other things. But it's not unethical, not if we don't deal in weapons or stolen goods. It took me a while to realize that after the years I spent in Fleet, but Jon convinced me that people have a right to buy and sell without government interference."

Jon frowned. "You're overlooking a big problem," he said. "It's one thing for local miners to sell ore to the interstellar traders and offer them contraband goods on the side. But the traders' ships carry crews to defend their cargo. There are plenty of pirates in deep space who'll try to get their hands on it, or so I understand."

"I know that," Terry declared. "They'll assume we do have a crew—they won't attack as long we brazen it out if we're challenged."

"What makes you think so? We'll be unarmed—"

"No, we won't. We've got a laser cannon mounted where it can be seen." The Elders had done this for him, agreeing that the appearance of strength was necessary, and had included the necessary permit when they forged the ship's registration.

"My God, Terry! Do you know how to use it?"

"Yes, but I've never had to. The trick is *not* to use it so that they don't find out that we're no match for them. I was captain of a small starship in Fleet, you know. There were just three of us in the crew and we couldn't have won in a fight, but the pirates didn't know that. I've had dealings with some in the past." He did not add that those pirates had wanted the passengers for ransom and therefore could not blast the airlock. With cargo the situation might be different.

"Will we go to Earth?" Alison asked.

"No—that's one of the only two places I *can't* go." He could never again go to Earth because he had promised the Elders to avoid any world where there were mentors who might draw their secret from his mind. Unlike his pledge to stay away from Maclairn, this was not a grief to him; Earth wasn't a pleasant place to be. "We'll just visit colony worlds," he told her.

"I'd like that—traveling, seeing new places, being free instead of confined."

Terry smiled. "I hope so. A ship's confining in its way, but not like this planet where you've never had a look at the stars or even the sun." Sensing her exultation at the prospect, he reminded himself that he hadn't yet told them about the biggest danger they'd be facing, a far more serious threat than pirates. "There's a lot more you need to hear, but first—Jon, you said you're meeting a cargo courier. How much do you have invested in what he's selling you?"

"All I could swing except for some platinum ingots I'm holding for the next starship to show up. I wish I could have bought more from him—he's supplying legitimate pharmaceuticals not affordable on worlds where biochemistry's less advanced. I'm told patients who can't pay what the legal importers demand generally get stuck with counterfeits."

"Are you positive that they're the real thing?"

"Absolutely. I wouldn't touch them if I didn't trust my source; you know how I feel about the drug traffic."

Terry hesitated. It was ironic—Maclairn had been founded by colonists who rejected all medication, and most other medical care, because it was imposed by force on the planet they were escaping. It was the antithesis of their belief that humans aren't machines. But people in other colonies didn't have the mind training the Maclairnans did; in many cases prescription drugs were essential for them.

"What sort of pharmaceuticals are they?" he persisted.

"Antibiotics, antivirals mostly—more versatile than what's produced for specific environments. The biochemists here have developed things nobody else has."

Terry shuddered. He knew that all too well. "Okay," he said. "Drugs to combat infectious disease, or cancer, or anything chronic such as heart problems. But no psychiatric drugs; I won't carry those on my ship."

"Not even those meant for treating mental illness?"

"Mental illness," Terry declared, "has different definitions in different societies, and when real psychosis does exist, drugs do more harm than good. I'd just as soon push cocaine. Can you pick and choose from what he's offering?"

"Sure, if you want me to."

"All right, then. Call him and tell him you've raised more cash. We won't be able to access our funds where we're going, so spend the rest of what you've got, and most of Alison's, too."

"And yours," Alison added. "I still have what your backup hackers put in my name to prevent its being confiscated when you went to prison."

"Great—leave just enough money in your account to make it took as if you hadn't planned to leave. The government knows Jon invests in cargo, but for you to draw out too much would raise questions." He turned back to Jon. "About that platinum—is it hidden aboard your ship?"

"It's not concealed like stash was; I wouldn't dare try that again. The inspector inventoried it when I landed, but as long as I won't be coming back maybe I can risk adding it to what I pay for the pharmaceuticals."

"No," said Terry. "Bring it along; we may need cash before we can arrange a sale. Just transfer our credits."

Jon nodded. "I'll call him now."

"Is this guy totally reliable?" Terry asked.

"Yes. He's an Estelan activist."

"Then when you see him, arrange for him to pick up your personal stuff, and Alison's, before he makes the delivery. Whatever won't fit into his van we'll have to leave behind." Control tower agents would be watching the cargo van cross the field to *Bonanza* while pretending not to know about it, and would be suspicious if it went back for a second load. They might assume that Darrow intended to sell more than he planned to report to the government racketeers.

"How are we going to get onto the ship ourselves?" Alison asked. "If the police see us, and ask questions—"

"You and Terry will have to be disguised as miners," Jon said, "and I'll tell my regular mining crew not to show up. I'll say I'm postponing the trip because of some mechanical glitch."

Terry said, "You realize that you'll have to abandon *Bonanza* in space? You can't transfer ownership to anyone; not only would that give us away, but whoever you left it to would be accused of complicity in our escape."

"Can't be helped," Jon agreed. "And it makes no difference since whoever gets it, either from me or by salvage, will be roped into smuggling for the government just as I was. Much as I love that ship, I don't mind trading it for a berth on a starship. Which reminds me, Terry, I still don't know how you got hold of a starship and why you're so sure it's where you left it. If it's not, we'll be in big trouble."

He was sure because he trusted the Elders to guard it, but he could not tell them that. The time had come when he had to tell them *something*, Terry knew, and he hoped he would not have to lie too much to the only two friends he now had.

~ *4* ~

ALISON FIXED BREAKFAST while Jon called the cargo courier and the mining crew. When they sat down to eat Alison said, "I'm waiting to hear how you got out of prison and into space."

"Well," Terry began, "while I was in there my interrogator was a man named Quaid. We despised each other, I for obvious reasons and he because he was afraid of me, not only on account of the influence I'd had at the trial but because he saw I really was able to turn off pain and bleeding. He'd assumed that my reputation for healing pain at the clinic was a scam, as the prosecutor claimed, and he was horrified by finding out that it wasn't. People like Quaid are scared by evidence that so-called paranormal mind-powers exist.

"He didn't want to believe I was a pilot either, since according to Ciencian records I'd had no training, but as I'd gotten *Bonanza* to *Freerunner* he had to concede that I must be. He laughed at everything else I told him and I amused myself by baiting him. So when people started demonstrating outside the prison gates, demanding my release, he had to find some way to get rid of me without turning me into a martyr. And that fit right in with his own plans. You know, don't you, Jon, that the government racketeers sometimes deal directly with smugglers' starships?"

"I've carried shipments for them without being in on the negotiations," Jon agreed.

"Well, one night Quaid led me out of the prison secretly, drove to the spaceport, and ordered me to shuttle him to a starship he'd arranged to rendezvous with. I figured out that he was selling something valuable his colleagues didn't know about and he didn't want to cut them in, but I thought it was odd that we took no cargo; I knew whatever it was had to be concealed in his clothes. And the starship wasn't one of the smugglers' ships I'd heard of—it was a little charter ship named *Venture*.

"Once we were aboard Quaid disappeared into a stateroom with the only two men in sight, and when they came out the captain showed up and said he wasn't willing to go where they'd told him to because that star had no inhabited planets and he wasn't equipped for an expedition, he didn't even have a crew. He declared they couldn't force him—since starship shuttles aren't allowed to land on Ciencia, if they killed him they'd be stuck in orbit till their life support ran out. So I spoke up and told them I was a pilot and I'd go wherever they liked."

"You mean these guys made Quaid release you to them?"

"He was glad to see the last of me. He'd said he didn't believe I'd ever piloted a jump ship, but I don't think that was true. I'm now convinced he wanted the men to get where they were headed and wanted me to be the one to take them. Anyway, he let *Venture*'s captain fly him down in the shuttle we came in. And the two passengers ordered me to proceed to the uninhabited solar system."

"What a lucky break!" Jon exclaimed. "You've always

managed to pull off things nobody else could—I assume you overpowered them and took the ship."

"It wasn't as simple as that," Terry said. "To explain what happened next I've got to fill in some background." He drew breath. This was the big revelation, the thing he had kept from them through all the years they'd been his friends.

"What I'm about to say is secret," he went on, leaning forward. "I'm sworn three times over never to reveal it, but if you're going with me on *Estel* you have to know. Will you give me your word not to repeat it to anyone?"

Surprised by his intensity, they nodded, and Alison said, "I have a feeling this is what you've been hiding as long as I've known you, the thing that made you so sad."

"Yes, part of it. There is another part I can't reveal under any circumstances, the identity of the group that brought me here. But no harm will be done by filling you in on what I was doing before that, something known to just a few people in the League. When I was a young officer in Fleet, it transformed my life."

They waited expectantly. "There is a world that's not on the charts," Terry continued, "not shown as an inhabited one at least, though it was colonized more than two hundred years ago. And on that world, everyone—the whole population—has the mind faculties in which I've been trained. Its people maintain their health by voluntary control of inner biochemical reactions, and they are able to feel physical pain without suffering. And they also have psi gifts, some greater than mine. Because they're all telepathic there's no misunderstanding among them— no unawareness of each other's feelings—so they get along without having to conform to rules. The name of that planet is Maclairn. It is the world where I lived with Kathryn, and though I can never go there again, I will always think of it as home."

He would, Terry realized with a pang, in spite of the fact that he had resigned himself to permanent absence.

It was the only place he had ever felt any attachment to, and its mark on his heart was indelible. Maclairn, a golden world as seen from space, arid and inhospitable on its surface except for the oases of its few small settlements, yet the focus of everything that had mattered in his life apart from flying. . . .

"Why can't you go there if you have your own starship?" Alison said with sympathy.

"Because of the other secret I know. The strongest telepaths would sense it in my mind, though they wouldn't intentionally pry; it's too fundamental for them not to. Kathryn surely would if we slept together, and then they'd sense it in her mind, too. That's why I was sent here by the people involved, and I don't blame them anymore. At first I was bitter, but now I see that they had no other choice."

"Did you come from Maclairn, then?" Jon asked. "I thought you said once that you were born on Earth."

"I was, but I left when I finished school and joined Fleet. Maclairn wasn't discovered by the League until shortly before I arrived there. At that time I was pulled off explorer duty and given the mind training I've mentioned before, but I wasn't told why. None of us assigned to the project were informed until we were aboard the cruiser enroute to it. Only high officials knew it existed, and Fleet's job was to make sure that no ship got close enough to find out."

"I don't see why it's so secret," Alison protested. "Proof of such capabilities is a wonderful thing that people should rejoice in! Are the authorities trying to profit somehow by keeping a monopoly on the healers' services?"

"No," said Terry. "On the surface, they're trying to protect Maclairn from exploitation. But underneath most of them don't want to believe in psi—it's too upsetting to their premises. They wish no colony where it's normal had ever been found. Think—would most people here on Ciencia, those who agree with the banning of all unscientific literature, want to see evidence that their beliefs about the nature of the human mind are wrong? Our followers are a minority, after all."

"That's true," she admitted. "But I thought that in other places, where the public has access to fantasy and speculation and religion—"

"They have access, but the majority don't take such ideas seriously. They enjoy fiction, but they view speculation as the equivalent and turn religion into mere dogma. Average human beings have a deep, innate fear of any threat to their view of reality. I found that hard to understand, too, until the Maclairnans explained it to me. In the late twenty-first century, when science had begun to establish undeniable evidence of psi, there was a backlash. The so-called paranormal was ridiculed more than ever before and it became taboo to mention the subject, even though it wasn't illegal to read about."

"I suspect that a lot of our recruits seek out forbidden stuff simply because it *is* illegal," Jon said. "I admit that I did, at first. What attracted me to it was just the idea that I should be free to read whatever I wanted."

"Yes. And that's the other factor—governments and other authorities don't like to have people discover the power of their own minds. It makes the public harder to control."

"So they hide the fact that there's a world where such powers are acknowledged, I see that. But you, Terry— why do you go along? I'd think you'd be spreading that secret as widely as possible, speaking out as you did at your trial."

"To make it known," Terry said, "would be dangerous. People often try to destroy what they fear."

"You mean Maclairn would be placed at risk?" Alison questioned.

"Absolutely; that's why a cruiser is needed to guard it. I'll say more about the danger in a minute, but first you need to know the Maclairnans' long-term goal. They intend to pass on their abilities—they believe the next step in human evolution is for everyone to have them. But it has to happen gradually.

"You've heard me talk about the collective unconscious," he went on. "Well, the aim is to spread acceptance of mind-powers slowly, without arousing antagonism, until it's so well established in the collective unconscious of Earth that the majority won't oppose their open use. And there's a plan for doing that." Soberly he added, "It's important, tremendously important, because Earth's civilization is on the verge of collapse and if we don't succeed in arousing hope for a changing future—one where people will have more autonomy—it may be too late to save it."

"And you were involved in the plan?"

"In furthering it, yes. To begin with I was in command of a small ship responsible for placing sensor stations throughout Maclairn's solar system to warn of any intruders. Only one interstellar ship, a privately-owned one named *Promise*, was allowed to come and go. Its role was to take Maclairnan emissaries called mentors to live in Earth's cities and give mind training without revealing where they came from. It also brought small groups of carefully chosen observers to visit Maclairn.

"Kathryn had been a member of the private expedition that discovered Maclairn, and she was its ambassador to the League as well as the guide for the observers. When the civilian crew of *Promise* retired it was decided that Fleet should crew it, so I was promoted and made captain. We traveled back and forth between Maclairn and Earth many times, and I learned first-hand that Maclairn has enemies within the League government who don't hesitate to use violence."

"What kind of violence?" Jon inquired.

"At first, just subtle threats. As I mentioned, I encountered pirates once—not real ones but hired thugs paid to make it look like piracy."

"Good God—what did you do?"

"I did what was necessary to save my passengers," Terry replied, hoping not to be pressed for details. He couldn't say that they had cut off two of his fingers and threatened to go further, since the Elders' full restoration of his hand couldn't be explained.

"Soon after that," he went on, "they murdered one of the mentors by planting a bomb in the building where he worked. And later I learned—from the message you brought me shortly after we met, Jon—that they'd murdered Kathryn's grandfather, who was head of the foundation that owned *Promise*. Both those men were my close friends."

"And so you're looking for revenge."

"Not revenge exactly, but I'm still pledged to defend Maclairn, and the danger has gotten worse, much worse. You'll understand when you hear the rest of what happened to me, but first there's more I've got to explain."

~ 5 ~

THEY LISTENED, FASCINATED, as Terry continued, "I committed myself to Maclairn's goals in a solemn ritual there; I can't tell you the details." Thinking of it, Terry could barely keep back tears. "It involved magnification of psi power, and for a little while afterward I was more sensitive psychically than usual. I had been trained in remote viewing—clairvoyant perception of things at a distance, even on the other side of a planet or in space—and for weeks I'd had a feeling that there was some sort of ship in Maclairn's solar system that the sensors hadn't picked up. The morning after the ceremony the feeling was stronger than ever, and of course I was quite young and reckless then—"

"You've never stopped being reckless," Jon remarked. "You took fantastic chances all the time I knew you, and now you're here again, though you know damn well that if you're caught on this world you'll end up back in the prison you just escaped from."

For a moment Terry sickened, thinking of the dim solitary cell in which he had expected to spend the remaining years of his life. Going back there would be intolerable; he refused to consider such an outcome. Hastily he continued, "I took off alone in a shuttle with exceptional range . . . and I found the intruding ship, or rather, it found me.

"As I've said, its crew had no choice. I knew about them and for their existence to become known to anyone else would—still would—do great harm I'm not free to describe to you, harm not to them but to Earth's society. They couldn't allow that to happen, yet they weren't willing to kill me; so they brought me here to Ciencia from which no one has ever escaped. I never saw Maclairn or Kathryn again."

Alison said sadly, "That's more tragic than anything I imagined—for you to suffer for having tried to protect your world."

"I spent a lot of time cursing fate for the unfairness of it," Terry agreed. "It wasn't just that I'd lost everything I cared about—the worst was thinking I could never serve the cause I was pledged to. It was hell being stuck here instead of taking action to support Maclairn's effort to win acceptance of new mind-powers."

"But Terry," she protested, "you did take action. That's what the whole Estelan conspiracy is about. You risked yourself for years to give such ideas a foothold here, and it's only because you inspired people to read and to talk about them that we have hope of changing Ciencia's laws."

"Yes, I know that now," Terry said. "But at the time I didn't look at it that way. Leading the conspiracy was just a way of keeping occupied when I was barred from my real aims."

"If you thought there was no more to it, you were

wrong," Jon declared. "You were dedicated to spreading subversive ideas right from the start—you lit up like a landing beacon when you talked about them. I always wondered where you got the energy and the nerve to take the risks you did."

"Well, for awhile I felt I had nothing to lose," Terry confessed. "Getting back to what happened aboard *Venture*, the two men who'd chartered it gave me coordinates of the star they were heading for, the one the captain had said didn't have inhabited planets. And I thought maybe I was dreaming the whole crazy episode, that I might be still in prison, drugged so that I couldn't tell fantasy from reality. Because the star they told me to go to was Maclairn's star."

"But that's incredible!" Alison burst out. "It couldn't be coincidence, and yet if Quaid hated you, why would he send you where you wanted to go?"

"That wasn't what he had in mind," Terry said bitterly. "There's no way he could have known I'd come from there, or even that I was aware that it existed. I was just a tool in a scheme I didn't suspect at that point. What I found hard to believe was that I'd come into contact with men who knew that star's location, which was top secret—I knew it myself only because I'd been captain of *Promise*. It all seemed surreal, and if I hadn't been so overcome by the prospect of going home, of maybe seeing Kathryn, I would have tried harder to figure it out. It wasn't till after I'd jumped, when we were halfway through the approach in normal space, that it dawned on me that I was breaking my oath of secrecy by taking strangers there."

"They must already have known about the colony if they were headed for it," Alison pointed out.

"Yes, when I finally thought it through, I realized that Maclairn's enemies in the League government had access to files that contained its coordinates. We'd feared all along that they might send spies; that was the main rea-

son Fleet was patrolling the solar system to turn ships
away. I knew I should have jumped somewhere else even
if they threatened to kill me. But it was too late to do
that, and besides, there were only two men and I thought
they couldn't be carrying anything more dangerous than
sidearms. Fleet would detain them, and I decided it was
just as well I was in control of the ship instead of some
other pilot, because I could disable the hyperdrive in case
they tried to escape."

Jon frowned. "Obviously you didn't. If Fleet let the
ship get away, won't the spies or others like them find
some way to go back?"

"They weren't spies," said Terry grimly. "They turned
out to be terrorists. Do you remember once telling me
that Ciencia's racketeers export biochemical stuff useful
only for warfare?"

"Oh, my God."

"It's a good thing you'd informed me. Because I kept
feeling more and more that something was wrong, something a lot worse than spying, and telepathically I could
sense evil in those men as well as fear. They were expecting death.

"And then my psi faculty kicked in, the kind that had
alerted me to the strange ship's presence long before,
and I saw that beneath their clothes they were wearing
vests full of vials. God only knows what was in them,
but because Ciencian biochemists are more advanced
than those anywhere else, I had to assume it was a
nerve gas or virus that might wipe out the whole colony.
All the pieces fit—League officials surely know Ciencia's
reputation, and I was sure Quaid would be happy to sell
something like that if he was told about the Maclairnans'
mind-powers, even apart from what he must have been
paid."

Jon and Alison were silent, too horrified to comment.

"At first I tried to persuade myself that all I'd have
to do was warn Fleet," Terry went on. "Patrollers had

already challenged us; we'd be taken into custody and even if I couldn't prove my identity, I'd be on the surface of Maclairn. I'd be home. But it was too great a chance to take. The terrorists were shuttle pilots; they'd needed me only for the jump. They might kill me and elude Fleet— they might get to the surface briefly, and that would be long enough. They were on a suicide mission, after all. I was unarmed, and I hadn't time to program a jump to another star. I did the only thing I could think of. I headed for a nearby asteroid, one I'd landed on in the past. And I crashed."

"That's understandable, considering the stress you were under," Jon said. "Very few pilots could land successfully on a chunk of rock in a situation like that—I didn't think starships could land at all."

"Small ones can, in emergencies. It wasn't from lack of skill, Jon. I crashed on purpose. It was the only way I could kill the terrorists and make sure whatever was in their vials stayed in space, where it was harmless."

"But you might have been killed yourself!" Alison protested, "Or been stuck there with a damaged ship."

"I expected to be. I didn't think I'd live through it, and at that point I didn't care." Terry hesitated, for now he must fabricate. The ship had been totaled and he'd been mortally injured past any possibility of self-healing, but he could not say so, for he could not reveal that the Elders had rescued him.

"The hull cracked open and the two men were exposed to vacuum," he said, "but the pressure seal on the bridge held, and the AI was operational. I was able to push the bodies out and get away. But my comm wasn't functional and I'd ignored the patrollers' hail when the ship was near Maclairn, so I was afraid they'd fire on me if I approached again. The only thing I could do was jump and hope I'd emerge from hyperspace close enough to the world I headed for to get there before my life support ran out." Terry guessed that neither Jon nor Alison knew enough about interstellar jumps to doubt this story, unreasonable though it was. Nor did they know how recently he'd been taken out of prison, so they would assume his crash injuries had healed naturally.

"I had friends I knew would help me," he continued, "friends who owed me because of something that happened in the past. I can't say who or where they were—some of their ops are illegal, and you've no need to know the details. But they treated my injuries and repaired *Venture*. Since it had been in the possession of the dead terrorists and its original captain had been paid a charter fee high enough to cover its value, no one but me had any claim on it. So they hacked League records to give me a new ID and register the ship in my name as *Estel*."

"That's awesome—it almost makes me believe in fate," Alison said.

"Fate has done stranger things in my life than give me a ship," Terry said seriously, "Aldren, the mentor who began my mind training, said he'd seen in a dream that I had some extraordinary destiny, and it turned out to be true. Everything that's ever happened to me led up to my saving Maclairn from the terrorists, starting with my being chosen by Fleet to go there. If I hadn't become captain of *Promise* I wouldn't have known enough about Maclairn's enemies to understand the danger. If I hadn't been pledged to defend Maclairn I wouldn't have sought out the intruders who captured me, and if they hadn't sent me to Ciencia—and made it impossible for me to leave—I wouldn't have known about its misuse of biochemistry, nor would I have been in the right place at the right time to deal with the threat. In fact, if I hadn't been caught trying to save Jon from prison I wouldn't have been in Quaid's hands."

"It's hard to believe it could all have been just chance," Alison agreed. "To think how we grieved over your being stuck here—"

"And how sure I was that my usefulness to Maclairn was over." Slowly, with deep feeling, Terry continued, "I've thought a lot about this. I almost died in that crash—at first I believed I *was* dying. Fate had brought me to the climax of a long sequence of events, and if that was my destiny my life should have ended there. Yet I'm still alive. I think there must be a purpose in it. I believe I've got a responsibility to go on working toward Maclairn's goal." It was the Elders' goal too, he knew, and he owed his survival to them—but that was something he could never disclose.

"To help with what the Maclairnans are doing on Earth?" Jon asked.

"No, I can't go to Earth because if I came into contact with the mentors there, they might sense the truth I'm bound to hide. For awhile, aboard *Venture*, I convinced myself I could keep it from them; but that was wishful thinking."

"Then how can you work toward their goal?" Alison protested. "You couldn't go on doing it here even if you wanted to, not when you're an escaped convict. And if you become a smuggler you'll have to stay out of sight."

"Smuggling's just a way of earning funds to live on and maintain the ship," Terry said. "My real work will be to do whatever I can to achieve acceptance of psi and other advanced mind faculties on as many colony worlds as I can visit."

"Well, I'm for that," Alison assured him. "As Captain of *Estel* you're already a symbol. We can spread belief in that symbol to other worlds."

"Perhaps. But it means danger, and not only of arrest for smuggling. The opponents of psi must have grown strong and gained influence if they were able to recruit terrorists for a suicide mission. I'll be targeted by Maclairn's enemies if I go public, as I must. You need to understand that, both of you, before you commit yourselves to coming with me."

"Count me in—I'll be proud to go with you," Jon declared. "I committed myself to your aims long ago."

"So did I," said Alison quietly. "We've been putting ourselves in danger here for years, haven't we? I never felt my life had much meaning until I joined the conspiracy."

"It won't be just prison we're risking," Terry warned. "These people were willing to wipe out a whole colony to stop the spread of the ideas we'll be promoting. They won't hesitate to murder us if they get a chance."

"Which is another reason we can't go to Earth."

"Yes, but the instigators are League officials, remember, and the League has a long reach. Unlike Ciencia, the other worlds aren't isolated. They're tied together by ansible as well as starship traffic, and word will get around. That's great for circulating our message, but it will make us vulnerable wherever we go."

"Then we'll have to watch our backs," Jon said. "I sure as hell won't let another government's threats rule me after escaping this one's."

They rose and Terry gripped Jon's hand, then embraced Alison. He hadn't doubted that they'd support him, but it was good to know that they shared his conviction. Perhaps, he thought uneasily, he shouldn't be leading them into peril; yet his own choice had been made when he took command of *Estel*, and he couldn't travel alone.

~ *6* ~

TERRY SPENT THE day tense with impatience, feeling, somewhat unreasonably, that every hour spent on preparation increased the risk of not getting away. He felt no real precognition about it; still, that was a form of psi he'd rarely experienced and had never been able to distinguish from telepathy, so he couldn't count on it to warn him of impending trouble.

Jon went to arrange for delivery of his cargo and personal stuff, then to do a preflight check of *Bonanza*. Alison sorted through her belongings and Terry's old ones, choosing the few they would be able to keep. She lacked bags to pack them in; since people on Ciencia had no place to go, most didn't own any. "I might be able to find something we could use at the clinic," she said, "if you don't mind my going over there."

"You'll need to go anyway," Terry said, "because we've got to take the neurofeedback gear with us."

"Whatever for? We aren't going to have therapy clients."

"No, but someday, somehow, I might be able to get hold of the kind of brain sensors used on Maclairn. I know I could adapt the software if we had the right input, and then I could help you and others gain at least some of the abilities I was trained in." They'd be taking a risk by making a stop at the clinic, he thought nervously, but the mind training was too important not to pursue.

So Alison went to the clinic—now closed for the weekend—to pack up the equipment, leaving Terry, who couldn't venture out where he might be seen, to deal with the other stuff. Jon, he knew, would have duffel bags, as all spacers did, though much of what he owned was kept aboard *Bonanza*. Posing as miners, Terry and Alison would be expected to carry duffels, too, and Jon had agreed to stop and buy two new ones as well as a flight jacket for Alison. Lacking any other means of carrying the rest of their possessions, Terry rolled them in blankets. He could only hope that nobody would be watching when they had to transfer them to and from the van.

Jon arrived before Alison got back, and Terry immediately sensed that he was worried. "Is there a problem with the pickup?" he asked.

"No, it's all set. But something else has come up. When I checked over the ship I found a glitch in the instrument panel and I had to call Gwen. The job won't be finished till after the time our transport's scheduled for."

"Who's Gwen?"

"Gweneth Morrell, my maintenance engineer—the best one I've ever had. She works for one of the big mining companies but does other jobs on the side."

"Is she trustworthy?"

"I'd trust her with my life, as in fact I do every time I fly."

"Sure, all pilots depend on reliable maintenance people. That's not what I mean. If she's still around when we arrive, will she keep quiet about anything unusual she notices?"

Jon frowned. "She will if I ask her to. She's an avid Estelan; that's how I met her. What worries me is that if she's there this evening, she'll be suspected after we disappear whether she knows anything or not. When *Bonanza* doesn't return the police will question everyone connected with me. I'd expected Gwen could say she hadn't seen me since last week."

"And if they have cause to think she does know something, she'll be arrested." Terry had not stopped to consider the danger to Jon's friends, especially those who were members of the conspiracy. The authorities overlooked his likely involvement as long as they were getting their sizable cut of his smuggling activity, but once that stopped, they might well track down his past associates.

"Jon," he said reflectively, "we've been focused on getting away without giving any thought to what's going to happen here after we're gone. If *Bonanza* is found abandoned, it will be obvious that you left this solar system aboard a starship. Yet the racketeers' stranglehold on interstellar trade, not to mention the government suppression of half humankind's heritage, depends on the public's belief that contact with starships is impossible. They're not going to want it revealed that your ship was found empty. If the police discover it first they'll probably destroy it in space, but if a mining crew does—"

"They'll try to silence anyone who can attest to my having been aboard," Jon agreed grimly. "And if it gets around that I was, they'll go after my known friends to focus attention on my alleged criminal background. They might even learn who the current hackers are. God, Terry—I can't be responsible for that! Much as I want to go with you—"

"If your ship was never found they could say you'd been lost in an accident," Terry pointed out. "In fact they might believe it."

"But as you said, a mining crew may bring *Bonanza* in."

"Not if we destroy it ourselves instead of abandoning it."

"I'd hate to do that, considering how I feel about that old ship, but you're right. The catch is that I don't see how I can get hold of enough extra mining explosives to pulverize it without arousing questions—certainly I can't this afternoon, and you shouldn't stay here any longer."

"We don't need explosives. Remember, *Estel* has a laser cannon."

"Oh, my God. It could work—but what about Alison? How do we account for her disappearance?"

Terry had been wondering about that. Originally he'd assumed it wouldn't matter after she was gone. But she, too, had known connections to the conspiracy, and her disappearing at the same time as Jon's "accident" in space might seem too odd to be a coincidence.

"We need to change the plan," he declared. "Alison should board the ship openly so it will be assumed that she died, too. It wouldn't be illegal for you to hire her as a member of your crew, would it?"

"No, though it might seem strange when she hasn't any similar work experience. Mining is hard physical labor."

"That won't matter after they think she's dead. Even if they suspect she was trying to reach a starship, they can call it evidence that such attempts are ill-fated."

"Okay, but if Gwen's still there when she boards, she'll have a hard time explaining. They're friends, and Gwen's space-struck; she's been begging me to let her come along for weeks. She won't be happy to see me take Alison instead of her."

"Well, that's awkward," Terry agreed. "But later when she hears the ship's been lost, she'll feel it was a stroke of luck."

Frowning, Jon said, "I don't like to think of how she'll feel. She's fond of Alison—and of me, too, maybe. I know we have to fake an accident, but hurting someone I care about—"

Terry cringed, remembering the people on Maclairn who must have believed that he had died in space twelve years ago. He'd had no choice about leaving them to grieve; Jon and Alison did. Yet they could not reject the chance to escape Ciencia for their friends' sake.

Alison, when she heard the new plan, agreed. "Gwen will be devastated, both when she thinks I'm in space and after we're reported lost. That can't be helped, though it makes me sad. Gwen is one of the nicest people I know, and one of the most enthusiastic about Estelan goals. But she's young and a little too intense—once she sets her mind on something, she doesn't let go of it."

There was nothing to do with the rest of the day but wait. At dinnertime they forced themselves to eat something; then Alison arranged everything in the apartment neatly, disposing of all perishable food, so it would look as if she had gone on a trip from which she planned to return. She had no clothes appropriate for mining work, but fortunately was tall enough to adjust warm pants and a shirt from Terry's closet in such a way that their poor fit wouldn't be obvious when covered by the new flight jacket. She would be seen in them for only a few minutes, after all.

The cargo courier arrived on schedule after dark and stopped directly in front of the building; groundcars weren't plentiful enough in the colony's compact city for there to be a parking problem. The blanket rolls were a tight fit with the boxed pharmaceuticals, so they had to squeeze one of them between the seats. As there wasn't enough room for four people Jon drove, leaving the courier to take the bus to retrieve his van. After quick stops at his rooming house and Alison's clinic, they headed for the spaceport.

Terry was silent, recalling the many times he had driven that route while smuggling in data chips containing forbidden literature. He was used to the tension of his trips to and fro, but this one was more nerve-wracking than any other. If he was caught this time, Alison and Jon would be arrested too for aiding an escaped convict. And if he was sent to prison again, it would be forever.

~ 7 ~

BONANZA'S PAD WAS lighted, and with a sinking feeling Terry realized this meant Gwen was still there. He had hoped not to meet anyone. "Don't talk to her," Alison warned as they approached, "or to us in her presence any more than you have to. She's listened over and over to the recording of what you said at your trial, and she might recognize your voice."

"If the instrument panel's taking this long to fix, that's bad news," Jon said. "I don't want to have to stick around after we load up."

But Gwen came out of the ship as soon as they arrived—a short, stocky woman with reddish hair nearly hidden by the hood of her jacket. "I'm through, but I waited for you," she said with enthusiasm. "I've never gotten a chance before to be here when you lift off."

Terry pulled his skullcap down, half-covering his darkened face, thankful that the freezing cold required them all to be bundled in heavy clothes. Not that this would be enough to conceal Alison. "You came to watch too!" Gwen said when she saw her. "Let's go to the hotel for something hot to drink afterward."

Jon said quickly, "We've got to hurry. Goodbye, Gwen, and thanks for coming this afternoon on short notice. I really appreciate the great work you do maintaining *Bonanza*."

"I enjoy it. I'll help you load if you've got stuff to put in the hold."

Gwen was aware that he smuggled cargo, Jon had told Terry, but she didn't know about the government's role in it, which he was forbidden on pain of arrest to reveal. She would assume that he must load the ship fast in case police observers showed up, and since she obviously didn't intend to leave the pad, he had no choice but to let her see how much more than usual they were carrying.

"Where's your crew?" Gwen asked. "Shouldn't they be here by now?"

"Well, they wanted time off," Jon lied, "so I'm taking this other guy, Ernie, as a replacement." Reluctantly, he opened the van's rear doors. They made quick work of moving the cargo, making sure that Gwen was too busy with boxes to notice the transfer of the blanket rolls.

"Would you take the van back to the observation deck so that I don't have to, Gwen?" Jon asked when they were ready to board. "The owner's going to pick it up there, and it will save you the walk."

"Sure. Coming, Alison?"

"I'll be along later," Alison said lamely. But Gwen simply stood there, looking puzzled, and the inevitable could be put off no longer.

"Alison's coming with me," Jon announced. "I need an extra hand this trip and she's been wanting to get a look at the sun."

"*Alison?* But Jon, you've known I want to go since the day we met! You know I wanted to be a pilot till I lost the training lottery when I was sixteen. I'd be useful in space—more so than Alison, because I could make repairs if something went wrong with the ship."

"Nothing's going wrong; you've signed off on it and so I know it's in top shape. Anyway, your company wouldn't be likely to give you time off on such short notice, which is why I didn't ask you."

"I'll quit! I've got plenty of freelance jobs, I'm thinking about quitting the company anyway."

"Then maybe some other time soon." Jon exchanged glances with Terry. It was risky to stand and argue, but on the other hand, Gwen would now be able to testify that Alison had boarded the ship; they wouldn't have to leave other evidence for the accident investigators.

Gwen seemed about to explode. She was a good deal younger than Alison, Terry realized, and much younger than Jon. She wasn't used to disappointment. "It's not fair!" she protested. "Alison, you're working, too—are you going to just abandon your clinic clients?"

Something had to be said, and Alison, in desperation, used the only plausible lie she could think of. "I'm taking a short vacation," she said. "Jon and I want to be together. We're—lovers."

Astonished, Gwen stammered, "I–I'm sorry, I didn't know." She was sorry for more than one reason, Terry saw. His telepathic sensitivity told him that she had feelings for Jon despite their age difference, and to his dismay he perceived that the feelings were mutual. No wonder Jon had been upset by the prospect of letting her believe he'd died.

"It's time we got going," Jon said gruffly. As he turned toward the ship, Terry, still facing away from it, saw what the others did not.

"There's a car approaching," he said, keeping his voice low. *Not now,* he was thinking—*not twice!* The other time he'd boarded *Bonanza*, the time he'd flown it while Jon was injured, he'd had to lift off hastily just ahead of the police. Reason told him that whoever was in this car had no reason to suspect him of anything, but his heart rate accelerated.

The car stopped beside the van and the man who got out strode purposefully toward them. Jon said, "It's my boss miner—not the one that flew with you, Terry—and I told him this morning I'd postponed the trip. Thank God he didn't see us load cargo. Come along while I talk to him, and act natural."

Gwen drew back. "I must have dropped my phone in the hold," she said, "and since its outer hatch is sealed now, I'll have to go in through the cabin. I'll be quick so you can leave as soon as you're through placating him." She headed for the main hatch while the others went toward the parked car.

"What's going on, Darrow?" demanded the miner, obviously angry. "Did you think I wouldn't see your pad lights on my way into the hotel bar?"

"Cool it, Mendoza," Jon said. "I got the repair done sooner than I expected so since I'd said you'd be free to make a night of it, I decided to fly with some friends this weekend. This is Alison—she's well, more than a friend, and she's been wanting to go up with me. And Ernie here has agreed to help me out just this once."

Mendoza scowled. "That might be once too often. I wouldn't want to think you were cutting someone else in on a cargo deal."

"Of course not, nothing like that. You don't believe I'd take my woman anywhere near a starship, do you? She's not immune from prosecution like registered crew members, so I'll just show her my asteroid claim and pick up some high-grade ore. There's no free trader in orbit now, so you can be sure I won't be selling any till later, when you're aboard."

Though contact with starships was illegal, only the

mining ship's captain was liable, Terry recalled. The crew, being powerless to choose where they were taken, were officially assumed not to know unless they told someone. That was the only way the authorities' smuggling racket could be made to work. Most miners spent the time while docked getting drunk or pretending to sleep, but they had to be paid shares; otherwise, if displeased with their captain, they might report him—which meant his inevitable arrest and imprisonment since the government could not ignore a report once it was filed.

Mendoza must know plenty about Jon's past dealings with starships, Terry thought nervously. He might call the police if he felt Jon was planning to hide a sale from him.

"Well, okay," Mendoza conceded, "as long as you've got a woman with you. She doesn't look like the type for mine labor."

"He'll remember her," Jon said quietly to Terry as Mendoza departed. "So it's a good thing he came; it'll provide evidence that she was aboard. Gwen's testimony wouldn't have been needed, and I'm sorrier than ever that she's involved."

"Especially since she helped load the boxes," Terry agreed, "though I assume she knows better than to reveal that you were carrying cargo."

"Gwen can look out for herself," Jon assured him. "She may be impulsive, but she's too sharp to let anything slip."

Terry frowned. "Does she know what you told Mendoza? They might run into each other in the hotel bar, and if she mentions that you called on her for repairs only this afternoon, he'll know you lied to him earlier. He could be reporting you to the police right now, for all we know."

"God, you're right," Jon said uneasily. "Gwen had gone back for her phone and didn't hear the excuse I gave him for not taking the crew. We'd better get out of here fast."

They boarded the ship hastily, glad that the preflight checking had been done earlier, and Jon started the liftoff sequence. Terry settled into the copilot's seat, remembering the night less than two weeks ago when, still a prisoner, he had flown secretly from this spaceport with Quaid. He had not imagined then that he would get away, much less that he would come back and escape again. He let out a deep breath. It was over—he was leaving Ciencia for the last time and from now on, whatever dangers lay ahead, he would be free!

Alison leaned forward from her seat behind the pilots. "We never said goodbye to Gwen. Did you see her get into the van, Jon?" The spot where it had been parked wasn't visible from the cockpit.

"No, she must have left while we were with Mendoza. The inner hatch to the hold is sealed; I'd have a warning light if it wasn't." Mining ships were devoted almost entirely to cargo space; the cabin contained only seats for four people besides the pilots, two triple-deck bunks, a toilet and a small galley. Since the hold was unpressurized it could not be entered during flight except in case of an emergency requiring spacesuits.

Jon had spent most of his adult life in cramped quarters like this, Terry thought. A stateroom in *Estel* would seem luxurious to him. Alison, on the other hand, would find it hard to get used to. Was he crazy, asking her to live aboard indefinitely? Excited though she was to be going into space, that might wear off; not everyone shared his love of flying.

The ship shuddered and rose gently from the pad, then picked up speed as more power flowed to its antigravs. Within seconds the pad lights were a small circle below. Through the viewport, now filtered, the sun appeared as *Bonanza* broke through the thick cloud cover. Dazzling against the black backdrop of space, it filled Terry with the surge of elation he'd always felt on emerging from a planet's atmosphere.

"God, Terry!" Alison cried out. "The sun! From the vids I didn't guess—" She had never seen it before. Born on a world perpetually enshrouded, she had been unable to envision its brilliance.

From behind Alison another voice broke in—Gwen's voice. "It's awesome!" she exclaimed. "Brighter than I ever imagined."

~ 8 ~

"OH, MY GOD." Jon twisted around in the pilot's seat, his face white. "*Damn* you, Gwen!" he burst out furiously, "I trusted you, vouched for you—how could you pull a stunt like this?"

Taken aback by his anger, Gwen said reproachfully, "I didn't think you'd really mind. It's not as if you and Alison could have any privacy in here with another man aboard, and on the asteroid you'll be in spacesuits." Then, sensing that this wasn't what had infuriated him, she added, "I knew you won't be doing anything illegal like contacting a starship with her along—I wouldn't have risked interfering with that."

Alison, too, was white with dismay. "I should have checked, I noticed that we hadn't seen you leave—I suppose you were hiding in one of the bunks, behind the curtain. You couldn't know you'd be putting us in danger."

"What harm can I do? You've got more than enough consumables for four people; I was working in here all afternoon, and I saw Jon stow the supplies."

"God help us," Jon said despairingly. "We can't go back now; it would attract attention. If we landed so soon we'd have to fake engine trouble and stay around for it to be investigated; the police would start asking questions."

"I don't understand," Gwen protested.

"No. You don't."

"Why would you want to go back? I won't be that much of a nuisance, I'll stay out of your way if I can't be useful."

Neither Jon nor Alison dared to answer. It was time

for him to take charge, Terry realized. "What's done is done," he said decisively. "We can't return now and we can't spend days in orbit and then take right off again. It's too big a risk—if I were caught the rest of you would be considered accomplices. Gwen's made her decision and she'll have to live with it. Tell her the truth, Alison."

"Gwen," Alison said soberly, "We're not planning to go back, ever. We're leaving Ciencia for good."

"Leaving? But that's impossible—where is there to go?"

"We're going aboard *Estel*, to other worlds."

"*Estel*! But even if it's real, its captain's in prison."

"Not anymore," Terry said, "but I would be if someone saw through my disguise. My name isn't Ernie. I was warned not to talk to you, Gwen, because Alison thought you might recognize my voice."

Gwen stared at him incredulously. "I–I do," she mumbled, awed. "I guess the police must be looking for you."

"Then you see what this means. We can't take you home, so you'll have to join us. For me that's great; *Estel* can use an engineer—it will save us from having to show ourselves at spaceports often. But I wouldn't have chosen to expose you to the dangers we'll be facing."

"Don't worry about it. If Jon and Alison don't mind them, neither do I."

"Well, with Alison there's more to it."

"I lied to you about me and Jon," Alison said. "I hoped it would keep you from sticking around where you might be implicated in our getaway. It's Terry I'm with. He's been to *Estel* once since escaping from prison, but he came back for me."

"I wasn't sure there really is an *Estel*," Gwen admitted. "Some people think it's imaginary, as the government claims."

"It was, until recently," Terry said. "But there's a ship with that name now, and I own it. There's a lot I can't tell you till I know you better, Gwen, and some things I can't ever tell anyone. You're going to have to accept the fact that I have secrets you don't share. But you do need to know about the risks."

Gwen nodded. "What can be so dangerous after we're gone from here?"

"For one thing, we'll be smugglers, so wherever we are we'll have to avoid being captured either by the authorities or by pirates. And for another, I have enemies who will try to stop me from spreading the word about mind faculties that aren't acknowledged by science."

"Even on worlds where they're legal to read about?"

"Yes, people don't always believe what they read, or bother to read about such subjects in the first place—and there are some who don't want them to. My aim is to counter that."

"I want to help," Gwen declared. "Only—I don't know much about starships; I'm not qualified to repair one."

"You can't work on the hyperdrive, of course. We'll have to take it to a starport for that anyway, but, barring some catastrophe, no oftener than we need to refuel. The rest of the maintenance work is the same as on any ship, and you'll have access to all the specs."

There was a long silence while Gwen absorbed this. Then, turning to Jon, she said, "I had no right to push in when you made plain that I wasn't wanted. Now you're stuck with me, and I can't pretend I'm not happy to be here. But I'm sorry I betrayed your trust."

"I do want you," Jon said in a low voice. "I was mad because I was afraid for you—and because I don't like your being forced to leave everything in your life behind without having chosen it."

"The only things I cared about back there were my work and what I was doing to promote Estelan ideas," she said. "It looks like I've still got all that. As for people—" She broke off, blushing.

It had turned out well in more ways than one, thought

Terry. He had worried about Jon feeling lonely while he himself was with Alison, as well as about his having to stay aboard alone when they went to a planet's surface and go down by himself when it was his turn. Besides, some of what had to be done might require an extra person. Gwen's courage and initiative would be an invaluable asset.

"What sort of things did you do in the Estelan party?" Terry asked. "Besides read, I mean." Alison had mentioned that Gwen was enthusiastic about its aims.

"Well, I talked to people, brought in recruits. And monitored some of the files in the cloud."

"That's great. You can help keep track of the response to the hacking I do in data clouds of other colonies.

"I thought all the texts are already in their knowledgebases," Alison said, "and that people can freely discuss them on the Nets. So why will you need to hack?"

"Well, I don't have all the details worked out yet," he admitted, "so let's wait till we're underway to talk. Right now we should get some sleep. It's been a long day and as soon we rendezvous with *Estel* we'll have to work hard moving everything in this ship over to it."

"I'm too excited to sleep," Gwen said. "I'll just sit here and enjoy seeing the sun."

"Gwen, there's one thing you need to get straight right away," Jon said. "You're part of *Estel*'s crew now, and Terry is captain. What he tells you to do isn't just a suggestion."

Jon had been Captain Darrow for the past twenty years, Terry thought ruefully; until this morning he'd expected that he would have that status for the rest of his life. Now, unless they parted ways at some time in the future, he would never be a captain again. It would be a hard adjustment to make, yet he'd showed no reluctance, though part of him would surely grieve over the destruction of *Bonanza*.

All four of them lay down on the bunks; unlike larger

vessels, mining ships normally carried only one pilot and didn't require a continuous watch to be kept. Terry fell asleep quickly but was wakened by the AI's insistent warning horn, aware that a red light was flashing in the cockpit. He was instantly alert and got there fast, with Jon right behind him.

The long-distance comm had recorded a message; Jon played it back. "Ciencia control, this is HS *El Dorado*, inbound from New Afrika, requesting permission to approach. Over."

"Of all the luck," Jon growled. "There was a ship here only a week ago; I didn't think there'd be another so soon." Permission to approach Ciencia would be denied, of course, since no starship traffic was permitted; the transmission was simply a means of informing local smugglers that *El Dorado* was in the market for cargo. The government, which secretly profited from smuggling, would ignore it, and the ship would stay around waiting for miners with ore or goods to offer. "If *Estel*'s in high orbit, at least one of them may detect it," Jon declared.

"No," Terry said. "It's playing dead electronically; it won't be seen unless someone happens to come close enough to spot it visually, which is hardly likely. But they'll detect *us*, because we've got to use a beacon for *Estel* to find us, and their AI will pick it up."

"Do you know just where in its orbit your ship is right now? Maybe we can keep on the other side of the planet."

"I have no idea, and it wouldn't make any difference if I did; *Estel*'s faster than any mining ship and it's programmed to rendezvous when it gets the signal from the tracker I'm carrying. I haven't any way to control it from here."

"In other words, there's a chance that the rendezvous could be detected."

"A small one—but yes, it could happen. What would a mining captain do if his AI showed a local ship in contact with an unknown starship?"

"Some would ignore it; they wouldn't want to get involved. Others, if they hadn't sold all their own cargo, would want a piece of the action. And," Jon added grimly, "there are a few who'd hope to cash in by reporting it to the police—the government would pay well for information about a rendezvous with a starship it's not monitoring. I've been suspected of concealing transactions ever since you were caught flying my ship to *Freerunner*, after all."

Terry heart lurched; that was an episode he didn't want to relive, and its outcome would be the same—worse, because this time Jon would be convicted too, not to mention Alison and Gwen. "We can't risk it," he declared. "When we reach high orbit I can't turn the tracker on."

"How are we going to connect with *Estel*, then?" Jon asked.

"We'll have to wait until *El Dorado* is gone. Our only option now is to proceed out to the asteroids as you normally would, just as you told Mendoza we'd do."

Jon said slowly, "We may have another problem. If Gwen did tell anybody that I called her this afternoon, Mendoza may get wind of it. And if he hears that there's a ship soliciting cargo, he'll assume that I meant to deceive him when I said there isn't."

"You think he'll be mad enough to turn you in?"

"Probably. We could be pursued, just as you were last time."

"But we won't be anywhere near *El Dorado*. They can't come after you for what you haven't done."

"They can arrest me for what I've done in the past if Mendoza files a report. They suspect me of holding back profits, and we've got platinum aboard plus cargo that's technically illegal for me to carry. The fact that I'm not in the process of selling it makes it worse, because there's no potential gain for them in letting me go through with it."

"Well," Terry said, "the first thing is to find out if

we've got reason to worry." He called out to Gwen, who had stayed in her bunk as ordered, and she came to the cockpit. "Did you mention to anyone—anyone at all—that you were going to work on *Bonanza* this afternoon?" he asked her.

"I said hello to the guy who runs the hotel café, like I always do."

"Oh, God," Jon said grimly. "Mendoza said he was going to the bar. He's likely to ask if anyone's seen you, and whether you started the repair job earlier."

"If he finds out you didn't, he'll know Jon lied when he called off the crew," Terry explained. "We've got to assume he'll suspect he's being cut out of a cargo sale, and may sic the police on us."

He kept his voice steady, but inside his head was whirling. History was repeating itself; he had run from the police in *Bonanza* before, and last time they'd caught him. Now it would be prison for the others, too; shut away in the cramped cell, never again to see daylight, he would not know when, or if, any of them were released. Jon wouldn't be; ironically, he would receive the life sentence Terry's first arrest had saved him from. And he, Terry was to blame; if he hadn't come back to Ciencia. . . .

Gwen had turned pale. "It will be my fault if they arrest you," she said contritely.

"You had no way of foreseeing this," said Alison, coming forward to join them. "I'm just as much to blame; if it weren't for me Terry wouldn't be here—"

"And if I'd handled Mendoza better he wouldn't have cause to be suspicious," Jon said. "But I suggest we stop blaming ourselves and figure out what we're going to do."

"Can't we outrun them?" Gwen asked. "We've got a head start."

"Their ships are faster than this one; eventually they'll catch up."

"I thought the police didn't have jurisdiction past high orbit," Alison said.

"They do over local ships, just not over starships."

Resolutely Terry put aside his remorse, but the memory of his other flight from the police nagged at him. "Jon," he asked after a pause, "Do they track ships they're after, or just guess where they're going? Last time I assumed they were expecting me to head for your asteroid claim. I thought that when I changed course to rendezvous with *Freerunner*, they'd keep going in the opposite direction. But they didn't. They were waiting for me when I left the starship."

"They heard you talking to *Freerunner* on the comm, I suppose."

"Yes. So they stopped following and went where they thought I'd turn up. If that's how they operate, we shouldn't try to hide. We should contact *El Dorado* and make it look as if we're going there."

"You're right!" Jon exclaimed. "They'd prefer to catch me in the act of smuggling, of course, and they'll wait for the cargo sale to be completed so they can confiscate the proceeds. By the time they figure out we're not going to show up, we'll be aboard *Estel*."

"We can hope so. We'll be much farther ahead of them, anyway. Hail *El Dorado*, Jon, just as you normally would when selling to a smuggler."

Jon hesitated. "We could be asking for trouble. Mendoza may have friends who'll hear the transmission, and if by any chance he hasn't guessed I'll go there, this will clinch it."

"In that case, they'll be too far behind for it to matter."

"Unless there's a police ship already in orbit."

"We have to gamble one way or the other," Terry said. "Make the call."

Jon did so, assuring the starship captain that he had cargo of exceptionally high value, and arranged a rendezvous. Meanwhile, *Bonanza* continued at maximum speed toward the asteroid on which he had staked his claim.

During the hours it took to get there Terry sat tensely,

clenching his hands and with difficulty controlling his heart rate and inner biochemical reactions through the use of his mind training. Luck had been with him so far, he told himself. Surely it wouldn't run out now, with the freedom of everyone he cared about at stake. . . .

And with the fulfillment of his mission at stake, too. He had committed himself to spreading hope to the colonies. That might have some impact on the future of humankind. Was his belief in its importance just an illusion? If not, then perhaps returning to Ciencia hadn't been justifiable, yet it had *felt* right, which might have been precognition—but on the other hand, so might his irrepressible fear.

~ *9* ~

IT WAS EVIDENT, once *Bonanza* reached the vicinity of the asteroid, that if the police had indeed been called they were no longer in pursuit. Presumably they'd waited in vain near *El Dorado* and then decided that they couldn't be sure of Jon's destination. It would be easy enough, after all, to intercept him on his way back to Ciencia; there being no life support anywhere else in the solar system, every local ship had to return sooner or later.

Actually, the threat that had made them contact *El Dorado* had been a benefit, Terry reflected, somewhat awed by the way fate had repeatedly helped him out. Since the police couldn't have known that Jon suspected a trap, they'd see no reason for his failure to meet the starship as he'd arranged to do—and that would support the assumption that his ship had met with an accident.

No one had gotten much sleep, and by now they were hungry as well as tired. As they ate, Terry said, "I'm changing the original plan. Since we're far past the range of the local ships' tracking systems, I can turn my tracker on now and bring *Estel* out to us. I'd expected to board it as close to Ciencia as possible, but it's not safe to go back where we might be caught and in any case, by rendez-vousing here we'll save the days that we'd have to wait to stay clear of *El Dorado*."

"If the other ships can't detect us, then how can *Estel*?" Alison asked.

"Its comm facilities are much better, and more sensi-tive—and of course it's searching for my signal."

"But if our sensors can't pick up *Estel* until it's closer, how can we tell whether it's headed for us?" Jon said skeptically. "At least now we know more or less where it is—though I still wonder why you're so positive that it hasn't been tampered with. Once it breaks orbit we can't find it if it fails to appear."

"It will obey the signal it gets," Terry said firmly. Would it, he wondered, or would the Elders who were guarding it think the signal was false? They wouldn't ex-pect him to have come all this way past the planned ren-dezvous area. And they had the ability to take over its AI at a distance.

On the other hand, they also had far greater remote viewing capability than his. They might be able to sense his location by psi, or at least sense that the signal was authentic. He would have to trust that they wouldn't in-terfere. Reaching into his pocket for the tracker, he clutched it and pressed the switch.

It didn't take *Estel* long to get within range of *Bonanza*'s tracking system, and Terry drew deep breaths of relief. He had been away from it only three days and had not doubted that it would be waiting for him; never-theless, the separation had been painful, not to mention the recent fear that he'd be recaptured and would never see it again. *His* ship, the starship he had always wanted and never believed he would acquire—the miracle of it was still new enough to excite him.

They watched through the viewport once the AI an-nounced that *Estel* was near enough to be observed. At the first sight of it Alison exclaimed, "It's beautiful! I never imagined starships were like this, clean lines instead of pieced together like the mining ships."

"It's quite new," Terry said, "and was built as a charter vessel. So it's better designed than most."

Jon agreed. "I've boarded plenty of smugglers' ships," he said, "and this one has them all beat for looks. Of course they're mostly old interplanetary freighters converted to hyperdrive, with parts cut off to stay within the legal size limit."

Alison looked puzzled and Terry explained, "Private ownership of large starships isn't allowed—Fleet has a monopoly on interstellar traffic to prevent any world from developing military ships." And, he thought, to provide ongoing work for the trained officers whose existence kept the galaxy free of armed conflicts. Fleet's merchant starships far outnumbered its explorers and police ships.

"Why does *Estel* have solar panels?" Gwen asked. "I thought hyperdrive ships didn't need them."

"Small ones use them when near a sun to save as much fuel as possible for multiple jumps."

"You'd never know it had crashed," Alison said. "Your friends who repaired it must have been experts."

"It crashed?" Gwen asked. "Were you on it?"

Terry froze, and Alison gave him a look of contrite dismay. Only now had she realized that mentioning the crash would lead to questions that would be difficult to answer.

"That's one of the things in my past that I can't discuss right now," he said. He could not tell her about Maclairn yet. He wasn't sure he could trust her to keep the secret, though more and more he was inclined to feel that he wanted to. It was going to be very awkward for the three of them to avoid referring to it in her presence.

The reminder of the crash triggered another thought, and he wondered why it hadn't immediately occurred to him. "There's something else I want to do differently," he said. "Jon and I have agreed that once we've moved everything into *Estel*, *Bonanza* must be destroyed so the authorities on Ciencia will believe we all died in an accident—that's necessary to protect friends who might be suspected of having helped us escape. We've been planning to do it with *Estel*'s laser cannon. But since we're near the asteroid, it will be much better to crash it there so that to people who don't know about the smuggling, it will look like we were on an ordinary mining trip. There won't be any mystery about our death, and no one will guess that we'd had any idea of leaving."

"That's true," Jon said. "They'll search there when we don't return, since they know where my claim is; they may even send a rescue ship. And the evidence of an accident will be conclusive."

"They won't find our bodies, though," Alison pointed out.

"We'll plant mining explosives to make sure the cabin is completely demolished," Terry said.

"I assume you're not going to be aboard this ship when it crashes," Jon said. "So how are we going to keep the AI from preventing an impact? We can't turn it off; we've got to program a course that will collide with the asteroid at high speed."

"We can program a time-delayed shutdown."

"Not on my ship, we can't. Its AI isn't that smart."

"If you're going to use explosives, why crash at all?" Gwen asked. "Can't you just land, and then plant them?"

"You're right," Terry said. "I had crashing on my mind, and didn't think it through. We wouldn't have had enough explosives to destroy the ship without a trace, which was why we were going to use the laser cannon. But on the asteroid we want to leave the bulk of it to show we were there."

"But what will they figure caused the cabin to explode?"

"It doesn't really matter," Jon said. "Mining ships carry explosives and crews are sometimes careless with them. Nobody's going to investigate once they see we're not around to be rescued. And anyway, there won't be much left to investigate; an asteroid's gravity is so low that debris from an explosion will just float off into space."

"Right now we've got to transfer all our stuff into *Estel*," Terry said. He waited impatiently in the captain's seat while the two ships rendezvoused and then docked—an AI-controlled process, but one that required a pilot on hand to deal with emergencies. Once the airlocks were safely joined, he told his crew to bring the stored platinum ingots plus everything they could carry and led them triumphantly into their new home.

"There are four staterooms," he pointed out. "Alison will share mine, and you two can take your pick of the others. We'll use the fourth one for storage to keep the clutter out of the lounge."

He and Jon got into spacesuits and started moving cargo from *Bonanza*'s hold to *Estel*'s, taking Jon's mining equipment—except for the store of explosives—as well as the boxes and blanket rolls. "Some of it's set up on the asteroid," Jon said. "I leave it there between trips. If you think you'll want to do any prospecting in the future, we'd better retrieve it with the shuttle when you pick me up, though using it may not be practical for so few of us."

"We're in this for the long haul," Terry said, "and all my life I've wanted to explore uncharted worlds. So let's leave the option open."

Meanwhile, Alison and Gwen stripped *Bonanza*'s cabin of everything not fastened down. When they had carried out all they could, they remained in *Estel* while Terry sealed the joined airlocks, turned off the artificial gravity, and took the heavier equipment, along with the loose oxygen tanks and extra spacesuits, through the rear hatch into the hold for transfer. The ship was soon an empty shell.

They gathered around the table in *Estel*'s lounge to rest and quench their thirst before proceeding. He and Jon should sleep for awhile, Terry thought; they had done so only briefly and they had a difficult job ahead of them. There was no real need to hurry now that they were far from Ciencia. But he was too restless to delay, and he knew Jon wanted to get the painful part over with.

"Friends," he said seriously, "this is the point of no return. Until *Bonanza* is destroyed you three are still where you're legally entitled to be, and if you were to go back you might find the police weren't chasing us after all. You don't need to be concerned about my safety now that I'm aboard my starship. So if anyone's having second thoughts, now is the time to speak up."

"Of course we wouldn't go back, even if we hadn't been pursued," Alison said.

"I'm where I belong, police or no police," Jon declared, "and where I'm honored to think I'm needed. But Gwen—" He looked at her with concern. "I still don't feel right about your not having had a choice."

"You needn't worry," she told him. "If I'd been offered a chance to work on *Estel* I'd have given up everything else for it without any hesitation."

"Okay," Terry said. "I'm going to approach the asteroid, but not too close because orbiting an asteroid is tricky and *Estel* won't have a pilot aboard while I'm down there." He went to set course for the coordinates Jon had given him.

Alone on the bridge, he thought of the Elders who had silently guarded the ship during the days he'd been gone. They would have departed when they observed the rendezvous with *Bonanza*; they'd bent their strict policy of noninterference by keeping watch for him, and they would not protect him in the future. He would never have any contact with them again. Yet his life had been shaped by the two past contacts, and though during his exile on Ciencia he'd suppressed his longing to know more about their vast alien civilization, since meeting them for the second time it had begun to emerge. How many worlds— shielded, he'd been told, from detection by human technology—did their Federation encompass? What was it like to live in a culture more advanced than Earth's, one where mind-powers even greater than those of the Maclairnans were universal? He alone knew the stakes in the effort to achieve acceptance of such powers by society. It was going to be hard not to reveal those stakes to the three people who had agreed to share his commitment.

When they were as close as Terry dared go to the asteroid, Jon took the controls of *Bonanza* for the last time and made a successful landing at his usual site. To minimize the time when *Estel* would be pilotless, Terry did not follow in the shuttle until the explosives were in place. It would be unwise to be involved in their deployment anyway; Jon was experienced with them while he was not, and inept handing would endanger them both. Worse, what would become of Alison and Gwen if he never returned?

Setting the shuttle down on the rocky surface, he was surprised by the intense emotions that surged through him. Memories of the many asteroids he'd landed on in the past were overwhelmed by the last one, where after deliberately crashing he'd crawled out of the ship to die. The terrain of this asteroid was similar. Above its nearby horizon, he saw the stars just as he had then, and was awed once again by the miracle of his unlooked-for survival. He could not doubt that there had been meaning in it. From this day forward, he would dedicate his life to working toward the future the Elders foresaw for humankind.

Working quickly, they retrieved the rest of the mining equipment and stowed it in the shuttle's hold. Then, after a last wistful look at *Bonanza*, Jon climbed aboard. "That ship's been the same as family to me," he said. "If I'd guessed when I got out of bed this morning that by the time the night was over I'd be blowing it to space dust, I'd have thought I'd lost my mind. Well, let's get it over with."

"We're your family from now on," Terry assured him. But he knew it wouldn't be the same, because *Estel* was his ship, not Jon's, and its mission was his no matter how strongly Jon supported it.

The detonator would work from above the surface, so he lifted off and hovered as Jon removed it from the case strapped to his belt. "Want me to push the button?" he asked quietly.

"No," Jon declared. Without further discussion he pressed it himself, and a cloud of rock and dust rose from *Bonanza*, not settling enough to give them a clear look at the remaining shell. As the asteroid had no atmosphere there was, of course, no sound. There was no drama in the explosion, only a pang of regret mixed with the thrill of the journeys to come.

~ *10* ~

"so, how soon do we jump?" Gwen asked when they were back aboard the starship.

"We have to get farther away from the sun," Jon told her. "How much farther, Terry?"

"About nine hours," Terry replied. "But there's something else I have to do first. I'm going back to orbit Ciencia."

All three of them stared at him in astonishment. "Whatever for?" Alison exclaimed.

Terry had expected that they would protest against what he was about to tell them. They would probably consider his plan rash. But he was captain, and a ship in flight was not a democracy.

"There are a lot of people on Ciencia who've been putting themselves at risk because of what I said at my trial," he said. "They need inspiration to go on trying to change the censorship laws. They need more supporters. And they need to believe in the ideal of *Estel*—if we're going to make it into a symbol elsewhere, we have to ensure that it remains a symbol here. That may not happen if they think the Captain of *Estel* is permanently out of the picture. To have hope, they need to know that I escaped."

"What are you saying?" Alison burst out. "We've just gotten away; you can't go back and *tell* anybody—"

"No farther back than high orbit. We'll be in no danger there; we're in a starship now and the Ciencian police can't touch a starship unless it descends lower. In any case, they'll have no idea that Jon is aboard."

"But if you speak as Captain of *Estel*, they'll know *you* are."

"You'd be crazy to take the risk," Jon declared. "Sure, they have no legal authority over starships, since officially the ones in orbit don't exist. But since when has Ciencia's government obeyed its own laws?"

"There are starships in high orbit half the time—*El Dorado* is there now. Have the police ever interfered with them?"

"How about when they arrested you at *Freerunner*?"

"It was docked with *Bonanza*. They wouldn't have approached it otherwise."

"Do you know that? They don't bother the smugglers' starships because they're profiting from the transactions locals make with them and they don't want to discourage them from coming. The only potential profit from *Estel* would be in capturing you again."

"If they can't touch you when you're aboard a starship, why didn't you just stay in *Freerunner* and get away?" Gwen asked.

"I thought about it. But I knew Jon would be imprisoned if I did."

"Even a friendly captain like *Freerunner*'s wouldn't have given you sanctuary," Jon said. "If people could leave aboard free traders I'd have gone years ago. But no amount of money could persuade an interstellar smuggler to take a Ciencian along, because afterward his ship could never trade here again. The local ships wouldn't be allowed to reach it."

Alison reasoned, "The police believe *Estel* is just a myth. So won't they assume you're in some other ship— and if starships don't give sanctuary, mightn't they suspect it's a stolen one that isn't even a starship? Quaid won't have told anyone that he took you aboard *Venture*, after all."

"They could tell this one isn't local once they sighted it," Terry pointed out, not admitting to himself that in the case of an escaped convict in a stolen ship, they might fire from a distance to kill. "Anyway, they couldn't board if they tried; we're better armed than the police ships. But I have no intention of getting into a fight. I'll make one broadcast over the comm and be gone before they can see us."

Alison and Gwen sat silent, torn between fear for Terry and admiration for his daring. "Terry," Jon said, "either you think you're living on borrowed time since that crash or you believe your survival of it means you're leading a charmed life, I'm not sure which."

Was that true? Terry wondered. Underneath perhaps there was a little of both. But mainly he felt that bold action was his only hope of succeeding in the task he had set for himself—and the sooner he got started, the better.

"I warned you that we'd face danger," he said.

"Yes, but we haven't even smuggled anything yet— and your opponents on Earth don't know you're alive. Why rush into it before you have to?"

"Will people who hear your broadcast believe it's really you?" Alison asked.

"Of course they will," Gwen said. "Those who don't recognize his voice from the trial recording will have the evidence from comparison with the new one. And it will make a big difference to recruiting—If I were still there I'd be so fired up that I'd draw a crowd of demonstrators."

"I guess so." Hesitantly, Alison continued, "Terry, are you sure that revealing your escape won't lead to your supporters being suspected of helping you? After all the trouble we took to make it look like the rest of us didn't know about it—"

"I'll make plain that they weren't involved," Terry assured her. "There's no way anyone outside the prison could have aided me, and the police know it. The danger was that if the authorities were aware that you left Ciencia with me, they'd assume that I'd been in contact with the underground after I got out. I'll give them a reason not to think that." It was best not to be specific before the broadcast, Terry decided. Jon would be sure to declare that what he intended to say was foolhardy.

He met their eyes, one person at a time. "Will you trust me on this?" he asked soberly. "I've got to do it, and I'd like your backing."

Jon nodded. "Any spacer knows that there's no worse place to be than aboard a ship whose crew doesn't trust the captain's judgment," he said. "If I doubted yours, I wouldn't have agreed to serve under you. So let's get on with it."

During the hours it took to get back to orbital distance, Terry sent his crew to their staterooms to arrange their belongings and rest. He himself stayed on watch, pondering what he was going to say. It was hard to express; at the trial his words had come naturally, impelled by the urgency of the moment, and he would have to rely on that happening again. He recalled with chagrin that the effectiveness of his courtroom speech had been enhanced by his telepathic connection with the listeners; not until then had he perceived the power of telepathy to stir a crowd. Mass telepathy would not work from orbit. The Ciencians would pick up what he said aloud, and nothing more.

The others joined him on the bridge once orbit had been established. He couldn't afford any delay, Terry knew, if only because merely being there made everyone edgy. He fought a sudden surge of doubt. Was he doing the right thing, or was he endangering his friends pointlessly?

Resolutely, he grasped the comm's microphone. "Ciencia control, this is HS *Estel*, outbound to Centauri, the captain speaking. Stand by to record."

"*Estel*?" The voice that came over the comm was incredulous; they had, after all, been searching in vain for the mythical *Estel* since long before Terry's arrest. "If this is some kind of prank, can it!" said a second voice sharply. "Identify yourself!"

The ship's transponder should identify it, as did those of the smugglers' ships, Terry realized suddenly—and if so there could be no doubt he was aboard a starship. But it had been registered only a few days ago and Ciencia's files might not be up to date.

"This is the Captain of *Estel*," he repeated. "My name is unimportant since the one you know me by is not my real one. You can verify my identity from my voiceprint. Make sure you are recording, because I will say this only once.

"People of Ciencia, remember the words hidden on the Net, the words passed from one to another among those of you who haven't personally seen them: 'There is a ship, and its name is *Estel*, which means hope. Its captain came from the stars and his heart is there, but at times his ship descends to bring the knowledge that's rightfully ours. And someday this knowledge will no longer be hidden.'

"I am that captain, and I tell you that those words are true. You believe that I am in prison, for you saw me sentenced at my trial. The government has told you that *Estel* is only a myth. But it is not, for I am aboard it now. They could not keep me in prison any more than they can keep you from reading the books and stories that are your rightful heritage. My friends and I brought those books to your world and many of you know where on the Net to find them. I will not be bringing more; I am going now to give hope to other worlds. You need me no longer, for you are freeing yourselves from the tyranny of your government's false view of humankind.

"You now know that your own minds are far more powerful than your government would have you believe. You have become aware that human beings have abilities that science does not yet acknowledge. Those who don't wish to acknowledge it are your oppressors. They hope to keep you in ignorance because, were you to learn how to use the full power of the human mind, they could no longer control what you think and what you do. And in fact they too prefer to remain ignorant of these things—they are imprisoned by the fear of discovering that their beliefs are wrong.

"Just as beyond the clouds that cover this planet there is sunlight bright enough to dazzle those never before exposed to it, beyond the facts known to science there is a reality that would overwhelm those who want to think that those facts explain everything. People of Ciencia, are you satisfied to live with the dark cloudy sky under which your laws confine you, or would you rather see the sun?"

Terry drew breath, realizing that although he was only broadcasting and could feel no response from his intended audience, he was nevertheless being elevated by a surging telepathic current. It came from his own crew, their latent psi capability enhanced by his projection of conviction that they shared. Gwen sat watching him, rapt; Jon's worried frown had faded; and Alison's eyes were bright with tears of emotion.

"Your government can no more hold you to those laws than it could hold me in prison," he went on, "for human destiny lies in freedom to travel between the stars, as your ancestors did, and as I will do when this broadcast ends. Now some of you may be thinking that it is not possible for a man to escape from prison unaided, and that somehow my underground friends must have contrived to help me. But the prison authorities know that this is not possible either; there is no way anyone could have gotten in, let alone out again. It was fate that freed me from those steel walls, because I was destined to return to the stars in *Estel*.

"And so I say to the authorities, don't waste your time hunting for accomplices you know cannot exist. Look instead to one of your own, and ask him what he was paid for the enterprise that required him to set me free. He is not my friend. He merely used me in secret for his evil ends, so as to avoid splitting a very large sum of money among colleagues who might feel entitled to share it. You will know who you are when I tell you his name is Quaid.

"I am leaving Ciencia now for good; *Estel* will not come here again. But the hope it has offered you these past years will remain with you, and in time, perhaps I will meet some of you on the worlds of other stars."

Terry switched off the comm and sank back into the pilot's seat, shaking with released tension. He was not sure just what he'd said; he'd spoken without conscious deliberation. But he knew it had come from deep within him.

"My God, Terry!" Jon exploded. "What were you thinking? Get us out of here fast, before Quaid hears the recording."

"He won't have time to think about *Estel* if his cronies hear it before he does," Terry declared with satisfaction. "And they'll be too busy making him pay up to worry about looking for Estelan conspirators."

"Maybe so. Still, if they don't kill him he'll come after us."

"He can't. We're faster than any local ship, and Ciencia has no starships."

"But he has connections. You know he does—he arranged in advance to sell to offworlders, after all. That means he has access to the government ansible and he knows how to contact your enemies on Earth."

"I suppose so," Terry admitted. "But I'm betting that he'll be neutralized before he gets a chance. At the very least he'll lose his position and be prosecuted for letting me go—perhaps be put in prison himself. I want him to *pay*, Jon! Not just in money but suffering for what he aimed to do to innocent people."

"And to you," Jon agreed. "It's natural to want revenge—"

"Just what did this guy Quaid do, aside from freeing you?" Gwen inquired.

"He was Terry's interrogator," Alison said with a shudder. "He tortured him."

"That was nothing," Terry said. "As you know from my work as a healer, Gwen, I can protect myself from physical pain. I did hate him while he was trying to break me, mostly because of his derision of everything I believe in. But that's not what he deserves to suffer for. Later, he sold a biochemical weapon to terrorists that would have wiped out a whole colony and tricked me into piloting the ship that was supposed to deliver it."

"Which put you in a position to prevent its use," added Jon.

"Yes, but no thanks to Quaid—looking back, I realize that he wanted me to observe the destruction of that colony and feel responsible, because he'd been unable to shake my faith in its people's goals."

On the verge of further questions Gwen held back, realizing that this touched on secrets she wasn't supposed to know. They said goodnight, exhausted from the length and stress of the day.

But Terry was too keyed up to sleep. He remained alone on the bridge, torn by elation about the impact his words might have had on listeners and fear that some should have been left unsaid. Had he indeed made himself vulnerable by naming Quaid? he wondered. Suddenly uneasy, he recalled past times when he'd been struck by the feeling that now spread through him, a sense of something ominous just beyond his reach—perhaps a trace of true precognition. He had never been sure. In principle, precognition could rarely be distinguished from other forms of psi, if the possibility of long-range telepathy was assumed; and there was little doubt that Quaid now wished him dead. Yet the foreboding seemed more than a personal warning, and it was stronger than ever before, suggesting that events more momentous than his own death had been set in motion.

Still, fate had favored him in the past even when it had led him into peril, Terry told himself. There was little use in worrying that it might not always be so benign. Happy that his mission was at last underway, he began programming the jump that would take them far from Ciencia, sure that whatever dangers lay ahead would pale beside his gladness in being free.

Part Two: Centauri

~ 11 ~

THE JUMP TO CENTAURI was experienced with relief by everyone and as something of an anticlimax by all except Terry. "Is this all there is to it?" asked Alison in surprise. "We're already orbiting a different star, when you said we were about to jump only a few minutes ago?"

"I programmed the AI while you were asleep," Terry told them, "so all I did on the bridge just now was authorize execution of the maneuver. Jumping through hyperspace doesn't take any perceptible time. We're in the Alpha Centauri system, but of course it will take several days to get to the colony."

"Why?" asked Gwen.

"Because if we emerged too close to a star there'd be a risk of falling into its gravity well. Jumping isn't precise enough to aim for a particular planet's orbit."

They celebrated with a meal made no less special by the lack of anything but standard rations to eat or drink. And then, Terry knew, planning his next move could be put off no longer.

He had avoided making specific plans while preoccupied with reaching Alison and escaping from Ciencia. Actually, he had very little idea of how to proceed. "I don't know a lot about the smuggling business," he confessed to Jon, "except that in most colonies it works differently from what you've been doing so far."

Jon nodded. "On Ciencia the smugglers' starships put out a call for cargo, and since the government looked the other way, all we had to worry about was getting a good enough price to avoid being suspected of shortchanging the racketeers. The captains never told me what they did with what they bought. For all I know they may have sold some of the electronic stuff legally; the fact that it was illegal to export doesn't mean it couldn't be imported on other worlds. But my source told me that smuggled pharmaceuticals are contraband everywhere, and so making contact with someone who deals in them may not be easy."

"Centauri won't be the best place for that," Terry said, "because it gets plenty of freight traffic and it's got the largest Fleet installation anywhere besides Earth's moon."

"Then why are we going there?" Jon inquired.

"Because it does have a big Fleet center, which means we can get current information about conditions on Earth. We need that—it's been over twelve years since I've had any contact with the League. Also, I know my way around Centauri City; I was stationed there for more than a year while I was in Fleet. And I know how to hack my way into its Net."

"Why do we need to do any hacking if everything's legal to read?" asked Alison.

"A lot of our readers on Ciencia were hooked by the mere fact that our texts were secret," Terry said. "Secrets are more appealing than what everybody has easy access to. So I've been thinking that the fastest way to develop a following in another colony would be to insert easter eggs just like I did before—some leading to existing texts, but also some new ones. If we're going to make *Estel* a symbol, we have to introduce it in a way that will be noticed."

"This is going to be fun," Gwen said.

"Especially since we can't be arrested for it," Alison agreed. "That will be a nice change."

"We can be arrested," Terry pointed out, "because hacking—especially hacking a public system like a knowledgebase—is illegal everywhere. I'm pretty good at it and I've been lucky so far, but it's a long way from safe, even without counting the danger from self-appointed watchdogs who don't like what we say."

"Our ship will be obvious if it's in low orbit," Jon pointed out. "If the police want the Captain of *Estel*, we'll be sitting ducks, won't we?"

"I'm starting to worry about that," Terry admitted reluctantly. "I probably made a mistake when I registered the ship as *Estel*. All I cared about when I first realized I owned it was that the imaginary ship could be made real. But if the word's to become a symbol everywhere, I don't want it associated with smuggling even among people who won't report us—and certainly it would be dangerous to identify our location to those who will. I think we've got to orbit under a false name."

"That's not a bad idea," Alison said. "That way *Estel* can be kept mysterious, as it was on Ciencia, a ship no one ever sees."

"But it's got a registered transponder like any other ship, hasn't it?" Jon asked.

"Fortunately, it has two," Terry said. "The one for its original registration as *Venture* was deactivated but not removed."

"It looks like your outlaw friends who repaired the ship had foresight," Jon remarked dryly.

Perhaps the Elders had indeed foreseen the need for camouflage, Terry realized. It had seemed strange at the time that they hadn't just ripped the old transponder out. "Can you deactivate one transponder and activate the other?" he asked Gwen.

"Sure, if you've got the right tools."

"I have basic ones. We'll have to buy more for ongoing maintenance."

"And some clothes for Gwen," Alison added. "She hasn't anything but what she's wearing."

"Which brings up the question of what we're going to use for money," said Jon. "It may take a while to convert our platinum to credits."

"I have money—enough for the tools, too, if Terry doesn't," Gwen declared.

"We can't draw on Ciencian accounts," Alison reminded her. "We're supposed to be dead."

"It will be easy enough to find a dealer in platinum, that's a legal business here," Terry said. "But we'll have to sell at least part of our cargo soon, too. Getting your IDs modified is going to be expensive, and we don't have life support or provisions for more than a few weeks; the consumables have to be replenished."

"Do we have to change our IDs?" Alison asked. "Why? Since Ciencia has no official contact with the League, word that we're alive won't reach the authorities there, will it?"

"It could very well be reported through the free traders that Ciencians had been seen elsewhere, and that would alert them to the fact that *Bonanza* escaped. Besides, you all need worldless status just to bank credits, so you can buy food in cafés even if not to shop."

"Must we change our names, too?"

"No, that's not necessary, but there are other things to be fixed. Jon doesn't have a League pilot's license, which he might need to show. Gwen will need an official engineer's rating to use port repair facilities for the shuttle. And since it's illegal for me to carry passengers who don't have transit permits, you'll need crew status too, I guess as a comm technician."

"I thought you told me long ago that you couldn't alter an ID file," Jon said.

"I can't. It takes a forger with access to an ansible,

which couldn't be obtained on Ciencia, and even here it's a Class A felony—meaning that the fee will be very high."

"So getting in touch with a buyer for the cargo is our top priority."

"I can probably locate a black-market drug dealer by poking around the Net," Terry said. "The problem will be finding one who doesn't push street drugs along with legitimate medical ones. All moral considerations aside, it's best to steer clear of such contacts if we don't want to be double-crossed."

"How close to reality is the old space fiction you sneaked onto Ciencia's Net?" Jon asked. "The captains I dealt with were honest free traders, but I judge from the stories I read that on most planets there's a lot of swindling and killing, and no one can be trusted."

"Well," Terry said, "the stories are exaggerated; not everyone in the underworld acts like Jabba the Hutt. But there's certainly some truth in them. We might be wise to carry sidearms when merchandise changes hands, if only for the sake of appearance."

"Have we got sidearms?" Alison asked in dismay.

"Any starship carries a few. As a Fleet officer I practiced with them, but never had occasion to put that skill to use."

"Are there really bounty hunters?" Jon persisted.

"Yes," Terry replied, catching himself just in time to avoid saying in front of Gwen that shortly after the colony on Maclairn was founded, bounty hunters had nearly put an end to it.

"Well, then, what's to prevent Quaid from hiring one to come after you?"

"He doesn't know my new name," Terry pointed out. "There's no way his contacts on Earth could connect it with the one I used on Ciencia. And if we don't identify the ship as *Estel,* they can't find me that way, either."

"But if we identify it as *Venture*, word may get back to him that *Venture* still exists, and the last time he saw you, you were piloting it. He probably assumes that's how you returned to make the broadcast."

"True," Terry agreed with a sinking feeling. He hadn't thought about that. Nor had it occurred to him that the original captain of *Venture*, to whom it was still registered, might want it back despite having been paid more than its value for falsifying its flight plan. Above all, he did not know whether either Quaid or the backers of the plot to destroy Maclairn had learned why their plan had failed. They might not be aware that the two terrorists were dead; they might think they'd gotten cold feet and fled instead of attempting to go through with the suicide mission. In that case Maclairn's enemies might well be on the lookout for *Venture*. And since they were League government insiders, they would know if it appeared near Fleet's Centauri base.

"I guess we've got to call it something else," he decided. "Gwen, can you damage the transponder in such a way that it looks accidental, so that if the port authorities board us to check on it, they won't suspect anything wrong?"

"They'll want us to replace it," Jon said, "and that'll cost plenty. There may even be a fine. Not to mention the fact that whatever we name it won't be found in the registration files."

"It will be when we need it to," Terry said. "We'll have bought enough time for me to hack the records."

"In an official League database? You'd need ansible access for that too, wouldn't you?"

"They're not as secure as ID files—they're Fleet records kept in two-way mirror files linked to Moonbase. I worked some on Fleet's computer system when I was stationed here; all explorer pilots had to have a secondary skill and mine was AI maintenance." The passwords would have changed, of course, but he knew a backdoor.

He had not intended to go anywhere near Fleet. Of

course he wouldn't need a physical presence in order to hack; still it seemed a bit more chancy than he'd have preferred. But there wasn't any alternative.

"We've got to think of a name that can't possibly be in use," he said. "None of the obvious ones, or one from mythology or well-known literature, or a famous person. And of course names connected with Ciencia or Maclairn are off limits."

"What's Maclairn?" Gwen inquired.

Oh, God. He had slipped. It probably couldn't have been avoided much longer anyway since he didn't have to be careful around Jon and Alison. "It's the name of a colony that must never, never be mentioned except among the four of us," he said. "Can I count on you for that, Gwen? I can't tell you yet why it's so secret, but it's important not to reveal that it exists. A lot of people might be hurt if that got out."

"Are we ever going there?"

"No," Terry said sadly. "I'm pledged to stay away."

"As to a ship name, practically everything has been ruled out," Alison said quickly, trying to change the subject. "Can we just pick an uncommon girl's name and hope no one has used it?"

"I suppose we'll have to. How about *Coralie*? It's my mother's name, but no one knows that." No one had known except Kathryn. He had not thought about his mother in years; it was too painful. He hadn't contacted her during his trips to Earth with *Promise*, as it would have been difficult to tell her of his marriage without mentioning Maclairn. Fleet would have notified her of his presumed death on an exploratory mission without saying where it occurred.

He sensed Alison's rush of sympathy. "I didn't know your mother was alive," she said softly.

"I don't know either, but she's not old enough to have died naturally. She's probably still grieving for me, unaware that she has a grandson."

"You have a son, Terry?" exclaimed Gwen in surprise.

"It's a long story," he told her, "but yes, I was married on Maclairn. My son was unborn when I left there, but I learned recently from friends that he's well and happy." The Elders had told him this when they rescued him.

"Yet you can't go back? That's awful!"

"It's the price that had to be paid for saving Maclairn from harm. I have a new life now and I'm looking forward to it. I'm legally dead under my old identity and my former wife is with someone else; I wouldn't intrude even if it were possible. But you see, Gwen, that's why I have to keep on spreading hope to other worlds, in spite of the danger we'll be walking into. I lost too much not to make my exile count for something."

Confused, she protested, "Hope? I thought that on other worlds life is better than on Ciencia, like you said at your trial."

"Better because there's less censorship. But people aren't happy anywhere—they don't look ahead the way they did when they were establishing new colonies. They haven't anything to reach for, and they know how everything's declining on Earth. They've lost interest in searching for new frontiers."

"And new faculties of the mind are the frontier that's needed," Alison added. "What was it you said, Terry—that it's the next step in evolution?"

"Yes. And it's vital, because if human civilization doesn't move forward, it will die."

"I—I didn't know," Gwen whispered. "I thought we were just escaping, and that what you said in the broadcast to Ciencia was only about winning freedom there."

Terry opened his shirt and drew out the tiny flame pinned to its inner surface. "This is a symbol of the human mind's power," he said, "that was given to me long ago by friends I cared about. I can never show it publicly because on Earth there are people who would recognize its origin, and some of them might have come to colonies.

Nevertheless I wear it, in remembrance of the pledge I made to serve the cause it stands for."

He paused. Now that the time had come for action, he wondered why he had ever thought that he and a few others could have any influence on humankind at large. "I'm not sure how to begin," he said, "and we'll have to move one step at a time. But this is why we're here."

"And," declared Jon, "whether or not we can accomplish anything, we're damn well going to try."

~ *12* ~

THE THREE DAYS spent in transit were busy. Gwen switched the transponders, hiding one and disabling the other; Terry taught Jon how to pilot *Estel* in normal space; and Alison learned what she could from the onboard knowledgebase about the colony they were headed for. In his spare time Terry prepared the texts he was going to plant on its local Net, wondering how he could manage to attract readers without also attracting security agents. But at night, alone with Alison in their stateroom, he gave himself over to the joy of lovemaking, elated by the telepathic link—unconscious on her part—that was forming between them.

His darkened skin had nearly faded by the time they arrived at Centauri, leaving it close to its natural color as determined by the Elders' restoration of the genes they had previously altered; the pallid skin of a Ciencian would be too conspicuous in other colonies. Since his companions' Ciencian citizenship was to be concealed, this was true for them too, so it was necessary for them to acquire a light tan through very careful exposure to the ship's sunlamps. Terry allowed them to believe that his own disguise had been the result of long hours under the bright sun of the world where his crash injuries had been healed; having no experience with tanning, the inadequacy of this explanation wasn't apparent to them—nor were they familiar enough with skin variations to ask how he had been made to look Ciencian during his exile.

The colony Centauri was located on Centauri Prime, the largest planet of the double star Alpha Centauri, which was the closest habitable exoplanet to Earth and therefore the first to be settled. It had taken the name of the entire system, though a small settlement on one of the other planets had been established later. Centauri served primarily as a maintenance and supply base for Fleet's starships so as to keep them out of the way of the heavy interplanetary traffic within Earth's solar system. But its civilian residents were fiercely proud of its status as the first extrasolar society and, Terry recalled, they had a thriving economy based on the production of plastic resin pellets for industrial use. These were legally exported, but since the demand elsewhere exceeded the supply, a good many were bought up by smugglers.

Authorization to orbit under the name *Coralie* went smoothly, with his lie about a damaged transponder readily accepted; he was used to lying to traffic controllers, after all, as he'd done it every time he'd flown to Earth from Maclairn. Now the most pressing need was to get the false name into Fleet's files.

Because privately-owned starships were rare and there wasn't much local shipping either, Centauri had no civilian spaceport; Terry had to land the shuttle in the designated area of Fleet's. It brought back memories; he had set down at this port often during his time as a lieutenant. Coming in, he circled above the familiar buildings that surrounded the vast field and could almost imagine that he'd crossed the gulf of years and become a hot young pilot again, eager to prove himself worthy of commanding an explorer mission. What would he have thought then, he wondered, if the precognition with which he was occasionally gifted had hinted at how differently his life would turn out?

He took Gwen down to the surface with him, much as he'd have preferred to show Alison her first new world. She would need to choose tools for maintaining *Estel* herself. Moreover, she could keep an eye on the shuttle while he went into the city, whereas Alison knew nothing about ships or spaceports; he would have hated to leave it untended. Fate had again proved helpful, Terry realized, when it forced him to add Gwen to his crew.

He had his own tablet computer with him, the one he'd used on Ciencia, which Alison had managed to hide after his arrest to prevent its being seized. Far more powerful than a phone and equipped with a variety of sophisticated hacking tools, it was a state-of-the-art machine that would serve his needs on any planet he visited. He and Gwen went into a civilian-owned café with a good view of the landing area and, holding his breath, he logged on to Fleet's database through the backdoor he remembered.

He hadn't much time, Terry knew; security could trace his location if his presence in the system was detected. But since he was connected through a router in an area under Fleet's authority, there wouldn't be an immediate alarm, as there would if he were in the city. After a quick search to make sure that the name *Coralie* was in fact not already in use, he created a new record, saving a copy of the newly-assigned ID on his tablet for use on the new transponder he hoped to get cash to buy. It was impossible to identify an owner since he had no access to ID files; that was something else he'd have to pay a professional forger to provide—plus a record of his having chartered the ship in case his right to possession of it was ever questioned.

As he logged off and took notice of his surroundings, he became aware that Gwen was staring at him in admiration. "I knew you were good," she said. "But so *fast*—"

"You have to be fast if you don't want to get caught. And in a public place like this, you have to make sure to stay inconspicuous." Looking around, he saw that the room was full of Fleet officers and that for a moment he'd forgotten that he wasn't dressed like them as he had been in the past when in their company. He suspected that civilian ship crews weren't seen frequently at this port.

Sometimes the best way to be inconspicuous was to attract notice. Rising, he went up to the nearest group of lieutenants and said, "Excuse me, but we're just off *Coralie* and we haven't landed here before. Can you tell me where to find transport into the city?" He already knew, having gone into the city often on leave; but the question would establish him as an innocent transient.

After accepting a lieutenant's friendly directions with thanks, he left Gwen to watch the shuttle—a natural enough role for a young member of a free trader's crew—and boarded the bus. His most difficult test was beginning, Terry thought nervously. He had never met any underworld people apart from the pirates who had once captured him, and he wasn't sure he could present himself convincingly as an outlaw. But ordinary free traders did not seek out ID forgers, so he would have to give it a try.

The first thing to be done was to sell the platinum he'd brought with him. He deliberately chose an establishment in the worst part of the city, a part he found easily from having avoided it in the past. Although the sale of platinum ingots was legal in Centauri, there were bound to be dealers who had sidelines, and information about their contacts was what he needed.

His own ID was legitimate; it had been forged by the Elders, who had agents at League headquarters. When swiped, his implanted chip revealed him to be Terry Steward, worldless, and a fully-licensed star pilot. "Captain Steward of *Coralie*," he added.

The man who greeted him frowned. "Never heard of it," he said gruffly.

"Well," said Terry, "today it's *Coralie*, and you don't need to know what it was in my last port."

"No, I guess I don't." The dealer looked at him with new respect. "I'll just weigh these ingots, if you don't mind."

"I mind if you're planning to do it in the back room."

"Then you'd better come along and watch." The man headed for a door behind the counter.

Unhesitatingly, Terry followed. It could, of course, be a trap, but that was a chance he would have to take. His telepathic sensitivity told him that if this man was a thief, he was an honest one; and dealers would not stay in business long if they robbed customers of whom they knew nothing.

As the ingots were being weighed, he said casually, "I wonder—I've got a problem, you see. I left my last port in something of a hurry, and then found I had a stowaway." The closer he could stick to the truth, the better; the telepathy would work both ways, for most people had unconscious sensing ability. "Anyway, I've taken this person into my crew, but her ID shows her citizenship and I don't want it known where we came from. Do you suppose there's any way I could get that fixed?"

"Not by me, there isn't."

"No, of course not. But you know the city, and I don't, so I thought—"

"I hear things, naturally," said the man slowly.

"Perhaps," Terry ventured, "you've made a mistake in the weight of that last ingot; it may not be quite as heavy as the others."

"My scale's accurate. But you might want to think twice about selling all your platinum. Some businesses prefer metal over credits." Shoving some of the ingots back across the table, he added, "If your stowaway needs outfitting, look up Zach's Emporium."

"Thanks," Terry said. "I'll do that." The dealer would hardly make such a suggestion out of interest in a crewwoman's clothes, he realized; and since the man had refused not only the offered bribe but the potential profit on a larger purchase, he was undoubtedly expecting a substantial cut from the ID forger.

He consulted his phone for the address of Zach's and made his way there. Surprisingly, the building was in a respectable area; it was one of the better prefab ones clustered around the city's central ring of steel-framed structures. Inside he found a store that carried top-quality gear. Seeing a chance to kill two birds with one stone, he began picking out a duffel and clothes for Gwen.

"Need help?" asked the sole clerk in sight, a big man who looked more as if he belonged in a construction crew.

Terry repeated his remarks about a stowaway. "She can't even buy her own clothes without worldless ID status," he said pointedly. "She doesn't dare draw on her homeworld account; the police have a watch on it."

As he had suspected, the word "ID" was the trigger, and his mention of police reinforced it. "I think we may have some more suitable merchandise in another part of the store," the clerk said. Again, Terry was ushered into a back room.

The older dark-skinned man at the desk there smiled pleasantly, but behind the smile Terry sensed something else—not malevolence or even intent to cheat, but nevertheless alarming. This wasn't a matter of telepathy, he realized. It was more like precognition, although normally there was no way to distinguish between the two. He had experienced precognition rarely, and then only in connection with potential trouble. Still, it didn't seem likely that the police would pay enough to an informer to be worth the risk of turning in a customer merely for soliciting a criminal act.

"I'm Zach," the man said, "and I believe you must be Captain Steward."

"Then I guess you've heard what I need done. Actually I could do it myself, because I've had quite bit of experience with databases; but I don't have the—facilities."

"That's interesting. If you're looking to rent ansible access, you're in the wrong place. I charge by the job."

"How much?" Terry realized unhappily that if Zach knew his name, he had also been told how many platinum ingots he was carrying.

"It depends. Citizenship status, that's one thing. Names, biomarkers, are something else."

"Nothing like that. Just citizenship and some licenses for three people. And I need an owner ID for my ship—a dummy not linked to anyone's chip."

Zach named a figure considerably higher than the available funds; Terry named one considerably lower. After lengthy bargaining they came to an agreement. "But it'll be more if I find they're wanted," the forger warned. "If you're not prepared for that, now's the time to back out."

Sure, Terry thought. If they were wanted for something serious there might be a bounty for which he would have to compensate; Zach didn't know yet that they'd come from a colony that couldn't be contacted. "No problem," he said. "You won't find anything out of line except that they may be officially dead by now."

God, what if they were marked dead later, wiping out the status he was buying for them? If they'd come from any colony but Ciencia that would be a real danger. Ciencia's isolation laws, however, were so strict that it might not send death notices to League Headquarters at all. He could only hope that if it did, there had been no delay.

Drawing a deep breath, he handed over the agreed-upon platinum ingots and the ID numbers of the crew and the soon-to-be-purchased transponder. "Okay," said Zach. "I don't let anyone watch me work, so Henson will show you where to wait."

The clerk from the store reappeared and as instructed, Terry headed for the door across the room. He didn't have time to feel the blow from behind that knocked him unconscious.

~ *13* ~

WHEN TERRY CAME to himself it took a while to grasp the fact that he was really in darkness, not just suffering from concussion, and that although he was lying flat, the ceiling was only a short distance above his head. With a sudden rush of panic he realized that he was in a box-shaped space that must be hidden beneath the store's floor. Reaching out, he could feel that the walls surrounding him were mere rough-hewn rock. There wasn't enough light to make out the composition of the top, but the general effect suggested a coffin. Perhaps, he thought in horror, it *was* his coffin.

The air in such a confined space couldn't last much longer. He remembered the cave on Maclairn where he and Kathryn had almost suffocated—that had been much larger, and high enough to stand up in. He had stayed alive there only because of the mind training that enabled him to lower his metabolism by slowing his heart rate and avoiding all motion, even speech. Resolutely he shifted into that state, wondering how long it would take to die.

But he wasn't dying. Air was coming from somewhere; the space was ventilated. He could hear the whir of the fan. They didn't intend to kill him, then, at least not yet. For some inexplicable reason they wanted to keep him captive in a place impossible to find.

Why? he wondered in despair. He had already given Zach most of his platinum; they hadn't needed to knock him out to get it. They wouldn't have feared that he might report them to the police in any case, not when they knew his crew's identity and could be expected to take revenge.

His crew—oh, my God, Terry thought. Gwen would be frantic when he didn't return. She would inform *Estel* by comm, of course; then Alison and Jon would be frantic, too, and if he never came, what would become of them?

Gwen couldn't fly the shuttle; they would be stranded and would eventually have to call the authorities for help. The cargo would be confiscated, and if the ID changes hadn't gone through, they couldn't acquire credits even for food. . . .

There was no way he could escape from a hole like this, Terry realized. He knew better than to beat uselessly against the stone walls; ventilated it might be, but not to the extent that he could afford to expend energy. There had to be some kind of opening in the top through which he had been lowered, but it would be locked or barricaded, invisible from above. That such a cage existed meant that Zach had trapped people before, perhaps repeatedly. What could he gain from it?

The obvious answer burst into Terry's mind. Ransom. A free trader captain with platinum to spend would be presumed to have cargo, it didn't much matter what kind. Zach surely had friends in the smuggling business. He knew that *Estel*—under the name *Coralie*—was in orbit, and he knew by whom it was crewed. All he had to do was contact Gwen and demand payment in exchange for her captain's life.

What would Gwen do? She had no money and the starship didn't have another shuttle for Jon to bring down, so they couldn't comply; Zach would have to send some other pilot. . . .

An even more horrifying possibility struck him, searing his heart. Why would they even ask the crew? Perhaps they'd assume the ship was armed, as in fact it was; but Jon didn't know how to use the laser cannon and in fact none of them had been trained to use sidearms. When Zach and his men discovered that, they could take whatever they wanted. They could take the whole ship. They could take *Estel*, and even if they didn't kill him afterward, he would never see it again.

That was a worse prospect to contemplate than the likelihood of his death.

If they took the ship, would they keep the crew aboard? Probably not; it would be obvious that they lacked enough experience with starships to be useful. Nor would Zach arrange transport back to the surface for them, where they could report the theft to the authorities. He would kill them. He would have no reason not to.

Alison—oh God, Alison . . . how, Terry wondered, had he ever imagined it was okay to take her and the others into danger? With remorse, he became aware that he had rushed blindly into dealings of which he knew nothing, putting his fanatic devotion to the course fate had set for him ahead of everything else that mattered. He'd been willing—was still willing—to die for it, but he was not willing for harm to come to Alison. Or to Jon, or to Gwen, whom he scarcely knew. He had not seriously feared that any of them would die soon.

Or that he would lose *Estel*. His possession of it had seemed too good to be true, and evidently it had been. There had simply been a short interval—less than two weeks—when he'd believed he could travel between the stars forever.

In agony, Terry struggled to manage his physiological reactions. He'd been trained to control his body's response to stress; that was how Maclairnans preserved their health. It really made no difference now, since no escape was possible, but instinctively he felt that to give up would violate the pledge he'd made. Even in the Ciencian prison he had not given up. Recalling the tiny cell that had felt unendurable, it seemed huge compared to a rock-walled box where he could not even sit erect. The walls pressed in on him, making him want to scream despite his certainty that no scream would be heard, let alone heeded, from above. How long? he wondered. How long before he cracked and lost all vestige of self-control?

Time passed. He longed to retreat into sleep but despite his usual command of unconscious functions, sleep wouldn't come. Eventually his mind grew hazy, only to be startled into alertness by nightmares. It would be better, he thought, if he were in pain—he knew how to turn off physical suffering, and the mind-pattern required for that would free him from thinking. When he felt that he could not bear awareness one moment longer, he bit down hard on his tongue and focused on suppressing the resulting anguish.

One thing kept nagging at his thoughts, something plainly incongruous. He had not sensed any evil in Zach. There had been the feeling of premonition that had proved all too accurate, but the man himself had seemed straight-forward—without scruples with regard to breaking the law, but not violent, not cruel, and not even lacking in integrity. Usually, Terry reflected, what he perceived by telepathy was reliable. He couldn't pick up private thoughts, but ever since learning of his psi gift he had been capable of judging people's feelings. How could he not have known that Zach intended to harm him?

He found himself wishing they would hurry up and get it over with.

Surely they would have learned by now that they had no need to demand ransom. Since keeping him alive was no longer serving any purpose, they would come back and shoot him. Or would they? No, Terry realized, his horror mounting. They wouldn't go to the trouble of shooting him; they would simply turn off the ventilator. He'd imag-ined many ways his life might end during the twenty years since he'd joined Fleet, but being buried alive was not one of them. He hoped that he would not die insane.

When, after a long while, he heard sounds above, he did not at first believe they were real. Then, suddenly, the top of the box was thrown off and the sudden glare of light nearly blinded him. As if from a distance he heard Zach say, "Come on up; I'll give you a hand. If you'd called for backup the police would be here by now."

~ 14 ~

UNCOMPREHENDING, TERRY SAT up, stretching his cramped limbs and adjusting to the light. After a few moments he took the hand extended to him and climbed out of the box. He did not speak; there didn't seem to be any words strong enough.

"This is a rough business," Zach told him, "and I have to be careful—one wrong move and I'd end up in a League penal colony. If you want anything done on the level of ID tampering, you have to expect it will cost you."

"My cargo, my ship, maybe the lives of my crew? I don't think so," Terry declared, keeping his voice even.

"Your ship? You thought I was going to steal it? Hell, no, man, I don't go in for larceny. All I do is protect myself." The man's amicable smile seemed genuine. "I've been under suspicion for years, but the police can't arrest me because sending in agents doesn't pay off. Anybody I have doubts about gets the same treatment you did, and if it's an undercover cop, he wakes up far from here with no memory of what happened to him; I've got drugs to ensure that."

"Why," Terry ventured, "have you decided I'm not a cop?"

"They use implanted trackers they can set off, or sometimes they arrange with buddies to move in if they're missing too long. If a team shows up, this is just a clothing store—they'll never find the hole through a legal search. The box is unlined rock so a metal detector won't show it; they'd have to demolish the building."

The hole undoubtedly contained more than one box, Terry realized; there would be another for stashing platinum, and the ansible terminal was probably down there, too. "You keep all suspicious-looking new customers buried for hours on end, just on the chance that they might be police agents?" he asked incredulously. "I wouldn't think you'd get much business that way."

"Well, I don't want business from people I can't trust to keep their cool. The average client doesn't stay in there very long; most of them start yelling to be let out, which a cop wouldn't do."

"How do you know if they yell? I'd have sworn the box was soundproof."

"There's a mike in the ventilator linked to my earphone. I don't aim to give anybody a hard time when there's nothing to gain by it; I haul them out, put their money back in their pockets, and dump them in the nearest tavern after a shot of the drug that erases memory. It's harmless—just a sedative that by then they're glad to get."

"I imagine they are," Terry said dryly. "Are you going to drug me now, by force?"

"God, no—you're something else. When I'm lucky enough to find a man or woman who doesn't panic at being confined down there and doesn't freak out with rage when brought up, that's somebody I know is reliable. This is a bigger operation than just forging IDs, and I'm always on the lookout for more partners."

Astonished, Terry declared, "You're mistaken if you think I'm going to become a partner in this sort of thing. I'm a trader and an explorer with no desire to get involved in crime."

"Oh? You're not above buying doctored IDs for fugitives. You implied that you're a hacker. And you mentioned cargo, which I'm willing to bet you don't plan to sell legally."

Terry was silent. Zach did have a point.

"I don't mean an active partner in my own enterprise," Zach went on. "It's a network, see? There's no boss, people just make referrals. Some need ID work, or a registration changed, or a particular kind of merchandise; others want to sell services or cargo. I'm picky; I don't handle stolen goods or deal with those who do, and I don't shelter killers. But I don't honor bureaucrats' laws, either. Free traders have my respect."

Was it possible, Terry wondered, that fate had again aided him by means of a seeming disaster? He had not known how to find a buyer for smuggled cargo; he hadn't even known how to start.

"It's true I've got merchandise to sell," he said slowly.

"Of course you do. That ship of yours is no mere yacht."

Terry froze. "What do you know about my ship?"

"I checked you out, soon as I saw you were the kind of man I might do business with. I have a friend in traffic control. And by the way, he said something about a broken transponder—you need that handled?"

"I've already taken care of it, except for the owner ID I asked you for."

"Oh, yes—you said you'd had experience with data tweaking, I assume you meant unofficial experience. You must be good, because you've got the cleanest ID I've ever run across. According to your file you've never attracted any attention, so my guess is that it was fixed somewhere along the way. If you'll be onworld for awhile I might have some work for you."

What would Zach think, Terry wondered, if he knew that he'd spent the past twelve years inserting subversive literature into a public knowledgebase, not to mention the prior hacking experience he'd acquired during his high school years on Earth? "Thanks, but I have my own agenda," he said, "and right now I've got to get back to the port before my crew gives up hope of ever seeing me again. I don't suppose it occurred to you that I wasn't the only one your tactics were hurting."

"Your crew's fine—I sent Henson to see the very competent young woman who's guarding your shuttle and give her a message from you saying you'd been unavoidably delayed. I wouldn't have wanted her to report you as a missing person, after all."

Thank God, Terry thought with relief. She'd have talked to Jon and Alison on the comm, so they weren't suffering as much as he'd feared.

Zach went on, "He tried to get her to open up about your business, but she's a cool one; he couldn't get anything out of her. We were only asking out of curiosity—their ID files showed that your crew came from Ciencia, so I'm confused. Ciencia's a closed world. I've been told there's no chance of getting closer than high orbit."

"That's true," Terry said. "No one's allowed to come or go, which is why I needed it wiped from my people's records."

Zach stared at him, his respect increasing. "*You* managed to pick up passengers."

"Not exactly," said Terry, trying to decide how much to tell this man, who was going to have to know that he carried Ciencian goods to sell. "My copilot Darrow brought up some cargo in a local mining ship and chose not to go back. The two women came with him, and if they're missed, it will be assumed that his ship was lost, which is how I want it to stay."

Puzzled, Zach persisted, "You mean you'd been flying alone till then? How did you get sole possession of a starship?"

"That's not for you to know. It's legally mine, however, in case you're worried that I might have stolen it."

"I'm not. I know straight talk when I hear it," Zach assured him. "Now about your cargo, what have you got to offer?"

"Pharmaceuticals," Terry said. "Top Ciencian quality."

"What kind?"

"Not the kind you're probably looking for."

"Psychoactives? I employ them when I need to, as I told you, but I'm not a user and I don't encourage street dealing. I don't care what's legal or illegal, a person has a right to free choice about what drugs to consume—but too much that's sold on the street isn't genuine; customers get jolts they're not expecting, and some die. I only refer traders to legitimate clinics."

"That's good, because I've got mostly antivirals."

Zach burst out, "*Antivirals*? Ciencian antivirals, the ones that don't have to be tailored?"

"Yes. You know anyone in the market for them?"

"There's an outbreak of something new on Toliman," Zach said, "and the legal supply has run out. I know half a dozen traders who'd pay twice the usual wholesale price, but I like you, Steward, and what's more, I don't hold with gouging a clinic with an epidemic on its hands. So I advise you to skip the middlemen. You've got a ship; go and sell direct."

"Go to Toliman?" Yes, he could do that easily, Terry knew; it was a small colony on another planet in Alpha Centauri's system; the name was taken from an old one sometimes used on Earth for the star Alpha Centauri itself. "How would I make contacts there?"

"I'll give you a name. She'll be wary, but you tell her you've been in Zach's box and she'll be willing to deal. Anywhere in the galaxy, that's all you have to say—if a guy knows what you're talking about, you can trust him like a brother."

"It's that big a network?" Terry exclaimed, overwhelmed.

"Traders move around a lot; usually they're just one jump ahead of the law, as I'm sure you know."

"I'm new to the smuggling business," Terry admitted, "though I've done other things I could be nailed for."

"Well, you're part of a family now. My screening method works; you can call hazing if you like, but I don't know any faster way of finding out who's got enough self-control to be trustworthy."

Impressed, Terry memorized the name and instructions he was given. He hadn't thought it would be so simple.

"One other thing before you go," Zach said slowly. "There's a rumor starting up about Ciencia. I met with another free trader a couple of days ago, captain of *El Dorado*, and he told me an odd story. Seems he picked up a transmission from orbit, some guy speaking directly to the people of the planet about how they should start a revolution—even implying that they *had* started it. If that's true I'm glad, because I don't like any government telling citizens what they can and can't do, censoring what they read and not letting them ship out if they want to. Would your crew happen to know anything about it?"

"If they do, they're not likely to say so. Not everyone on other worlds would be as understanding as you are." God, Terry thought, he hoped he was judging Zach rightly—but his initial impression, which had stuck even while he'd thought the man would kill him, was now stronger than ever. And he'd have to trust his own psi perceptions if he was going to spread ideas among the colonials he interacted with.

"I have heard the rumor," he declared. "It's said there's a ship named *Estel* that no one ever sees, and the word Estel means "hope," and the Captain of *Estel* has special powers that people everywhere will someday possess. If there's a revolution on Ciencia, that's probably what sparked it."

"I'll pass the word around," Zach said. "Nobody's thinking much about the future anymore, but if there's anything in it worth hoping for, that's something my network would be happy to hear."

~ *15* ~

WHEN TERRY GOT back to the shuttle and had assured Gwen, and the others via comm, that he was okay, he transferred some credits to her and told her to purchase a new transponder and any essential tools as quickly as possible. The port had a hardware outlet, fortunately, and he'd bought enough clothes for her from Zach. He didn't want to waste any time. If there was an outbreak of disease on Toliman, people might be dying.

While Gwen was gone he grabbed some protein bars from the emergency stores in the shuttle, having had nothing to eat since the day before, and then got busy with his tablet. He would have to hack the colony's knowledgebase from where he was; it would take too long to go back into the city, though it might be less risky from there.

They would come back to Centauri after delivering the antivirals to Toliman; still he wanted to make the rumor about *Estel* public immediately—encouraging though it was that Zach planned to spread it to the underworld, that wouldn't reach ordinary citizens. He was excited by its having gotten started already; *El Dorado* must be a faster ship than *Estel*, or else it had emerged from hyperspace closer to Centauri.

He used the same wording as he'd used on Ciencia, which had proved effective: "There is a ship, and its name is *Estel*, which means hope. Its captain came from the stars and his heart is there, but at times his ship descends to bring the knowledge that's rightfully ours. And someday this knowledge will no longer be hidden." But now he added, "It is knowledge of the powers of the human mind, which are greater than is generally guessed. With these powers we can defeat sickness and pain and misunderstanding, and all who gain them will interact with each other in harmony—the childhood of humankind will end and a new phase of history will begin."

This was, of course, looking rather far ahead, Terry thought ruefully. He was thinking of the era when the Elders would appear, which wasn't going to happen in his lifetime. But people *needed* to look ahead. That was what they had stopped doing, thereby letting civilization go downhill. They needed to believe there was something worth reaching for, as once they had reached for the stars.

And at least a few people could gain what the Maclairnans had, what the Maclairnan mentors were teaching in secret on Earth. There could be a beginning.

Earth . . . he hadn't found out what was happening there, though Centauri was the place most likely to have people who would know. He should have asked Zach, Terry realized. He hadn't been in a mood to stick around after his release from Zach's box, but probably the man had contacts on all the settled planets in the galaxy. In fact he'd as much as said so. Did they include anyone aware of the conspiracy on Earth that was trying to suppress awareness of psi? Would it have been safe to ask him? Zach would certainly oppose that effort; even if he knew nothing about psi powers, he would instinctively feel that suppression of them wasn't compatible with his dislike of government authority.

It didn't take Terry long to crack the knowledgebase and plant the easter eggs leading to his text, and to some relevant speculative books, in several places that the people most apt to be receptive would be likely to see. Since the existence of such a comment wasn't illegal in itself here, it would probably find its way into some blogs, and certainly there would be comments in public forums— in fact he inserted a few under anonymous screen names to get the ball rolling. Initially there might be a few readers curious enough to wonder about his text's origin. Once it spread, however, nobody would bother to trace it, and in any case, by that time he would be gone.

He hadn't yet told the crew about his experience, feeling it would be too hard to explain from a distance. Once aboard *Estel*, he set course for Toliman before sitting down with them to say why. "It was a real break," he concluded. "We'll sell the whole cargo for sure. But when people are sick and suffering, I don't want to profit from that. I think we should ask just what we paid for the stuff. Do you agree, Jon?"

"You'll never be a big success in the smuggling business," said Jon, smiling. "But yes, I agree. The only thing is, this guy Zach is expecting a cut, isn't he? Presumably he'll collect from the courier he referred you to, and if it's true that he knew dealers who'd pay twice wholesale, he's likely to feel shorted."

Terry frowned. Zach had trusted him to contact the go-between rather than seek out a clinic himself and disappear with the entire proceeds of the deal. It would be wrong to cheat him, even if it weren't that his friendship might prove valuable in the future. "He doesn't know how much cargo we have," he said thoughtfully. "Let's hold some back and charge enough for the rest to give him a fair cut—and then donate the rest directly to people who need it. As long as we don't pocket profits he's entitled to share, I don't think he'll mind."

It took less than a day to reach Toliman. Terry wished Jon could be the one to negotiate the price for the pharmaceuticals, but it wasn't possible since he himself had to make the contact and one of them had to stay with the ship. It didn't really matter this time when they weren't aiming for maximum profit. They loaded the cargo into the shuttle and he headed for the surface, taking Alison with him.

It was dusk when they landed, the strange brilliant dusk dominated by the second sun Alpha-B, which gave too much light for the sky to turn black. "It's like this only half the year," he told Alison. "During the other half Alpha-A and Alpha-B are on the same side of the sky so Alpha-B appears only in the daytime when it's too dim by comparison to be visible."

"It doesn't look like a sun," she said, "at least not like what I saw through the filters on *Bonanza*."

"Well, it's a small one. Tomorrow morning when Alpha-A rises you'll see real sunlight." What a thrill that would be, he thought, to someone who had never before walked on a world that wasn't enshrouded. This one was not an attractive example, being made of featureless rock; but he knew the absence of clouds would seem awesome to her.

Toliman's spaceport was no bigger than Ciencia's and served a similar purpose; only mining ships were based here, and what little other traffic it got consisted of supply ships. Ostensibly, *Coralie* was carrying plastic resin pellets from Centauri; that was what Terry had told the port authorities. He knew they would not inspect the shuttle's cargo. Though in theory imports were taxed, he'd been told that it was done at the point of sale and that everyone knew that smuggling went on. Toliman, which was merely a base for orbiting metal refineries, needed goods more than it needed tax revenue.

Legally imported pharmaceuticals had to be ordered from suppliers on Centauri, who in turn ordered all but the most common ones from Earth; this meant several transactions involving both tax and dealers' profit on top of the manufacturer's price. If medical drugs were needed, nobody would question the source of cheaper ones except for assurance that they were not counterfeit. That, Terry knew, was what the contact to whom he'd been referred would be wary of. Had Zach not been aware that *Coralie*'s crew came from Ciencia, he reflected, he would have been taking a big chance by making such a referral. People could die from counterfeit medication, and a dealer who'd been stung might well take revenge on the person responsible.

He called the number he'd been given. "I'm just in from Centauri," he told the woman who answered, "and I've got something a friend of yours said would be of value to you. Can we meet?"

"I'm not interested in imports right now. Nobody's buying." Her tone wasn't friendly.

"So I understand. I know there's illness here; that's why he thought you'd be in the market for antivirals."

Angrily the woman declared, "If you think I'm going to fall for a pitch like that, forget it. There are no antivirals on Centauri; we've exhausted every possible source. There's nothing lower than a scammer who'll take advantage of suffering, and you can tell my alleged friend not to send me any more."

"He said to mention that I've seen the inside of Zach's box," Terry said quietly.

After a short silence she conceded, "Maybe we'd better meet. Where are you now?"

"The spaceport. There's a woman with me; we're on the porch of the spacers' hotel." At a small port like this one, frequented only by miners and local traders, he knew it would be safe to leave the shuttle unattended.

While they waited he explained to Alison about epidemics—there had been no such thing on Ciencia, of course, considering the advanced skills of its biochemists and the fact that it allowed only rare, surreptitious contact with offworlders. Nor did contagious disease exist anywhere in the League except on backwater worlds with no stock of vaccines and antimicrobials on hand. "At the first sign of anything new, the rich colonies treat everybody," he said. "Whatever's broken out here must have been brought by a trader who'd been to the outskirts."

"But where could it have come from originally if the first settlers of each colony are disease-free?" Alison protested.

"Bacteria and viruses evolve fast," Terry said. "Those native to new worlds adapt themselves to human hosts, and even if vaccines and drugs are developed to defeat them, ships get away without everyone aboard having been treated. A jump takes so little time that they may not get sick until later, or they may be merely carriers who don't get sick at all."

The dealer arrived in a dilapidated van that probably dated from the colony's founding. "Okay," she said. "I'm listening. But I'll need to know how you came by what you've got."

"We brought it direct from Ciencia," Terry said, "where we bought it legally."

"Ciencia? I've never been offered anything from there."

"It's a closed world. But if you handle biochemicals you must have heard of Ciencian expertise in that field."

She frowned. "Ciencian . . . yes, I've picked up rumors. If they're true, anything you have is worth more than I can pay."

"Not necessarily." Terry decided to trust her; he could tell she was honest and in desperate need. "Look," he said, "We're not aiming to profit at sick people's expense. We bought this stuff on speculation and we've got to recover what we paid, but that wasn't as much as it would have been if we were offworld dealers. We bought direct from a local supplier and transported it ourselves."

"From a closed world? There'd have been risk in that."

"No more than we were taking anyway by leaving the planet."

"I don't quite get it," she protested. "If it's illegal to export biochemicals, why do they manufacture more than enough to meet local demand?"

She was worried that the drugs might not be genuine, Terry realized, and her skepticism was reasonable. "The Ciencian government runs a racket," he explained. "They encourage illegal exports as long as they get their cut. Offworlders can't go to the surface and there's a leash on local captains, so any cargo picked up would normally be priced accordingly. But as I said, my crew was mainly concerned with getting away. We couldn't have transferred our credits so we invested in medical supplies."

"How much have you got, and what are you asking for it?"

"That depends on what percentage Zach expects from you."

"He won't expect anything on pharmaceuticals; he knows I don't profit from them. I'm a part-time accountant at the clinic—I do all their buying, legal and otherwise, and I don't add a markup."

"I just need to get back what we put in," Terry said. He named a figure. "That includes the antivirals plus some antibiotics, and I'll give you a hand transporting them to the clinic."

"We'd like to help out," Alison added, "if the clinic's shorthanded."

The woman stared at them. "How did a couple like you get mixed up with Zach? You're not much like his usual clientele."

"So I gathered," said Terry, "but my crew's Ciencian citizenship had to be erased."

"And Zach put you in his box for that?"

"I guess I looked clean-cut enough to be an undercover law officer."

She smiled. "I've never met him myself, but we've talked. He's not as ruthless as he may seem, but God help the man or woman who betrays him after being judged trustworthy."

"How widespread is the illness here?" Alison asked. "Has everyone in the colony been exposed?"

"No, only those who came into contact with the crew of a prospector that came in last week, and their associates. We've got it pretty well contained, but they're in bad shape." The woman pulled out her phone. "Let's get on with this. I've got to get back to the clinic; I'm volunteering as a nursing aide. My name's Claudia."

"I'm Terry, and this is Alison." He held out his arm for her to swipe his ID implant, and Claudia transferred credits from her phone to his. Then all three of them went out to the shuttle and moved the boxes of drugs to her van.

The clinic was a long, low prefab, more recently built than the adobe structures of the original colony and unshaded by the genetically-engineered trees that surrounded the older ones. As they entered Terry froze, struck by a wave of agony so startling that he nearly stumbled. Every muscle in his body screamed in pain.

"Oh, my God," he gasped, struggling to regain his mental balance.

"Terry, what is it?" Alison asked, sensing his distress.

White-faced, he murmured, "The patients—the ones

sick with the virus—they're hurting bad, all of them. I feel it just like I did with the neurofeedback clients."

~ 16 ~

IT WAS THE flip side of his telepathic sensitivity—when someone was suffering physical pain, he felt it in his own body. At least he had since becoming consciously psi-gifted, and according to his Maclairnan mentors it was probably why, as a child, he had suppressed his gift. Maybe he shouldn't call it the flip side, Terry told himself, because it enabled him to help people. That was how he'd gained his reputation as a healer in Alison's neurofeedback clinic.

He had never wanted that reputation. Ever since learning of his psi-giftedness he had shrunk from the idea of being idolized in such a way. But when clients came to Alison with the hope that psychotherapy and neurofeedback would lessen their pain from ills medical treatment hadn't cured, he couldn't refrain from helping; and though he'd never admitted to them that anything more than neurofeedback was occurring, before long some had caught on. Word spread, and to his dismay he had gone from a mere technical assistant to the clinic's central attraction.

It had proved fortunate not only for the clients, but for his own status among the Ciencians after his arrest. People whose suffering he had relieved had appeared at his trial, and his telepathic influence as the Captain of *Estel* had been magnified by his rapport with them. But he was not a miracle worker. The pain relief wasn't permanent; it lasted only during the neurofeedback session and for a little while afterward, though a few people had learned, after repeated sessions, to achieve it briefly on their own. They did not become immune to suffering from the physical sensation, as he and others trained by the mentors were. And he had worked with them one at a time.

Now, overwhelmed by the simultaneous agony of many people, Terry was close to panic. He had shifted easily into the mental state that eliminated his own suffering; that was second nature now. But to pass it on to a patient he would have to shift back. That was how the healing worked—only by briefly sharing the pain of the other person could he enable that person to make the transition. How could he do that for a whole clinic full of sick people, one by one?

Alison saw his turmoil and covered for him. "What does this virus do to people?" she asked Claudia, glancing around the large room into which far more beds than would properly fit had been crammed. The patients lay flat on their backs, yet their eyes were open and they were obviously all too conscious of what they were feeling.

"It attacks the muscles," Claudia answered. "Even the slightest movement produces severe pain. And there's no way we can lessen it; we ran out of painkillers long ago. They just have to wait it out."

"But they do recover?"

"Most of them. We've had a few deaths where breathing muscles were affected. Usually the acute phase lasts only a few days. They'll have aching muscles for weeks afterward, though."

Terry, dazed, was scarcely aware of Alison and Claudia recruiting orderlies to bring in boxes from the van, or of the nursing staff unpacking the antivirals and beginning to administer them. Once he managed to pull himself together he went to the nearest bed and crouched beside it, taking the hand of the girl who lay there staring up at him.

"Relax," he told her, forcing a reassuring smile. "You'll hurt less if you quit fighting it." Realizing that in the absence of a neurofeedback display she would need a tangible sign that something was happening, he added, "When you're relaxed enough to feel better, I'll squeeze your hand." Then he dropped back into normal consciousness and let her pain envelop him.

We don't have to suffer, he told her silently. *Follow me—go where I go, into a place where pain doesn't matter. Where you don't have to let it hurt you as nature programmed you to feel hurt when it warned you of danger. You're safe here; you can turn the warning off. . . .* When he sensed her response, knew she was in unconscious telepathic rapport with him, he shifted back to freedom from suffering and gripped her hand tightly, carrying her along.

"The pain just—stopped hurting!" she murmured incredulously. "What did you do?"

"I showed you how to turn off the brain programming that made you suffer from it. I can't stay with you because there are a lot of other people who need help, and I'm not sure how long the respite will last. But you know it's possible now. When your pain is really bad, relax and remember—perhaps it will happen again." He rose and went to the next bed, where he repeated the procedure with an old man.

Six hours later he had made the rounds of the entire clinic and was starting over with the first patients. Alison had come along behind him, comforting, reinforcing their relief with her calm reassurance as she always had with her own psychotherapy clients. They had lost track of time, and of the fact that they were both shaking with exhaustion from constant immersion in other people's agony.

Vaguely, Terry perceived that the psychic atmosphere in the room he'd first visited was different now. It was a makeshift ward, normally the clinic's cafeteria, and held about twenty beds lined up with barely space for nurses to walk between them. The patients, unable to sit up, could not see him or each other; only when he bent over someone was it possible to make eye contact. Yet he felt a linkage with them not only individually but as a group, and he sensed that they had begun to feel it, too. The telepathic rapport he'd established with each was spreading, so that they were soothed not merely by the memory of the short-term alleviation of their own suffering, but by what he was doing for others.

These people's latent psi capability had been enhanced by the stress of pain, as his own had been during his training, Terry realized. Their rapport with him had merged with the awareness of each other's response—and had thereby been magnified—in the same way as during his speech at the trial. It was likely that he could now reach them simultaneously.

He stood and raised his voice. "Pain doesn't have to hurt," he said. "What we feel with our nerves isn't what hurts us; it's how we process the sensation in our minds. That's automatic when we're born because we might get injured without a warning we couldn't ignore. It's got to stay automatic with animals and children—but we're grown up, now. We don't need a built-in warning and we can turn it off when we know there's no danger."

This was how it had been explained to him, long ago when his mind training had begun. Far more than the explanation was needed for a person to learn how to do it alone; but the clinic patients did not have to gain that capability. They needed only to believe that suffering was unnecessary in this particular situation. That when he was here to help, they could free themselves from it by just letting go. Only through mass telepathy was this possible. He had set the stage for it and, he thought dazedly, he must seize the chance to make them believe.

"The human mind has greater powers than most people know about," he declared. "Not just the power to learn and to reason. Ever since the first humans evolved on Earth, people have been developing more abilities—to speak, to use tools, to create ideas and technologies—step by step, we've gained conscious control of our thoughts and actions. But the process isn't finished. We can gain the ability to control things that are normally unconscious, so that we're no longer bound to the way animals and children are programmed to react. An animal's body readies itself to fight or run when threatened, but doing that over and over to no purpose leads to illness and pain. Instinct isn't helpful anymore. We can ignore it and make our own choices."

They were absorbing this from his mind more than from his words, Terry knew. They were receptive because he had shown them it was true. The ability he was giving them was only temporary, only an aid in coping with this emergency. But it was a start. And perhaps it could also engender the wider hope he was aiming to spread.

"There's more to be gained," he said. "Responses to danger aren't the only functions of our unconscious minds that can become conscious. We can communicate by telepathy, too, and we can perceive things we can't detect with our physical senses. Throughout history there have been a few people who could do this, and a time is coming when many will be able to. Some will find it frightening because it's new to them and changes the way they think; some may even turn against those who welcome the change. But you will know that it's good, because you have found it's possible to turn off suffering when you're in pain."

Terry, oblivious now to anything apart from the emotion he'd shared with these people, drew breath and plunged ahead without thought of possible consequences. "There is a ship named *Estel*, which means hope, and it travels from star to star to tell of the coming change—of the time when people will gain awareness of much that is now unconscious. Of the time when they communicate mind to mind, and live in harmony because there's no misunderstanding between them, no isolation from each other's feelings. And in days to come, when you hear rumors of that ship, remember me—"

He broke off, realizing just in time that he could not identify himself as *Estel*'s captain because if he did it would get back to Zach, and it was too soon for Zach to know. But at least, he thought, knowledge of the name *Estel* might plant a seed.

Claudia, who was still on duty as a nursing aide, had come into the room while he was speaking. As he turned to move on to another, she came up to him, obviously shaken. "Who *are* you?" she asked, awed.

"Nobody special," Terry said. "Just a guy who's been lucky enough to have training that's not widely available."

"Is there really a ship like you said, or was that only a figure of speech?"

"It's real, all right."

"Have you seen it?"

"Those who've seen it are not allowed to say so," he told her, avoiding a direct lie. "Someday, maybe, it will show itself. Meanwhile I'll go on believing in what it stands for."

Claudia nodded. "I knew from the start that you're no ordinary free trader. It must have been fate that sent you here from Ciencia just when we needed what you brought."

"Well," Terry said, "fate's had a way of thrusting me into all sorts of surprising situations that turn out to mean something. I've stopped trying to guess where I'll end up next."

~ *17* ~

FOR THREE DAYS and two nights Terry and Alison continued to make the rounds of the clinic, giving patients encouragement along with temporary relief of pain. They got a few hours of sleep in a small room vacated by the first few people to recover, and Claudia brought them something to eat from time to time. "The antiviral pills are working fast," she said on the third afternoon. "The incubation period's short and we've given them to everyone left who was exposed, so I don't think there'll be any new cases. Already most of the patients can sit up. It looks as if the crisis is nearly over, thank God."

Terry was by this time dizzy with exhaustion and unable to fly the shuttle without a full night's sleep. He had sent someone to the spaceport the first evening with a message to be passed on via the controller to *Coralie*, telling Jon they'd be staying on the surface for a few days. So when Claudia invited them to her home to rest up, he accepted gratefully.

They ate an early dinner, reveling in the warm sunlight that streamed in through Claudia's window—a novelty to Alison, deeply gratifying to Terry after his years on Ciencia and the days since in space. He had almost forgotten what it was like to be touched by the sun.

"I don't really understand what you did with the patients," Claudia said. "Did you hypnotize them?"

"No," Terry explained. "A person who's hypnotized can be made to believe things contrary to reality—a false memory, for instance—or in the case of surgery, won't feel the cut. It's the opposite of taking full conscious control of unconscious functions. I don't tell people they won't *feel* pain, I tell them they needn't *suffer* from it. They remain aware of the physical sensation; it just doesn't bother them. They switch their own minds into that state; I just show them how."

"Could you show me how?" she asked hopefully.

"No. For an untrained person it only works with severe pain. If that weren't true, the inborn purpose of pain would be defeated; little kids would learn on their own and their bodies wouldn't be protected from injury by a compelling warning."

"Then how did you learn?"

"I was taught through a procedure that was developed—in secret," he said, realizing that he was skirting the edge of a subject that must not be mentioned. "The instructor has to inflict extreme pain on the trainee, who has to be willing to tolerate it. And there has to be neurofeedback in addition to the telepathy involved."

"You never told me about the infliction of pain," Alison remarked. "You've always just said you had training."

"Well, it never came up. It's not at bad as it sounds— it's harder on the instructor than on the trainee. Only a few are qualified to be merciless, yet compassionate at the same time."

"I don't see why you think large numbers of people will consent to go through something like that."

"They'll need to be taught at puberty. It's—will be— easier for kids to absorb than adults because they don't have years of experience in believing pain can't be overcome. And by that time, they'll be developing telepathic ability as children, so the rapport with the instructor will be stronger." He would tell her later, when they were alone, that this was how it worked on Maclairn.

"You keep saying that people will have paranormal capabilities in the future," Claudia said. "What makes you so sure?"

"I can't answer that," Terry replied, not saying why. "I only know that if the human race doesn't keep moving forward, civilization will die out. I've been to Earth. I know how bad things already are there, and not just because it's so crowded. What kind of future will there be even here if there's nothing new ahead to hope for? You're just surviving, marking time. We're past the era where founding colonies like this one is challenging enough to be fulfilling."

"You're right," Claudia said sadly. "We know that underneath, we just don't admit it to ourselves. What good does it do to keep settling more worlds when there are already hundreds?"

"Humankind couldn't survive without expanding—if we hadn't done it, we'd have overrun Earth and destroyed ourselves long ago. But it's no longer enough. There always has to be a vision of something not yet within our reach."

Terry thought about it when, after dinner, he and Alison went to the bedroom prepared for them. Drained though he was, he spent some time with his tablet planting messages about *Estel* on Toliman's Net. They would be particularly effective here because the people he'd helped in the clinic would eventually come across them and pass the word around. And there would be cross contact between this world and Centauri since they were in the same system and communicated by ordinary comm channels.

"Come to bed," Alison said. "If you're half as bushed as I am, you'll need a long night before you're ready to fly."

"In a few minutes," Terry said. "I've just got to finish this."

"Don't wait too long now that the reaction's setting in. It's more than just fatigue—I feel giddy, halfway out of it, and I wasn't under nearly as much strain as you were."

Half an hour later he collapsed into bed for the rest his body craved, letting himself fully relax for the first time in days. Alison was already asleep.

Sometime during the night he dreamed that she was calling out to him. *Terry . . . Terry . . . oh, God, Terry, I need you. . . .* He came hazily awake, puzzling over it; he'd had the impression that she was frightened, begging for his help. That wasn't like her; Alison wasn't a dependent person. Was he subconsciously haunted by the memory of his anguish in Zach's box, when he'd believed he might have gotten her killed? Or was what he'd experienced in the clinic coming back to him in personal terms, as insistent as the shared physical pain? He'd felt that pain again in the dream. . . .

Terry . . . please, Terry—help me! It was more like telepathy than dreaming. Their past nights in bed together had strengthened the link between them, but never to the point of silent speech. Now it was as if she had cried out aloud. He rolled over and saw that she lay motionless on her back, her eyes open and filled with tears. In dismay, he reached out to draw her into his arms.

No! Don't touch me, it hurts too much to move! Show me how to stop hurting! The pain he'd automatically suppressed flooded into him as he grasped the fact that it was real. Alison had caught the virus, and she was in agony.

Instantly he projected comfort, aware that the intensity of the pain had completed the awakening of her latent telepathic capacity; he did not need to speak aloud. *Alison, I'm here. Relax—don't fight the pain. To make it stop you have to let yourself give way. Just relax, and follow my lead. We can feel it without suffering from it. . . .* He was able to convey the idea much faster through their established bond than to the strangers he'd helped in the past. When her mind meshed with his, she came easily along with him as he switched into the state where pain didn't hurt.

It does work! My body doesn't feel right, but I don't mind it! Only it's hard to breathe. . . .

Oh, God. Claudia had said there'd been deaths when breathing muscles were involved.

He could sense that Alison was worse off than the patients he'd seen had been. Was that just because they had already begun to recover, or did she have a more serious case? They had not stopped to think that she might contract the illness—he'd been so absorbed in others' pain at the clinic that it hadn't crossed his mind, while she, having come from a world without contagious disease, hadn't realized that she was vulnerable. He himself was not in danger of getting sick; his mind training gave him ongoing control of his body and his immune system was strong enough to withstand the stress that would otherwise have weakened it. Hers was not, and she too had been under great stress the past few days.

They had administered the antiviral to hundreds of people at risk, yet had not given it to her. Was there any left? There *had* to be—though Claudia had said they'd nearly run out, it was intolerable to think that the last dose might be gone.

~ *18* ~

HE WOULD HAVE TO wake Claudia, Terry decided; they could not afford any delay. Fumbling with his phone, he keyed her number and prayed she wasn't a sound sleeper. At last she answered. "It's Terry," he said shortly. "Alison's got it—got the virus. Can you bring me some of the pills?"

"I'll try. If there are any they're in a locked cabinet at the clinic. I may have to call one of the doctors."

"I think we should call a doctor anyway," he said grimly. "She's having trouble breathing. But she's in too much pain to be moved."

"They were all that way when it started," Claudia agreed, "and the doctors couldn't do anything after we ran out of drugs. It has to run its course. The difficulty in breathing is simply because of the pain—every breath is torture. If you can get her through that, she'll be okay,"

Terry bent over Alison and, being careful not to move her, he squeezed her hand. "If it starts hurting again, go ahead and cry," he said gently. "Struggling to be brave will make the pain worse. That was the first thing they taught me in training." In this situation her usual calm self-assurance would not serve her well, yet he couldn't induce her to give it up completely, which was the fastest way of getting the point across, for unlike the mentors he had neither the skill nor the equipment to bring her back from a breakdown.

If only they had the kind of neurofeedback helmets the mentors used! He had worked with the Maclairnan software and was sure he could recreate it; the computer they had brought from Alison's clinic was adequate. But the helmet was not. It didn't provide the detailed brain function output needed to transform states of consciousness into discrete mind-patterns a trainee could learn to visualize. So though he could help people temporarily when they were in pain, he could not teach them to shift mind-patterns by themselves—a process for which two helmets would be needed, since it depended on comparing the trainee's brain state with the instructor's. And without that training, they would never have the control over internal biochemistry that kept Maclairnans healthy.

More and more, it troubled Terry to think that neither Alison nor his crew could be given the same capabilities he himself had. And, he thought miserably, there was something else they would not have, something he'd never mentioned to them. . . .

The mastery of their bodily functions gave Maclairnans long life.

It was another reason the existence of Maclairn was being kept secret. If the public knew that the people of Maclairn generally lived to be a hundred twenty or older, its enemies would be more eager than ever to destroy them out of sheer envy, while its supporters would overrun the planet in search of the Fountain of Youth. Many of the people being trained by the mentors on Earth would outlive their contemporaries, but by that time, hopefully, mind training would be available widely enough for their longevity to be viewed as attainable. Meanwhile, it would not be among the promises he made as Captain of *Estel*. There was no guarantee of it for an individual anyway, only a strong possibility.

He did not expect that he himself would live to be much over a hundred; he hadn't had the advanced training Maclairnans got in middle life. But if he wasn't killed first, he might well live longer than Alison. And that meant he would be left to grieve for years after her death. He didn't think he could bear that. Now, in terror over the possibility that she might not survive the virus, he knew he couldn't. He had lost Kathryn; to lose Alison, even far in the future, would be too much. His heart aching, Terry lay back down beside her as renewed pain swept through them both.

The night wore on interminably. Over and over Terry let himself experience Alison's pain, leading her out of it into a brief respite. Her breathing was shallow in between those times, and she moaned in anguish. Whenever she slipped into unconsciousness the pain came back in full force, bringing her to full awareness. He knew that a seriously ill or semiconscious person could not avoid suffering; the programming provided by nature kicked in to warn anyone incapable of judging danger.

Claudia did not appear with the antiviral until nearly morning, bringing a doctor with her who could do no more than say he believed Alison would live. "She's strong," he said, "and she has courage. The cowards can't force themselves to breathe when it's as bad as this. But there are enough antiviral pills to bring her out of the worst of it."

There were not enough to cure her. She would be disabled for many days.

They were the hardest days Terry had known outside of prison—even worse, because there he'd had no one else's suffering to worry about. Alison's distress was much harder to bear than his own. He couldn't help feeling it was his fault. He had taken her away from a safe world into trouble she shouldn't have had to endure. Underneath, he knew this wasn't true; she hadn't been safe on Ciencia, she had been subject to arrest and happy to leave. Her life could no more be ruled by excess caution than his could. But sharing her pain took a toll on him, and he was too weary to be rational.

There was no lack of volunteer nurses; the people of Toliman felt nothing was too good for Terry, on whom they looked with awe as well as gratitude. More came to help than Claudia's house could accommodate, and she herself was kept busy tending to their needs. He was brought meals for which he had no appetite, and—in a genuinely helpful move—his phone was patched through the spaceport comm link so that he could talk to Jon aboard *Coralie*. Except for bathroom breaks, he was unwilling to leave Alison's bedside.

He had to sleep, of course, but allowed himself to do so for barely an hour at a time, unwilling to let Alison go too long without joining his mind to hers. Gradually, as she became experienced in shifting consciousness, she was able to maintain freedom from suffering for awhile; but she still needed his help in initiating it. The telepathy between them grew stronger, and they shared memories when her mind was clear enough. They rarely talked aloud; speaking was hard for her and had become unnecessary.

Eventually, she began to recover. Once she could sit up with assistance and could eat, Terry was impatient to get her back to the starship where the gravity could be lowered to make her more comfortable. Furthermore, the neurofeedback equipment they had, though inadequate, would be better than nothing. But he knew he was in no shape to fly.

You've got to rest, Alison told him silently. *My muscles just ache now—it's not unendurable. And there are plenty of people here to take care of me.* So at last he went to another room that Claudia vacated for him and, letting go of the conscious control of wakefulness that had kept him alert for all but brief naps during the past ten days, he slept for twenty-two hours in one stretch.

The next day helpers carried Alison to a van and from there to the shuttle, staying with her while Terry performed a thorough preflight check. With a feeling of relief he lifted off, rising gently from the pad and using as little acceleration as possible to reach orbit. It felt great to be in space again and he was eager to be back aboard *Estel*. Kind though the people of Toliman had been, he had felt trapped on the surface. Now, with Alison feeling better, it was like waking from a bad dream.

Jon and Gwen welcomed them aboard and helped Alison settle on the couch in the tiny lounge. Terry went immediately to the bridge and lowered the artificial gravity to a level just sufficient for stable orientation to the floor. It would ease the strain on Alison's muscles, and could be gradually raised as she continued to improve.

Next, he asked Jon and Gwen to move everything out of the spare stateroom and find someplace else to store stuff; he wanted to set up the neurofeedback equipment in there. "We needn't bother," said Gwen. "There's an extra stateroom you can use."

"An extra stateroom?" Confused, he failed to see what she meant until he saw her blush. Then it dawned on him: Gwen had moved into Jon's stateroom, and they intended to share it permanently.

He was glad. He had worried that they would be lonely and bored stuck in an orbiting ship for ten days with nothing to do. Evidently they had found something.

For the long term, a crew was better off with two couples than with one couple and two unattached singles. Jon was a lot older than Gwen, but that shouldn't matter. On Maclairn, where physical aging was slowed, people didn't know each other's ages unless they had been acquainted as children. It was considered impolite to mention the age of any adult under a hundred.

They had made good use of their time during his absence; between the knowledgebase and inspection of the ship they had become thoroughly familiar with its design and control board. Gwen was now qualified to make any necessary repairs not involving the hyperdrive engine, and Jon was ready to pilot it anywhere in normal space. So Terry let him handle the flight back to Centauri while he himself stuck close to Alison. When they arrived, he transferred the credits he'd received from Claudia to Jon and sent him to the surface in the shuttle to buy needed supplies and a cargo of plastic resin pellets to be sold at their next destination.

Terry set up the neurofeedback equipment in the stateroom vacated by Gwen, using the mattress from the folded upper bunk to turn the main bed into a couch with a back that Alison could lean against. He had only what they'd used in her clinic on Ciencia, but incomplete though it was, it had helped patients there, and here she could have several long sessions a day to speed her recovery. Through showing her how her brain was reacting, he taught her to perceive and maintain a relaxed state of mind despite pain, so that she was more open to his telepathic assistance than when merely trying to relax, and did not fall back into suffering as quickly when without it. "All those years when I watched you help others, I couldn't grasp how changes in the neurofeedback display *felt,*" she said. "At last I know."

He had not been alone with Alison in the daytime since before his imprisonment, and their new telepathic intimacy was a joy to him. Now that she could speak easily again, they did converse aloud; but the wordless undercurrent was there—the deep ongoing contact he'd craved desperately ever since his exile from Maclairn. He had gotten used to doing without it, but had nevertheless felt isolated and withdrawn. The lack of it had seemed an insurmountable barrier to union with Alison during his years on Ciencia, as he now confessed to her, admitting that he'd been paralyzed by fear of his own inability to love.

"Dearest, you don't need to explain," she assured him. "I understand so much more now about the void you felt, the torment it must have been to have this kind of contact with people and then lose it. And about why you want so much to make the whole human race aware that it's possible. It was almost worth my getting sick to gain the ability to join our minds."

"Well, I wouldn't say that," Terry told her. "But since

it did happen, let's make the most of it. In bed it will be even better, you know—sex between telepaths leads to a fuller merging of minds than what you've experienced so far."

"Then I'll hurry and get well fast," she said, smiling. They had to wait, Terry knew, until movement no longer caused her pain. But there was plenty of time ahead. He had Alison, he had *Estel*, and he was no longer in danger of imminent arrest. Life seemed totally good for the first time since he'd left Maclairn.

After several days on the surface Jon and Gwen returned and all three labored to transfer sacks of pellets into the cargo bay, after which Jon went back to pick up another load; he had bought more than the shuttle could carry. As exporting them was not illegal on Centauri, they could do so openly. Importing them elsewhere might be another matter. Terry had no idea how to locate a buyer, or even what planet to head for. But this time he knew where he could find out. He would visit Zach again, which he wanted to do anyway to get news of the situation on Earth.

"Be careful, Terry," Jon advised. "There are already rumors down there about what happened on Toliman, and some of them are exaggerated—you know what happens to stories when they spread. And if Zach guesses that you're the Captain of *Estel*, it may get around to this crime network you say he has."

"Why would he or anyone guess?" Terry asked. "Nobody on Toliman has heard of *Estel* except the patients and staff of the clinic; there's hardly been time for it to spread from the comments I planted on the Net."

"Time? God, Terry, there've been ten days," Gwen reminded him. "The text you put on Centauri's Net has gone viral, and that means it's all over Toliman, too, with responses from people who heard second-hand what you did there."

"Well, we want to spread the idea," Terry said, "so if it's happening fast, that's good."

"Yes, but as Jon said, the rumors are exaggerated," Gwen told him. "Some people are saying that the Captain of *Estel* can heal the sick—not just relieve pain, but cure whatever is wrong with anyone."

"I never meant to give that impression," Terry protested.

"Of course not, but stories grow in retelling. I recruited for the conspiracy on Ciencia, remember, and so I've seen what can happen."

Alison frowned. "And I know from my training in psychology how people can get carried away. We wanted to spread the symbol, the idea of future mind capabilities, but we didn't bank on your getting involved in mass treatment of patients too ill to be clear about what was happening. That put a whole new face on it. I should have warned you, Terry, but we were so absorbed in trying to help them all, and then I got sick myself—"

"I don't like the thought of *Estel*'s captain being viewed as some kind of miracle worker," Terry said, "but as long as no one's aware that it's me, I guess it's harmless. To whoever we meet I'll be just captain of *Coralie*, after all, and we'll be leaving soon."

"The people on Toliman know you came from *Coralie*," Jon declared. "Some will put two and two together. And if that gets back to Zach and he passes it on, sooner or later Quaid may hear about it. Which means he'll be able to follow your trail."

~ *19* ~

ON THE WAY down to Centauri, alone in the shuttle this time, Terry thought about what Jon had said. It was true that he hadn't been thinking clearly when he spoke out on Toliman about *Estel*. He'd been on his feet for many hours, sharing and then relieving the physical pain of more people than he could count; his head swimming with fatigue, he had acted on impulse. He had wanted to give those people hope for the future, just as he wanted to spread it from world to world—and he had sensed from the telepathic ambience of the place that they were in a state to absorb the message. It hadn't occurred to him that they were also in a state to confuse it with their memory of his aid.

Looking back, he realized they might not even know that it had been the antiviral pills that had cured them. Many had been semiconscious when the nurses passed out pills, a routine act that wouldn't have made much impression. Their contact with his mind, on the other hand, had aroused strong emotions. He had not told them his name or the public name of his ship. They had heard only the name *Estel*, backed by the deep feelings he himself had about it. Later, they or their friends had seen the prophecy about *Estel* he had posted on the Net. It wasn't surprising if they associated its captain with the mysterious respites from pain they'd experienced and credited him with special powers.

Oh God, Terry thought. He had botched it. He'd meant only to spread the idea that someday everyone would gain new and wonderful capabilities. Now they would be expecting some sort of supernatural intervention.

And the irony of it was that their conception of paranormal healing wasn't untrue. The mentors, and some other Maclairnans, were indeed healers. He himself could stop bleeding and heal minor wounds—which was actually a matter of showing people telepathically how to do it for themselves, just as he showed them how to stop hurting. He didn't have the gift for healing internal injuries or dysfunctions. But some did; on Maclairn there was no medical treatment because it was not needed. Healers couldn't defeat an external threat like a virus except to the extent of strengthening a person's immune system, and of course it wasn't possible for them to restore missing organs or limbs. Such problems were rare, however, so for all practical purposes, they could cure any illness that was likely to occur.

His first mentor, Aldren, had told him what a burdensome responsibility this was to those away from Maclairn where healing was normal. Mentors on Earth had to keep all their paranormal abilities hidden, but it was especially difficult when it meant refraining from helping people in need. He'd mentioned that he, Terry, might someday face such a situation—but that hadn't seemed likely enough to worry about. His only worry had been that if he learned healing skills he might be set apart from his peers by undeserved veneration. Now Aldren's warning made all too much sense.

As he brought the shuttle in to land, Terry noticed that something unusual was going on at the civilian edge of the spaceport. A crowd had gathered, and he could see Fleet officers holding them back. How odd, he thought. Civilian passenger landings were a rarity; a celebrity from Earth or some major colony would arrive in a Fleet transport. He'd heard nothing on the comm about any charter ship in the area.

He set down and secured the shuttle, wondering whether it was safe to leave it unguarded for even a few hours with so many people around. If he'd known a special event would be happening he'd have asked Jon to bring him down and come back for him. Perhaps he should find someone he could pay to keep an eye on it.

As he headed for the gate, people broke through the officers' barrier and rushed toward him. "Captain!" someone shouted, and others took it up. "Captain! Captain!" They swarmed around him, and a newscast crew's lights shone in his face. Bewildered, he stammered, "I'm not who you're looking for, you're mistaking me for somebody else—"

"You're not Captain Steward of *Coralie*?" demanded the nearest reporter. "We heard the controller authorize you to land."

Yes, nearly an hour ago he had identified himself and

announced his approach. But why would they care about the arrival of a free trader? Besides, Jon had been here twice in the same shuttle and had aroused no notice, not to mention his own first trip to the surface.

"We know what you did on Toliman," said the reporter. "We're honored to have you here; it's not often someone of your stature visits the Centauri system. Can you comment on how it feels to have saved so many lives?"

"I didn't save lives," Terry protested, "except in the sense that a few more people might have died without the antivirals I delivered."

"You're too modest. We've heard how you healed a whole clinic full of people. There are many here waiting for your help."

Terry realized with dismay that he was on camera. "There's no outbreak of disease here," he said. "The virus was contained."

"But there are people in chronic pain. Our stock of surplus painkillers was sent to Toliman, all that's left is reserved for accident victims and surgical cases, and it will be awhile before we get another shipment from Earth. In any case, painkillers won't cure them. It's a miracle that you've come just when you're needed most."

"Look," said Terry in desperation, "I can't cure anybody! I can help people stop suffering from pain sometimes, but that's temporary. The patients on Toliman were cured by the antivirals."

He realized that if he once started doing what he'd done for chronic patients on Ciencia, there would be no end to the demand—there would be far more than he could even begin to treat. There, the majority had scorned the idea of nonphysical treatment; those who came to Alison's clinic had been exceptions. Here, the public apparently expected him to provide it.

A woman rushed up to him and grabbed his sleeve. "Please! My mother has cancer that didn't respond to drugs—"

Sadly, Terry told her, "If I could help, it would be only for a few hours, and I couldn't see her day after day. So it wouldn't do much good."

"But if you touched her she'd get well," the woman insisted.

Horrified, Terry declared, "It's not a matter of touching! People have to stop their own suffering, I can only show them how." But he recalled how he had squeezed patients' hands to let them know their pain was about to ease.

Others pushed forward with similar entreaties, ignoring his words. There were several people in wheelchairs who begged him to help them walk. The newscaster had moved back to get video of the mob closing in on Terry. Then suddenly there was silence. Someone in the crowd had spoken the word *Estel*, and the murmur that rippled through it was clearly one of recognition.

"You came from *Estel*!" one of the women asserted. "You came to fulfill the prophecy."

Terry said, "What's written about *Estel* says that someday people will be able to use their minds in powerful new ways. It doesn't say anything about healing." He knew, telepathically, that he was not fooling anybody. Accurately enough, they had made the connection between the two concepts. "If you heard me speak on the comm," he added, "you know my starship's name is *Coralie*."

"But *Estel* is somewhere—you must have once come from it. Some on Toliman say it was the Captain of *Estel* who healed the sick."

Despairingly, Terry knew that denial was useless; he could not lie convincingly when emotion was enhancing their telepathic link to him. He must get away. But he couldn't leave Centauri before seeing Zach, for it was now more vital than ever to know what was happening on Earth and in other colonies to which the story might have spread. Zach might even be spreading it.

He stepped forward, but the crowd pressed closer,

barring his way. The murmurs grew louder and less deferential; these people obviously weren't willing to have their hope of immediate help thwarted. Then, to his relief, they fell back as two armed Fleet lieutenants appeared. Thank God, Terry thought. Fleet wouldn't be influenced by wild rumors, and would make sure he was let through.

"Captain Steward, you are under arrest," said one of the lieutenants. "You're to come with us, and don't try to stir up any more of a disturbance."

~ 20 ~

"THANKS FOR GETTING me out of there," Terry said to the officers as they escorted him across the field. "But arrest? I haven't done anything; I was mobbed by people who'd gotten a wrong idea about me."

"We don't take kindly to claims such as yours, Captain Steward. It's our job to maintain order at the spaceport, and to prevent fraud."

"Now look here," declared Terry. "I made no claims. I denied those people's mistaken ideas about what I did on Toliman, and it's not my fault that they wouldn't believe me."

"Just what did you do there?" one of the officers inquired.

"I delivered a shipment of antivirals. And I helped out at the clinic, comforting patients and trying to ease their pain." It was just as well, he decided, not to attempt an explanation of how he had eased it.

"And where did you get antivirals? We sent all that were available to Toliman days ago. If you were hoarding them secretly—"

Terry hesitated. They could not charge him with smuggling without concrete evidence that antivirals had been aboard *Coralie*; Fleet had authority only over ships and spaceports except when required to deal with armed civil conflict. All the same, it was not the kind of information to entrust to mere lieutenants. He had outranked them when he was in Fleet, and even after all these years it was hard not to feel that they should be saluting him.

They took him to an office in Centauri Base headquarters, which with a rush of nostalgia, he found familiar. He had walked through this building daily when stationed here, had been briefed for his last exploratory mission in one of the rooms they passed. In those days he had indeed been a lieutenant; his promotion to lieutenant commander had not come until he was on Maclairn. He wondered if any of the senior officers he had known were still around.

Not that they would recognize him if they were; the Elders had changed not only his appearance and voice, but his DNA. Nothing short of a retina scan could connect him to Lt. Cmdr. Terry Radnor, presumed dead, and that would be dismissed as coincidence. But he was glad that the commander to whom he was taken was too young to have met him.

"We don't tolerate disorder here," the officer told him, "and you seem to be the focus of it, whether or not you invited it."

"It was the last thing I wanted," Terry assured him. "I'm not what those people think I am. I'm just a trader."

"A free trader, I assume," declared the commander dryly. "In other words, a smuggler. As you know, I can't hold you without evidence, but I've sent officers to inspect your ship."

"We've just taken on a full load of resin pellets," Terry said. "That's legal."

"Nevertheless, we'll inspect. You will instruct your second in command to permit docking." He handed Terry a phone linked to the offworld comm.

Terry complied, trying not to worry Jon by what he said. God, he thought, what if they inspected thoroughly and found the hidden transponder that identified the ship as *Estel*? They could indeed hold him on a charge of falsifying its registration.

"Now, about the antivirals," the commander said. "You've nothing to lose by revealing where you got them, and I'm inclined to overlook any irregularities—I've done some checking and found that you didn't overcharge and donated a considerable amount of time to the clinic. But I'm curious. I tried all the sources I know of when Toliman appealed to me."

"I went to Ciencia," Terry said honestly, "and pharmaceuticals were the cargo I was offered."

"Ciencia! I'm familiar with the name, but I've never encountered anyone who's had dealings there. Is it true that they won't allow anyone to land?"

"Yes. Shuttles can't go below high orbit; local mining ships bring the cargo up, which is technically illegal. The government wants to keep the population in the dark."

The commander frowned. "I wonder . . . did you hear anything about a revolution starting?"

"I'm surprised if Fleet has heard that," Terry temporized. "I understood that you keep hands off that world." He was aware, as this officer probably was not, that Fleet was paid by Ciencia's government to do so, something the Elders had told him that he intended never to repeat. He still felt some loyalty to Fleet and any internal corruption was none of his business.

"There's a rumor going around in the city. Some trader who went to Ciencia heard a broadcast by a man who identified himself as the Captain of *Estel*. I don't suppose that was you?"

Terry froze; it was a moment before he realized that the officer was merely asking if he was the trader who had heard it, and that he evidently wasn't aware that the people in the crowd associated him with the name. "It wasn't, but I know of the incident," he said cautiously, hoping to find out what Fleet thought of it.

"I've got mixed feelings," the commander admitted. "If the people of Ciencia are oppressed, a nonviolent revolution would be a good thing, and I'm glad we have no arrangement with its government that would require us to step in. But apparently this man calling himself Captain of *Estel*—who, incidentally, has by now been mentioned in a posting that's gone viral on the Net—went further. He talked about some future time when people will allegedly gain abilities that might be considered paranormal. And that could lead to trouble if the rumor spreads."

"Trouble? Why?" Terry inquired.

"Well, you've seen that people can get wrought up over things like that. You know and I know that the paranormal doesn't exist—at least I assume you do, since you've convinced me that you made no wild claims to arouse that crowd. But on Earth some strange beliefs have been taking hold, and lately the situation has begun to get ugly. I was stationed there until a few weeks ago, and I didn't like what I saw."

"What sort of beliefs? Surely not supernatural healing of the sick." He knew that even if the mentors were teaching more openly than in the past, they would never have done anything to precipitate a misunderstanding like the one he'd just encountered.

"Not that, but notions equally foolish. The old fantasy of ESP is being revived, and along with it a claim that people can develop other powers such as the ability to stay healthy through some magical mental process."

"Foolish, of course," said Terry with a straight face. "But I'd hardly call it ugly."

"There's been a reaction," the commander told him. "First it was just a fanatic religious group that took such concepts literally and claimed all paranormal abilities are works of the devil. They began accusing law-abiding citizens of witchcraft. Then these relatively harmless zealots were exploited by a more sinister movement, a terrorist group with deep historical roots that thrives on the innate intolerance of humans for anyone unlike themselves. Its influence is growing, and there has been violence."

Terrorists. He had known, of course, that there must be more than the two he had killed. He had been aware that they must have backers, and that the kind of targeted violence in which Maclairn's enemies had long engaged must be continuing. But their attacks had been focused solely on Maclairn and its representatives. What he was hearing now, Terry realized with horror, was a great deal worse. It implied that open violence was threatening ordinary people who'd been taught by the mentors or simply influenced by the ideas they were subtly spreading.

Works of the devil? Witchcraft? He had read enough history to know how dangerous fear of them could be. And Aldren had warned him long ago that believers in psi would someday be endangered.

"So," the commander was saying, "this man from *Estel*, if there is such a ship, is playing with fire. He'd be putting the Ciencians at risk if it weren't that it's a closed world the fanatics can't reach—but if he's stirred up a revolution it may not stay closed, and once landings are allowed the troublemakers will get in. The same goes for any other colonies he may visit. If he ventures to Earth they may murder him, which might be just as well except that it would make him a martyr, and then we might have widespread conflict that Fleet would have to deal with."

"I don't suppose he's aware of what's going on there," Terry declared. "I got the impression from what I heard that his aim is merely to give people hope for a brighter future."

"No doubt. But encouraging them to believe in an illusion would be bound to backfire, even without organized opposition." The commander sighed, then reached for his phone. "I'll get you an escort back to your shuttle. You'll be mobbed again if you walk out there alone."

"I have business in the city," Terry said, "I've got to take care of it before I leave."

"Frankly, Steward, you are not welcome here; you've been seen on the news and we don't want another disturbance."

"I won't be recognized away from the port if I avoid public places."

"Perhaps not, but getting out of it, and back again, would be impossible."

Terry hesitated, debating whether he dared make the suggestion that came to mind. There didn't seem to be any alternative. "I was here many years ago," he said, "and I had friends among the junior Fleet officers. Some of them were, well, delayed in getting back from leave sometimes . . . and there was a tunnel—" He wasn't disclosing any secrets; all the officers had known about it. Young pilots were allowed a good deal of leeway.

With a smile the commander said, "I guess we can let you out that way. But you'll have to make your own way back after dark, and I want your shuttle gone by morning."

Terry refrained from revealing that he knew which corridor led to the tunnel and let the provided escort take him to its entrance. He recalled the last time he had been there, late on the night before his departure for the training base on Titan. With no knowledge of what lay in store for him there or the deployment to Maclairn that had followed, he had been bitter—he'd been due for command on his next explorer mission and the unexpected, seemingly senseless orders he'd received had outraged him. He had never wanted to be anything but an explorer pilot. That he might someday find himself committed to a more far-reaching goal would have been unbelievable.

As he left Fleet's building he looked back with a sudden surge of sadness. On receiving his commission he had sworn to uphold League law. By falsely identifying his ship and the crew's citizenship he had broken it, and now

he was embarking on a path that would involve more serious breaches. He had no regrets, considering the change
in his circumstances, but the memory of his uncompli-
cated former life was bittersweet.

~ 21 ~

ONCE IN THE city Terry entered the nearest place where
he'd be unlikely to be noticed, a dark, sleazy-looking
bar, and phoned Zach. "I'll pick you up," Zach offered.
"I've got some information for you, and after seeing that
newscast I'm damn sure you'd better not attract any more
attention."

When he arrived Terry moved quickly from the bar to
his groundcar. "How did a story like that ever get started?"
Zach asked as they headed for the Emporium. "I guess
you delivered the antivirals to the clinic personally, but
this other stuff—"

Terry told him as much as he could without implying
any psi capability. "Turning off suffering from pain is a
trick of the mind," he said. "Anyone can do it if the conditions are right; I just showed them how. It only worked in
that special case, for a little while—to do it consistently
takes special training."

"Which apparently you've had." Slowly Zach added,
"There are people who'd pay a good deal for that kind of
training."

"It's not for sale, Zach."

"No, I don't suppose it is. I suppose it has something
to do with your knowing more about the ship *Estel* than
I'd heard from the first trader who mentioned it. That
rumor has grown since you were here, by th way.It's all
over the Net. And when I passed it on by ansible, which you
didn't tell me not to do, I got back some interesting information from Earth. It seems there are people there with
the same sort of ideas this Captain of *Estel* talks about."

He went on to repeat the information Terry had gotten from the Fleet commander, but had details to add to it. "These guys opposing believers in paranormal stuff are a nasty bunch," he said once they had settled in his workroom to talk. "None of my contacts want anything to do with them. It's one thing to ignore laws, and I deal with plenty who break more than I do. But it's something else to stir up hatred and go after anybody with a different way of thinking. In any case, I don't hold with killing except when it's a matter of defense."

"They're actually killing people?" Terry exclaimed. "Like gangland shootouts?"

"Nothing so common as that. But there have been lynchings. And they work hard at terrorizing people they don't go so far as to kill. They burn houses, or crosses stuck up in front of a house. They cover themselves with white robes and masks so they can't be recognized and defy anyone to stop them. And no one does, unless there's evidence of murder. The police on Earth are too busy trying to trap rule-breakers like me to take on a bunch of weirdos that there's no way to identify."

"Oh, my God." What Zach was saying triggered a memory of something Terry had once read; since boyhood he had spent a good deal of time poking around knowledgebases, and ancient history had fascinated him. "Does this terrorist movement have a name?" he asked.

"Yes, as a matter of fact, but it doesn't make sense—it would be laughable if they weren't so violent. They call themselves the Ku Klux Klan."

Shocked, Terry said, "It makes all too much sense. That's the name of a group that existed way back in the nineteenth and twentieth centuries. Its tactics were just the same. And so were its motives—it aimed to foster hatred of anybody different from its members. At first they just hated dark-skinned people, who were underdogs in the area where they lived—"

"Dark-skinned people?" Zach scowled. "I know that hundreds of years ago my ancestors were treated unjustly, but you're saying they were targeted by terrorists?"

"Some were. The Klan also persecuted other minorities, Jews and Catholics and foreigners. Of course wars have been fought for similar reasons, but this wasn't on as large a scale as a war. Klansmen were just losers who took out their frustrations on those they treated as scapegoats. At times they had a lot of supporters, but after racial and religious prejudice became socially unacceptable, the organization died out."

"It should have stayed dead," Zach remarked grimly.

"But the revival is understandable," Terry said, "because living conditions on Earth are so bad now and for the first time in centuries, there is a group of natural targets."

"You think there are people who can really do paranormal stuff, not just talk about it?"

"Yes," Terry admitted. "At least a few, enough to arouse opposition from men seeking something to oppose. The Klan made its members feel important. It involved a lot of powerful symbolism that was turned to evil ends. Any movement, good or bad, needs symbols in order to thrive. So to stir up violence against people with new and frightening abilities, somebody without the imagination to create a new symbol unearthed an ancient one that fit."

"If that's true," Zach said, "then the good guys had better get a symbol, too." There was a pause. Then he said reflectively, "God, that's what's happening, isn't it? With the rumor about *Estel*?"

"I'd like to think so," Terry replied. "But I doubt if the Captain of *Estel* knew he was going up against the Ku Klux Klan."

"There's something else he doesn't know," Zach declared, "which is one reason I'm glad you came today, Steward. And I'm even gladder since I saw on the news that people are confusing you with him, because that's a dangerous position to be in."

"I don't like it," Terry said, "but I wouldn't call it dangerous as long as I stay clear of the Klan."

Zach said slowly, "I don't know who you are or what you've been doing before now; since your ID's so clean I'll wager it doesn't show your real name or anything about your past. But I could tell you were a special case from the moment I first I talked to you, and hearing that you didn't take a profit on the antivirals bears that out. You know something about this *Estel* business, and I'm willing to bet you've got a way to contact the man in charge."

When Terry didn't reply, he went on, "At first I thought there wasn't really any Captain of *Estel*, that it was all some kind of fantasy. I heard otherwise from my friends on Earth. There's a bounty on him. The word is out that unnamed sources will pay triple the going price; some in my network were set to go for it until I told them to lay off. You sure as hell don't want anyone thinking you're him, and so maybe you can warn him to lie low."

Terry drew breath. He had known it would happen sometime, but he hadn't thought he'd be targeted so soon. "Is the Klan behind it?" he asked.

"I don't think so—they don't operate that way, and they don't have that kind of money. I'd guess that it's coming from higher up, maybe even somebody with government connections. It's been hinted that rough stuff won't be prosecuted."

"In other words, he's wanted dead or alive."

"Yes, but there's a bonus if he's delivered alive, and that means either he's believed to have information of value, or somebody has a grudge that demands personal payback."

It had to be Quaid, Terry realized despairingly. He must have gotten word to his contacts on Earth after all. They didn't know his current name or his ship's—but the news that Captain Steward of *Coralie* had spoken of *Estel* on Toliman might be reported by ansible, and they would surely assume there was some connection.

Chilled, he recalled what Quaid had said to him when taking him out of prison: *If you ever suggest to anyone, in any way, that this trip ever happened, you will die in the most unpleasant way our biochemists can devise.*

Twice now he had let emotion blind him to caution; he had named Quaid in his broadcast, and he had revealed a relationship to *Estel* by his talk in the clinic. Twice, too, in Zach's box and on Toliman, he had been jolted by the fear that he'd led Alison into worse danger than he'd planned. Was it true what Jon had said, that he felt after escaping the crash of *Venture* that he was leading a charmed life? Would he pay for his recklessness, leaving her and the others stranded on some unfamiliar world to rebuild their lives without him?

"Either way," Zach was saying, "I wouldn't want to be in that Captain's shoes if he's brought in."

With difficulty, Terry concealed the extent of his dismay. "Thanks, Zach," he said. "I'll see that the warning is passed on."

~ 22 ~

THAT NIGHT, HAVING returned to the spaceport after dark and lifted off without incident, Terry boarded *Estel* in a quandary. "Gather around," he said to the crew. "We've got a lot to talk about."

He had spent a long time with Zach, waiting for darkness, and had learned a good deal from him about possible markets for plastic resin pellets and future sources of cargo, as well as about the climate of opinion in various colonies he might visit. Still, deciding on a destination was going to be hard.

The crew had seen the spaceport newscast live, and shared Terry's consternation. "We can't ever go where there's an epidemic again," Alison said, "or where people in pain are likely to be in contact with us."

"No. But my reputation may spread," he said. "So it may be that we can't go anywhere receptive to belief in psychic healing. And there's another factor that has to be considered."

He told them, then, what he had learned from the Fleet commander and from Zach about the situation on Earth. "It's a lot worse than I expected," he said. "I knew Maclairn had secret enemies in the League government. But the open, organized persecution of anybody who reveals an interest in psi is another matter."

"I don't see how a fringe group like this Ku Klux Klan can attract enough members to be a real threat," Jon argued. "Surely it's just a few psychos attracting excess publicity, the way serial killers do."

"Historically, the Klan attracted many members who weren't psychos," Terry said. "In some eras it was supported, theoretically in secret, even by community leaders; they acted anonymously but everybody knew who was involved. That's what hatred does to people. They lose all sense of decency and reason."

"But why would they hate anybody because of the color of their skin?" protested Gwen. "That's just senseless. A difference like that is too trivial to cause conflict."

"Well, there were complicated reasons why skin color was considered significant," Terry said, "because at that time skin variations weren't evenly distributed among the population. What's relevant now is that the people with the most power were afraid those unlike themselves would gain equal power—and the difference today isn't trivial. Humans who have, or want, psi abilities really are different from the majority who fear such a change. So it's easy to turn zealots against them."

"A mob, yes," Alison agreed. "The sheep will follow whoever leads them. But to create an organized hate campaign based on ancient symbols strikes me as a very

calculated process. It seems odd that people of the sort
to fall for it had the skill to do that."

"I don't for a minute think they did," Terry replied.
"As you say, it must have required some sophisticated
social engineering. And that didn't come from within the
Klan; the historical connection is too obscure for unedu-
cated bigots to have been aware of. I'm willing to bet that
they're just tools and that the movement was set in motion by the high-level conspirators in the League that I
told you about."

"You mean the ones who backed the terrorists you
killed?" asked Gwen. Terry had filled her in on the basic
facts about Maclairn during the flight to Toliman.

"Yes," he said. "This is just the sort of thing they'd
try. It must have started long before they made the attempt to destroy Maclairn, of course—it would take years
for such a movement to get well established."

"Then the terrorists were Klan members."

"That's unlikely," said Alison. "Most people who join
hate groups are basically cowards. They destroy and kill
from fear because it makes them feel stronger than those
they attack, but they generally avoid risking their own
necks. Fanatics recruited for suicide missions are of another breed."

"You're saying the League government is as corrupt
as Ciencia's" Jon said grimly. "I thought maybe we'd seen
the end of that, but if it's true that the police aren't putting down the violence—"

"The police on Earth gave up on stopping gang warfare long ago," Terry said. "It wouldn't take many corrupt
officials to keep them from making an effort to stop hate
crimes. But Maclairn's enemies are stronger than I
thought, and they're manipulating public feelings. I'd give
a good deal to know how the mentors on Earth are responding. It must be hell for them—there'd be no way of
doing the job they came for if they didn't keep their views
secret from everyone but their trainees."

"Then they probably isolate themselves from world affairs," Alison said.

"Yes, but mentors are far more telepathic than I am, and they'll feel the pain, even the emotional pain, of victims everywhere as if it were their own."

You're feeling it yourself, in your imagination, she observed silently. *It's going to be hell for you, too. . . .*

He clenched his fingers. "I can't *do* anything about it!" he mumbled. "Even if I were free to go to Earth, I'd be helpless—"

"You did a lot on Ciencia," Jon reminded him. "You can influence more colonies the same way."

Terry hesitated, then said, "That's what I've set out to do. But it's more complicated than we knew at first. I can't go where I'll be a public figure reputed to have magic healing powers; that rules out worlds where the ideas I've been promoting will be welcomed. Yet on worlds where they won't, I'm likely to run into what now seems to be a violent attempt to suppress them. The risk is greater than you people bargained for."

"I'm okay with that," Jon declared. "Don't worry about it."

"We have two choices," Terry went on. "We can go somewhere safe, sell our cargo, and probably make a good living for years by smuggling without anyone guessing that I have anything to do with the *Estel* rumors. Or we can go where we can spread them most effectively and sooner or later, encounter hostility."

"We always knew we would," Alison said calmly.

"But the danger isn't just to us. The man I talked to in Fleet made me realize that by encouraging the people of Ciencia and other colonies to adopt new ideas, I was setting them up to be threatened by the hatemongers."

"Terry," said Jon, "you can't have it both ways. Either you believe these new ideas are vital to the survival of civilization, as you told us, or you don't. If you do, then they're worth risk for everyone who cares, not just you."

"That's how civilization has progressed from the beginning of time, isn't it?" Alison added. "You know more
about history than I do—isn't it true that millions of people
sacrificed and died to get us where we are now?"

"Yes, of course," Terry said. "But I need to be sure
you all see it that way. Gwen?"

"When I heard the recording of your trial speech I
thought it was just about ending the censorship on
Ciencia," Gwen said, "yet it made me feel I'd fight for
anything you believed in. Now that I know it's so much
bigger than one world, and so important . . . well, it's a
matter of choosing sides, isn't it? A person can't be neu-
tral about something other people are being killed for.
And if I'm on your side, then I'm committed."

Terry nodded, deeply touched by their support.
"Okay," he said. "We're all agreed that we're going to keep
on promoting what *Estel* stands for. But there's one more
thing you're entitled to know."

He had not told them this part yet; he'd wanted to be
sure they'd back him for the goal's sake and not just out
of friendship or loyalty. Now he said soberly, "There's a
price on my head. Zach told me bounty hunters on Earth
are looking for *Estel*."

"Surely no one on Earth can have picked up on the
local rumors already!" Gwen exclaimed.

"No. News spreads fast by ansible, but nothing in them
suggests I'm a threat to take seriously. And there's too
much money involved for it to come from anyone but the
League government insiders. Which means someone on
Ciencia got word to them about my broadcast there."

"Quaid," said Jon. "Just as I feared at the time."

"Probably. I didn't think he'd survive the wrath of his
colleagues once they knew he'd held out on them, but he
must have sent a message that convinced his League contacts that I'm dangerous. I guess I should be glad they
think I may have an impact."

Alison's worry flooded into Terry's mind despite her

effort to hide it. "You mentioned to Ciencia's controller before your speech that you were headed for Centauri," she reminded him.

Jon nodded. "If Quaid checked the traffic control recording, he'll have passed that information on, and they'll question the port authorities here. We'd better get away soon."

"Can you change the name of the ship again?" Alison asked.

"No, because I can't go back to the Fleet base to hack the records."

"What would happen if we just changed the name anyway?" Gwen asked. "Will they check it against the registration at the next colony we visit?"

"Not if it's a small one. They check here because Fleet's records are on-site; they don't have to do it by ansible. But a backwater colony might not bother."

"They'll recognize *your* name, though," Alison said, "if the news about what you said on Toliman has spread."

"You could use a false name yourself, maybe," suggested Gwen, "except it's too late to get Zach to alter your ID—"

"I wouldn't want to do that even if it weren't," Terry said. "I'm already on my third identity, and the name Steward—means something to me. Besides, if it was changed again I could never prove in the future that *Estel* is mine."

After a long moment of thought he added, "It's a common name, so if I'd chartered a ship other than *Coralie* an outlying colony's officials might not report my presence to anyone likely to investigate. Zach said some of those places are friendly to smugglers. If I hadn't been so stunned I'd have asked him to change the name on our false registration when he informed me about the bounty."

"But wouldn't he have wondered why?" Alison objected.

"He told me I'm being misidentified as the Captain of

Estel. He's sharp, and he could figure out the need to rename the ship—even now, if I texted him with a hint about it."

"It seems to me you're placing a lot of trust in a man who's involved with a crime ring," Jon cautioned. "I suppose you're relying on this telepathic sense you've got, but when it comes right down to it, he breaks the law for money, doesn't he? Why would he do anything you can't offer cash for?"

"I have good reason to trust him," Terry pointed out. "I was with him all afternoon, in his car and in his back room—yet he advised me to warn *Estel*'s captain instead of trying to extract information that might give him a chance to collect the bounty himself."

"That's true," Jon admitted. "Why, I wonder? Not that you're not likeable enough to make friends with all sorts, but a professional forger—"

"Zach was fascinated by what I told him about the *Estel* idea," Terry said slowly, "and about my mind training, which I explained without any hint of where I got it. He hates the League government and the regimentation it imposes, so he shares the hope for the future I'm trying to spread. I owe him a lot, and his underworld connections may prove invaluable to us."

"I'm not sure I'm comfortable with your being indebted to him," Alison said. "He's an outlaw, after all."

"We're outlaws ourselves," said Gwen.

"Yes," Terry agreed. "And it may be that Zach will someday ask me to do him some favor in violation of the law. But I have a feeling that it will be a matter of helping *Estel* supporters that I'd want to help anyway."

Part Three: Vagabond

~ 23 ~

ESTEL LEFT CENTAURI as *Coralie* and arrived at New Afrika, a colony in the Epsilon Eridani system, under the name *Vagabond*. Terry had decided to use a name so familiar that it was unlikely to attract notice and told Zach to pick something else common if that one was already in use. There had been countless ships named *Vagabond* in the past, both on Earth's oceans and in space; but fortunately it was currently available. Although text messages were less likely to be intercepted than voice comm, he would have hated to exchange several even though he'd worded his request for forgery subtly.

Once landing was authorized, Terry took Jon with him to sell their cargo of plastic resin pellets. This was possible because on his last visit to Zach he had obtained a Class D pilot's license for Gwen, which permitted her to serve as caretaker for a ship in a stable orbit although not to break out of it. An engineer was fully capable of this, and she had thoroughly familiarized herself with the ship at the same time Jon had. He knew she had always wanted to be a pilot; she'd been kept from it only because relatively few of the young people who applied for pilot trainee jobs on Ciencia were hired. The Class D license would permit her to fly the shuttle as a student, and since his unrestricted license qualified him to instruct, he could eventually get her a legal upgrade.

The other major change in their roles was that to traffic control and on the surface, Jon was named as *Vagabond's* captain. This, Terry hoped, would mean that his own name would never have to be mentioned and the bounty hunters would have no way of locating him in an attempt to extract information about *Estel*. By delegating all financial transactions, too, he could avoid allowing his ID to be scanned. To be sure, Quaid had known of his friendship with Jon Darrow and if Darrow's death in the explosion of *Bonanza* had been questioned, a connection could conceivably be made; but that wasn't likely to happen.

So Terry was to be in all respects the elusive Captain of *Estel*, no more identifiable than the ship itself. And this, Alison said, was a good thing. "You are a symbol, just as *Estel* is a symbol, and you will always be mysteriously hidden—not just from your enemies but from your supporters. Mystery strengthens people's emotional response to an idea. Maybe they'll go on crediting the Captain of *Estel* with supernatural powers, but it won't matter as long as they don't know you're him."

New Afrika was a promising market for resin pellets as it had no arable land free for growing the genetically-engineered plants from which plastics were produced—all fertile soil not needed for food production was used to grow sugar cane, as refined sugar was the colony's main export. And its import tax was high. The custom here was like Ciencia's in that smugglers' starships remained in high orbit, beyond police jurisdiction, while local ships came up to trade; but since offworlders were permitted to land, the smugglers' shuttles also came down. It was rare for them to carry cargo, however. There was no point in taking such a risk when the demand for contraband goods exceeded the supply. The only tricky part was making contact with a trustworthy dealer.

Zach had given Terry several phone numbers. The first

man he called was unavailable; the second was suspicious, but agreed to meet. "What did you say your name is?" he inquired when he appeared at the designated café near the spaceport.

"I didn't," Terry said. "And I don't plan to, as I don't want certain people to find me. But I can tell you I've been in Zach's box." By now he understood that this was not literally true of everyone who said it; it was simply a password given to anyone Zach trusted, whether they'd had face-to-face contact with him or not.

The dealer glared at Jon. "I usually meet with only the captain."

"This is Captain Darrow of *Vagabond*," Terry said. "I came along to vouch for him because he's not acquainted with Zach."

He let Jon make the deal in view of his long experience, and observed that he was as good a negotiator as he'd always claimed; they got enough more than they'd paid for the resin pellets to make a larger profit than he'd expected. Once they had arranged a time for the pickup late that night, they decided to take a look at New Afrika before returning to the shuttle.

Jon, who had been to the planet's surface at Centauri only after dark—or what passed for dark when that system's second sun was above the horizon—exulted in the warm red sunlight of Epsilon Eridani. Though he had often viewed Ciencia's cold bluish sun from space, he had never before seen sunlight in an atmosphere or felt the touch of it against his skin. "And you mustn't let it touch you now," Terry warned, "or you'll burn, despite having been exposed to the ship's sunlamps."

As he would himself if the darkening of his skin for disguise had totally faded, he thought with dismay. It was easy to forget that he was more vulnerable to sunburn than he had been after awhile on Maclairn. The sun had been hot there, glaringly hot; once his mind training had enabled him to adapt to the extreme climate, he had spent much of his free time outdoors. There had been a lake with a beach where he and Kathryn went to swim. . . . Strange that he was picturing Maclairn now, on a world unlike it, when he'd believed the flashes of memory were long past.

Something had brought it to mind, Terry perceived, some vague stirring that he couldn't put his finger on. Not through sight; the settlement didn't resemble Maclairn—its large buildings were of steel and glass like those of most colonies, not brick and stone. The people weren't dressed like Maclairnans, and they were predominantly dark-skinned. It was just a feeling. . . . And then it stuck him: he sensed a presence that could only mean that there were telepaths among them.

Not many. It wasn't the same as on Maclairn where everyone was telepathic and his awareness of interconnection was constant. But on Ciencia and Centauri, he had felt nothing, and here he knew the psi faculties of at least a few others were alive.

Zach had told him that New Afrika would be more receptive to the concept of esoteric mind-powers than the average colony world. It had been originally settled by emigrants from Africa on Earth, who had a cultural affinity for ancestral traditions passed down through the centuries since a time when belief in the so-called paranormal had been widespread. They might now, Terry thought, be ahead of the game. There might even be people in this colony who had recently emigrated to escape the predominant anti-psi attitude on Earth. Certainly the Ku Klux Klan would have no supporters here.

And so, he realized excitedly, it was fertile ground for spreading belief in *Estel* and what it stood for.

Was there a chance he might connect with a telepath? It had been so long since he'd done so as a normal part of his life—there had been the recent few days with the Elders, and of course his growing bond with Alison, but those were special cases. His hunger for an ongoing link to others, which on Ciencia he'd learned to suppress, came rushing back, and he knew he would not leave New Afrika without trying to make contact.

The colony had been more completely terraformed than most, and there was a public park in the city's center that had grass and flowers as well as the fast-growing genetically designed trees found nearly everywhere with a suitable atmosphere. They settled on a bench and Terry, who had brought his tablet along, proceeded to plant his texts on the local Net. Here, it wasn't even necessary to hack; access was public and he established a new blog linked to all the likely sites he could find, creating several identities so as to initiate a lively discussion. It would be possible to continue it from orbit, something he hadn't dared to do when hacking because the origin of space transmissions could be traced.

Alison would be enraptured by this place—Ciencia was too cold for flowers and she had never seen any except in pictures. He could hardly wait to show them to her, but she wasn't yet fully enough recovered to walk far or to cope with the planet's slightly plus-standard gravity. Assuming that the cargo sale went smoothly, they would stay awhile before moving on, he decided. For the first time since escaping from prison, he had no need to hurry.

~ 24 ~

BACK ABOARD THE ship, Terry couldn't keep his mind off the hope of telepathic contact. It wasn't long before he began getting responses to his postings, which he had worded as an observer's comments on the rumors that were circulating in the Centauri system. A few people, he found, had already heard them by ansible or from other traders. Interest in *Estel* among New Afrikans was evidently high.

In the middle of the night, as planned, a shuttle—
much larger than *Estel*'s own—docked and took on the
cargo of resin pellets. If this was all there was to smuggling, he thought, it would be an easy life. But he knew
that on some worlds it would involve more action and
more danger, as might acquiring a new cargo even here.
Unauthorized export of New Afrika's sugar was illegal
and demand for it was insatiable nearly everywhere; suppliers had no need to risk themselves by delivering it to
free traders. He and Jon would have to pick up a load
without attracting the attention of the port authorities.

Since Alison wasn't quite well enough to go to the
surface, Terry stayed aboard to let Jon and Gwen go there
together for a few days. He kept busy conversing via the
Net with people curious about *Estel*. There was a good
deal of wild speculation about the abilities the Captain of
Estel had declared would become common; he was dismayed by the extent to which his original postings had
been exaggerated. But there were also hints that some of
the commentators knew more than what was in the rumors. A few of them implied that they were well aware
that esoteric mind-powers already existed.

Were they simply basing this on reports of the persecution on Earth? Terry wondered. Most of the other writ-
ers who had heard about it seemed not to take the idea of
psi seriously; they thought the actions of the Ku Klux
Klan were a literal witch hunt. Yet he was sure that in
the city he had sensed the presence of at least one nearby
telepath. . . .

Finally, after three days, someone who identified himself as Jamar wrote, "Do you want to continue this discussion by private message? Or get together, maybe?"

Terry had not given his real name, of course, nor had
he provided a messaging address for his screen name. He
had not even revealed that he was in space. He hesitated.
This could be a trap if the Klan had agents in New Afrika.
But he'd seen no evidence that it did, and if he was ever

going to contact anyone telepathically, he had to follow up every possible lead.

"I'll be in the city the day after tomorrow," he replied, and arranged to meet Jamar in the park. To his surprise he found that he was looking forward to it with boyish excitement.

Jamar proved to be a young man, dark-skinned like most New Afrikans, whom he immediately liked. He wasn't telepathic, or if he was, he didn't let it show; but he had poise and self-possession of the kind people got from mind training, making Terry wonder if perhaps he'd been taught by the mentors on Earth. Such people weren't informed about Maclairn, of course, and they didn't gain psi capability unless they were naturally gifted. But they had immunity to physical suffering and ill health—the capabilities he wished could be given to Alison. Not for the first time, he mourned his debarment from Earth, not for his own sake but for hers.

After a brief conversation Jamar said, "I wanted to warn you in case you don't know what you're getting into. On Earth what you've said online would be dangerous. A lot of the people in your forum are just repeating rumors, but your posts go beyond that, and I got the impression that you didn't set it up just for entertainment."

"I'd like to think," Terry said cautiously, "that the rumors are based on fact. Not literal fact, of course—not a real ship with a captain who's got supernatural powers. But a symbol of something that's not so far out as we may assume."

"Well," said Jamar, "it's been said for centuries that ESP exists. And if there are people who have it, maybe they should keep quiet about their talents, as I'm sure they do on Earth, because what's happening there might spread."

"Yet if it's true that such talents will become more common in the future, is it right to hide knowledge of them? Shouldn't the public be learning to accept the idea, so that in time hate groups will be squelched?"

Jamar paused, and then said with warmth, "Come home with me for dinner. There's someone I want you to meet."

Terry had flown to the surface alone once Jon and Gwen were back, not wanting to involve Alison in something that might prove dangerous; so he accepted the invitation gladly. He was welcomed into a modest apartment in one of the city's large buildings, where Jamar's wife offered him a tall sugary drink—something he'd not had since last on Earth—while Jamar made a phone call. After a few minutes of casual conversation, another guest arrived.

"This is my friend Deion," his host said, and Terry scarcely heard, overcome by the presence of the tall white-haired gentleman to whom he was being introduced. His first impression was that he must surely be one of the New Afrika's leaders, but that was not what mattered most. The man was telepathic! This, or someone like him, was the person he had sensed on his first day in the colony. Their silent communication was wordless, but within moments they knew without speaking that they shared a similar outlook on life and could trust each other implicitly. It was the sort of connection he had felt with Maclairnans, and now that he was experiencing it again, he did not see how he had borne the years without it.

Deion smiled. "I've read your postings," he said, "though I don't often write online myself. We seem to agree that there's hope for future progress, and that's something too rarely found these days."

"People seem to crave it, though," Terry said. "Look at the interest they've shown in the rumor about a ship named *Estel*."

"Yes, that's certainly encouraging. I'm impressed by the way it's taken hold, and I'm wondering how such a rumor got started."

He must be careful, Terry realized, or the man would

pick up the truth from his mind. Regretfully he closed it to sensing, and immediately perceived a trace of bewilderment in Deion's, as if suppression of telepathy was something he'd encountered before and found troubling.

"Are you from Earth?" Deion asked. "I thought I knew all the refugees, but there may be some here I'm not aware of."

"Refugees?"

"Yes, people interested in the paranormal who've emigrated to escape persecution. Many have come to New Afrika, some of them families who lost their homes to fire. We have a sort of community, a support group. You'll be welcomed into it whether or not you've been a victim."

"I haven't been to Earth for many years," Terry said, "but it's true that I've just arrived here." He did not say how; though these people surely wouldn't report him for smuggling, if he should be caught anyone he'd associated with might be placed under suspicion.

"That's a little surprising," Deion observed, "because you seem to have knowledge about the mind that's not widely disseminated. I'd thought that only here and on Earth were there people from whom you might have gained it."

"Maybe it's just instinct," Terry suggested. "If the time has come for humankind to start developing these abilities, wouldn't it happen in many places at once? For instance, if there's really a Captain of *Estel*, couldn't he be doing what apparently some on Earth have been doing?"

"Yes, I suppose he could. If so, his counterparts on Earth would be eager to meet him."

No doubt, Terry realized suddenly. He hadn't given any thought to how the mentors would react if the *Estel* rumor reached them, as of course it would. They would want to track it down. And it was quite possible that Deion was in contact with one of them; it was becoming more and more evident that he, at least, must have had mind training.

How long, Terry thought, could he himself conceal the fact that he too had been formally trained? Long enough to enjoy a few days of fellowship with the community of emigrés? It would be awkward if they found out, but not disastrous; not knowing about Maclairn, they would not suspect he was anything but a trainee like themselves. They would not press him to say where and by whom he'd been taught; it was understood among them that these details were not to be spread around.

They sat down to dinner and went on talking, Terry oblivious to everything but his joy in finding friends who fully understood the ideas he'd been trying to convey. When the meal was over, Deion said quietly, "What if it were possible to actually gain some of the mind faculties we've been discussing—would you want to?"

"Yes, of course," Terry replied. Was this a subtle approach to the issue of whether he already had?

"You're aware of what happened on Toliman. The man rumored to have helped the patients there obviously had such skills, including an ability to feel pain without suffering and to draw others into the same state of mind. To have acquired that, he must have gone through considerable pain while learning."

"I imagine he did. It could hardly have been inborn because children who don't mind pain would be in danger of injuring themselves."

Deion nodded. "If learning of that kind were essential to gaining other mind capabilities—if it involved a painful ordeal—would you be willing to go through it yourself?"

Terry nodded, confused. Perhaps Deion hadn't guessed after all; it didn't sound like a rhetorical question. But why ask, when the training was available nowhere but on Earth?

"This may surprise you, but I think you have faculties you're not conscious of," Deion continued. "That often happens when a person has a natural gift, and suppressing it can lead to emotional problems—"

Yes, Terry thought. He'd had his share of them in youth without knowing why.

"And so I think you would benefit from the kind of training I mentioned. I tell you this in strict confidence, of course—what I'm saying must never be passed on to anyone. But if you decide you want to pursue it, come to the Bramfield Health Club on Kenya Street and ask for me by name."

Bramfield Club? In shock, Terry was struck by vertigo and Deion's voice sounded hollow and far away. The Bramfield Clubs on Earth were where the mentors from Maclairn worked. They had been founded and financed by Arthur Bramfield, Kathryn's grandfather, for that purpose, though they also offered standard health club facilities to the public. If there was now a Bramfield Club in New Afrika, and Deion could choose people for special training there. . . .

That meant Deion was a Maclairnan. A mentor. And he, Terry, had given his word to the Elders that he would never visit a world where mentors might be encountered.

~ *25* ~

COULD DEION HAVE already learned about the Elders from his mind? Terry wondered in panic. The man had not probed; he would have felt that. And his mind had been closed to casual pickup of information so as to conceal the truth about *Estel*. But mentors were far more perceptive than people with less psi capability. The Elders had insisted that he could not hide his awareness of their existence from mentors; the course of his life—exile, the loss of his career in Fleet, his separation from Kathryn— had been determined by that assumption. It would be unbearable if because of one unplanned visit to a friend's home, that turned out to have been for nothing.

He calmed the pounding of his heart and with effort

steadied himself, aware that Deion was waiting for a reply. Of course the man could not have grasped such an incredible fact during a mere hour or two! The ban on contact had been meant to apply to ongoing interaction with mentors who knew Terry and were accustomed to communicating with him, people who could tell that he was not deluded. Mentors who would absorb the secret unconsciously even if there was no sudden revelation. His terror that he might have betrayed it had arisen from turbulent emotion rather than rational fear.

But he must leave quickly. And he could not come to the surface of New Afrika ever again.

"I'll certainly think about it," he told Deion. "I've got commitments that will keep me tied up for the next few days, though; in fact I'm running late, I'm supposed to be somewhere else right now—"

Deion looked at him closely. Obviously he was not fooled, and Terry knew that he'd sensed his dismay although not the truth that led to it. "It can be frightening to open your mind to new faculties, even when you believe they're good to have—especially if you're in the habit of repressing them. But it can also be a very exciting experience."

"Maybe so," Terry said. He would have to offer some excuse to break away, though the only one available was humiliating. "But I'm not sure I can take much physical pain. To do it in theory is one thing, but basically I'm a coward."

"It's not the prospect of pain that's bothering you," Deion declared.

"No," Terry admitted. So much for thinking he could get away with a lie.

"I'm a good judge of people," Deion told him, "and I believe you have great aptitude for the kind of training I can offer you—more than you suspect. That may account for your deep interest in the *Estel* rumor. Perhaps you feel such capabilities are just for the future you've written about, or for superheroes like the Captain of *Estel* who may be only a fantasy. Don't let that keep you from seeking them in real life."

Terry's heart ached at the need to deceive this man who was so much like the mentors whose friendship he'd valued in the past. To walk out on the only psi-gifted person he'd met since leaving Maclairn, letting him think he was too weak to act on what he'd claimed to believe. Would his Net forum continue? he wondered. He could never post there again, at least not under his existing screen name; would Jamar and others who'd valued his comments now be disillusioned by his apparent failure to follow through? He turned away from Deion to thank Jamar and his wife for their hospitality, and barely managed to get out the door before his eyes blurred with tears.

He was on his way back to the spaceport before it occurred to him that there was a more pressing reason to have left in a hurry than the remote possibility that Deion would instantly learn about the Elders. It was much more likely that he would have sensed that Terry knew about Maclairn. The mentors kept their origin strictly secret, sharing it only with the few observers who had been taken to their world—not counting the Fleet crew there and the handful of government officials who knew. If they thought that secret had gotten out, they would be justifiably worried, and so Deion might have probed him to discover the source of the leak. It had been a narrow escape.

He had not been aware that Maclairn intended to expand its network of training centers beyond Earth as soon as this. Were they being established in all large colonies? Would he have to find out before landing on a world whether it had a Bramfield Club? No, he decided. Undoubtedly, mentors had come to New Afrika to go on teaching the emigrés from Earth, whose training would have been incomplete at the time they fled. Advanced instruction often went on for years.

Sadly, Terry looked around at the New Afrikan city

where he had planned to stay awhile, thinking it might be a long time before he came upon another colony as pleasant. Passing the park that Alison would now never see, he grieved for her. She had never been to a physically attractive world. He had promised her a look at this one, yet they must leave when she wouldn't be in any danger here. . . .

His heart jumped as, suddenly, he was struck by what that implied. He could never set foot on New Afrika again—but Alison could. It wouldn't matter if she met mentors if he was not with her. She could spend as much time with them as she liked. Alison could get the training he so desperately wanted her to have.

It would be easy to arrange. The training, secret from the public, was offered only by invitation; ordinarily someone simply walking into a Bramfield Club would be observed for weeks before being approached by a mentor. But Alison had a good excuse to go there and to request neurofeedback treatment—her muscles weren't completely recovered from her illness and she still had some pain. Since Deion knew that a man with extraordinary ability to relieve pain had helped the virus patients on Toliman, there was no reason why she couldn't admit that she had been one of them, expressing interest in how he'd done it. She could also mention that she had operated a neurofeedback clinic of her own in the past. It would thus be entirely natural for the mentors to consider her a good candidate for mind training.

She couldn't get enough of it to protect her health and lengthen her life, of course; that took many weeks of practice with the advanced neurofeedback equipment mentors used. But she would have the beginning, the breakthrough. She would be free of physical suffering for the rest of her life, and would be able to control simple things like body temperature and heart rate. And her latent telepathic ability would be further enhanced.

Terry was so happy at this thought that it almost

overshadowed his dismay at his own close call and his sorrow about the loss of the lasting friendships he'd hoped to form in New Afrika.

Aboard *Estel*, he called the crew together and explained the situation. "I don't see any problem with your going," he said with enthusiasm. "That is, if you want to, Alison." Belatedly it dawned on him that she might not be eager to undergo the painful stage of training.

"Of course I do," Alison said. "I've wished for years that I had abilities like yours. Will I be able to relieve patients' pain as well as my own?"

"Maybe. You're not psi-gifted, but just knowing how it feels to control your mind's reactions should enable you to help people."

"Are you—sure I'm qualified to learn?" she asked hesitantly. "If I don't have a gift for it—"

He realized that he'd confused her. "Anyone who's willing can gain control of their own unconscious processes. Psi capability, if it develops, comes later, from having telepathic contact with the mentor during the training. A mentor's gift is strong enough for unconscious communication even with someone who lacks natural aptitude."

"If that's true," declared Gwen, "then I want to be trained, too."

Terry hesitated. It would increase the risk if two people with knowledge of Maclairn went to the Bramfield Center, yet neither of them could be connected to him in any way. And though she had never felt the kind of pain relief he'd given Alison on Toliman, the training didn't depend on prior experience. All the Fleet personnel assigned to Maclairn had gone through it successfully, and Gwen was certainly as brave as any young Fleet officer.

"I need to be sure you understand what it involves," he told her. Unlike Alison, she hadn't heard him talk about it before. "You have to go through a crisis intense enough to override your inborn genetic programming, the mental reaction to pain that evolved to prevent animals from ignoring injury. As a human adult, you can learn to turn that reaction off so that you don't suffer. But it's possible only if an instructor has shown you how, telepathically and through neurofeedback that displays details about how your brain is reacting. And for that to happen he has to subject you to very extreme pain at the beginning."

"Well, if other people endure it, so can I."

"I'm sure you can—but don't expect it to be easy. Some steps in the training are worse than what you'll anticipate." He couldn't offer a warning more specific than that; there was one step all trainees swore to keep secret from anyone who hadn't been through it, since its effectiveness depended on surprise. He cringed at the thought of Alison, or Gwen either, being purposely led to believe for a while that she had failed to qualify, yet only in that way could a person stop fighting the pain long enough to discover that doing so was counterproductive.

"Once you're past the bad part, the rest is fun," he assured them. "It's a wonderful feeling to be in control of your body's reactions. The only problem is that we can't stay here long enough for you to get much practice with neurofeedback."

"But you have a neurofeedback setup aboard," Gwen protested.

"Yes, but not the right kind of helmet. Ours doesn't show brain reactions in enough detail."

"Can't you get one?"

"I wish to God I could. But aside from those manufactured on Maclairn, they exist only in major medical centers. League doctors use them just for diagnosing neurological disorders."

He went on to emphasize how careful they must be not to let anyone find out that they knew about Maclairn, or were aware beforehand of the nature of the training—it would lead to questions that could not be answered. And especially, they must not reveal that they'd had personal contact with someone who'd written in the Net forum, or that they'd been told about the Bramfield Club by a newcomer to New Afrika. "Just say you've heard it offers neurofeedback and are interested because you've worked with it before," he said to Alison. "And that Gwen comes with you to work out at the health club simply as your friend. You'll be offered special training before she is, but after you're through the first of it, you can ask that she be invited."

"But if there's danger that the mentors could learn your secret telepathically, why can't they learn ours?"

"Because I'm concealing something major that's relevant to Maclairn, facts that would startle them. They won't sense commonplace information you want to hide—mentors respect privacy. For you, the danger is simply in what you might let slip in talking to them." He recalled how while getting acquainted with his first mentor Aldren, he'd been carried away by his liking for him and had said more personal things about himself than he'd intended.

"Will the man you met, Deion, teach us himself?" asked Gwen.

"Perhaps, but more likely it will be his lifemate—his wife, though marriage on Maclairn isn't formal. They work as couples and usually teach trainees of their own sex."

"Weren't you formally married to Kathryn?" Alison asked in surprise.

"We were married under League law by the captain of the Fleet ship. But that was only so we could share a cabin on *Promise* without shocking passengers from conservative cultures on Earth. Maclairnans don't believe personal commitments are any of the government's business."

He suddenly remembered one policy he'd neglected to mention. "Don't let on, either of you, that you're in relationships," he told the women. "Mentors won't train half a couple—during sex an untrained partner with latent psi capability might perceive things that would interfere with being trained later. Couples have to get the training at the same time."

"Won't Jon be coming soon, though?" Gwen asked.

Oh, God, Terry thought, she'd been assuming more than they'd realized. Nothing had been said about Jon getting the training, and he had been silent throughout the discussion. Naturally he would want it, but he had known without being told that it wouldn't be possible.

Brusquely Jon said, "I can't go, Gwen. Terry and I have been seen together; the dealer we sold the cargo to knows us."

"Does the dealer know Deion?" Gwen demanded.

"We can't be sure," Terry said. "He may know some of the emigrés and if he met Jon in their company, might mention that another man had come onworld with him. Not many ships arrive here, and it's important that it not be guessed that I'm from *Vagabond*. Deion sensed some mystery about me and might very well try to trace me."

"I would have to disappear suddenly when we leave, just as you will," Jon pointed out, "and if it were known that I'd had a companion matching Terry's description, a connection with his disappearance might be made. Maybe some time in the future we'll be back here, and enough time will have passed for me to get the training without risk. But it's more important for you young people to have it, anyway."

"I don't see the risk," Gwen persisted. "Surely none of the people who believe in *Estel* would turn Terry over to the bounty hunters, even if they identified him with its captain."

"It's not that," Terry told her. "I know you don't understand, and I'm not free to explain further. But there would be serious consequences if I were near a mentor long enough for him to sense the secret I'm sworn to keep from them."

"He can't reveal it even to me," Alison added. "When he asked me to leave Ciencia with him, he made me promise not to press him about it. So you mustn't either, Gwen."

That night when they went to their cabin, she asked, puzzled, "If a partner in a couple who hasn't yet had mind training learns too much about it during sex, why haven't I learned too much from you?"

"Because the training was a long time ago for me, and it wasn't relevant to you personally. But it's true that we can't make love tonight, when we've been talking about it and you're wondering what it will be like." He was stricken; they had made love every night except during her illness. And they would be separated for ten days or more. It would be hard to refrain now, when they needed each other's strength—but for her to grasp what he could no longer keep out of his mind would be worse. He couldn't take the chance that she might fail to experience the shocks necessary to a breakthrough.

In bed she nestled close to him without sexual provocation. "Terry ... I'm scared," she whispered.

"Everyone is, at the beginning. That's what makes it possible to learn—it shakes you up, forces your mind out of the rut of ordinary functioning." Alison was normally so calm, so self-controlled, that the mentor would have to push her hard, he knew, and that wasn't pleasant to think about. But what she'd gain would be worth it.

"It will turn out okay," he promised. "You can trust mentors—they've got a lot of experience and they don't let anyone come to harm."

In the morning the two women went to the surface, piloted by Jon. Terry transferred enough credits to them to pay for health club memberships and live on while there, glad that Alison wouldn't have to venture alone onto a planet new to her.

"I wish I could take you down myself," he said sadly when they boarded the shuttle. "But I gave my word that I'd never go to a world where there are mentors, and I'll not knowingly break it." He took Alison in his arms, aching at the realization that he would miss her terribly and wondering if he would sense her pain remotely while she was undergoing the ordeal.

~ *26* ~

DURING THE NEXT few days Terry was on tenterhooks, waiting for word that Alison had been selected for mind training. They couldn't communicate directly, but they had arranged a code whereby they could pass information to each other via the Net forum, in which they were both using new screen names. Finally the message appeared: "I'm hoping to learn more about what happened to me on Toliman," she wrote. "I've met someone who has a theory about it."

The first day, or night, would be the hard one, he knew. As the hours passed he found himself unable to focus on anything. What if it went wrong? What if she *did* fail—what if she didn't agree to face more pain after discovering that she couldn't tolerate it by means of sheer fortitude? That never happened; mentors could judge beforehand what a person was capable of, and they didn't invite anyone to start who wouldn't get all the way through. Nevertheless, he worried. She had not questioned his conviction that it would turn out well for her; what if it turned out that he'd misled her?

He recalled his own ordeal vividly—not so much the pain, which had receded from memory once he'd learned not to suffer, but the despair following the demonstration that endurance has limits. Only after a trainee gave up endurance as hopeless could he or she understand that the fight rather than the pain itself was what produced suffering.

At times of crisis, Terry knew, telepathy could work over long distances, even between orbit and the ground. When the moment of Alison's agony came, he did feel it—

in his own body, as he had with the clinic patients. Instinctively he switched into altered consciousness, ending the suffering, and then he remembered that he must not, just as the mentor who was instructing must not; a trainee couldn't learn do it for herself if someone helped at this stage. She was not telepathic enough to receive aid from this far away, so it didn't matter; all the same he refrained, and suffered with her.

"God, Terry!" Jon exclaimed from across the table where they were sitting. "What's come over you?"

The intense pain lasted only a minute or two, of course; mentors made sure it was severe enough to preclude its being needlessly prolonged. When it passed, Terry explained as much as he could without giving away the part that a candidate for future training couldn't be allowed to know. Jon frowned, troubled. "Will I feel it too, when Gwen—"

"No. Neither of you is consciously telepathic. Alison and I have communicated silently before, mostly in bed."

"Then later, when Gwen is back, will I learn too much about it from her? You said people in relationships weren't supposed to be trained before their partners."

"That would be a real problem if either of you were psi-gifted," Terry said. "But you're not. A mentor who hasn't met the partner doesn't know, so their policy is not to take the chance; but I can tell that whatever telepathic bond you develop won't be strong enough for her to leak information."

Whether he actually sensed it or merely assumed, Terry wasn't sure, but after some hours he became aware that the crisis was over and that Alison had experienced her breakthrough. From now on, she would be having regular neurofeedback sessions, to practice and to learn other skills, for as long as they could stay. He hoped Gwen would be able to begin mind training soon because every day they spent in orbit would increase their risk of being arrested for smuggling.

Jon had spent some time on the surface after landing with the women, finding out, in his role as ostensible captain of *Vagabond*, what smuggling sugar involved. It wasn't encouraging. On Ciencia neither he nor his suppliers had needed to worry about arrest as long as they avoided displeasing the government racketeers who encouraged illegal traffic. But New Afrika's government wasn't corrupt. When it declared that exporting sugar without a license was prohibited, it meant exactly that. Most of its revenue was derived from the export tax, which was lucrative because the offworld demand for sugar was great enough to support a virtually unlimited number of legal exporters as well as to tempt free traders. The law against unlicensed trading was therefore strictly enforced.

"Couldn't we just buy a license?" Terry suggested. "I don't want to endanger Alison and Gwen if we can avoid it, and if we're caught while they're aboard they'll be implicated."

"It's not so simple," Jon told him. "The legal exporters have a cartel; you have to pay a high fee to join before you can apply for a license from the government. They don't accept offworlders—if they did, they'd lose control of the interplanetary sugar trade."

"Well, then, we haven't much choice. How do other free traders get away with it?"

"I gather it's more or less of a crapshoot. The police can't board every shuttle that lifts off, day or night; we haven't been inspected so far. Which gives us an advantage, because now they're used to us. Smugglers don't stick around visiting a city."

"Besides, traffic control knows we're in low orbit, where I assume smugglers' starships don't come." After selling off their cargo of resin pellets he had descended to minimize the time spent making multiple trips to the surface.

"Yes, but even in high orbit, outside New Afrika's jurisdiction, there's danger because Fleet patrols the system to protect its own merchant ships from pirates. Not all sugar smugglers are honest free traders; some find piracy more profitable than dealing with a willing supplier. And Fleet treats smugglers the same as pirates except when a ship has been attacked."

True, Terry thought—while in Fleet he had not thought there was much difference between the two. The concept of an honest free trader had been unknown to him. "What's the penalty if the police catch us?" he inquired.

"A year in jail—as you probably know, according to League law no colony can hold an offworlder longer than that for anything short of murder. And confiscation of the cargo, of course."

Terry considered it. If arrested by Fleet they would face at least three years in a penal colony. "What would happen," he asked slowly, "if we stayed in low orbit, and took the cargo aboard here?"

"No smuggler would do that," Jon protested.

"That's the point. They know we've been here awhile, and we'll be staying even longer, making shuttle trips back and forth. It won't occur to them that we'd be carrying sugar while still under their jurisdiction."

"You're right," Jon said. "It might be our best chance—and the women won't be aboard while we're loading, so if we're caught at it they won't be involved. How much time should we allow for them to finish their training?"

"We should pick up the cargo now, Jon," Terry decided. "The longer the time between doing it and leaving, the less chance of being chased when we go." To be sure, they'd be vulnerable during that time, but Alison and Gwen wouldn't be. And breaking orbit without attracting attention would be easier.

So Jon went back down to find a supplier and make a deal, which was something in which he had long experience, while Terry stayed alone aboard *Estel* pondering their next move. Where to go? Sugar would bring a high price in all but a few colonies; he could take his pick of those where he was unlikely to encounter bounty hunters.

But he hated the thought of tearing Alison away before she had completed enough mind training to protect
her health. This was an even greater regret than it had
been before she had any training at all. Originally, he had
been sad that she lacked it and had known that as she
aged faster than he did, his worry would grow worse. But
he had realized that even if he had access to the indispensable brain imaging helmets, he could not bring himself to inflict severe enough pain on her to produce a
crisis, nor would he be qualified to lead her to a breakthrough—only a mentor possessed that skill.

Further training was another matter. Now that she'd
been given the ability to consciously alter her brain's responses, he could easily teach her to control the ongoing
reactions to stress that would otherwise result in aging
and illness. Complex neurofeedback software would be
required, but he was familiar with the source code of that
used on Maclairn and was sure he could recreate it. That
is, if he had sufficient data input, he could. . . .

Adequate helmets existed only in the hands of the
mentors and, as he'd told Gwen, in major medical centers
on Earth; colonies had neither the population to warrant
top-quality medical facilities nor the funds to acquire them.
And of course, even if he could go to Earth, there would
be no way to get hold of such an object. They wouldn't be
for sale and he wouldn't want to steal from a hospital,
assuming that were possible.

Only on Earth . . . but, Terry recalled suddenly, there
was one exception. There was one colony that prided itself in having what it claimed was "the finest medical
facility in the galaxy." Undine, the world from which the
founders of Maclairn had escaped. . . .

He had learned all about Undine when studying
Maclairn's history. The medical authorities there were
literally the government, a dictatorial government that
imposed treatment for all lapses from health on its
citizens, whether they wanted it or not. They were under

constant surveillance, even to the point of automated analysis of bodily functions by the equipment in their bathrooms. They were not allowed to do anything viewed as a health risk, nor were they even allowed to die—dead bodies were kept in stasis indefinitely.

Undine's hospital, Terry knew, was the focal point of the colony there. It contained the seat of government as well as medical facilities; its administrators were the only public officials, just as ambulance crews were the only police. All citizens were subjected to periodic medical evaluation even if they were not sick. Examinations were far more extensive than routine ones elsewhere, involving invasive tests as well as every conceivable type of scanning. They surely involved neurological testing, using the most sophisticated brain imaging equipment available. Ian Maclairn, who had developed the methods of mind training later used by the mentors, must have obtained his helmets from that hospital in the first place. And almost certainly he must have stolen them.

What had been done once might be done again! The hospital was wealthy, for Undine's citizens were heavily taxed to support it, and it possessed far more equipment than could be put to legitimate use. Undoubtedly it had many such helmets and employed them in "diagnosing" the rebellious tendencies of anyone considered politically unreliable. Terry knew he would feel no guilt whatsoever about stealing from such an institution if he could get away with it.

But could he? Could he even get to the surface of Undine?

The information he'd been given was, of course, more than two hundred years old; but the colony's government had been a stable one supported by the vast majority of its citizens, who wanted their health protected regardless of cost. Quickly he turned to the ship's knowledgebase and found that nothing had changed. What little it said about Undine confirmed what he already knew.

The world was closed to immigration; otherwise it would be overrun by people seeking free medical care who'd fallen for the claim that its population "lived" forever. Tourism was likewise forbidden, as was travel by citizens, which was legal but precluded by monetary restrictions that prevented them from spending any funds offworld. It was not as isolated as Ciencia, however. Messages got in and out by ansible, and they were not censored. Fleet's freighters brought imports paid for in diamonds from the planet's rich mines. Whether other ships went there was doubtful, since it was off the beaten track; still, he knew that the Maclairn group had smuggled in equipment for their hidden lab. It would be a prime market for smuggled sugar, certainly, since the people of Undine could not legally consume "unhealthy" food.

Underneath, Terry was aware that attempting to land there would involve high risk with little chance of achieving his goal. Still, it wasn't a place where bounty hunters would look for him. And like Ciencia, it was desperately in need of faith in the power of the human mind. Ian Maclairn's followers had spread belief in that power as best they could and had won converts; perhaps not all of them had escaped with the group. Perhaps they'd left descendants hoping they were not alone in their faith that people were more than machines requiring medical repair. He could confirm that hope, whether he got his hands on neurofeedback helmets or not. And so, he decided, Undine would be his next port of call.

~ 27 ~

MORE THAN A WEEK passed, during which Jon brought up several loads of sugar without incident. If they had been anywhere but New Afrika, Terry would have made at least half of these risky trips himself; but he dared not take a chance of being caught on the surface of a world he was sworn to stay away from. One pilot had to remain aboard *Estel* in any case, though they shared the job of moving the sugar sacks out of the shuttle.

Jon, who had formerly been in the habit of stashing refined platinum within *Bonanza*'s cabin so the inspectors wouldn't know he'd mined more than was in its hold, suggested that they conceal some sugar sacks in the same way. "As insurance," he said.

"Against what?" Terry protested. "If they board us they'll check the cargo bay and arrest us. Even if they don't search the whole ship, we won't get a chance to use what's hidden." But there was no downside to the suggestion, so he went along with it.

He kept his plan for their next destination to himself. There was enough to worry about without explaining to Jon why he'd chosen a course that meant asking for trouble.

Alison and Gwen sent regular coded messages through the Net forum, letting him know how their training was progressing, and once they reported that they were confident of their ability to turn off suffering at will, Terry reluctantly sent word that it was time to leave. It would be unwise to wait any longer in orbit, loaded as they were with illicit cargo.

On the night before the women were due to come aboard, the police arrived.

"HS *Vagabond*, this is New Afrika Control," the comm announced. "Stand by for routine inspection."

Keeping shock out of his voice, Terry responded, "New Afrika Control, this is *Vagabond*. We have been in orbit for many days now, as you know. What reason is there to inspect us now?"

"It's routine," the controller repeated. "Our policy is to make spot checks. We have a problem with smuggling here."

Argument was impossible, of course; it would only arouse suspicion that might not yet exist. If he and Jon were friendly to the inspectors, Terry wondered, could they possibly be talked out of entering the cargo bay? Was their work routine enough that they might be tempted to save themselves effort by cutting corners?

Helplessly they waited while the police ship approached and docked. A year in jail, Terry thought in despair. He could endure it; he'd experienced worse. Undoubtedly Jon could, too; but what would happen to Alison, to Gwen? New Afrika was a better colony to be stranded in than most, at least—Alison might get a job as a neurofeedback therapist at the health club and Gwen would have no trouble finding work at the spaceport, for maintenance engineers were in demand everywhere. But later . . . after losing the cargo he wouldn't have enough money for upkeep on *Estel*. What then?

"Terry," Jon said hurriedly, "you can tell what people are thinking, right?"

"Not specifically, unless they're telepaths and want to communicate. With others I can just sense feelings, attitudes."

"Well then, find out how these inspectors feel about their job. Are they strong for law and order, or might they be open to collecting side benefits?"

"A bribe, you mean? I thought New Afrika's government wasn't corrupt."

"It's not, but that doesn't prevent individual officers from taking advantage of their opportunities. You're used to being with people committed to upholding the honor of Fleet. I've been living in the real world since I was a kid."

"Not all Fleet officers fit the image," Terry admitted. It was quite true that some of them carried smuggled items alongside the cargo on the manifest. Not having been in the merchant branch of the service, he was not sure what else they might do. "We haven't enough platinum left to tempt anyone," he pointed out.

"But we have sugar hidden away. Why do you think I suggested stashing some?"

"They can get all they want from the hold," Terry protested.

"No. They have to produce vid evidence of the inspection if they make one, and then they get nothing but their regular pay. If we can convince them not to enter the cargo bay—offer a story that will sound convincing to their superiors—who can say how much they've carried away and sold to dealers?"

It was worth a try. Though it would be a mistake to insult police officers if they were dedicated to law enforcement, the moment they emerged from the airlock he could sense that they were not. They weren't dishonest men, he perceived. It was just that they didn't care any more than he himself did whether the rules against free trade were obeyed.

Jon was ostensibly *Vagabond*'s captain; Terry signaled a go-ahead and kept quiet. He did, however, project the idea of potential profit, just in case the inspectors had enough unconscious telepathic ability to pick up the thought.

"I can't stop you from searching my ship," Jon said to them, "so I may as well come clean and save you the trouble. We're here because a couple of crew members were overdue for shore leave; we've no plans to take on cargo. But, well, with sugar so cheap in this colony I couldn't resist stocking up on some. We can't afford it anywhere else, and I wanted to give the women a treat. I know exporting it's illegal, but do a few sacks for our own consumption count?"

"Yes," said one of the inspectors. "Sorry, but they're forfeit. How much have you got?"

Jon and Terry proceeded to haul sacks out of the spare staterooms. "Do I have to pay a fine or something?" Jon asked innocently. "I'd just as soon do it now; we're leaving tomorrow when our crew's back, and I don't want to waste time going down to the city."

The inspector hesitated, estimating how much he could

get in hard metal; an electronic transaction would do him no good since it would be recorded. Finally he named a figure low enough to make sure it would be forthcoming. Jon obliged, saying, "The women in our crew will be disappointed, but I guess you have to follow the law."

"Yes," said the inspector. "We appreciate your cooperation." He and his partner carried the sacks through the airlock, which required several trips, and then departed.

Weak with relief, Terry sat down at the table. "They weren't fooled," he said to Jon.

"Of course not. But we gave them an out."

"You knew all along this would happen. How?"

"There was no other way so many ships could be escaping. Think of the amount of sugar being smuggled into other colonies—it all has to come from here. The police confiscate a few loads from time to time to make it look good, and there was real danger ours would be one of those taken. But underneath it's just like it was on Ciencia—the colony supports itself by interstellar trade. The only difference here is that some of it's legal."

"But the government doesn't get anything from the share that isn't."

"No, but the suppliers do, and they wouldn't support the government long if it enforced restrictions on how much they could sell. Their cartel has more political clout than anyone else on the planet because sugar is the sole cash crop suitable for export."

The next morning Jon went down to pick up Alison and Gwen, who returned elated by the skills they'd gained and impressed by the sunlit world they had seen, so unlike the dark, frigid one they'd been born into. They'd had plenty of free time between neurofeedback sessions and had taken advantage of New Afrika's park, gardens, and outdoor swimming pool. "I never dreamed people lived like that," Gwen said. "The stories I read on Ciencia didn't do other colonies justice."

In bed that night Terry and Alison made love exuber-
antly, thankful that the separation was over. "Was the
training worth it?" he asked her afterward, as they relaxed in each other's arms. "The moments of pain, I mean,
and the hours of despair I couldn't warn you about."

"That was terrible because I thought I'd failed you,"
she admitted. "That I couldn't live up to your expectations. But later, when Deion explained and I realized that
you'd had to fail at the beginning too, I was happy because going through what you did makes us closer. There's
so much I've always wanted to understand about you,
Terry. I know there are things you still can't tell me, but
sharing your mind skills helps a lot."

"I'm glad," he whispered, pulling her to him again and
caressing her shoulders. "It was hard sending you away,
yet I wanted you to have what only mentors could give."

"The only trouble," she said hesitantly, "is that I do
wish I could go on learning, like I was told I would—"

"That may not be impossible," Terry told her. "If
I'm lucky, I may find a way to teach you more skills
myself."

~ *28* ~

AFTER DEPARTURE FROM the Epsilon Eridani system, *Estel*
was still in danger of being intercepted by Fleet patrollers, or worse, by pirates. Terry held his breath until they
were far enough out from the sun to jump. Once they
emerged in Undine's system, however, they were free and
safe—at least until his effort to acquire the neurofeedback
helmets thrust them into danger again.

When making his plan he'd had no idea how he could
get to the surface of Undine, considering that privately
owned ships never went there and it had only a minor
spaceport to serve Fleet shuttles. But his conversation
with Jon about black market dealings had set him to

thinking. Fleet freighter captains did sometimes carry contraband; though as a young officer he hadn't wanted to believe that, it no longer shocked him. Why shouldn't they? They weren't stealing and it didn't interfere with their work, nor did it cost Fleet anything as long as a ship didn't deviate from its scheduled route. He knew that smuggled cargo got to Undine somehow, and if no other ships landed, that was the only way it could.

So all he had to do was contact a Fleet freighter and sound out its captain, who would undoubtedly be well aware of the high value of sugar.

But this might not be easy. He didn't know how often freighters came to Undine. He would have to wait in high orbit until the comm picked up a ship's transmissions to the colony, hoping that would happen before *Estel* got too low on life support to stick around. And he would have to think of an excuse to rendezvous that would hold up if the captain wasn't receptive—something he would have to judge telepathically, as he had with New Afrika's police inspectors.

Predictably, Jon was dubious. "If we try to rendezvous with a strange ship they may assume we're pirates," he pointed out.

That was indeed a problem, Terry realized. In this case it was not good that *Estel* was visibly armed. "I know Fleet's comm codes," he said, "so their AI won't raise an alarm. I'll just have to take the chance that they won't do enough of a visual scan to notice the laser cannon."

"But if they do?"

"They won't fire first, and no real harm will be done if we're captured. Once they get us aboard they'll find sugar instead of weapons, and they'll know that since we already have a rich cargo we'd have nothing to gain by stealing theirs."

"You're overlooking the possibility that they may assume we stole it in the first place."

"To get them to rendezvous you could say we're in

trouble, that we need some kind of assistance," Gwen suggested.

"No, I couldn't. Pirates do that all the time; it would confirm any suspicion a captain had."

Jon sighed. "I may have done too good a job of convincing you that not everyone in uniform follows the law. What if you meet one who feels it's his duty to arrest us for smuggling?"

"He couldn't accuse us without evidence," Terry declared. "Mere possession of sugar isn't a League offense, and we're a long way from New Afrika; they're not under contract to enforce its local laws at this distance."

"Didn't you say importing it to Undine is illegal?" Gwen put in.

"Yes, but we haven't imported it yet, and we can't be arrested for mere intent even if it's obvious."

"Terry," Jon said, "I've known you long enough to know that once you make up your mind to do something, you'll do it. Just be sure it's not just from wishful thinking about helmets that you probably can't lay hands on even if you get down there."

"I shouldn't have told you I'd like more mind training," Alison said with remorse. "I never thought it would mean putting you in danger."

"This isn't just about what I may be able to do for you and Gwen—or for you, Jon, if I ever get good enough at instructing to handle the initial sessions," Terry said. "It's about what I can achieve on Undine. We agreed that we'd go where our ideas about the future would do the most good. Well, the situation's as bad on Undine as it was on Ciencia as far as people's ignorance about the mind is concerned—worse, in some ways. They think there's no more to a human being than a body. They keep dead bodies hooked up to machines, their hearts beating forever, as if it were keeping them alive—"

"That's awful!" Gwen protested.

"Yes. Ian Maclairn gave up his life prematurely so his

group could escape from there, and his body may be still in stasis after more than two centuries—the Maclairnans don't like to think about it, but they all know. Well, I can't change that, but maybe I can continue what he started, making people believe their minds have power. Giving hope to those who care by telling them what they feel inside isn't as foolish as the medical establishment teaches them it is. If what I'm doing with the *Estel* symbol is important anywhere, surely it will be on Undine, where the idea for Maclairn started."

"I guess you're right," Jon conceded. "I guess considering the history, you have to follow through."

It was left at that. Terry put *Estel* into high orbit and waited, inwardly in turmoil because he had no real idea how to proceed. He would have to take one step at a time.

As the days passed he occupied himself with work on the neurofeedback software he planned to develop, simulating the inputs. In addition, he taught Gwen to fly the shuttle, though the most difficult part, landing, couldn't be tackled until they reached some other colony. Jon and Alison were less busy and their nerves were on edge; for their sake he hoped the suspense would end soon.

Finally, the comm picked up the transmission he was counting on, a freighter's announcement to Undine of its ETA. Using the same frequency, Terry responded indirectly, requesting permission from ground control to land, which was, of course, denied.

"You already knew they wouldn't grant it," Alison said, puzzled.

"I did, but hopefully it will work the way it does on Ciencia in reverse—free traders who arrive there transmit requests to approach just so ships in the area will know they're present and ready to buy cargo. The freighter will assume that if I want to land here I've got cargo to sell."

"A pirate ship wouldn't announce its arrival to the base, anyway," Gwen said.

The strategy worked. "HS *Vagabond*, this is FHS *Peregrine*. We heard your request. No private ships are permitted to land in this colony. Do you need to take on consumables? Over."

"Not at present, *Peregrine*. But I had hoped to do business here. Over." He was not talking to the captain, he knew; it would be some junior officer with no authority to make decisions. Their taking the initiative was nevertheless a good sign.

"What sort of business, *Vagabond*? Are you a free trader? Over."

"I have cargo to sell, yes. Over." They could draw their own conclusions about its legality; some free traders carried legitimate loads.

After a pause a different voice came over the comm. "*Vagabond*, this is *Peregrine*, the captain speaking. What have you got? Over."

Terry drew breath. "I have sugar, direct from New Afrika. Over."

"I might be able to take it off your hands. Do you wish to rendezvous? Over."

"Affirmative, *Peregrine*." After agreeing on a position, he switched off the mike and spoke to Jon. "I'll let them know I'm captain, since I need to talk them into taking me along when they land cargo. While I'm gone you're in command."

"What if they recognize your name? A Fleet ship may have come straight from Centauri; they could have heard rumors."

"They won't have to scan my ID till the sugar's been sold and they pay me my share of the proceeds. They'd have no reason to demand it sooner when we're dealing outside the law."

"How long are you going to be down there?" Alison asked unhappily.

"I have no way of knowing. I'll make them promise to provision you if you run low." Suppose he never got back?

Terry asked himself privately. Jon couldn't jump the ship and Undine wouldn't let them land. . . .

When docking was complete he went aboard *Peregrine* alone, where he was welcomed with some enthusiasm by Captain Garick. It wasn't often that a load of prime contraband was delivered to a ship with no danger of discovery either by export authorities or by Fleet. Terry knew at once, from sensing Garick's mind, that he was an honorable officer who simply saw no harm in such a transaction. He didn't have to worry that such a man would cheat.

"There's just one thing," Terry said when they came to negotiate. "I have personal business on Undine. I want passage to and from the surface, and I want some sugar stored where I can access it—to be deducted from what's owed me, of course, if I dispose of any."

Garick eyed him, obviously doubtful. "I'd need to know what kind of business. I have nothing against free trading, but I won't be a party to other crime."

Terry hesitated. "How much do you know about the government of Undine?"

"It's democratically elected, though I understand it has some peculiar policies."

"People sometimes vote away their own freedom, and I see nothing wrong in attempts to make them aware of that. Subtle attempts, of course. I don't plan to start trouble." At Garick's noncommittal nod, he added, "Maybe you've heard what's happening on Earth, people being harassed, even killed, because they believe unorthodox ideas about the power of their minds aren't just fantasy. That sort of thing could spread, and dissidents in colonies like this one, where the government treats any sort of deviation as an illness, would be helpless against it. If the going gets tough they'll need to know they're not alone."

"Unorthodox ideas about mind faculties?" Garick surveyed him thoughtfully. "Did you come from Centauri, by any chance?"

"I was there recently, yes. For a short time."

"I'm wondering if you heard the rumors that are going around. When I left Centauri Base just a few days ago, they'd become a hot topic, talk about postings that had gone viral on the Net—not in Fleet, of course, but in the city. It seems that some guy known as the Captain of *Estel* made a broadcast to an outlying colony claiming people can do more with their minds than they think, paranormal things, and telling them to revolt against any government that says otherwise."

"I did hear that," Terry said, keeping a straight face. "But I got the impression that he didn't advocate violent revolt. It was more that they should elect a government that doesn't dictate what they're allowed to believe—which I'd call good advice."

"I agree. If the notions being spread along with it weren't so crazy, I'd say it should be encouraged. But it's gotten out of hand; this Captain of *Estel* is said to have supernatural healing powers. He's being identified with a real captain who delivered antivirals to Toliman and helped out during an epidemic. And as you say, the trouble on Earth over weird beliefs could spread."

"Is there actually a ship somewhere named *Estel*?

"Who knows? Fleet's on the lookout for one, but without a transponder ID we can't trace it. A guy at Headquarters did track down the origin of the name—it appears to have come from a classic fantasy novel called *Lord of the Rings*, where it's said to mean 'hope.'"

Terry had wondered how soon someone would discover that. He'd told his friends on Ciencia, but he wasn't sure how familiar the book was on Earth. "Plenty of ships are named after mythological characters," he said. "That doesn't mean it isn't real."

"No, but if it is, it's odd that these new myths are centered on it." Garick continued slowly, "It's almost as if someone is deliberately trying to stir people up. And from what you've said, it looks as if you might be aiming to do just that on Undine."

"Would encouraging change be a bad thing?" He knew, telepathically, that Garick wasn't opposed; it was merely a matter of getting him to admit it.

"I'm not sure," Garick reflected. "Fleet's afraid the troublemakers on Earth—the gang that calls itself the Ku Klux Klan—will get a foothold in the colonies, so the brass wants to stamp out ideas that might lead it to try. But it seems to me that for us to suppress them would be the same as what the Klan wants to do. A lot of the notions going around are silly, yet they create hope for the future, and people need hope nowadays. Otherwise we're all just on a milk run, like I am with this freight route. Besides, the League government is getting more and more intrusive, and I don't like that."

"There are government insiders behind the Klan activity," Terry informed him. "They don't want people to know how much power their minds have to resist authority."

"My God. That's news to me, but it makes sense."

"Undine's government intrudes into every detail of people's private lives," Terry went on. "It puts bioanalysis units in their home toilets. It implants GPS-enabled heart monitors in their bodies. Did you know natural conception isn't allowed there? Men are required to bank their sperm, and women can't have babies except through IVF after geneticists have created embryos meeting specified physical characteristics. And the kids are raised in crèches, seeing their parents only a few days per week, because the authorities don't want them doing anything bad for health."

"Hell, no—I hadn't heard that. I know about the heart monitors, though, because when off-duty crews leave the spaceport, we have to wear badges that signal we're exempt. Otherwise we'd be picked up by the ambulance police if we were spotted."

Terry swallowed. He'd overlooked that possibility. He'd pictured himself getting access to the hospital by blending into a crowd. Evidently he would need more help from Captain Garick than he'd planned on asking for.

"Look," he said, "I'm familiar with the *Estel* myth and I intend to pass it along wherever I think it might encourage people to question authority. But I'm not going to lie to you—I've got a personal agenda besides that, and it involves breaking the law. I won't tell you how because if I'm caught you'll need to say you didn't know. But it's harmless. You have my word on that."

"Okay," said Garick slowly. "I don't know why, but I can tell you're more trustworthy than the average guy in the smuggling business. You can go to the surface with us, and I'll say you're part of the crew; but we have to keep to our schedule. If you're not at the spaceport when our last shuttle leaves, you'll be left behind."

"That's fair," Terry agreed. "But I want your word that if I get into trouble and don't show up, you'll take care of my crew. See that they get my share of the sugar sale proceeds. What's more, my second in command isn't a jump pilot; he's only flown in normal space, mining asteroids. If our shuttle's not allowed to land, they'll be stranded without life support unless you bring them aboard."

"How many are you carrying?"

"A man and two women."

"No problem. Hell, I could bring your whole ship aboard—we're at the end of our freight run, so the cargo bay's empty till we reach our first stop on the way back to Earth. But I hope it won't come to that."

"So do I," Terry said fervently, "but it's good to know. I love that ship and I'd hate to think of it being abandoned for salvage." At least in another colony Jon and Alison would be able to sell it. He pushed away the thought, stricken by what it meant. He might be stuck forever in a colony with tyrannical laws under which his body would no longer be his own. Was he crazy, risking the loss of his freedom, of Alison, of *Estel* in a venture unlikely to succeed that wasn't even essential?

Perhaps. Yet it came to him, suddenly, why getting the helmets mattered. He needed proof that the future he was encouraging people to believe in—perhaps endangering them by his encouragement—wasn't just talk. If his own crew couldn't be given the mind-powers he said were latent in everyone, then he couldn't be sure that the hope he was trying to arouse was valid.

By its very nature the life he'd chosen demanded risk; he couldn't pull back or he'd never accomplish anything. And besides, Terry realized, he did feel an obligation to the present inhabitants of the Maclairnans' ancestral world.

~ *29* ~

AS *PEREGRINE*'S SHUTTLE circled Undine, Terry was first aware of what a beautiful planet it was. Though he had known it was a water world dotted with small islands, he hadn't pictured the vivid green-speckled blue expanse as seen from low altitude. It had been terraformed, and the islands were covered with the genetically-engineered trees common in all colonies where they could be made to grow. Most of it was uninhabited, however. Only a small region was occupied, and as they approached the spaceport he saw that the islands near the center of it were devoid of everything but stark, tightly-packed buildings.

At the time the Maclairnans escaped there had been only one city, filling a single island, with mines, farms, and a few private settlements on others nearby. Now, two centuries later, there were several. On some islands the buildings were low, probably factory farms; but on the residential ones most were tall. Two islands in particular stood out, the first of them covered with high box-like structures arranged in neat rows with virtually no space between them, the function of which was a mystery. And then the main island where the port was, laced

with canals in lieu of streets and dominated by a vast
cluster of glaringly-white skyscrapers. He realized at once
that this must be the hospital.

Even in the earlier era it had been huge, and since
then the population of the colony had grown. As everyone
was required to have regular high-tech examinations, it
was in no way comparable to hospitals elsewhere that
merely served the sick, especially since its interconnected
towers housed the entire administrative branch of the
colony's government as well as medical facilities. Its bulk
was monstrous. No doubt it contained fast-moving walkways so that people could get from one part of it to another in a reasonable length of time. And, Terry recalled
with a shudder, a significant part of it was devoted to the
vaults where dead bodies were kept in stasis. . . .

But even a vast complex such as this surely couldn't
hold all the people who had died in the past two hundred
years along with the generations before them. Since pro-
creation was strictly controlled the colony's population
increased slowly, but still. . . . Abruptly it dawned on him
what the boxlike structures on the other island were for.
They contained more stasis vaults.

Or did they? The machinery and consumables required
to keep hundreds of bodies "alive," even considering the
reduced oxygen supply required for stasis, had always
been prohibitively expensive by the standard of any other
colony; but by now the cost would have grown past all
reason. Surely the authorities could not have kept up the
system this long.

But they might say they had. The general public did
not see the maintained bodies; they were merely told about
them. So it was possible that as people died and were
placed in the hospital's vaults, older bodies were moved
to the other island—and that the structures there were
not stasis vaults at all, but tombs.

Before he could absorb the implications of that, the
shuttle was above the spaceport; it hovered, then settled

gently to the surface. Only one other ship was visible; Terry realized that this small base possessed only a few and they had all gone to get cargo from *Peregrine*. The ground crew started loading bales into the trucks that were waiting to move them to the port's warehouse, where they would be picked up by city buyers. The sugar wasn't included; it would be retrieved from *Estel* with Jon's help and brought down by Captain Garick later, surreptitiously, after he'd made arrangements with a local dealer.

The half-dozen men and women aboard the shuttle were officers on shore leave, except for the pilot who would go back for another load; fortunately they wore civvies so Terry wasn't conspicuous. They had been told by the captain not to question his presence and of course they knew why, but nothing was said about it. Garick had arranged for him to share a room with Lt. Harris, as he could not register at a hotel himself—his name wouldn't be recognized here but to allow his ID to be scanned would reveal that he wasn't employed by Fleet and was thus on the planet illegally. They boarded the bus for the city together; it left them at the small park in its center, to which Terry returned after getting his keycard from Harris. He had three days to do what he had come to do and be back at the spaceport in time for departure.

The park ran along the sides of the city's main canal, lined with docks for water taxis—there were no ground vehicles on Undine except for trucks. Across the canal from where he stood was the hospital, looming against the sky and blocking the sunlight, dominating everything within sight as it dominated the lives of Undine's citizens. Terry did not plan to enter it. He'd read too much about it on Maclairn not to be repelled, and in any case he would have no way to locate neurofeedback helmets once inside. He would have to make contact with someone who worked there.

On his side of the bridge was a strip of small stores plus an attractive café that was undoubtedly frequented by hospital workers. If anyone was in the market for a few bags of illegal sugar, it would be the proprietor of a popular café; fingering the badge that exempted him from heart monitoring, Terry went in. To pay for food he would have to present his ID, but a restaurant's scanner, unlike a hotel's, probably wouldn't check anything beyond the validity of his credit. He had no choice, since there was no way to judge whether the proprietor would be receptive without lingering awhile over a meal.

The café was crowded. Terry ordered the most promising item on the posted menu—a tasteless synthi-chick sandwich on what proved to be dry bread—and sat at the table furthest from the counter. If anything containing sugar was being served it wouldn't be done obviously, though it was unlikely that health police would be watching the diners; they would inspect only the kitchen. He, on the other hand, could sense telepathically if any people around him were enjoying illicit snacks.

Some were. There was no mistaking their emotions—pleasure at the taste mixed with the thrill of getting away with something they knew was not allowed. Since their government treated them like children, the adults of the colony felt childlike excitement about disobeying the rules. Small crimes like eating sugar, Terry decided, gave them an outlet for repressed resentment over having to submit to invasive and unnecessary surveillance of their bodies.

He went back to the counter and ordered what passed for coffee, first removing the badge that identified him as an offworlder; it would protect him from electronic monitoring even when hidden. "The bran muffins on the menu don't appeal to me," he said to the server. "Have you got anything that's not listed?"

The woman smiled knowingly. "Maybe. I could check with the kitchen. Sometimes things with scarce ingredients aren't posted, so as to avoid disappointing people when we run out of them." She made no move to do it, but simply stood there.

It didn't take telepathy to know what she was waiting for. Terry extended his arm to be scanned, saying, "Five times the top price I see for the regular ones, is that right?"

She deducted the credits without comment and retreated into the kitchen, returning with a box containing a small thinly-frosted cupcake. Turning his back on the other customers near the counter, Terry bit into it to be sure it was genuine. He waited until the server was free and then said in a low voice, "You ought not to be selling these; someone might report you. I think I'd better speak to the person in charge."

"He's not available right now," she declared firmly.

"Tell him to make himself available. I'm sure he wants to avoid trouble."

After disappearing again briefly she beckoned to Terry from the kitchen door. From there he was ushered into a back office.

"Are you the owner?" Terry asked the dark-haired man seated at the desk. "If so, I have a proposition that's in your best interest."

"If you're trying to muscle in on Paco's territory, forget it. Paco doesn't like competitors."

The man wasn't nervous; evidently the health police didn't work undercover. "I'm not acquainted with Paco," he said "but I doubt if he'd ever hear about a small transaction on the side."

"What, are you from Verge Island or something? He hears everything in this city and if you tried to turn me in he'd come after you; he guarantees I'll never have to pay anyone else."

For not exposing him, no doubt. "I'm not what you think," Terry said. "I've gotten hold of some white stuff and I'm looking for someone interested in acquiring it."

"Well, that's different," said the man. "How much?"

"Five, maybe ten kilos. I'm not a supplier; this is a one-time offer."

"How do I know it's not been cut?"

"I can tell you it came straight from New Afrika. You'll have to take my word." Terry hoped this man had enough latent telepathic ability to sense sincerity; he had no other proof.

The café owner nodded. "What's your asking price?"

"Here's the thing," Terry said. "I'm not asking for money. I want a favor. Nothing that will cause trouble for you, just setting up a contact for me."

"A contact with who?"

"Some person who works in the hospital. Employees come in here all the time, you probably know one to recommend. I need somebody willing to lift a couple of small items from a lab and pass them on to me. They'll be only for my personal use."

"Drugs? I steer clear of that business."

"No, not drugs. Some electronic equipment I can't find anywhere else."

"That's theft. You'd be sentenced to the psych ward if I reported you."

"But you won't, considering what I know about your menu. I could talk before Paco finds out I exist." At the man's hesitation Terry went on, "There are two ways of thinking about the hospital. Some people accept the official story—they assume the administration cares only about their well-being and all the laws should be obeyed. I don't think you're one of them."

"Hell, no. There's no harm in sugar; I wouldn't serve it if there were. And there are a lot of other laws I know are stupid. But I don't steal."

"Yet the government steals from *you*. You don't think all the taxes it collects for health care are spent on curing sickness, do you? Some of the money goes to enforcing stupid laws and some gets into the pockets of the bureaucrats, and one of the ways it does is through kickbacks from importers who sell more equipment to the hospital than it has any legitimate use for. A few excess items more or less will never be noticed."

"You've got a point." The café owner hesitated again and then said, "Okay. I know a guy there who's always bitching about corruption. Just last week he told me they made him put through purchase orders for stuff he knew damn well would never even be delivered. Next time I see him I'll sound him out."

"I have to meet him by tomorrow night, or the deal's off."

"That's not much notice."

"I can't help that; I won't have access to the sugar beyond the next day."

"How much of it are you offering him?"

"That's between the two of you. You get the sugar; you can share it with him or pay him in credits—or in hard metal, if you've got any."

They agreed on a meeting time and shook hands. Terry knew the night and day of waiting would be nerve-wearing.

~ *30* ~

WITH HARRIS OFF someplace in the company of fellow officers, Terry spent the evening in their room alone, investigating the local Net. He went to bed late and rose early, for he wanted to do more on Undine than acquire the helmets. This would be his only chance to spread the *Estel* symbol to its people, who were more desperately in need of real hope than they knew.

At first he planned to do his hacking from a bench in the park, but it was a bright sunny morning and he longed suddenly for a closer look at the sea. So he took a public water taxi to the island's waterfront, where a wide esplanade separated a long row of well-kept historic homes from the low concrete wall at the water's edge.

Boats and seaplanes, bright-colored ones, were moored at piers for as far along the esplanade as could be

seen. He had been told that many people on Undine had
private planes because the islands were too widely scattered for quick boat trips to be practical. Ian Maclairn
had owned a lodge on one of those islands, where mind
training had been given and where some of his group had
spent leisurely weekends. It no longer existed, for they
had destroyed it when they left to prevent the smuggled
equipment it contained from being traced to their offworld
contacts. Maclairn's founders had grieved over that, and
had built the Council Head's house on their new world in
its image. Thinking of it, Terry was struck once more by
the vivid memory—it was where he had gone through the
Ritual. . . .

Maclairn would always be a part of him, no matter
how deep his love for Alison, however happy he was to
own *Estel*. Being on Undine brought it all back. Had the
founders felt nostalgia for this world in later years, knowing that they would never see it again? They'd hated its
government and ugly city, but the sea and the islands had
beauty—and they, too, must have felt pain at exile from
the place where their first Rituals had been held. What
had it been like, remembering when they were old?

Hacking Undine's Net was not difficult; Terry knew
the Group had done it routinely even for altering hospital
records. He set to work with his tablet, inserting his usual
texts in places where they were likely to be noticed, including oblique references to the ship *Estel*. Here, more
than anywhere else but Ciencia, the idea of the mind having power over the body was foreign. Some of the
Ciencians, starved for the mythology to which they had
never been exposed, had taken to it like caged birds to
free air; but here the worship of bodies was tied to the
denial of death.

He found himself thinking again of the island full of
unacknowledged tombs, which he'd learned from the Net
was called the Isle of Sleep. The citizens of Undine were
assured that they would "live" forever. Even government

officials had once believed this, but at least some of them must now be aware that it was a false promise, whether or not they thought the bodies in actual stasis were still alive. Yet if people were allowed to stop believing that the restrictive health laws of their colony led to immortality, they might start objecting to them. They might become unwilling to pay exorbitant taxes and vote those who imposed them out of office. The medical administration and the bureaucracy that supported it might be endangered.

The prospective Maclairnans had defied the stasis system and buried bodies in the sea at the risk of arrest for "murder," yet they had not been able to convince more than a handful of people that calling permanent stasis "life" devalued the real thing. That a human life depended on a mind—whether conscious or unconscious—and not just a brain-dead body. But their contemporaries had known nothing of death. The natural cycle of life and death had not been part of their experience. What, Terry wondered, would have happened if they'd been aware that permanent maintenance of the farce was impossible, that death occurred sooner or later no matter how hard society tried to deny it?

What would happen now, if in his texts about *Estel* he suggested that the presumed stasis vaults outside the Hospital were not what they seemed? If even a few people investigated and managed to publicize what they found, it might bring down the government. He had already planted the seeds of revolt on one world; why not another? Why not this one, that had tyrannized the founders of Maclairn? It would be fitting. They'd have been happy to know that their indirect influence would bring about its downfall. . . .

Yet they had not tried to overthrow Undine's government. They had believed that because it was democratically elected, they had no right to do so by any means other than the manifestly-impossible task of persuading

the voters to demand change. And that was all he'd aimed
to do on Ciencia. It would be a different matter here; the
people had been not merely suppressed, but deceived;
and they would be angry. A revolution here would be a
violent one. Very likely there would be a great many
deaths besides the natural ones that could no longer be
hidden.

Terry's mind whirled. It was frightening to realize how
much power he had, how much he was purposely seeking
to gain as the mysterious Captain of *Estel*. His goal was
to set people free from false beliefs about human nature—
that was the point of telling them about the capabilities
inherently theirs. It had been the reason for giving the
Ciencians access to literature they weren't allowed to read.
It was what the mentors were doing on Earth, and the
Elders had told him the future of civilization depended
on the mentors' work. So shouldn't the people of Undine
be made aware that mind was life's essence and that it
didn't reside in dead flesh? That might put them in danger, but he'd been warned that he might have put the
Ciencians in danger, too, and hadn't Jon said that if
spreading truth was worth risk to him, it was worth risk
to everyone who cared?

"The ship *Estel* travels from star to star spreading
knowledge," he wrote, "knowledge that will someday be
possessed by everyone—knowledge of the powers of the
human mind, which are greater than most of you have
ever guessed. With these powers we can defeat sickness
and pain and misunderstanding. But such powers belong
only to the living. If you think the bodies in the Vaults
can ever attain them, you are deceived, for those bodies
are not living, but dead; and what powers the dead have,
no one knows. Death is a mystery that the Captain of
Estel himself cannot unravel, but he knows a living body
from a dead one. And he knows that the difference has
nothing to do with whether or not it contains a beating
heart."

Terry thought for a moment, and went on writing, "Some of you think a heartbeat defines life, and that is because you know too little of mind; but when people gain more mind faculties, they will see that making hearts beat in dead bodies is foolish. It is not even possible for very long. Your government has told you that your hearts will beat forever, that the hearts of your ancestors still beat, and that is not true. Go to the Isle of Sleep and tear down the walls, and you'll see that it's not. Those interred there are not asleep. Many of them may be mere bones by now. What then was the good in keeping their bodies warm in the Hospital for so long? The government knows, but it will not tell you. If you became aware that there was no benefit except to the bureaucrats, you might question the exorbitant taxes you have been paying and the outrageous laws you have been tolerating in the hope of eternal life. Those who questioned in the past had no proof of deception, but now you can find proof on the Isle of Sleep."

Not everyone would be swayed by this, of course. Most people would go on believing that death could be permanently avoided. But if rumors about *Estel* went viral, some would follow through. The tombs on the island weren't guarded; there had been no need for that. The government wouldn't take the rumors seriously. So a few walls *would* be torn down, and then. . . .

Then the conflict would begin. Some people would be angry at the government; others would be angry at the doubters—and it wouldn't be a matter of mere debate. His hand on the Enter key to post the message, Terry drew back. He had asked himself what difference there would be between encouraging such a revolt and what he had done on Ciencia. But there *was* a difference. For one thing, he wouldn't be around to lead this one. More than that, it would involve the same sort of resistance to new ideas that was being exploited on Earth. Fear of death was as deeply emotional, if not more so, as fear of unsettling facts about the paranormal. To foster beliefs that would make people vulnerable to persecution by evildoers was one thing; but to set them up for violence against each other was something else.

Reluctantly, he erased the second paragraph and posted only the first one, plus similar statements elsewhere on the Net. It was not his job to tell the people of Undine that they would someday die. Hopefully, by the time new mind faculties were widespread they would have figured that out for themselves.

Late that evening he returned to the café as arranged and found the proprietor with a young man dressed as a hospital lab technician. "This is Brad," the proprietor said. "I've told him what you want."

"I'll be glad to help you out," Brad said with enthusiasm. "Any way to put one over on the bastards, I'm willing to try. They've been ripping off the taxpayers and they've got it coming to them."

Terry described the helmets. "They'll be in the neurology department," he said, "and I'll be surprised if there's not a spare or two, though they're not used often."

"All that stuff is used," Brad told him. "They do full brain exams on everyone who acts eccentric. But they won't be doing one late at night, and anyway they've got plenty of duplicate equipment."

"You won't have trouble getting into that lab?"

"Hell, no—I'm on the graveyard shift, and nobody checks where I go on my breaks. The thing is, though, I'll have to stash them till I get off work—I can't carry them around with me. They'll be too big."

"They're foldable, the layer with the nanoelectronics is thin." That would make no difference, unfortunately; Brad wore a short-sleeved lab coat and its pockets weren't large. He couldn't hide helmets under it while working.

"Don't sweat it," Brad told him with assurance. "I've got a safe place to put stuff." It was likely that this wasn't his first theft of hospital property, Terry realized. He apparently had no scruples about it, which was no more due to lack of morality than the Maclairn group's circumvention of hospital rules had been. A bureaucratic institution that tyrannized people was fair game.

Once they'd finalized the plan, Terry went back to his room. He slept because his mind training gave him control over sleep, but not for long. He was back at the café well before Brad's shift was due to end, waiting impatiently and barely tasting the free meal with which the proprietor provided him. Time passed; Brad was late. At long last he appeared—but without what he'd promised to deliver.

"I'm sorry," he said. "I stashed them, but I couldn't get back to pick them up. Some of the guys came by my lab and wanted me to go for breakfast, and I couldn't make an excuse to detour—they'd have tagged along with me. Don't worry, I'll bring them tomorrow morning."

"Can't you go back for them?" Terry protested.

"God, no! I'd run into people who know my shift's over, and they'd ask questions. You'll have to wait till tomorrow."

He wouldn't be here tomorrow. The last shuttle would leave this afternoon and if he wasn't on it he'd be stuck on Undine permanently, with Alison and the others stuck in space. Sick with dismay, Terry didn't reply. To have come so close to acquiring the gear he needed and then leave without it! He couldn't bring himself to do that.

There was only one solution. He would have to walk into the hospital and retrieve the helmets himself.

~ *31* ~

"I HAVE TO HAVE them today," he declared firmly, "Tell me where they are and I'll go and get them."

Brad stared at him. "You're crazy, man. You'd never get away with that."

"The public can go in and out, can't they?"

"Sure, but if you don't know the layout you couldn't find your way around. And it's not in an area where visitors belong."

"Let me borrow your lab coat. I'll stay under the radar."

"Well, okay, but I wouldn't want to be in your shoes if they catch you—no matter how current your physical, they'll do a full invasive exam once you're an inpatient." Brad took off the lab jacket and handed it over.

You'd be sentenced to the psych ward, the café owner had said . . . the police and the hospital authorities were one and the same. He was indeed crazy, Terry admitted to himself. It was too big a risk, with too much at stake; the sensible thing would be to forget the helmets and head for the spaceport right now. He'd already done what he could to offer hope to the people of Undine—and giving more mind training to his crew was not really essential, disappointed though they would be.

But he had never backed off from a challenge before, and it wasn't in him to refuse this one.

"Where did you hide the helmets?" he asked.

"In my gym locker—the ninth floor gym, for low-level employees only. They're in the top row of Aisle C, number 9C-1067."

That might be a problem. "Will they scan my ID on the way in?"

"Not unless you present it to log your time. They don't check—people aren't likely to forget, and some don't bother about recording extra hours."

Terry recalled that all citizens were required to exercise for an hour per day unless away from the city, in a public gym or, evidently, one provided at their workplace. To remain inconspicuous, he would have to work out like everyone else there.

"There's a sweatshirt in the locker you can wear instead of the lab coat when you leave," Brad said. "That's what I was going to do."

After getting detailed instructions from Brad on how to reach the right area and find the locker, Terry headed for the door. "Hold on," the café owner said. "You're forgetting something. I haven't got my sugar."

"It has to be picked up from a warehouse. If I haven't enough time left to do it, I'll give you the claim code when I get back with Brad's shirt."

"If you're caught you won't be coming back. Give it to me now."

That was a reasonable demand; the man had done his part, and Brad had done as much as he could under the circumstances. Terry took the phone handed to him and keyed in the address and code that Captain Garick had provided.

"Hey," said the man, "that's my regular supplier's place! If I go there Paco's going to get wind of it."

Terry paused, nonplused. He couldn't afford the delay of collecting the sugar himself, yet if these men didn't get what they'd been promised they could prevent him from leaving. In desperation he said, "Tell Paco I'm a friend of Zach Dyllon." He did not give the password.

"Will he know the guy?"

"A lot of people do, on a lot of worlds. And they know he doesn't like to hear that friends of his friends have been hassled." Zach would not have included a protection racketeer in his network so his name might not mean anything, but the mere suggestion of a connection with an interstellar underworld would make Paco think twice before starting trouble.

On leaving the café, Terry went into one of the adjacent stores and bought a roll of tape. Then he walked rapidly toward the canal, beyond which rose the massive hospital. This had to be gotten over with fast. Crossing the bridge, he joined the stream of people heading for the doors and, drawing a deep breath, he passed through.

There was a vast, white-walled lobby with moving walkways branching off in various directions. Most of these people had appointments for treatment or exams, he realized; every day was busy here when the entire population had to report for checkups at regular intervals. Then too, some came to the city's administrative offices—tax assessment, issuing of permits, and all the other red tape handled by bureaucrats on any world. There were too many reasons for citizens to be present for him to be noticed in areas open to the public.

He strode purposefully toward the bank of elevators. The ninth floor, Brad had said. It consisted of offices and labs, reached by a succession of cross-corridors. With luck, the lab coat he wore would identify him as an employee on the way in. Several others emerged from the elevator at the same time he did, paying no attention to him. He followed them down the long main corridor to the gym at its far end.

This being the morning rush hour, it was crowded, and he passed the desk without attracting scrutiny. There were many aisles of stacked lockers; he scanned them quickly, hoping to spot 9C-1067 before anyone observed that he was searching. It was on the top row. Terry punched in the keypad code he'd been given and beneath the folded gym clothes inside, he saw, to his relief, the stolen helmets.

It was all he could do to keep from touching them. But he couldn't take them yet; if anyone was watching, it wouldn't look natural to remove something from the locker and leave immediately. Resolutely, he put the lab coat over them and changed into Brad's gym clothes. Then he proceeded to the nearest free treadmill and spent one of the longest hours of his life pushing himself close to exhaustion in the effort to avoid worrisome thoughts.

A terrifying possibility had occurred to him when it was too late to change his strategy—what if the treadmill was linked to the implanted heart monitor he did not have? What if it triggered an alarm when it got no normal signal from it? Since this did not happen—at least nobody came to check on him—he judged that the badge he wore under his shirt sent some sort of "all clear" to every device programmed to detect a citizen's heart status. But he was careful to keep his heart rate within the range that might reasonably be expected.

When the hour was up he returned to the locker room and got back into his own clothes, but left the lab coat in the locker, covering the helmets, while he put on Brad's sweatshirt. Apparently workers often left the gym so dressed; it must be assumed they worked out after their shifts ended—he'd been too absorbed in getting there undetected to notice people on the way out of the building.

Now for the hard part, Terry thought. He stood close to the locker and carefully reached inside, pulling the folded helmets out from under the gym clothes and—when he was sure nobody was looking his way—dropping them into the neck of the sweatshirt. They would not stay there, of course; they would slide down as he walked and eventually fall out. But he should be able to get as far as the men's room, where he'd have enough privacy to reposition them.

The men's room, too, was crowded; there were men in line for stalls. Terry joined them, growing more and more nervous at the wait. He could feel the helmets slipping beneath his shirt. Once behind a locked door, he retrieved them just in time and spread them out, securing them to his torso with the tape he had bought.

When he reached the ground floor he drew a deep breath of relief and headed jubilantly for the main exit. He'd gotten away with it! Nobody would know or care what he was carrying outside the hospital. He had left his duffel at the café, since Harris, who'd been sleeping, had planned to check out of their hotel room during the morning. Now he just had to collect it and wait in the park for the bus—the sooner he was off this planet, the better. . . .

Abruptly, with shock, he saw what was happening at the hospital exit. They were scanning IDs.

He had noticed when he arrived that the exit was screened from the entrance by a barrier he'd thought merely decorative. It hadn't occurred to him that they were actually separated. Now he realized that there was a force field of some kind to prevent people from going in the opposite direction. People could enter freely, but not leave.

It should have been obvious, Terry thought in despair. He had known the hospital detained people it did not choose to release. It was a prison both for unwilling patients and anyone accused of a crime. Naturally there was a security checkpoint—the IDs of people to be held were flagged by the system, while everyone else was let through.

But he would not be let through. His ID was not in the system at all; when examined by the security officer it would reveal that he was not a Fleet officer and was therefore on Undine illegally. Whether or not the helmets were found at the time he was detained, he would be imprisoned.

He had not told either the café owner or Brad that he was an offworlder, so they'd had no reason to warn him. He'd been trapped the moment he came into the building, Terry thought despairingly; the checkpoint was not visible from outside. How could he have been such a fool? What he knew of the hospital should have told him what to expect.

He broke away from the line moving forward, aware that he must head somewhere purposefully to avoid looking nervous. It would do no good to search for another exit, though considering the number of people employed in the building there were surely many—they would be guarded and the same software would control them all. He couldn't tell what he might meet in the ground floor corridors; he no longer had the lab coat and a sweatshirt would undoubtedly be out of place there. So he returned to the elevators and held back when one opened, at a loss for what to do.

There must be fire exits. He could in fact see one on the opposite side of the lobby. But of course he couldn't just push it open; he'd be observed, and in any case it would have an alarm. His only chance was to use one on another floor and hope he could get down the stairs before being pursued. It was a slim hope; if getting out were as simple as that, prisoners could escape easily. Yet he had no choice but to try.

He went up just one floor to minimize the distance he'd have to run. He couldn't move quickly—the precarious taping of the helmets under his sweatshirt wouldn't withstand that. It was no real problem; speed now wasn't necessary and after the alarm went off he'd get out before they loosened, or he'd be caught and it wouldn't matter. Whether he was held for theft or merely for being on the planet wouldn't make much difference; either way, he'd be unable to reach *Estel*.

The fire exit sign was in plain sight when he left the elevator, and seeing no people around, Terry rushed it, throwing his weight against the door so as to push through fast when the inevitable alarm bell began to ring.

Nothing happened. The door was locked.

In horrified desperation, he tried again, feeling the handle this time—maybe there was some particular place to press? Fire doors weren't locked. Even aboard starships it was against regulations to seal fire doors.

Except in prisons. Of course they'd be locked in buildings used as prisons. They would be programmed to open only if there was a fire.

So there was no way out. Common sense told him that fire detectors would not be placed in such a way that prisoners could fool them by setting things on fire. They would be in ceilings, too high up for anyone to reach, and there would be no combustibles left around.

Terry slumped down against the wall, slipping his hands up the front of his sweatshirt to check the taping of the helmets. The corridor remained deserted; evidently it was not public and was used only between shifts by employees going to and from work areas. Sooner or later, he supposed, he would be found. There was no place he could hide and why bother, when in a few hours the shuttle was going to depart without him?

He stared up at the ceiling. There was indeed a fire detector there, out of reach. He had nothing to start a fire with anyway... or did he?

He could set candles alight, after all.

Long ago on Maclairn his mentor Tristan had taught him to light and extinguish flame by means of psi. Terry had been initially reluctant to acquire that ability; it had frightened him to think how much power it might give him. Some Maclairnans could melt metal with their minds. He suspected that all mentors could; certainly they could light torches in the Ritual. He was psi-gifted and might well be able to do the same, but he had chosen not to pursue that path—a choice that had given him some understanding of the public's widespread fear of psi in general. He'd become confident, however, about lighting candles.

"It may someday prove useful to you," Tristan had said. Was that true? There was no magic in the generation of fire; it was simply an intensified form of controlling temperature. Something combustible was needed, and if it got hot enough through use of psi it would burst into flame just as it would if heated some other way. There was nothing combustible here that would make enough of a blaze to set off a fire alarm—but fire detectors didn't detect fire directly. They simply sensed smoke or heat.

Which type was this one? He had no way to create smoke, but if heat was all that was needed, he might be able to trigger it.

He closed his eyes and visualized the pattern, the indelible mind-pattern for generating heat that he'd been taught. As with any form of psi, emotion would intensify his power, though paradoxically it would be necessary to set aside—but not fight—all conscious doubt and fear. This was what the training had been for. It was why he'd risked so much to get the helmets, so that Alison and others could have the training, too. If he could not make use of his own training when he needed it, what good had it done to take that risk? How could he claim that the beliefs he was spreading were valid?

He focused on the fire detector, seeing it not with his closed eyes but through clairvoyance. He imagined the air around it getting hotter, and hotter. . . .

And then suddenly the alarm was ringing and he was soaking wet from the stream of the automatic sprinklers. Jumping to his feet, clutching the helmets, Terry threw himself against the fire door again. It burst open and he ran down the stairs to the now-unlatched outer door, and freedom.

~ *32* ~

HE DID NOT tell Captain Garick the details of his adventure; aboard *Peregrine*, Terry merely thanked him for his help and accepted his share of the sugar sale proceeds. Garick, however, informed him that monitoring of Undine's Net from orbit had revealed that comments about his *Estel* postings were now circulating there. He didn't seem surprised or displeased.

Terry bade him farewell and returned triumphant to *Estel* and reunion with his crew. He didn't like to think how close he had come to losing everything, to betraying their trust in his ability to keep them going. But of course they insisted on knowing how he'd gotten hold of the helmets, and Alison grasped enough telepathically to make hiding the facts pointless.

They were nearly out of provisions, so they would have to jump soon, and he had no plan as to where to go. Only two more jumps could be made before it would be necessary to service the hyperdrive engine and replenish its fuel, the second of them to the starport where it would be done. And, since he had split the money from sale of the sugar with Garick, he had barely enough to pay the cost. If he had to spend all his credit on ship maintenance they'd be destitute and unable to acquire more cargo. He and Jon would therefore need to invest in something that could be profitably sold at the starport.

More sugar would be ideal, but returning to New Afrika was out of the question. Terry couldn't land there, nor could they count on being lucky with the police again if they reappeared so soon. The colony Stelo Haveno, where the port was located, had a thriving electronics industry and was in no need of high-tech imports. So it would have to be some other luxury food.

Wine, maybe? Almost all wine traffic was handled by smugglers, as the few worlds with climates suitable for growing grapes didn't produce enough to be included on regular Fleet trade routes. Being agricultural colonies, they didn't need to import food and couldn't afford to import much else. So they welcomed free traders, who bought wine from them legally; but importing it legally was impractical everywhere—the tax was higher than all but the wealthiest free traders could pay. Could he sneak it past the Fleet starport controllers? Terry wondered. He would be taking a serious risk of arrest by Fleet for the first time, and it still made him uncomfortable to set himself against the organization to which he had once sworn loyalty. But wine was a harmless commodity, and he could not see any other way to earn enough money to keep flying.

After consulting *Estel*'s knowledgebase, he decided on Eden as the most promising destination. It was one of the first worlds discovered that had a temperate climate and soil that could support terragenic crops, which accounted for its preemption of a name expressing the hopes of all pastoral colonies. But from what he read about it, he gathered that its society was far from Edenic. Pleasant though their surroundings might be, its people apparently clung to an outdated form of religion based on literal interpretation of ancient texts, a dogmatic interpretation that allowed no room for new ideas—which explained why it hadn't attracted more settlers despite its favorable environment. He could see that it wouldn't be a place where he could promote belief in psi or other mindpowers. It had vineyards, however, and it could be reached without depleting the ship's power reserve. He had little choice but to head there.

During the days of transit in normal space after the jump, Terry continued his work on the software for processing input from the newly-acquired neurofeedback helmets, an absorbing task that left him no time to worry about the obstacles ahead. He remembered the design well from having studied what the mentors had shown him on Titan and on Maclairn; it was just a matter of implementing it. He could hardly wait to try it out with Alison, but that would have to come later.

Eden didn't have a real spaceport; like Maclairn, it offered merely a few pads for shuttles surrounded by open ground, in this case grass-covered. There wasn't even a controller on duty. He was guided in by an automated beacon and met on the ground by a small committee of farmers. For a moment Terry came close to panic; what if they didn't have any cargo to offer? *Estel* didn't have enough power to go somewhere else; he must head for the starport directly. He'd seen flourishing green vineyards from the air, but maybe no aged wine was available. . . .

The farmers didn't seem too friendly; they didn't introduce themselves and Terry decided that although he doubted that bounty hunters would come here, it would be best not to give his own name unless pressed. "I assume you're wanting to buy wine," said one of the farmers brusquely. "My own stock's gone, but I'll put out the word to nearby settlements."

"Thanks," said Jon, still playing the role of captain. "We're in the market for it, yes. Do you have ground transport to a place where we're likely to find some?" Terry wondered what kind of transportation they had on Eden; it looked like something out of a history book and he half-expected to see horses—though of course there were no horses on colonized worlds. It would depend on their source of power, which evidently wasn't space-based. And he had seen no wind turbines.

They turned out to have a standard power grid, fed by a fusion reactor like any large colony that lacked satellite power. The people weren't the hypocrites he'd feared they might be; though they lived simply due to limited imports, they understood that survival on new planets required technology and didn't pretend that high-tech facilities could be rejected. They wouldn't have lasted this long if they did, he realized. There had been many failed colonies whose residents had tried to duplicate ancient lifestyles.

"Whoever has wine to offer will phone here," the farmer told them, "and after you arrange terms, his truck will bring it to your ship. I'm afraid we can't allow you to leave it, though we'll provide food and camping equipment if necessary. The last traders here caused some trouble, and I don't want any more outsiders mingling with our people."

"Trouble?" Terry was astonished; traders who were rowdy or rude to a colony's residents would not stay in business long. If they wanted to get drunk they would wait until back aboard their starship. "I assure you that we'll behave ourselves," he said.

"That may be, but I'm taking no chances, not after what was done to my daughter," the farmer replied grimly.

Shocked, Terry protested, "You can't judge all of us by one man's offense! If your daughter was harmed by a trader you should have called on Fleet; they're tough on offworlders who commit violent crimes. Don't you have an ansible here?"

"We do, but her contamination was not the result of violence. She was exposed to evil ideas, and we may never be able to drive the devil out of her, though God knows we've tried." Sorrowfully, he said, "I've been cruelly hard on my own daughter, but it's failed to restore her soul. All I can do is make sure that no one else is lost."

"Well, they won't be through us," Jon declared. "We have our own partners aboard our starship and we've no interest in seducing local women."

"You misunderstand. For her to take a lover would be sinful, but in time the sin might be forgiven. To be seduced by the devil is worse, since if she never renounces him she will be doomed to hell for all eternity—as are outsiders who have fallen for his lies and aspired to his powers."

Terry did not know quite what to make of this. He was aware that some religious minorities believed literally in a personified devil, but what evil had the girl been exposed to if not illicit sex? An evil with which any outsider might contaminate others? It didn't really matter when the father was adamant about not letting them near the settlement, but he was curious.

They were given a locally-programmed phone and settled on the grass near the landing pad to wait for a call. After several hours it came, and Jon negotiated the price of the wine they were offered, which was to be delivered at dawn the next day. Though they could have gone back to *Vagabond* to sleep, Terry decided that camping out would be less effort and a rather pleasant novelty. They didn't need shelter; it was a warm, cloudless night and Jon had had too few opportunities to see the stars from a planet's surface.

Late in the night, they were wakened by a soft voice only a few meters from them. "Please, traders—wake up! Wake up!"

Terry sat up, startled, and saw a young man—really no more than a boy—crouched next to the tarp on which they'd been sleeping. "I snuck out," he said. "Becka's dad will kill me if he finds out. But he's killing *her* already— he's beaten her with a belt every day since the last traders left, and she won't give in. I've got to get her away from here."

"Beaten her!" Terry exclaimed in horror. "Why?"

"To cast out the devil. I–I think he really might kill her sometime, because the Bible says 'Thou shalt not suffer a witch to live.'"

"You mean he thinks his daughter is a witch? Why does he believe such nonsense?" Surely, in a colony with technology as modern as this one's, the people knew better.

"She can tell what people are thinking," the boy said. "She always could—it didn't feel like the devil's doing but everyone says he deceives people, so she didn't tell anybody but me. Then the traders came, a man and a woman, and we went to look at their ship. We asked about Earth, and the man said there's trouble there over people being attacked because they can hear silent thoughts, or believe others can. And then the woman said she read on the Net that a prophecy says someday more people will be able to do it—that it's a *good* thing that will make the world better."

Oh, my God, Terry thought.

The boy went on, "I told Becka her parents wouldn't believe that, and she'd better keep quiet, but she insisted she'd known inside it wasn't evil and now she had proof. She got the traders to talk about it when they came to her house for dinner, and her dad got into a rage. He made them leave and locked Becka in her room, and he says he'll keep on beating her until she admits she's possessed by the devil—but I know she won't. She told me that if other people are suffering for the same thing, she's not going to be the one to lie."

With a sinking heart, Terry realized what had to be done. Indirectly, he was responsible for this girl's plight, and even if he hadn't been, he couldn't let a psi-gifted

young woman—or any young woman—be beaten to death.
Yet if he found a way to help her escape, she'd have no
place to go . . . and the boy who'd helped might be in danger, too. He would have to take them both offworld.

~ *33* ~

NO INTERSTELLAR TRAVEL regulation was taken more seriously than the law against transporting unauthorized per-
sons from one world to another, Terry knew. A starship
captain who violated it would lose his license and, in most
cases, would serve time in a penal colony; that was why
he'd needed forged crew status for Jon, Alison and Gwen.
All passengers without such status must have transit
permits. No colony was willing to accept tourists or immigrants who might be fleeing the consequences of crimes
committed elsewhere, and many did not allow their own
citizens to emigrate. A transit permit must therefore be
obtained from Fleet, by ansible if there was no local base,
before a traveler could embark. No exceptions were
made.

Obviously, these young people could not get transit
permits. They might not even have IDs; some colonies
didn't register anyone but those who did business with
offworlders. So he'd have to not only get them onto the
shuttle unobserved, but sneak them off it in Stelo
Haveno—and what would they do after they were there?
Without IDs they'd be arrested. He didn't know anybody
who could hide them. . . . And all this presupposed that
he could somehow get Becka out of the room in which she
was locked without alerting her father.

Inwardly, Terry cursed the traders who'd had no more
sense than to talk about psi powers to people in a colony
such as this one. Still, they couldn't have known the girl
was psi-gifted, and in any case they'd probably had no
idea how the adults would react; he had read much more

widely than most people and knew more about ancient beliefs and customs. In any case he had been actively spreading rumors about the "prophecy" symbolized by *Estel*; he couldn't complain when someone followed his lead.

To the boy, Josh, he said, "Do you know what room Becka is in? From the outside of her house, I mean."

"Sure. I've talked to her from under her window, that's how I know what's happening to her."

"Is it big enough for her to get out through?"

"Yes, but somebody's got to help her, or hold me up while I do—I can't reach it. And she's hurt. I don't think she's strong enough to jump."

Well, he and Jon could handle that, Terry thought, but they'd be taking their lives in their hands if the farmer was within hearing distance. "What kind of place is it?" he asked. "Just vineyards, or are there outbuildings?"

"There's the one where they process the grapes. And a chicken coop."

"How close to the house? Can you see the coop from Becka's window?"

"No, it's around back on the other side of the driveway."

Frowning, Terry considered it. He hated to do any real damage, but a man who beat his daughter with a belt repeatedly had it coming, and the chickens were destined to be killed anyway. "If the coop caught fire," he said slowly, "her parents would try to put it out, wouldn't they? They wouldn't go back inside until they did."

"There's a fence around it with a locked gate. We couldn't get close enough to set it on fire."

"Well, I think I could." A chicken coop was full of dry straw that would be easy to ignite with his mind, even from outside a fence. "Do they suspect that you've been in contact with her, Josh, or that you'd try to help her escape?"

"No, I made a big show of asking to see her and

slinking off defeated when they wouldn't let me. Her dad doesn't think anybody would dare defy him, even about other things. He's used to being obeyed."

"I won't insult you by asking if you're willing to take a risk," Terry said, "because you already have, by coming to us. But I've got to be sure you realize that you may have to leave here for good, and you may not be safe from trouble where we're going."

"That's okay," Josh said. "I don't like this place much. I don't want to be a winegrower, I want to see other worlds."

"And if there is trouble you'll stay with Becka, take care of her as long as she needs you?"

"Of course. We want to get married."

Terry had assumed this was the case, but was relieved to hear it stated. Running away to get married would be more understandable to Fleet than running from an accusation of witchcraft, which was so ludicrous as to sound fabricated, and married couples had more rights than unattached young people—although not many when it came to unauthorized transit. "Okay," he said. "We haven't any time to waste if we're going to hide Becka in the shuttle before the truck comes to deliver our wine. Will you follow my orders even if you don't understand what's happening?"

"Yes," Josh promised.

"All right, then, after you show us Becka's window, come with me to the chicken coop. We'll have to be quiet and so I'll say this now—when the coop catches fire, I will go back for Becka. Wait till you're sure it'll be hard to put out, then run to the house and pound on the door to tell her parents that it's burning. You'll have to help them fight it and keep them at it as long as you can without letting them suspect you of anything."

"But Becka's never seen you," Josh protested. "If I'm not there, she won't dare try to escape with someone she doesn't know."

"She will know me. I hear thoughts just as she does, Josh, and if she's been telling the truth about herself, she will be able to hear mine." He hoped she would, anyway; even if psi-gifted she might be too inexperienced or too scared to grasp them.

He and Jon loaded their camping gear into the shuttle, ready for a quick getaway once the wine arrived. "We're crazy, you know," Jon said morosely.

"I know. But have we got a choice?"

"No, I don't suppose we do, though it's an uglier situation than I'd choose to get mixed up in."

"Even if they catch us, they can't kill us or even detain us when they don't know how many people are aboard our starship," Terry pointed out. "They can't be sure an armed party won't come to our rescue in a second shuttle. Anyway, while fighting the fire they'll be too busy to think about us; it won't occur to them that we might meddle in their affairs. I'm more worried about what's going to happen when we get to Stelo Haveno."

Noiselessly, they set off toward the farmhouse, Josh leading the way. No light shone from it at this late hour, so they had to trust his familiarity with the path; Terry didn't dare use a flashlight. When they got close enough to see the windows, Jon stationed himself as close as possible to Becka's while Terry and Josh went on around to the other side and crossed the wide driveway to the chicken coop. Fortunately there were no trees around and the ground was bare; there was no danger of a fire spreading.

Terry pressed close to the wire fence that surrounded the chicken yard and focused on the coop at the center of it. He had warned Josh to ask no questions and to do nothing to distract him. Straw, he told himself—think about the straw, not the chickens that would be prematurely roasted. He had done this once not long ago; to save an innocent girl he could do it again. . . .

With all the intensity he could summon, he envisioned

a small circle of heat within the straw getting hotter . . . and hotter. . . After a few minutes flickering light from within signaled the kindling of flame.

Josh stared at it, bewildered. Under his breath he murmured, "How did you—"

"Never mind!" Terry whispered. "Wait till it's past control, then run to the house and wake them. Yell 'Fire!' as loud as you can when they come out, but not before, so I'll know it's safe to take action." He headed back to where Jon was waiting.

They approached the window, which was a dormer high above the ground. *Becka!* Terry called silently. *Becka, wake up! Wake up and come to your window!* If she was latently psi-gifted she would hear him more clearly in her sleep than if she were already awake. *Becka! Becka, Josh sent us to free you . . . We'll take you to Josh. . . .*

Before long a faint stirring could be seen behind the glass and the window opened a crack; she had sensed his presence. *Josh sent us*, Terry repeated. *We're going to get you away from here. Speak to me in your mind if you understand.*

Josh? Josh, are you there? He had come to her window before, so she wasn't surprised by the possibility. But she was aware that this was different.

We're Josh's friends. He's not far off, and we'll take you to a place he can find.

I can't get out! she protested despairingly. *And if my dad hears me try, he'll beat me again.* Terry could tell that she was suffering not merely from fear, but from pain; but he could do nothing to relieve it while she needed to be alert.

Your dad won't hear you. He'll be out of the house in a minute, and then we'll help you climb down.

But my mom—

She'll be outside too, around front. The chicken coop is on fire.

On fire? How could it be? I think I'm dreaming this, I

*have strange dreams sometimes. I'd better get back into
bed.*

No! No, don't do that! Terry burst out in dismay. *You
have to open the window wide and climb out just as soon
as Josh lets us know it's safe.*

"*I'll fall. And I'm hurting too much to run, even if
there were someplace to run to. If it weren't for that, I'd
have jumped out before now.*

At that moment Josh's yell startled her into full wakefulness. "Fire! Fire!" Terry rushed forward, urging, *Now,
Becka! Open the window now and climb out onto the roof
where I can reach you!* With a lift from Jon, he scrambled
up to a place from which he could catch her.

Becka had heard Josh's voice, and that galvanized her;
she climbed over the sill into Terry's waiting hands. *I
have to pass you down to Jon,* he warned. *Just let go, and
we'll keep you from falling.* Silently, she complied.

Somehow they managed to get her onto the ground,
where it became evident that she was indeed too weak to
escape under her own power; with shock, Terry perceived
that she had been not only beaten, but starved. They would
have to half-carry her to the ship. There wasn't much
time; the sky was already brightening. At least there was
now enough light to see their way. With Becka in a daze,
supported between them, they retraced their path as
quickly as they could. Not until they were safely inside
the shuttle was he able to examine her injuries.

She was wearing a thin shirt that clung to her back,
and to his horror he saw that there was blood on it. She
winced at his mere touch. "Where's Josh?" she asked
weakly. "You said you were taking me to him."

"He'll be here as soon as the fire is out and your parents have gone back inside," Terry said, hoping it was
true. Surely they'd expect him to go home when he was
no longer needed; for him to disappear wouldn't raise suspicion. But it wouldn't be safe to wait for him past the
delivery of the wine shipment. They would have to lift off

immediately, before Becka's father discovered that she was gone.

He turned to relieving her suffering, reassuring her, connecting with her mind as he'd done with the patients on Toliman. Being psi-gifted, she responded and went quickly into rapport with him, letting the pain of the belt lashes drain away. He made sure her back was no longer bleeding, but left the raw wounds for Alison to bandage once they were back aboard *Vagabond*. Jon went out to complete the wine transaction; not until it was time to load the boxed kegs did Terry have to leave Becka's side. Shortly after that, Josh showed up, and he knew that for a time at least, his own presence was no longer needed.

Which left him free to acknowledge, for the first time, the enormity of the mess he'd gotten himself into.

Part Four: Stelo Haveno

~ 34 ~

ONCE ENROUTE TO Stelo Haveno, the problems Terry had
pushed from his mind closed in on him. Mustering his
limited healing ability, he did what he could for Becka's
lacerated back and dealt with her remaining pain during
frequent neurofeedback sessions. But where in God's name
was he going to take these kids? Well, not actually kids,
at least he hoped not. Becka had told him they were sixteen, the age at which children became adults in most
colonies—but in a culture as hidebound as Eden's, where
parents evidently claimed the right to tight control over
adolescent offspring, it might be higher. In that case he
would be guilty not only of unauthorized transport but of
kidnapping.

Assuming he was caught at it. Fortunately, he had not
told anyone on Eden his name or the name of his ship, so
its authorities couldn't put out a specific alert. If he were
headed anywhere but Stelo Haveno, he could buy forged
IDs for them and drop them off. There, however, it wouldn't
be so simple. Starships putting in for maintenance at Stelo
Haveno were closely observed, and there were few civilian
residents of the colony; it was mainly a Fleet installation.
Moreover, he wouldn't have money for forged IDs or anything else until he could smuggle in the wine.

And of course, the maintenance facilities at Stelo

Haveno being a magnet for starships from all over this part of the galaxy, it was also a place frequented by bounty hunters.

On top of this was the question of how he could get the money to keep flying. His intention had been to buy more wine, several shuttle loads; but they'd had to get out fast with just one. Assuming it was sold immediately, it would bring enough pay for provisions and hyperdrive maintenance; but there would be very little left to invest in cargo, and what would happen if he couldn't make enough on the next trip to support himself and his crew?

Despite these worries, they were not what bothered Terry most during the slow days spent in normal space after emerging from the jump. Becka's suffering at the hands of a fanatic disbeliever had left him shaken, for it was a reminder that on Earth many were undergoing even worse ordeals as victims of the Klan. And about that, he could do nothing. He was pledged to promote hope for the future spread of advanced mind faculties, yet when people did believe in them, they sometimes got hurt. Whether or not he was responsible for endangering them—and Alison insisted that he wasn't—they were vulnerable to harm he was helpless to prevent.

The situation on Earth haunted him more and more. Besides, he was all too aware that Maclairn's enemies might try bioweapons again; the fact that they were strong enough to be instigating Klan action made it even more likely that they would find another pair of suicidal terrorists, and this time he wouldn't be around to stop them.

"If only there were some way I could warn Fleet," he said to Jon when out of the kids' hearing. "The plan has been to keep intruders on Maclairn so they couldn't get away and reveal the secret. It didn't occur to anyone that taking unarmed men to the surface could pose a danger. But now that should never be allowed, at least not without a strip-search and perhaps a CAT scan."

"But if no one but the mentors knows Maclairn exists, and you can't contact any mentors—"

"There are a few Fleet officials who know—and the people connected to the Maclairn Foundation, of course, including former visitors taken there to observe. The trouble is that I can't reveal that *I* know. Any warning would have to be anonymous, and it couldn't mention Maclairn specifically or they'd fear the secret was out. So they'd dismiss it as coming from some crackpot."

"I thought you said there are psi-gifted people who can foresee the future. Mightn't one who'd seen a disaster coming try to contact psi experts?"

"Perhaps. It's public knowledge that the Foundation does research on psi; that's their cover. But they wouldn't connect such a report with Maclairn. Unless—" Terry pondered it, his excitement rising. "Unless the person had picked up some identifying feature through remote viewing, something that no outsider could have known."

That night, alone with Alison in their stateroom, he began composing a message. "I don't dare approach you openly," he wrote, "since if it were known that I have psi powers I'd be targeted by the Ku Klux Klan. I'm too much of a coward to risk that, or to risk my loved ones, so don't try to find me—you can't, and even if you could I wouldn't admit having written this. It may mean nothing to you, yet I know that the Maclairn Foundation studies psi phenomena, and if what I've seen has any substance, someone ought to know about it. I have been blessed—or cursed, some would say—with psi all my life, and my precognitive flashes have often proved to be true foresight. I hope this is an exception, because it's worse than any of the others.

"For six nights now the same vision has come to me. There is a world—I don't know its name—with just one small colony, and a ship approaches it, and it is captured by patrollers from a larger ship; but then a shuttle lands. And I know, in the vision, that the shuttle has brought evil, because everyone begins to die. All the people in the colony sicken and die, and there are piles of bodies—I try to close my mind but I can't, I can't see the world from space anymore, just the decaying bodies of its people. They lie where they fall, for the sickness strikes too fast for there to be any help for it; they gasp for breath, but the air is poisoned and they writhe in agony as they collapse. And the crew of the large ship can do nothing, because once the shuttle reached the planet's surface it was already too late."

Terry paused, wanting to delete the words from his tablet as he'd tried to delete the image from his mind. What if it *was* true? What if it had come through his own precognitive gift rather than from his memory of what had nearly happened? For too long he had suppressed his knowledge of the danger, telling himself that it was out of his hands. . . .

"Each time it happens I come to myself in horror, knowing that if this is true the colony must be warned," he continued. "But I don't know where it is. I've looked through the atlas in the knowledgebase, and I don't see any world like it—a golden planet with just one settled area, and a dam that holds back a long, narrow lake in the center of a deep canyon. I can't find a lake like that in any pictures of colony worlds. So maybe it is a false seeing, as precognitive ones often are; but if anyone else has reported something like it, this message may have value as confirmation. The people of that world, if there is such a place, must be told never to let strangers land."

He passed his tablet to Alison, and she read it frowning. "Do you have to put in the part about how people die? If they take it seriously they'll be terribly scared."

"They should be! I am. Oh, God, Alison . . . it's been less than twelve weeks since I stopped the last attack, and there's no reason to think Maclairn's enemies have given up. I've kept so busy being Captain of *Estel* and planting hope on the Nets, and taking crazy chances like

I did on Undine, that I didn't have to remember that killing those terrorists might not have done any permanent
good."

She pressed close to him on the bed where they were
sitting and put her arm around his slumped shoulders.
"It doesn't help to remember it. You couldn't do anything
to stop the conspiracy even if you were free to go to Earth,
any more than you could defeat the Klan. But you're helping a lot of people by spreading the *Estel* symbol."

"Am I? Look what it did to Becka."

"Becka chose to stick by what that symbol led her to
believe in, knowing the price she'd have to pay, and she's
better off for it—won't she be happier away from Eden
than being dominated by men like her father all her life?"

Miserably, Terry protested, "What if we hadn't happened along to save her from that?"

"You can't look at it that way. Fate has helped you
many times—do you think you're the only person it helps?
Some are spared harm and others aren't, and it's not up
to you to decide who. Nobody is happy without believing
in something, so when you give them that, they're ahead."

Terry turned to her and held her close, allowing himself to be comforted by her warmth, and after awhile they
made love. But his depression did not lift. Though he did
his best not to let it engulf them during the telepathic
merging of their minds, he knew that Alison was not fooled,
and that she grieved over it.

The only thing he felt sure of was that someday, somehow, he would have to take action; otherwise he would be
crushed by what he alone knew of the danger. Not just
Maclairn's danger, but humankind's, because if belief in
new mind faculties was stamped out, the bright future
the Elders had told him about would never arrive. . . .

The first thing was to send the message to the Maclairn
Foundation. But how could he? It would have to go either
by ansible or by courier, and he had access to neither. To
transmit it via public ansible would cost more money than

he could raise. He should have sent such a message when he was with Zach, he thought in dismay. It would have been impossible to explain, but he could probably have talked Zach into taking his word that it was important.

Would some friend of Zach send it? Probably not, not for free. All ID forgers had ansible access; that was one reason they charged high fees for their work. He was going to have to pay plenty to get IDs for Becka and Josh, if and when he acquired some credit from sale of the wine. He had the name of a dealer in Zach's network, which Zach had given him knowing he'd eventually need to re-fuel his ship at Stelo Haveno. But getting in touch with the man was not going to be simple. First he would have to get *Estel* into a maintenance dock without letting any-one discover that he had unauthorized passengers aboard.

~ *35* ~

TERRY HAD HAD plenty of experience in lying to starport controllers, since when bringing mentors to Earth in *Prom-ise* he'd had to conceal the fact that it had visited a planet not on the charts. So he decided it would be best not to mention Eden, just in case the kids' flight from home had been reported. He stated that he'd last been to Undine but had been denied permission to land, which was verifi-able if anybody cared to check.

He also lied, of course, about the number of passen-gers aboard. If there was an inspection, Becka and Josh would have to hide, but he hoped it wouldn't come to that. And finally, he lied about *Vagabond*'s captain, again nam-ing Jon. This was going to be awkward because while the captain would be expected to make the arrangements for maintenance and refueling, Jon knew nothing about the hyperdrive; some excuse would have to be offered for his delegating the necessary paperwork.

That was not the biggest problem, however. More

difficult was the fact that neither of them had enough money to pay more than a deposit on the bill. If they couldn't sell the wine before the work was finished, *Estel* would be held as security until they could come up with it—a thought Terry found too dismaying to dwell on.

As soon as orbit had been established and landing clearance for the shuttle had been obtained, Terry and Gwen went to the surface of the planet to pick up provisions, leaving Jon aboard as "captain." Supplies had priority over other expenses—they'd been low on them in the first place, since they'd obtained none on Eden, and for the last few days two extra people had been consuming not only food but water and oxygen. *Estel* was too small a ship to have a self-sustaining life support system.

Gwen piloted the shuttle; she was by now experienced in everything but landing, which at a spaceport was handled mainly by the AI. To get a license to fly solo with passengers, she would have to learn to land on rough terrain, but that could wait. Her student license authorized her to carry cargo for their own use and she'd had plenty of practice in docking, so with the purchase and loading of supplies taken care of, Terry sent her back to *Vagabond* alone and went in search of the dealer whose name Zach had given him.

Stelo Haveno was a domed colony, the thick atmosphere of its planet being unbreathable without the respirator masks that all starships carried as standard equipment. It had little function beyond housing the Fleet personnel who worked on the starships in port for maintenance plus the services that supported them. There were a few civilians employed in high-tech industries, and there was a thriving recreational district that served everyone, composed of the usual assortment of gyms, cafés, bars, arcades, and brothels. From the initial greeting of the woman who answered his call Terry half-expected the latter, but once he mentioned Zach's box, her tone changed and he was directed to a respectable-looking restaurant with several wine kegs in plain sight behind the bar.

Serving wine was not illegal in the colony, he realized, and apparently no questions were asked as to where restaurants got their stock, though surely everyone knew that it came from smugglers since official Fleet cargo ships rarely carried it. The woman, Jenna Fenway, and her husband Walt—warm, friendly people who reminded him of the retired couple who'd lived next door during his childhood on Earth—explained to him that there was nobody authorized to check. Because the charter of the colony stated that importing consumables without a license was forbidden, Fleet prevented their transport to the surface; but it had no jurisdiction on the ground except over violence, and the colony had no police since Fleet did control any violence that occurred. Therefore, if a shipment of wine or some other luxury got past the inspector at the spaceport gate it was safe from challenge.

Nevertheless, getting it to the ground and past the gate would not be easy. And, Terry thought grimly, getting Becka and Josh past the gate would be even harder.

There was no way to contact an ID forger except through this couple, and he did not know how to broach the subject—they weren't the sort of people likely to be acquainted with the underworld. Though they bought smuggled wine, they weren't breaking the law once it was out of their van and sold only by the glass. Zach had vouched for them, which meant they would not turn a lawbreaker in for any offense short of murder. But they struck him as too wholesome and unsophisticated to have friends among forgers.

Which was just as well, since they were also unlikely to be watched by bounty hunters. All the same, he had no choice but to make some attempt at getting information. After the terms of the wine deal had been agreed upon, he ventured, "If there are no police here, I suppose there's a lot of crime—nonviolent crime, that is."

"Well, that depends on what you call crime," Walt said. "Just about everything is legal here except for League offenses, and most of us aren't too particular about obeying bureaucrats' laws."

That explained Zach's approval of them, Terry thought. "But surely, stealing, forgery—"

"We don't tolerate thieves; Fleet transports them offworld once they're convicted in our local court. There's no way they can escape, after all, with no breathable air outside the dome. As to forgery, though—I suppose you mean ID tampering—that's under League jurisdiction and there wouldn't be enough demand for it here to warrant the risk."

"You see," added Jenna, "Fleet checks IDs coming and going, and if someone boarding a ship didn't have a record of having arrived, or the records didn't match, it would show that there'd been tampering. We have only one public ansible, and it would be easy enough to find out who'd had illegal access to it." She seemed rather uncomfortable with the topic, Terry noted.

"How do you communicate with Zach?" Terry asked. Surely a mom-and-pop restaurant business wasn't profitable enough to support ansible fees.

"When he contacts us, we reply collect, and he'll also accept collect messages in emergencies. I gather he's got an ansible terminal of his own in the hidden box he told us about. He's a wealthy man, you know."

Surprised, Terry said, "I didn't. He lives in the back room of a store."

"But I've heard he's got millions in investments—the kind of forging he does pays well, and he doesn't do it for the money, he only cares about defying the League government's red tape. And about helping people he feels have gotten a raw deal."

"He wanted a contact here because it's a hub for traffic from all over, and a wine smuggler he knew recommended us," Walt explained. "That was years ago. We pass on messages to captains if he asks us to, and he sends us sellers that we can trust."

And they could send text to Zach without paying, Terry thought hopefully, thinking of his letter to the Maclairn Foundation—but how could he explain that it was an emergency? The rest of what they'd told him was even less promising. He had realized that Becka and Josh would either have to sneak off the ship and stay at Stelo Haveno permanently, or else be given IDs and transit permits without leaving the ship to receive them, in which case he would have to smuggle aboard a device for implanting the chips. But if there were no local ID forgers, they couldn't get IDs at all. They couldn't stay here without identification, and he would face the problem all over again wherever he went next.

Walt agreed to have his van at the spaceport before dawn the next morning, and Terry prepared to leave. "Before you go," Jenna said, "there's something I want to ask you—I ask everyone I meet from offworld. There's a rumor on our Net, and I don't know where it came from, or whether there's any truth in it. It's said there's a ship called *Estel*, and its captain helps people in trouble, and he promises that someday humans will be better off than they are now, happier, because their minds will have new powers and won't be so vulnerable to control by the government. Have you ever heard anything like that?"

Terry's spirits rose. So it had reached even here—of course it would, since ships from everywhere came and crews on leave would talk. And from here, it would be passed on to many other colonies. "Yes," he said. "I've heard it, and I believe it's true."

"This Captain of *Estel*—does anyone know how to get in touch with him?"

"Why would they want to?" Terry hedged.

"Well," Jenna said, "on Earth, I've heard, people are being attacked by gangs of terrorists because they have paranormal powers, powers like what the rumors say we'll all have in the future. Some of their homes have been burned and they've had to hide their families, and they want to get away from Earth. But of course most of them haven't got transit permits or money for passage. And I wondered if what I've read about the Captain of *Estel* helping people in trouble means he takes them aboard his ship."

Terry froze. He had helped two people escape persecution for psi, but from Eden, not from Earth, and she couldn't possibly have guessed unless she was telepathic herself. And she wasn't—her mind wasn't open like a telepath's, nor was it intentionally closed. Yet the emotion he sensed in her suggested that her question involved more than mere curiosity. "I don't think," he said slowly, "that *Estel* ever goes to Earth."

"I don't suppose it could," Jenna agreed. "It would be caught by Fleet, wouldn't it? But if a few people were smuggled aboard some other ship, a ship that couldn't transport them to a permanent refuge, maybe *Estel* could be taking them on to a world that would welcome them. It's—sort of a fantasy I have, because I don't like the thought of those people being in danger."

A world that would welcome them? He wished he knew of one where he could take the kids. If they could stay here, Jenna would watch out for them, he thought ruefully; she was just the kind of person they needed. But without IDs, they couldn't escape detection for long.

He pushed the thought aside, knowing that he had more immediate concerns to deal with. The wine had to be delivered tonight—once the ship was in the space dock, its cargo bay would be under seal. Fleet couldn't arrest him for carrying wine as long as he stayed in orbit, but if he was caught transporting it, or if the seal was broken, the game would be up.

The shuttle hadn't been inspected or challenged on the trip down; could he rely on that at all hours, or would they suspect someone landing at an unreasonably late hour of trying to avoid notice? Terry decided that they might. If he came at a time when he could have legitimate business and left the shuttle unattended with the wine stashed in its hold—something no smuggler would be expected to do—they'd get used to seeing it on the ground and wouldn't bother to investigate.

There remained the question of how to unload it and get it through the spaceport gate. Walt did it regularly, so it must be possible, unlikely though that seemed. Yet he too would be at risk as the driver of the van, even if they couldn't prove he was a buyer. Why hadn't he told him how to trick the Fleet inspectors? Terry wondered as he waited by the gate for Gwen to pick him up with the shuttle. He'd had to let his ID be scanned coming and going, and could only hope there'd be no permanent record that might fall into the hands of bounty hunters.

He had no choice but to follow Walt's lead. If the wine kegs weren't sold before the ship went into the space dock, he wouldn't have the money to get it out. There was no way to sell them without delivering them to Walt, and Walt hadn't seemed to doubt that he could collect them. Either he trusted Zach's recommendation of him—and his own telepathic impressions—or he didn't. What good did psi-giftedness do him if he couldn't rely on it?

When he got back to *Estel*, Alison was at the airlock to meet him, obviously shaken out of her usual calm. "They're inspecting all the ships," she told him. "They'll get around to us any time now—we were afraid you wouldn't be back soon enough."

"It's no big deal," he said reassuringly. "They can't accuse us of smuggling when we haven't smuggled anything yet, and simply having wine on board isn't illegal."

"You don't understand. It came over the comm—there's a report of two underage kids missing from Eden. They're searching ships in all the ports within easy range."

"Oh, my God." He'd been hoping against hope that sixteen was Eden's age of majority.

"What are we going to do, Terry? There's no place to hide them."

"There's the cargo bay," he said grimly.

"I thought of that, but Jon says it's not pressurized."

"That's why they won't search it. We've got spacesuits to spare, all those from *Bonanza* as well as our own. They won't notice that any are missing."

"You mean to say you're going to put those kids into an unpressurized compartment?" Alison protested. "Becka can't possibly deal with a spacesuit—even I couldn't, without training."

"There isn't any alternative short of sending them back to abusive homes." Not to mention his own situation, Terry thought silently; there was no chance that he wouldn't be arrested if they were found.

Jon said, "I agree, but we don't know how long they'll have to be in there, and they certainly don't know how to change tanks. Somebody's got to stay with them, and I guess that's me."

"It can't be you," Terry said. "Supposedly you're captain, and the inspectors will expect you to appear. I'll go in myself."

"You *are* captain, and we can't spare you—some crisis may arise that you'll have to handle."

Gwen spoke up. "I'm the logical person—Jon taught me how to use spacesuits while we were waiting for you to get back from Toliman, and the kids like me."

That was true, Terry realized. They did like Gwen and would feel comfortable with her, and an engineer's absence wouldn't be noticed. "Okay," he said. "Call them in here, and we'll get started."

Becka and Josh were in their stateroom—he had allowed them to share one because he hadn't wanted to let himself think that they might be underage. Gwen went to get them, explaining the situation as they returned to the lounge. Becka was dubious. "A spacesuit?" she protested. "All sealed up in it where I can't breathe?"

"You can breathe. I'll be there and I'll make sure you always have enough air."

"Hey, it'll be fun," Josh told her. He had explored the ship during the past few days and had decided he wanted to become a spacer.

"If you don't do this, they'll send you back to your father," Terry told her, adding silently, *I know it's scary, but you're a brave person—you stood up to your dad, and you climbed out that high window to escape.*

She nodded. "I guess so. Can you . . . talk to me in your mind while I'm in there?"

"Maybe. But I'll have to focus on talking to the officers."

They got Gwen and the kids suited up and into the airlock for the inner entrance to the cargo bay, first taking through a generous supply of oxygen tanks. Nervously, Terry pressed them to hurry; Jon had received word that the inspection team was on the way. When the lock closed behind them and the light showing it was occupied finally went out, he drew a breath of relief. *Are you okay, Becka?* he asked silently. Gwen had a comm unit, but they hadn't dared give them to the kids lest they speak into a live mike accidentally.

Yes . . . I'm all right. . . . Then, almost immediately, an officer's voice came over the comm requesting permission to board.

During the next half hour two grim-faced Fleet officers searched the entire ship, even taking up the cushions of the couches in the lounge to inspect the storage lockers underneath—a place large enough for a young girl to hide in, which Terry had known better than to use. "Don't take this personally," one of them said to Jon. "We have orders to be thorough; the missing kids may have left Eden voluntarily, but even so, kidnapping can't be tolerated. When the ship that has them is found, its captain will soon be on his way to Draconis."

Inwardly, Terry cringed. Draconis was a League

penal colony on a desolate world in the Sigma Draconis system.

"What cargo are you carrying?" the officer asked.

"Wine," declared Jon honestly. "We know it's not legal to import here; we're just in for hyperdrive maintenance."

"Then you won't mind if we seal your cargo bay here and now to save the trouble of doing it when you go into the space dock. We'll get the outer hatch before we cast off, and the inner one right now."

As Terry and the others watched in horrified dismay, the man snapped an official seal onto the bay's airlock and departed—with Gwen, Becka and Josh locked inside the airless cargo bay.

~ 36 ~

"DO YOU THINK they suspected anything?" Jon asked when the officers were out of hearing.

"Maybe. On the other hand, they would have had to seal it when we entered the space dock and they may be shorthanded there."

"It doesn't look too hard to get off," Alison said. "Will they notice when we go into the dock that it's gone?"

Terry broke the news as calmly as he could. "It's electronic," he said, "and when it's tampered with it sends a signal to the control base. If we break the seal, they'll be back in half an hour to find out why."

"Well, we haven't any choice—we'll have to take our chances, and the sooner the better," Jon said. Terry could feel the surge of desperation in him; *Gwen* was in there.

They had not understood. "It's not a question of chance," he said. "There's no other place to hide the kids. I'll be arrested for kidnapping and illegal transport, and on top of that for breaking the seal, which is another felony. I'll end up on Draconis, as they said."

Alison paled. Jon stared at him for a moment and then declared, "No, you won't. You're forgetting that they think I'm captain, and only the captain is liable."

"The record shows I chartered the ship, and in my presence I'm in charge," Terry pointed out. "You can't be held accountable for my decisions."

"Terry," said Jon firmly, "long ago on Ciencia you gave yourself up to save me from spending the rest of my life in that hellhole of a prison there. Do you think I've forgotten? You're always talking about how fate's put you in the right place at the right time. Well, now it's put *me* in the fortunate position of being able to pay back a debt I never thought I could repay. I'm believed to be the captain of *Vagabond* and we're not going to tell them otherwise."

"Jon, I can't let you—"

"Of course you can. *You* went to prison for *me*, so it's only fair.

Jon had questioned the wisdom of rescuing Becka in the first place, Terry thought; it wouldn't be at all fair for him to suffer the consequences. And in any case, he himself was captain of *Estel,* under whatever name it flew, and he was responsible for the welfare of his crew. *Estel.* . . .

"There's an alternative," he said. "It's legal to break the seal once we're out of orbit, beyond the range of its signal. So all we have to do is leave as *Vagabond* and come back as *Estel* with its true transponder."

"But we decided that it's too dangerous to reveal *Estel,*" Alison said. "Word's sure to get around if it's known to have come here."

"That may be, but it's a risk of bounty hunters finding me versus a sure prison sentence. I'd rather take the risk."

"What good can it do?" Jon protested. "They're checking all the ships in orbit, so they'll inspect *Estel* when it arrives."

"Not in the first half hour. I'll take the kids to the surface—I'm pretty sure the couple I met there will shelter them. There'll be trouble later because they don't have IDs and there doesn't seem to be a forger available, but it's better than for them to be sent back to Eden immediately. And by the time they're discovered we'll be gone."

"You're forgetting that when Fleet does inspect *Estel*, they'll recognize me, as well as the ship's interior," Jon pointed out."

"It won't be the same officers," Terry declared. "Except aboard starships, Fleet personnel have at least sixteen hours between shifts. So they can't be back on duty that soon."

"How long will the oxygen tanks in the cargo bay last?" Alison asked.

"Nine more hours, but we can't go that far away because I have to meet the buyer on the ground fourteen hours from now. So it's six hours out, break the seal, and six hours back, allowing time to establish a new orbit and go down in the shuttle." It would be cutting it close, Terry thought unhappily, but that was all the time they had. If he was more than a few minutes late, Walt might not wait for him.

He'd had a strange feeling during his conversation with Walt and Jenna; his telepathic sense had told him they were concealing something from him. Yet there was no ill-will. Their friendliness had been genuine; he was sure of that. And Zach had assured him that anyone he recommended was trustworthy. Perhaps they didn't trust *him*—though that was unlikely, since they'd said Zach sent them reliable wine sellers.

He piloted the ship out of orbit, heading as far from Stelo Haveno as it would be possible to get in six hours, while Jon explained to Gwen what was happening. Steady, unshakable person that she was, she took it in stride, saying she felt she could keep the kids from panic. Six more hours would be a long time for an inexperienced person to stay in a spacesuit, and since they didn't have comm capability she could talk to them only by touching helmets. Becka, however, responded to Terry's telepathic reassurance with surprising serenity. She had discovered during the past week that she was equal to just about any situation.

At last, when the time was up, he broke the seal and the prisoners emerged, suffering more from hunger than from stress and eager for the meal Alison had ready. When they finished it Gwen got to work changing *Estel's* transponder back to its original one, hiding the *Vagabond* transponder for future use. Terry and Jon spent the return trip laboriously moving the wine kegs from the cargo bay's interior airlock into the shuttle's hold via the lounge, since it would have been impractical to take the shuttle out of its bay while the ship was under power.

"Okay," said Terry when they were back at Stelo Haveno and ready to land. "Here goes—let's see what sort of reception we get." Rumors about *Estel* were on the local Net, he knew. Furthermore, Captain Garick had said that Fleet was on the lookout for such a ship. He didn't know if an official policy had been established; he would have to play it by ear.

"Stelo Haveno Control, this is HS *Estel*, now establishing orbit. Request permission to land our shuttle. Over." Fortunately Jon had done all the comm for *Vagabond*, so there was no danger that his own voice would be recognized.

After a long pause, Control responded, "Unidentified ship, please state your real name and the name of your captain. Over."

"This is HS *Estel*," Terry repeated, "Captain Terry Steward speaking. If you doubt my word, please check your readout for our transponder." Captains' names were always stated and he had known he would be required to give it, but after having hidden it for so long, he did so regretfully.

He waited again for a reply. Finally it came: "HS *Estel*, we have verified your identity. Permission to land granted. You are welcome here and officers will be on hand to greet you. Over."

Oh, God. He hadn't stopped to think that he might draw a crowd even before dawn. "Stelo Haveno Control, we ask that our arrival be kept confidential and that we not be met," he said quickly. "Our shuttle will be unmarked and we wish no publicity. Over."

"HS *Estel*, that may be difficult. Many have been searching for you, as you no doubt know. Over."

"Are we under suspicion of any crime? If not, I am entitled to the same privacy as all other League citizens. I will be on the ground only a short time to arrange for hyperdrive maintenance. Over."

Another pause. Finally Control conceded, "You are not under suspicion. We will honor your request, but we would appreciate the courtesy of a call at Fleet headquarters before you leave. Out."

He would have to move fast, Terry knew. The kids were already in the shuttle, wearing Gwen's flight jackets, her old one and another she had bought on New Afrika. Since the respirator masks would cover their faces, hopefully they could pass as crew members except for the check at the gate. For that, he must trust in whatever scheme Walt had for getting the wine kegs through; reckless as that seemed, they had nothing to lose by gambling on it.

Coming in to land he could see that there was little traffic. Fleet would undoubtedly recognize his shuttle simply by the fact that there were no others coming in at this hour, and they would see it being met by a van; it was too bad he'd had to abandon his original plan to arrive inconspicuously and unload the wine only after a long wait. On the other hand, since they'd acknowledged that *Estel* was not under suspicion, it probably hadn't occurred to them that its famous captain might turn out to be a smuggler. They might ignore a shuttle unloading cargo in their eagerness to spot a pilot who looked like a possible celebrity.

Walt's van was waiting by the landing pad nearest the gate, as Terry had seen from above. Once the shuttle was stabilized he got out quickly and got to work unloading the hold. Merely bringing in cargo was not grounds for challenge; the wine kegs were boxed and not easily identifiable. Walt helped, and because of the respirator masks they did no talking. When they got into the sealed van, however, the presence of the kids had to be revealed.

"I hope Jenna was serious about wanting to help refugees with psi talents," Terry said, "because I have two in the shuttle who need sheltering."

Walt stared at him, astonished. "Refugees? You already—?"

"We were in a bind and I didn't have a chance to ask you; within an hour they'd have been picked up. The girl is telepathic, and her father beat her half to death trying to drive out the devil. Unfortunately they're underage, so Fleet's searching all ships for them."

"How did you expect to get them through the gate, then?"

"The same way you get wine kegs through, whatever that is. They haven't got IDs so they'll have to be hidden in the back of the van."

"My God, you're a bold one. Zach was right about you."

"Zach told you about me specifically? He couldn't have known when I'd be here."

"Nearly all ships in this region of the galaxy turn up sooner or later. He told us to watch for *Vagabond.*"

Walt and Jenna had reacted to the ship's name as if it meant something to them, Terry recalled. But if they'd been watching for *Vagabond*, why hadn't they said so? Why had they treated him as a total stranger? "I'm sorry to get you involved in this mess," he said, "but after what Jenna said—"

Slowly, Walt said, "You made the right choice. Your

refugees can get in back with the wine kegs—no need to hide. The cargo area won't be inspected."

"Why not?"

"Because I have an ongoing arrangement with the officer on this shift; he comes around afterward and picks up a keg. Most sellers, I don't tell before they deliver because I can't be sure they won't give us away. In your case, I was afraid you might be too honest to go along with bribery."

"I'm not that honest. So far, besides a variety of things in a former life, I'm guilty of evading arrest, forgery, operating a starship under a false name, buying forged IDs for my crew, smuggling, illegal transport, kidnapping, breaking an official cargo seal—oh, and theft, if you want to count relieving a corrupt institution of a couple of items it didn't need. And of hacking more public knowledgebases than I can remember offhand."

"I don't care about any of that," Walt said. "What I do want to know is if Zach was right when he told us you might know how to get in touch with the Captain of *Estel*."

~ *37* ~

"YOU BELIEVE THE *Estel* legend?" Terry asked, not knowing whether to feel jubilant or dismayed. He wanted people to believe in the idea it symbolized, not in a man with supernatural powers.

"Zach does. He thinks it's literally true, that otherwise there wouldn't be a bounty on the man. He said he told you about that, thought you might be in a position to warn him."

With a sinking feeling Terry inquired, "Has he sent you a message about the bounty, something more to add to the warning?"

"Not exactly." Walt looked him in the eye. "You haven't given me your name."

"It's best if I don't, Walt. It could get you in trouble." Although he trusted the Fenways not to expose him, they could very well be sought by bounty hunters themselves if any connection to him was suspected, and outlaws of that kind would not hesitate to use unpleasant methods of forcing them to tell what they knew.

Terry escorted Becka and Josh over from the shuttle and made sure that no evidence had been left of their presence. The van was waved through the gate without inspection, as Walt had expected. Once inside the dome they were, temporarily at least, safe.

Jenna welcomed them with warmth, seeming more confused than amazed. "I don't understand," she said. "How can you already have picked up refugees? I got the impression that you hadn't been in touch with Zach lately."

Terry, equally confused, repeated what he had told Walt. "What has Zach got to do with it?" he asked. "He didn't mention knowing anyone on Eden."

Walt and Jenna exchanged glances, but said nothing until the kids had been settled in the kitchen for an early breakfast and the adults had withdrawn to the restaurant's office.

"I think under the circumstances it's time you were let in on our secret," Walt said. "We've been sheltering people who've been victimized by the Ku Klux Klan on Earth. Zach sends them to us—he has contacts among captains, some of them Fleet captains, who will bring them this far when they're coming in for maintenance anyway. We have a family with us now, a couple with two little girls. But of course they can't stay here; this colony doesn't accept unskilled immigrants, even documented ones. So we can help only a few, depending on who we can find to take them to a world that does. That's why he told us to watch for your ship."

Stunned, Terry said, "Why didn't Zach say anything about this when I was with him?"

"He's only been doing it for a few weeks. The situation on Earth keeps getting worse, and after he learned one captain had broken the rules, he began looking for others. He didn't have a way to reach you, but he thought you might be willing."

"And what's more," Jenna added, "he thought you might reach the Captain of *Estel*. A man like that who knows how to stay out of sight would be able to take refugees to many worlds—maybe all the way from Earth itself. And he's a symbol, you see. If people heard the Captain of *Estel* was rescuing victims, just the idea would give them hope, because they've suffered for the beliefs that he stands for."

Terry's mind was spinning. She was right, of course. It was the sort of thing he was committed to do, and to hell with the risk. But there was an obstacle she hadn't thought of.

"Where would the funds to operate and provision his ship come from?" he asked. "Unless he's got a lot in savings, he must work at something—he couldn't keep making trips to carry refugees without some way to meet the cost." As he said this, he was thinking that Zach had contact with buyers and sellers on many worlds; if it were possible to communicate with him, smuggling deals might be prearranged.

"I don't know about the Captain of *Estel*," Walt said, "but Zach has sent us enough money to compensate some captain for taking the family that's with us now. Which could be you."

"I wouldn't do it for money," Terry said, "but expenses—well, with what you're paying me for the wine, I'll have enough credits to get my hyperdrive engine serviced but not much more, so I'll have to go someplace where there's a demand for what little I can buy here." This worry had resurfaced now that the time had come when it must be faced. If he spent all he had on cargo and failed to sell it, they would run out of consumables.

"Call it a charter job," said Jenna. "There's nothing underhanded about that."

True—there was no reason why Zach shouldn't use his illegally-earned wealth to bankroll a rescue operation. He could well afford to charter a ship.

"There's another problem," Terry pointed out. "I'm willing to take passengers without transit permits, but what are they going to do if I can't get forged ones for them later? Any colony's immigration authorities will require documentation, and so will Fleet's gate officers. Becka and Josh don't even have IDs."

"They'll have IDs by tomorrow, and transit permits, too," Walt assured him.

"I thought you said there was no one here who can provide forgeries."

"I implied it. At that point we assumed you had no need to know. Actually there's a hacker who sometimes helps people—those in real trouble, I mean, not criminals on the run."

"You can put me in touch with him?"

Walt smiled. "You're already in touch. It's Jenna."

"I used to be a programmer at League Headquarters," she told him, "and I know their system, including a few backdoors. I keep quiet about it because there are some who'd demand my services at gunpoint, considering that I'm the only ID forger in Stelo Haveno."

And he had thought her too unsophisticated to have underworld connections, Terry thought ruefully. His telepathic faculty must be failing him. "What about ansible access?" he asked.

"I contact Zach collect and work remotely through him. Of course it's just an occasional thing; it wouldn't be practical on a regular basis."

Perplexed, he said, "You told me that forging IDs would be useless because IDs are checked at the gate and departures have to match arrivals. Hiding people in the back of the van is fine for private shuttles like mine that you can meet or deliver supplies to, but how do people sneak in or out on Fleet shuttles?"

"Our friend Warrant Officer Lorenski at the check-point doesn't like what's happening on Earth any more than we do," Jenna said. "He's been helping us smuggle wine for years, but this other business, he does just because it needs doing. The captains are told what time it's safe to bring passengers, and when someone with an ID I've coded leaves, a mismatch doesn't trigger an alarm."

For a warrant officer to do this was risky, and not only for himself, Terry thought in dismay. What if some-day he was given a different assignment? What if he was transferred out? Jenna, seeing his skepticism, added, "He's not a young man—he's been here for decades, and took the night shift rather than be forced to retire. I gather he's considered a fixture, so nobody watches him too closely."

It might work, Terry thought with excitement. He might be able to get the kids and the other refugees onto *Estel*—but that would have to wait until it was out of the space dock. He liked the idea of putting it in for mainte-nance under its own name less and less—but what choice had he? The hyperdrive engine hadn't enough fuel for an-other jump, at least not with enough reserve to go any-where after that, and if stuck where it couldn't get anti-matter it would be stuck forever. He had heard of starships permanently stranded in solar systems where no hyperdrive maintenance could be done, and the thought of such a thing happening to *Estel* filled him with dread.

With the kids safely in the Fenways' care, it was time he got over to Fleet's technical office to schedule a space dock appointment and make the down payment on the work—at least now he was assured of having enough credit to reclaim *Estel*. And, he supposed, he would have to visit Headquarters as Port Control had requested; it would look odd if he didn't and he couldn't afford to become the focus of attention.

Yet, he thought suddenly, what if he was already under surveillance? Word might have been passed by the officer who'd evicted him from Centauri that he was an undesirable; that officer had known his true name. Or the rumors about *Estel* alone might have branded him as persona non grata on the theory that his presence might cause trouble. Perhaps their courtesy had been a trap; they might intend to hold him and his ship. . . .

In an agony of apprehension, Terry was unsure what to do. His instinct—perhaps precognition—told him to get out while it was still possible, and take the refugees with him. Reason told him that it was *not* possible until the hyperdrive engine was serviced.

And then, suddenly, the situation became critical.

Walt answered a knock on the door and admitted Warrant Officer Lorenski, who'd come to collect his keg of wine. "You'll want to get out to the port right now," Lorenski said. "A rumor's spreading that the ship *Estel* is in orbit, and that the Captain of *Estel* has landed in a shuttle. A lot of people want to get a look at him."

"Oh, I hope it's true!" exclaimed Jenna. "Walt, let's both go—we can get back before it's time to open the restaurant."

Oh, my God, Terry thought. He sat paralyzed, not knowing what to do. "I'm going back on foot," Lorenski said. "I just came to tell you folks, and to get the wine into my groundcar in case they close the dome entrance to vehicles—they're not going to want it blocked by traffic."

"We'll come along," Walt said. "If he's really here, we don't want to miss him."

Appalled, Terry stood up, trying to catch Walt's eye. *Don't!* he thought desperately, hoping he or Jenna had enough latent telepathic ability to catch the gist. *I can't speak in front of Lorenski, and you need to hear what I have to say. . . .*

Jenna turned and abruptly changed course. "On

second thought, there's something we have to take care of first. Thanks for telling us, Lorenski."

The minute he was out the door they converged on Terry. "You do know him—I could tell from your face. Are you planning to meet him here?"

"He doesn't want his movements known," Terry said, not answering the question. "He certainly doesn't want to draw a crowd. There was an unfortunate incident on Centauri a while back—people had gotten the idea he could heal the sick, and he was mobbed. That kind of thing has to stop. He never meant to become an idol, and in any case, you know what will happen if bounty hunters locate him."

"*Can* he heal the sick?"

"No. The reports were exaggerated, as many of the rumors about him are."

"But if there's a real *Estel*, it could carry refugees. Can you tell us how to reach the captain privately?"

"First, some way has to be found for him to escape the crowd at the spaceport. Any ideas?"

"If he's already in the dome, he doesn't need to escape until after we've met him," Walt pointed out. "Except that when the crowd discovers an empty shuttle no one recognizes, people will guess that he's here. If you know how to contact him, you'd better tell him to hide in our place before they hunt him down."

God, he's right. Terry thought. There was no way out—he would have to tell them the truth. "Can I count on you to keep his identify secret?" he asked slowly.

"Of course."

"And you'll hide him until the crowd goes away?"

"Yes. We'll help him any way we can," Jenna declared. "I can hardly believe all this is real, and that we might be lucky enough to have that honor."

"Okay, then," said Terry, drawing a deep breath. "I've never told anyone this except my crew—not even Zach, though I now think Zach has a right to know. My name is Terry Steward, and I am the Captain of *Estel*."

~ *38* ~

WALT AND JENNA stared at Terry in astonishment. "You? You're the Captain of *Estel*, and yet you work as a smuggler?"

"I'm not some sort of superman, you see," Terry said. "I'm merely a star pilot who happens to have some uncommon mind skills, many of which anyone could learn if the proper training were available. And as I told you, Walt, I've done a lot of things that are against the law. But I've made a commitment to spread what I know about the powers of the human mind."

"People sometimes get hurt for believing in such powers," Walt said slowly. "People like the ones being persecuted for it on Earth. And like Becka."

"Yes. There's always opposition to anything new because some are afraid of it and don't want to know that their old way of thinking might be wrong. And there are always evildoers who strike out against anybody different from the herd. But what's true is true—no good can come from denying it, only harm. So standing up to those who try to suppress it helps humankind evolve toward a time when people won't put up with the kind of thing that's going on now. They needn't go on thinking there's nothing ahead to look forward to. Anyway, that's what some very wise people have told me."

"You write like that on the Nets," Jenna observed, "and it's said that you make speeches. And those who hear are convinced, and are happier for it. Now I see why— it's more than what you say, it's what you feel inside."

"You're entitled to know that there's more to it than that," Terry said. "I've got a gift like Becka's for communicating directly with minds, so that they sense what I'm trying to convey."

"Why has nobody ever seen your ship?" Walt asked after a pause. "We weren't even sure it was real."

"And I wish it could have stayed that way, for one thing, because I don't want bounty hunters to know where it is. So it flies under a false name. But I've had to use its real identity this time to keep Becka and Josh safe. Now Port Control knows it's here, and I asked them to keep it confidential, but evidently they didn't."

"That's odd," Walt said. "They must know you're famous, and they should have foreseen what would happen."

Terry nodded. "Fleet banished me from Centauri when the crowd got disorderly there, and the same thing will probably happen here, if not worse. Yet I can't just leave, even if I can get back to *Estel*, because the hyperdrive engine hasn't been serviced yet and it hasn't enough fuel for more than one jump."

"There's a maintenance dock at Moonbase," Jenna said.

"Yes, but there are reasons why I can never go to Earth or the Moon. Besides, hyperdrive service there is more expensive than it is here, more than I can afford. And anyway, I can't take the refugees back where they came from."

"We can hide the refugees for awhile," Jenna said. "And just going to a space dock isn't the same as landing on the Moon or on Earth, is it?"

He had not thought of that. He wouldn't have to land, any more than he'd landed on New Afrika after he'd learned there were mentors there. There would be no mentors in orbit, and if any business had to be done on the Moon, Jon or Gwen could take the shuttle down. But there was still the cost—although, Terry thought suddenly, cost was no longer an insuperable barrier. He would have the charter fee from Zach.

Except that he wouldn't have the charter fee if he didn't take the refugees; he could hardly expect payment in advance. He might be caught by bounty hunters and killed, or the ship might be destroyed, and they would be stuck here with no money to pay some other captain. He explained this to Jenna, but she was unperturbed.

"How many refugees does *Estel* have room for?" she asked.

"Well, the legal maximum is twelve, and there are four of us in the crew, so we can take eight."

"Which is two more than are already here. You could pick up another couple, or even a family, from Earth and take them all to a new colony together. Small children wouldn't need separate beds, so they wouldn't count against the maximum."

They would, but since he would be carrying the passengers illegally anyway, that scarcely mattered. There were only eight bunks in staterooms, but some people could sleep in the lounge. He'd have to replenish the consumables on every trip, but again, the expenses were going to be covered. . . . And if he went to Moonbase, he could send the message to the Maclairn Foundation over an ordinary comm channel without having to pay for ansible access.

"If *Estel* were destroyed or its captain killed, a lot more would be lost than a little of Zach's money," Walt declared. "I'll take a chance and give it to you now, and if for any reason you can't use the space dock here, then go straight on. We'll trust you to come back for the refugees."

"I won't be able to come back under the name *Estel*," Terry realized, "and *Vagabond* may not be safe either—they may have figured out a connection by then, or suspect that Becka and Josh were on *Vagabond*. Can you forge ship IDs, Jenna?"

"I'm not familiar with that database, but Zach probably is."

"Yes, he changed my former false name to *Vagabond*, so he can change it again, if your ansible connection is secure. It better be done now before I leave, in case the name I suggest is already taken."

Jenna went off to the ansible office to communicate with Zach, while Walt took Terry along with Becka and Josh to the Fenways' apartment. There they met the other refugees, Pavek and Eurika Bartel and their daughters aged three and five. Their home had been burned to the ground by Klansmen and a note had been left threatening the lives of the two girls, targeted because Eurika had used remote viewing to help the police find a neighbor's missing child. The police had not appreciated the help; to his horror, Terry concluded from the details he heard that they might have alerted the Klan. He spent the afternoon listening to a first-hand account of its activities, feeling sicker than ever about his inability to do more than transport a very few psi-gifted victims to safety.

The crowd at the spaceport had thinned by afternoon, Jenna told him when she returned between the restaurant's busy lunch and dinner hours; but there were still more people there than seemed reasonable in view of the fact that Terry hadn't shown up. Surely he was not important enough to justify curiosity-seekers sticking around all day—this time, the issue of healing had not even arisen. Furthermore, Fleet officers were not doing much in the way of crowd control; there were only two at the gate, Lorenski reported, and Terry began to worry about the shuttle; if it was identified as his, people might attempt to get in and take souvenirs.

It was evident that there would never be a time when no one was watching, so he waited for Lorenski's shift and got through the gate in the back of the van. Walt drove it directly to the shuttle; Terry scrambled in quickly and sealed the airlock behind him, unable to do a pre-flight walk-around despite having left the shuttle unattended. He'd contacted the crew earlier by comm, but had been unable to say anything that would identify him although Alison, speaking as if she were a disinterested observer, had described the crowd. "What did you do to tip them off?" she asked when he boarded *Estel*. "I thought Fleet was going to keep our presence quiet."

"So did I," Terry said. "They weren't happy about the crowd on Centauri, where they didn't even know I'm really *Estel's* captain. I'd have thought they'd want to avoid attracting attention to me—the League government wants to suppress awareness of psi, after all."

He was more uncomfortable than ever about entrusting the ship to Stelo Haveno's maintenance dock, and decided to take the Fenways' advice and go to Moonbase. After explaining his new commitment to the crew and informing them that from now on *Estel* would fly under the name *Bright Hope*—chosen by Zach from traditional ship names he thought appropriate—he prepared to depart, glad that he hadn't scheduled the work. But he'd been back in the ship no more than an hour before the comm announced the presence of Fleet officers requesting permission to board.

"They've already searched us for the missing kids, haven't they?" Terry asked, puzzled. "I thought they'd do that within a few hours of our arrival."

"They did," Jon told him. "And they were different inspectors, as you said they'd be. They didn't act suspicious."

"Well, I don't know what they could want from us now, but I guess we'll soon see." A request for boarding permission from Fleet was not a request, but an order.

Two officers including a lieutenant commander appeared at the airlock, looking anything but friendly. "Are you Terry Steward, the captain of this vessel?" the younger officer asked without preamble.

"I am," Terry replied, suppressing his annoyance.

"And this is the ship named *Estel*?"

"If you've checked its transponder, you know it is."

The commander stepped forward. "Terry Steward, otherwise known as the Captain of *Estel*, you are under arrest and this vessel is impounded," he stated coldly. "You are to come with us now, and in due course your crew will be taken to suitable quarters pending deportation to Earth."

~ *39* ~

IN THE PATROL ship, Terry was so stunned that he could scarcely hide his feelings. *Estel* impounded? Alison, Jon and Gwen sent away fundless to a world none of them had ever seen before, where he himself could not go even if he managed to break free?

The officers would tell him nothing about the charges against him. He didn't see how they could have discovered the connection between *Estel* and *Vagabond*, but they must have, since the smuggling hadn't been detected and apart from that, he had not done anything illegal here besides transporting and hiding Becka and Josh—and, he supposed, "kidnapping" them. Plus operating a starship under a false name, if they did know the connection. All these things were felonies, and he had been well aware of the consequences if he was caught. He hadn't expected to be caught.

After being informed that he had the right to remain silent, he was taken to Fleet headquarters on the surface of the planet. As on Centauri, he had a strange feeling of déjà vu on mingling with uniformed officers and hearing their manner of address, but this time he was too preoccupied to notice. Draconis, he was thinking in horror. It was not merely a penal colony, but one where most prisoners were assigned to hard labor. . . .

It would not be as bad as the prison on Ciencia, of course. He would not be condemned to lifelong solitary confinement in a cramped cell, wondering when they were going to start testing illicit drugs on him. But he had gotten out of that prison. Could he possibly have such luck a second time?

They left him alone in a holding cell for several hours. Then he was led to an interrogation room to confront an officer who introduced himself as Commander Flanders.

"Don't expect my sympathy, Steward," Flanders

declared. "You have caused too much trouble for us, for too long, to receive leniency, and I for one have not been taken in by your claims. Fraud is fraud, however altruistic it is made to sound."

Fraud? Bewildered, Terry managed to say, "I have the right to know the charges against me."

"If you insist, although you're well aware of them. You are charged with fraudulently claiming to have supernatural powers, with inciting revolution on Ciencia with the intent to extend rebellion to other worlds, and with hacking various public databases to promote your lies. Not to mention lesser charges such as escaping from legally-imposed imprisonment on Ciencia and creating public disorder in Fleet installations, both here and on Centauri."

At a loss for words, Terry addressed the last point first. "I had nothing to do with attracting the crowd at the spaceport today—I wasn't even there. I took pains to avoid being there."

"No doubt, but you engineered it to gain exposure for yourself and your wild claims. We know how you work your scheme. You don't show yourself, which makes people all the more likely to believe the foolish ideas you try to foist on them."

Though there was an element of truth in this, Flanders' distortion of it was startling. About to protest, Terry suddenly grasped what was happening and knew he had no recourse.

He had not engineered the disorder at the spaceport—Fleet had. That was why they'd leaked the information that he was in Stelo Haveno, and why they had made no attempt to control the crowd; probably they had gone on fostering rumors of his presence all day. They had needed a specific, verifiable incident in order to arrest him, but they had been preparing their case for a long time, waiting for the ship named *Estel* to turn up.

Why had he not foreseen this? He had known that conspirators within the League government wanted to suppress awareness of psi, that they had been behind the attempted terrorist attack on Maclairn and were now surreptitiously backing the Ku Klux Klan in an effort to discourage people from believing in the so-called paranormal. He had suspected that they were funding the bounty Quaid had put on his head. How had he imagined that they wouldn't try to stop further action by the Captain of *Estel*?

At least Fleet evidently didn't know about the alleged kidnapping or any of his actual crimes. They could put him away for those far more easily than they could convict him on these other charges.

"You accuse me of inciting revolution on Ciencia," he said, "but Fleet has no jurisdiction over Ciencia's internal affairs. In fact, you have no official knowledge of anything that happens there, as it's a closed world."

"It's closed no longer, since a few days ago the revolutionary party there—the party that bears your ship's name—seized control of the government. And we indeed have jurisdiction, because you have declared that your advocacy of such revolution is interstellar in scope."

"I have never advocated violent revolution, and I don't for a minute think that's what happened—the Estelans must simply have won an election. And I've never suggested that people should oppose their government anywhere else," Terry protested. How fortunate that he hadn't posted all that he'd started to write on Undine. . . .

"No? Let me quote from the transcript of the speech you broadcast from orbit. 'I am going now to give hope to other worlds. You need me no longer, for you are freeing yourselves from the tyranny of your government's false view of humankind.' The implication is very clear."

Oh, God. He hadn't meant it that way, but it was true enough that if he happened to be in another colony with unduly restrictive laws, he would encourage its people to work toward changing them.

There being nothing more he could say on that point,

Terry tried another approach. "As to my supposedly fraudulent claim to have so-called paranormal powers, I do have some, as I will demonstrate anywhere not within sight of the Ku Klux Klan. The reports of my abilities have been exaggerated, but that is not my fault. And in any case, how would I profit from encouraging others to believe they have them?"

"There are no such powers—they are all fantasy, as you very well know. Profit? How does any demagogue profit? By receiving the adulation of the people taken in. In your case you receive it mainly online rather than in person, but the satisfaction you seek is the same."

It was quite possible that Flanders believed this. The majority of the population, after all, assiduously avoided letting themselves think that psi might exist, all the more because any slip might put them within the purview of the Klan. Terry knew better than to try to convince him. "Whether you call them fantasy or not isn't important," he said. "Under the League Constitution I have a right to my own beliefs. That's known as freedom of thought."

"You have a right to believe whatever nonsense you wish," Flanders agreed. "But you don't have a right to push it on the public."

"Oh? Religious evangelists do it all the time. That's in the Constitution, too."

"Are you claiming that your notions about the mind are religious?"

"Certainly not, not unless you use a broad definition of 'religion' as including any idea about the fundamental nature of human beings."

"That's fortunate, because there are specific laws against public proselytizing via interactive media, which were passed when mass conversions got out of hand."

"Those apply only where collection of money is involved," Terry reminded him. "I have never asked people for money or anything else of which they'd be deprived by believing me, so I don't think the claim that I've committed fraud by misrepresenting myself will hold up in court."

"We'll see about that. In any case our claim against your ship will hold up, and without it you won't be able to cause any more trouble."

Terry froze. *What* claim against his ship? He hadn't been tried yet, let alone convicted, so they couldn't impose a fine.

"According to the laws of civil forfeiture, an asset is forfeit if used in the commission of a crime whether or not its owner is convicted of anything," Flanders said. "That's an old principle of law, dating at least to the twentieth century in America if not further back, that you should be familiar with if you're as knowledgeable as you think you are."

Terry did recall having seen something about that, and about the protests against the unfairness of it, when reading history. He hadn't known it was on the League books. But *Estel* hadn't been *used* in the acts with which he was charged, it had only been *mentioned*. At the time of his underground work on Ciencia it hadn't even existed. Except . . . oh, God. The later broadcast had been made from *Estel*, and the transcript said so. Therefore, according to Fleet's reasoning, the ship had been used to incite revolution.

He doubted that the officers at Stelo Haveno could have dug up an obscure law in the hours since he'd arrived here, or even that those at Fleet Headquarters could in the few days since the Estelans had officially opened Ciencia to communication with the League. This whole scheme to discredit him had obviously been initiated by Quaid in league with his like-minded friends on Earth—a backup plan, no doubt, in case the bounty hunters failed to locate him. And Quaid had known very well what would hurt the worst. He'd be happy to see him back in prison, but even happier to know that he'd lost *Estel*. . . .

It was not true that he couldn't achieve anything more without *Estel*. It had accomplished a lot as an imaginary ship, and then as a real one that no one had ever seen. If he were free, he could keep the legend about it alive—unless Fleet destroyed it publicly, and even then it might retain its symbolic value. But he himself would be crushed by the loss. He was not sure he would feel up to any more campaigning.

And in any case, he was not free, and was not likely to be free for a long time.

~ *40* ~

APART FROM THE prospect of losing *Estel*, what concerned Terry most in the days that followed was worry about what was happening to Alison—and to Jon and Gwen too, of course. They had virtually no money; there hadn't been much credit left and he had transferred nearly all of it to his own account for a down payment on servicing the hyperdrive engine. They had no knowledge of Earth or how to get work there. Their new League IDs might not even entitle them to work; since unemployment was high on Earth, non-citizens couldn't often get work permits, and in fact those for the Maclairnan mentors brought to Earth in *Promise* had been forged along with their League citizenship. Would Fleet really dump his crew without means to support themselves? He thought of the endless hordes of homeless street people on Earth, and shuddered.

On top of these problems was the fear that if Ciencia was now open to League contact, their past might catch up with them. Presumably, they had been listed as dead on Ciencia, and he had not gotten new names or histories for them when Zach forged their worldless citizenship. So if and when Ciencia's records were transmitted to League Headquarters, a mismatch might turn up, and then they would be subject to arrest for ID tampering if not for whatever crimes Ciencia might charge them with.

It was even possible that Jon's name might be connected with his alleged captaincy of *Vagabond*, and then, since he was known to have been aboard *Estel*, the whole string of Terry's crimes and the crew's implication in them would come to light.

If he could get in touch with Jenna, Terry thought, she could create new IDs and work permits. But Jenna and Walt would probably never know what had happened to him. They would wait in vain for him to return for the refugees, and when he didn't keep his promise, they could only assume that he had made off with Zach's money. In their eyes, and those of anyone they talked to about *Estel*, the reputation of its legendary captain would be tarnished.

He was housed in a secure compartment of the warrant officers' barracks, Stelo Haveno's Fleet installation being too small to need a separate brig. It was a large step up from the prison on Ciencia, but confinement itself was galling enough to bring him to desperation. He could not believe this was happening to him, not after all he'd gotten through in the past. When he was spared from death after crashing *Venture*, he'd believed it meant something—meant he could help ensure humankind's future. What good could he do locked away here, awaiting a trial that would serve only to condemn him to long-term imprisonment? The Elders had thought he could serve Maclairn's cause when they gave him *Estel*, yet he'd had it for mere weeks before it was taken from him. And he'd been with Alison so short a time, when he'd expected they'd be together for the rest of his life. . . .

On the sixth day of his confinement, Alison was permitted to visit him, having described herself as his common-law wife. Terry was taken from his cell to a guarded room at headquarters to which she was escorted; they were not allowed to talk alone. She and the others were not prisoners. she told him. They had been given decent though spartan accommodations and were free to go anywhere in the dome while awaiting deportation. They would be unable to stay after transport was available, however, as the colony did not accept immigrants. They had applied to go to New Afrika where they knew people and believed they could get jobs, but Fleet didn't have a scheduled flight to New Afrika from here and it did not intend to make a special trip for them.

Terry explained the charges against him, warning Alison silently to show no surprise and above all, to say nothing to Fleet that might suggest she'd expected different ones. He felt her amazement and relief, and sensed that they had all believed his arrest was due to discovery of Becka and Josh, though they'd been careful not to reveal that they knew about the kids. They had maintained to Fleet that he was totally innocent of any wrongdoing, hoping that there were no telepaths among the officers they encountered.

I've got something else to tell you, Alison ventured with silent intensity, and Terry realized that their weeks of telepathic contact during lovemaking, while not in the form of conversation, nevertheless would enable her to convey information she could not give him aloud. He perceived it as if she were communicating words, although she really wasn't, and his heart rose as he grasped the gist of them.

We remembered you'd sold the wine to an older couple who run a restaurant . . . When we found one with managers who looked right, we asked if they'd been in the crowd looking for the Captain of Estel. And I could sense that the woman was hiding something so I told her we were from his ship and that he'd been arrested . . . And she wanted to know what for and I didn't tell her about Becka but I could see she was terribly upset. . . .

Thank God. *Go back!* he told Alison. *Go back and tell her you're afraid of going to Earth because I once said it wouldn't be safe without a new name and a work permit. Tell her I mentioned something called Zach's box, so she'll know the message is from me. She can get you new IDs like she's getting for Becka and Josh, and if she offers to, you can trust her and tell her everything. . . . Nod if you understand!*

Alison nodded vigorously, then came into his arms. A few minutes later the guard said their time was up and took him away.

Much relieved by the thought that Alison and the others would be given a chance to survive on Earth, Terry resigned himself to imprisonment. The days dragged but he was allowed read-only Net access, so for a few minutes at a time, at least, he was able to occupy his mind with something other than the loss of *Estel*. It always came back if he raised his eyes from the screen, though, and at night it became a torment. What did Fleet do with forfeited ships? Would they sell it, hopefully as a charter vessel but more likely to some disreputable smuggler who might turn pirate? What would the Elders think if they knew?

As he was not considered violent, the guard arrangement was informal; he'd been allowed to keep his own clothes and warrant officers who lived in the barracks sometimes brought his meals. Three days after he'd seen Alison, his empty dinner dishes were picked up by Lorenski.

A rush of hope surged through Terry. Here was a way to communicate with Walt and Jenna—a way to know for sure that his crew was taken care of. "Have you seen our mutual friend lately?" he asked.

"I have," said Lorenski. "He said to tell you your wife and friends are okay." He continued in a low voice, "No need to be so careful, this place isn't bugged and there's no camera. They're not set up to deal with spies or gangsters here." Then, casually, he took off his uniform jacket and handed it to Terry.

As Terry stared, he went on to say, "We've got to exchange pants. This is where I live and it's normal enough for me to wear civvies in my own barracks. On the other hand, nobody will notice if an officer in uniform walks out. Your wife says you once were a Fleet officer, so I assume you know how to act like one."

Flabbergasted, Terry took off his pants and put on the smartly-styled black ones he had worn throughout his youth. They were a bit loose, as Lorenski had gained weight in his later years, but the fit wasn't bad enough to be noticeable; and though the jacket wouldn't have passed muster on a formal occasion, it was unlikely that anyone would take that close a look at him.

No one would check his cell before breakfast time, he knew. If he left just before lights out in the barracks, he could pass as an officer heading for a late work shift, as in fact, Lorenski told him, he himself did every night. "You'll have to wait somewhere till I've had time to re-lieve the guy on gate duty before me," the warrant officer said. "Once you're sure I'm there alone, just come on through. Walt's van will be waiting nearby."

It was chancy—but Lorenski was taking an even more terrible chance. He was close to retirement. If caught aiding an escape he would spend his last years in some prison light-years away from Stelo Haveno and the job he'd been unwilling to retire from. To be sure, he took chances frequently by letting smugglers and refugees pass the gate, but none so great as this. "Why?" Terry asked in awe. "Why are you doing this for me?"

"Because you're the Captain of *Estel*," Lorenski said, "and I hope to live long enough to see you change how people think about the future."

~ *41* ~

THE STANCE AND stride of a Fleet officer came easily to Terry even after more than twelve years. Just act like you're on routine duty, he told himself. Don't worry about what's going to happen if somebody speaks to you. They can tell if you're worried, even if they're not consciously telepathic.

In the barracks all compartment doors were closed and the corridor lights had already been turned down. His cell was at the end farthest from the exit and it seemed like a long walk, but no one appeared. Out in the dome, it took him a few minutes to orient himself; he hadn't seen much of the Fleet area when taken through it, as there had been more crucial things than sightseeing on his mind. Off to his left was the residential district, on the other side of the business and entertainment establishments. He would have to cross the concourse to get to the thoroughfare that led outside.

It was unlikely that he would be noticed in the dome's civilian sections. What he feared was meeting other Fleet officers who might ask his name; Terry wasn't sure whether there were so few at Stelo Haveno that they would all expect to recognize each other. If so, he would be unable to bluff, and whether they suspected him to be a prisoner or not wouldn't matter; merely by impersonating an officer he was adding yet another item to his long list of crimes. But since even the few on his record were enough to convict him, he supposed one more would make no difference.

His first crisis came as a lieutenant approached; in his worry about being identified as a stranger, he nearly forgot that he wore the insignia of a warrant officer and was therefore required to salute. He was, after all, used to having lieutenants salute him first. But he reacted in time and was not challenged.

Getting out of the dome was not especially risky, Terry realized. The danger would come tomorrow, after his escape was discovered and a search began. Presumably, Walt and Jenna intended to hide him, but for how long? Did Fleet have the authority to search private residences? They hadn't searched the dome for Becky and Josh, but then, they hadn't known for certain that they were here;

it was merely one possibility out of many. His own presence was another matter. How could he ever get onto a shuttle—and even if he could, where would he go? He couldn't leave *Estel* in Fleet's hands. . . .

By the time he reached the dome's foot-traffic airlock, it was well past midnight. Being a large lock, its operation was totally automated; he had to wait nervously until the next cycle. Entering, he put on the mask from the beltpack Lorenski had given him and watched the hatch slide shut behind him. There were no other occupants at this hour, which gave him a break from vigilance that served merely to provide time for worry. What if some other officer was with Lorenski? Terry thought in dismay—or what if something had happened and Walt's van wasn't in sight after he passed through the gate?

When the airlock opened he calmed his heart and dried his sweating hands, using the mind skills that rarely needed conscious attention. As he approached the lighted gatehouse he could see that only one officer was there; he must assume it was Lorenski since he dared not pause for a close look. When he was not stopped, he knew that he was free.

The van was a short distance away, barely visible at the dark edge of the cluster of lighted shuttle pads. He walked purposefully toward it, knowing he must take as little time as possible getting inside. Silently Walt, in the driver's seat, raised his hand in greeting and the cargo doors opened; Terry was barely inside before they closed behind him. The van started to move and though he couldn't see out, he knew that they were retracing the route by which he had just come. After a nerve-wracking pause, during which he assumed Lorenski was checking and recording Walt's ID, the sound of the vehicle airlock's pump told him they had reentered the dome.

"I wish I could say we knew what to do next," Jenna said, when Terry was safely inside the Fenways' apartment and had changed into pants they provided. "I can give you a fake ID, of course, and if we had a way to get our refugees onto a ship, you could go along with them. But so far we haven't found any captain but you who's willing to take them, and Lorenski says we may be searched."

"You shouldn't have risked yourselves for me," Terry said contritely. "There's not much hope I can get offworld, and in any case I wouldn't leave here without *Estel*. So sooner or later I'll be recaptured." He had known this; he cursed himself now for having been unable to resist the temptation to take action that couldn't end well for any of them. He hadn't stopped to analyze it; he had simply fled when given the chance. But what if Becky and Josh were captured because of him? What, then, would have been accomplished by taking them away from Eden at the cost not merely of his freedom, but of his ship?

"There's always hope," Walt declared. "*Estel* stands for hope. It would be a betrayal of all you stand for to say it's not true."

Yes, Terry thought. Perhaps he should do what he'd done on Ciencia—address the public, give one last speech proclaiming that people should look toward a better future. He could probably rig a broadcast setup, tell people to go on believing no matter what they heard about him. The problem was that if he did that, it could be traced to the Fenways' location.

He hated the thought of changing the ID the Elders had given him. If he ever did get *Estel* back, he couldn't prove his ownership, and besides, he was sick of constantly becoming someone else. He had resisted doing so when it meant inconvenience and even danger; but now there was no alternative. This time he couldn't keep even his first name—reluctantly, he allowed Jenna to link his ID number to the record of Tom Ryan, the name Zach had given to the fictitious owner of *Vagabond*. At least the bounty hunters wouldn't be looking for him under that name, any more than Fleet would if he got away from this world where he'd be recognized. And if he didn't, Terry thought grimly, they would identify him through a biometric search and he would become Terry Steward again in prison.

"We have to go to the restaurant this morning, but Alison will be along soon," Jenna said. "She'd have spent the night here if I hadn't convinced her that overnight absence from her assigned quarters might raise suspicion."

"I don't think she should come," Terry said resolutely, realizing that his longing to see her was another potential trap. "I don't want to take the chance that they might find her here and assume she's implicated in my escape."

"They will assume that no matter what she does," Walt said gravely. "She and your two friends will be the first people they question. That's why we didn't tell them any details."

Oh, God. He would have realized that, too, if he'd stopped to consider the consequences of what he was doing. From the time he'd landed on Eden, he'd gotten them deeper and deeper into trouble from which there was no way out.

He needed rest, not knowing what the day would bring. Jenna finally got him to lie down on the couch—all the beds being occupied by refugees—where, using his mind training, he let himself slide into a despairing sleep. When he woke, Alison was beside him. He sat up at her touch and they clung to each other, aware that it might be for the last time.

Jon came after a few hours. Fleet had already questioned him and had finally concluded that he knew nothing. Gwen was still in their hands, but since she knew nothing either, he expected that she would soon be released. Officers were looking for Alison; she had better stay hidden, Jon said, because conceivably they might use her as a hostage for the escaped prisoner's voluntary return. At this thought, the last traces of Terry's youthful loyalty to Fleet were finally and irrevocably extinguished.

Estel, as far as anyone knew, was still in the orbit where they had left it.

Estel . . . all of a sudden, while again mourning its loss, he was struck by a sense of urgency. "I've got the strangest feeling," he said in bewilderment. "I think . . . someone is searching for me."

"That's not strange," said Jon. "Half the Fleet officers on this planet are searching for you."

"No, that's not what I mean. It's someone friendly, someone who wants to help." It was like precognition—or if not that, some other form of psi. Maybe remote viewing, maybe he was supposed to *see* whoever it was—or perhaps simply telepathy. He had not sensed such a presence anywhere but in New Afrika.

"Do you have any idea of how to find this person?" Alison asked.

"I think . . . maybe there's some clue on the Net. In the comments written about *Estel*." He picked up his tablet, which Alison had managed to conceal among her own belongings during his arrest, and searched for keywords.

The message wasn't hard to find. Fleet had publicized his arrest with the hope of disillusioning people who believed he was invulnerable, but this strategy had backfired; indignation had gone viral. As on Ciencia, people were rising in his defense and were on the verge of gathering for a demonstration. In the midst of the hundreds of forum comments in his support, Terry spotted one that stood out. "If the friend of Aragorn wishes to regain what he has lost," the writer said, "he should pray in the temple of Vesta, goddess of fire, for she aids all stewards of the sacred flame."

"Oh, my God," Terry burst out.

"What? What do you see?" Alison asked, looking over his shoulder.

"Aragorn is another name for Estel, though the Fleet officers here aren't likely to know that," he said excitedly. "I could hardly fail to notice the comment."

"But it doesn't make sense—the two names in it aren't related. Aragorn is a character in a classic novel, and Vesta was an ancient Roman goddess, wasn't she? "

Walt and Jenna were still at the restaurant and all the refugees were in their bedrooms, where they'd been warned to stay in case someone came; Terry could speak freely. "The reference to Vesta is just an excuse for mentioning stewards of the flame," he said. "Readers will dismiss this as a crackpot posting because it's a hodgepodge and because no one worships Vesta today. But it couldn't be coincidence. It has to have been written by someone who knows about Maclairn."

"Oh . . . the flame pin you wear in secret—you still have it?"

"Yes, thank God. I was what's called a Steward of the Flame there, which the pin symbolizes. Whoever wrote this knows enough about Maclairn to have guessed that I may know the phrase, which only the few chosen to visit that world do—I suppose because what I say about mind faculties matches how Maclairnans live." He hadn't thought of that possibility before. It didn't mean his secret had gotten out. Though a mentor would know that he had not been among the observers, another observer wouldn't.

"Is it simply a way of letting you know they're on your side, then? There isn't any temple of Vesta, after all."

"Perhaps there is," Terry said thoughtfully. "There's a Chapel of All Faiths in every colony, and that could be interpreted as meaning ancient faiths as well as modern ones. I think I'm supposed to go there and meet someone."

"That could be dangerous," Jon pointed out. "Your enemies in the government also know about Maclairn."

"Not that there are still Stewards of the Flame; that's not spoken of except within the colony." He had not previously mentioned it even to Alison; he'd simply told her what ideas the flame pin stood for. "In any case," he went on, "I was led to this either by telepathy, which our enemies don't have, or by precognition. So it can't be a trap. The person who wrote it may know some way I can escape."

And get my ship back, he thought with elation. Regaining what he'd lost couldn't have been mentioned for no reason. Whatever the risk of venturing out into the dome, he would have to visit the chapel just as soon as he could get there.

~ *42* ~

WALKING THROUGH THE dome a second time, without the anonymity of a uniform to protect him, was more nerve-wracking than it had been before. It was daytime, with more people who might notice him, Terry thought apprehensively. And Fleet was searching for him now. Officers must have been shown his picture. At any moment he might be recognized.

The Chapel of All Faiths was near the center of the concourse. Like all structures in domed colonies, it was attached to others and not imposing from the outside, but its interior walls were covered with illuminated art so as to create the illusion of stained glass windows. In the dim light of the sanctuary the effect was inspiring, but he was not in a mood to feel inspired.

There were only a few people in the pews, engaged in private meditation. Having no idea when whoever he was supposed to meet would arrive, Terry had no choice but to wait, realizing that the chapel had probably been chosen as the one place in the dome where sitting quietly by himself wouldn't attract attention. He closed his eyes and tried to think hopeful thoughts, telling himself that miracles do sometimes happen—had not fate intervened on his behalf several times before? After awhile he became aware that this was a form of prayer.

But then, when he looked up, he saw to his horror that a Fleet commander was about to sit down beside him.

Oh, God—it had been a trap after all. Fleet officers didn't meditate in chapels in the middle of the day; he must have been followed here. There was no possibility of getting away—if he started to leave he would simply be seized. His brief period of freedom was at an end.

At the same moment, however, the sender of the message must also have arrived, for Terry was suddenly overwhelmed with unmistakably telepathic input, overriding his fear. *Don't panic*, he was being told. *You have more friends than you know.*

Thanks for your offer of help, he responded, *but it's too late. I'm about to be arrested.*

No, you're not. Terry's eyes searched the room, wondering who could see him without seeing the officer—and realized with shock that the officer himself was in rapport with him. The commander, a slender man with close-cut sandy hair, turned to him with an enigmatic smile. *I think* Estel *is too important to be left in the hands of anyone but its rightful captain.*

At first incredulous, Terry realized that it wasn't so strange after all. There were Fleet officers who knew about Maclairn; a cruiser had been stationed there for nearly fifteen years and there must have been many crew rotations. Those assigned there were sworn to lifelong secrecy, as he himself had been when he was chosen; but they could discuss it with people who already knew of the colony's existence, and the message would have been meaningless to anyone who didn't. All such officers were given mind training, which led to psi capability in those with a natural predisposition. This man had it in full measure.

Taking a close look at him, the first thing Terry noticed was how young he seemed. Despite his evident poise, he appeared to be no more than twenty. That wasn't surprising; he himself had been a skilled shuttle pilot at that age and a starship pilot before he was twenty-two. But commander rank normally wasn't attained by anyone under thirty. And it was odd that a young officer who favored Maclairn would have returned so soon; to keep the number of people in on the secret to a minimum, transfers were voluntary.

"It's safe to talk here," the commander said in a low voice, "but there isn't much time. I'm a pilot and I can get you back to your ship—it's fueled and ready to fly. But there will be risk. If you have any other way of escaping from Stelo Haveno, you'd be wise to use it."

"I can't give up *Estel*," said Terry. "I won't leave here without it unless I'm taken by force."

"So I thought. But you'll have to trust me not only with your own life but with those of your wife and crew, assuming you want them to come with you."

Terry nodded. He was torn; he wanted them desperately but was hesitant to put them in danger. They could go to Earth safely, and later meet him at the Moon's orbiting transit station. . . . Well, he would leave it up to them to decide, but he knew perfectly well how they would choose.

"I can borrow a groundcar if they're coming," the officer went on. "They have the freedom of the colony so they won't be stopped at the gate, but you yourself will have to hide in the luggage compartment and hope it won't be searched."

This was a harder choice, Terry thought in dismay— did he trust this man far enough to betray Lorenski? Telepathically, he perceived that the commander was totally reliable, but had he the right to make that judgment, considering what Lorenski had done for him and for the refugees?

The refugees! He was committed to taking them offworld and there would be no possibility of coming back to pick them up. If stuck here, Becka would be found and sent back to her father, and the events leading to his arrest would have achieved nothing. Yet there wouldn't be room for them in a groundcar, nor could they be hidden in it.

The officer looked at him quizzically, obviously sensing some new problem, and said, "It might help to know my name—Holden, Commander Liam Holden."

It was offered as proof of mutual trust, and Terry decided to accept it as such. "There are other people I've got to bring," he said, "refugees I'm responsible for. They can get out the same way they got in, in the back of a van. If we go after midnight it won't be inspected."

"How many refugees? The shuttle I'm appropriating can carry only eight people."

Oh, God. Counting the pilot there would be eleven, ten even if the smallest child sat illegally on her mother's lap. He would have to leave the Bartels behind. That would mean breaking his word to Walt and Jenna, abandoning the new role he'd envisioned for the Captain of *Estel*— and they had suffered so much at the hands of the Klan that the thought of letting them down was devastating.

He didn't have a choice; no other escape route was open. "Then, with the crew, I can bring only two extra," he said. "Tell me where to come."

"If you have a van with a trustworthy driver, meet me at the closest shuttle pad that's occupied, soon after midnight."

Terry nodded and held out his hand. "I don't know how to express how grateful I am." There was risk for Holden, too—tremendous risk, even though he ranked high enough to lift off in a Fleet shuttle without being questioned as to his purpose.

"Just keep on with what you've been doing with *Estel*. You're needed, and will be needed even more in times to come."

Silently Holden departed, warning that they must not be seen leaving the chapel together. A few minutes later

Terry made his way back to the Fenways' in a daze. Walt and Jenna were there, worried about his having gone on some mysterious errand that Alison wasn't free to explain to them. "I can't tell you how I made the contact," he said, "but we're leaving tonight in a shuttle—assuming, that is, that you're willing to take us through the gate, Walt."

"Of course," Walt said, and Jenna asked quickly, "Are you taking the refugees, too?"

Sadly Terry told her, "We'll only have room for Becka and Josh because the shuttle will hold just eight people."

She frowned. "I suppose you've got no choice, but I don't know what we're going to do with the Bartels, Terry. They've been cooped up in that little room so long with the kids sleeping on the floor, not daring to come out except a few minutes late in the evening—and there isn't any hope on the horizon."

"What will happen to them if they're caught?" Gwen asked.

"They'll be convicted of traveling without a transit permit and deported back to Earth. Since they were burned out and have no money, they'll end up on the street—and the Klan may hunt them down. Of course that would have happened anyway if Zach hadn't gotten them out, but after they've thought they were safe—"

"Would the government really leave them at the mercy of the Klan?"

"If you think not, you don't know much about governments," Jon said grimly.

"The League government as a whole isn't corrupt," Terry said, "at least not under the current administration. It's closing its eyes to the Klan because a certain group of bureaucrats has taken power by default; nobody's responsible for oversight, and those who do see what's going on don't dare stick their necks out. Unfortunately that element seems to have gained influence over Fleet, too; otherwise they wouldn't be trying to silence me." It couldn't have happened when Admiral Frazer was in charge, he thought. How long before the new brass recalled *Shepard,* leaving Maclairn unprotected?

"We wouldn't be able to save more than a few people even if we were free to do it openly," Alison said miserably, "no matter how many colonies were happy to accept them."

"But we can save the Bartels," Gwen declared. "Jon, you and I have new IDs and legal transportation to Earth. Terry can pick us up at Moonbase later on."

"I could," said Terry dubiously. "but what if I don't make it? What if I'm caught again and *Estel* is seized?"

"Then the same thing would happen if we were with you," Jon pointed out, "and we'd be arrested too."

True enough, Terry concluded. "All right," he said reluctantly. "There's a problem, though—Gwen, you won't be around to switch the transponders after we leave here, and we can't arrive anywhere else as *Estel.* You'd better tell me how to do it."

During the evening she spent some time explaining the process in detail; considering his expertise in AI, the only new thing he needed to learn was how to make the physical hookup. Terry also transferred enough credits to her and to Jon for them to live on while waiting for him to arrive. They agreed to meet at the transit station in Moon orbit where all passengers bound for Earth were processed, making contact through the new names they would by that time be using.

At midnight they said their farewells, all four of them hugging each other with full hearts. "Jon, I don't like being without a copilot, and there's no one I'd ever want but you," Terry said. "So stay where I can reach you, okay?"

Then while Jenna stood watch to make sure the coast was clear, they got Becka, Josh and the Bartel family into the van along with Terry and Alison. "Godspeed, Terry," Jenna said as Walt closed the cargo door. "In case you need to contact Zach, his friends use the arcade at the transit station as a message drop, so check from time to time. The next time I hear from him I'll let him know he can get in touch with you there."

Zach would try, certainly, when word got around that the Captain of *Estel* had appeared at Stelo Haveno. And, Terry thought, if he could stay free long enough he might indeed continue smuggling refugees. It would be a fitting occupation for the hero people imagined, and—now on his fourth identity—he could never show them his true self again.

~ *43* ~

COMMANDER HOLDEN WAS waiting at the shuttle pad he'd designated, having completed his preflight check. As Terry settled into the copilot's seat, he watched the officer's expressive face. There was something compelling about this man, some inner mystery that transcended the fact that he was risking his career and perhaps his freedom to help people in trouble. *Estel is important*, he'd said. It was almost as if he glimpsed an even greater destiny for it than Terry himself had seen.

"Want me to get liftoff clearance from Port Control?" Terry asked. It was a copilot's normal duty.

"No," said Holden. "Actually we wouldn't be given clearance; my rank got me past the lieutenants on duty, but Control would ask questions. We've got to be past surveillance range before they have time to frame them." He started the liftoff sequence without further preamble.

Well, he'd done the same thing the day he left Maclairn, Terry thought, and for a few moments he was back in *Skywalker*, ignoring the comm's furious hails from *Shepard*. But he had been headed outward, while *Estel* was still in low orbit. "How are we going to rendezvous without surveillance?" he ventured.

"We're going to wait till the next shift of controllers

comes on," Holden told him. "We'll head for high orbit and we may be chased because I don't really have any right to be in this shuttle—they'll suspect it's in the hands of pirates. While they're busy focusing on that, we'll turn off its transponder and sneak back to *Estel*. If the new controllers are watching, they'll have no reason not to assume we're a different ship assigned to check on it."

"Sounds like fun," Terry said, trying to sound as if he meant it.

"It's a bit iffy," Holden went on, "because we had to leave later than I planned and missed the midnight shift change, which means staying out longer than I expected. And we're carrying more passengers than I figured on, so we may run a bit short of power. Hopefully, the worst that can happen is that they'll catch you, which would have happened anyway sooner or later."

It wouldn't have happened to you, Holden, Terry thought as the lighted pad fell away below them. The man proved to be a superb pilot; he handled the shuttle effortlessly as if it demanded little attention, despite having used auxiliary lift power. He was wasted on a mere maintenance base like Stelo Haveno, and for him to have ended up here was no doubt another instance of Fleet's bureaucratic inefficiencies. Perhaps he sought adventures like this out of boredom.

The comm blared, "Unidentified shuttle, report please. State your captain's name and mission. Over."

Holden ignored it. After several repetitions, with low orbit past establishing, he replied calmly, "Port Control, this shuttle is now past your jurisdiction and its captain's name is of no concern to you. Out."

Unsurprisingly, Control warned, "Unidentified shuttle, patrollers are being scrambled to make visual contact. You are not authorized to leave orbit, repeat, you are not authorized to leave. Either return and land or stand by for boarding. Acknowledge, please. Over."

"Negative, Control. We do not acknowledge your ju-

risdiction and we will not permit boarding. Out." Holden
spoke with utter conviction, which was so strong telepathically that Terry could not doubt that he believed
what he was saying. Then he turned off the comm pickup
to allow Terry to speak.

"You have to land eventually, after you drop us off,"
Terry said in dismay. "They'll take you into custody."

"No, they won't," Holden said. "Don't worry about me.
I know a few tricks Control's not aware of." And Terry
realized, again through telepathy, that he would not be
made aware of them either. Bribery? Blackmail? This
clean-cut young officer didn't seem like the type to resort
to such things, but on the other hand, it would be in a
good cause. . . .

They kept going, heading for deep space in a shuttle
powered only to reach orbit, and Terry did not ask questions. Alison and the refugees, behind him, assumed all
was normal; they didn't know how long reaching *Estel*
*w*ould normally take.

Finally, with only seconds remaining in the controllers' shift, Holden switched off the transponder and put
on a surge of power. *Estel* appeared almost immediately,
and Terry realized that they *had* been in orbit—an ellipti-
cal orbit calculated to take them back to it at such an
unusual angle that it would not have been tracked when
the controllers were focused on the ship itself. Experienced though he was, he had not thought a shuttle's AI
was capable of such a calculation. He wondered how Holden
had known.

"When we dock, get your people aboard fast and don't
waste any time checking status," the officer told him.
"Your hyperdrive engine has been serviced, so don't hesitate to use it at minimum distance from the sun—your
main engine's faster than a shuttle's, of course, but they
may follow you in another starship."

"I'm never going to forget what you've done," Terry
said. "If I accomplish anything from now on, the credit

belongs to you, even though I can't say so publicly."

"The credit belongs to the Captain of *Estel*," Holden said. "I'll be watching for rumors about his success." And silently, unmistakably, *I think you and I may meet again someday.* . . .

The docking light came on and Terry turned to transferring the passengers. When the airlock cycled shut behind them, he realized with shock that the shuttle had detached and that Holden was already gone.

He made a dash for the bridge and got *Estel* moving at top speed, heading for the nearest jump point. It didn't much matter where it was, as long as the AI knew where, which it couldn't determine accurately until out of the sun's gravity well. Normally he would allow a couple of hours leeway to be safe, but the risk of being overtaken was greater than the risk of miscalculation; he would let the AI determine when it was ready to lock in the ship's position. Meanwhile, he set to work programming the jump itself.

He had decided to take the refugees to New Afrika; they would be welcomed into its community of expatriates, and Alison knew people to whom she could introduce them without revealing to the Bramfield Club that she was back onworld. He himself couldn't land, of course, except to drop them off at the spaceport and pick Alison up later; he would have to let her handle it alone. But Alison was very capable, and he knew he had no need to worry about her on a safe world.

The worry would come later. Earth was anything but safe, and he had not liked sending Jon and Gwen there. Any number of things could prevent making connections with them. . . .

Not the least of which, Terry admitted, was the possibility that he'd be caught before he could jump. He'd quickly passed out of shuttle range, but there were a number of starships in port, perhaps not Fleet ships, but they could legally commandeer a private one when in pursuit of a criminal. The AI had presented no alarms, but that didn't mean he was out of danger.

His readouts showed the hyperdrive had been checked and fully supplied with antimatter fuel, as Holden had said. It seemed strange, now that he thought of it, that Fleet had fueled a ship they expected to sell. As it was, it had been done at no cost to him, putting him well ahead financially provided they hadn't frozen his credit account—which it was extremely odd that they had not done at the time of his arrest. He'd been able to transfer credits to Jon without difficulty, yet Jenna hadn't had to unfreeze it and there hadn't been time for Zach to hear rumors that he'd been arrested. Terry wondered if perhaps Holden's mysterious ability to put one over on Fleet extended beyond his actions as a pilot.

Estel hadn't been pursued, he realized suddenly. Any ship capable of overtaking it would have caught up by now; Fleet probably didn't even know it was gone. They were busy pursuing Holden—they had said they would send patrollers, and undoubtedly he could lead them a merry chase. Terry vowed that he'd live up to what his extraordinary ally evidently expected of him. He hoped they would meet again, if only to be assured that the man hadn't gotten into trouble.

In due course the AI signaled that *Estel* was far enough out to jump, and Terry authorized it to execute. They were free! For the first time in weeks, he slept in peace with Alison close beside him. The days of normal-space approach to New Afrika were spent explaining to the refugees what they could expect there and, of course, switching the transponder to the one registered as *Bright Hope*. He would be hunted from now on; never again could the ship fly under its true name.

But when the Bartels asked what they should say if questioned about their escape, Terry said, "Tell everyone you were aided by someone acting in the name of the Captain of *Estel*."

Part Five: Earth

TERRY APPROACHED THE Moon with mixed feelings. He had not been here since the day he'd set forth on his last trip in *Promise*, carrying the experimental ship *Skywalker* that had been destined to transform his life. He had, during the week he'd been checked out on *Skywalker*, renewed his acquaintance with Fleet Headquarters and the Academy where he'd spent his first years as a spacer. The old excitement had come back that week, seeing the port with its vast array of ships, ships that had once been the symbol of everything he had aspired to. But he had still been a Fleet officer then, in command of a ship crewed by Fleet.

Now he was a fugitive.

And now there was no friendly Admiral Frazer with whom to discuss the defense of Maclairn. Now Fleet Headquarters was a place to avoid, and any nostalgia he might have felt for it had been destroyed by the discovery of what kind of leadership was taking over. Yet conflicting emotions lingered as he put *Bright Hope* into orbit. He had come to Moonbase with Kathryn, visited League Headquarters with Kathryn. That was part of a life he'd put behind him, and the memory was bittersweet. He did not want to revive it.

So he was glad that he couldn't go to the Moon's surface any more than he could go to Earth itself. There might well be mentors there; Fleet might have extended its mind training program beyond Titan during Admiral Frazer's tenure—though this would have been kept secret from all but a select few—and there might be a Bramfield Club for civilian residents. Even if the Klan was active on the Moon, mentors could be living there secretly, and he couldn't take the risk of encountering them. He'd explained this as best he could to Jon and Gwen, just as he'd explained his inability to go to the surface of New Afrika. The plan was for him to contact them by comm and then pick them up at the orbiting transit station, to which they would return on a commercial flight.

Since *Bright Hope* wasn't a licensed transport vessel, Port Control assigned it an orbit much higher than was convenient; free traders had low priority. Still, Terry decided, since he didn't plan to go to the surface anyway and didn't want it noticed that he was continuing to orbit without any stated reason for his presence, this was probably a good thing. He sent text messages to Jon and Gwen under their new names for retrieval from Earth's public system, which they had arranged to check every day. Then while waiting for a response, he considered what to do about his message to the Maclairn Foundation.

Its comm number was easy enough to find through a search of Earth's Net. But if he sent the message from an orbiting ship its origin could be traced, and they might very well want to trace it. Furthermore, the conspirators within the government might be conducting general surveillance that would detect keywords—if not any specific to Maclairn, then at least those revealing that the writer had psi powers. The excuse he'd included for not identifying himself—that he feared being targeted by the Klan—was all too valid. Being wanted by bounty hunters and by Fleet was bad enough without adding a third group of pursuers to evade. Yet somehow, he had to get the warning through.

He expected contact from Jon within hours after messaging him, but none came. By the time a full Earth-standard day had passed, he began to worry. Jon and Gwen would surely have been able to orient themselves enough by this time to check for messages, and he'd given them ample funds. They'd never been to a world where criminals and desperate panhandlers roamed the streets as they did on Earth, still, he'd told them how to find safe lodging. What if all the hotels had been full—or worse, what if Jenna's ID changes, which had been scheduled to go live after they boarded the Fleet transport at Stelo Haveno, hadn't taken effect?

By the end of the third day he was frantic. Could they have been attacked by muggers? He'd heard of ID chips being cut out of people's arms by thieves, sometimes for temporary identification and sometimes to access the victims' credits. Obviously, the victims were first rendered incapable of fighting back.

"Maybe the messages didn't go through—or the reply didn't," Alison said.

By this time Terry had sent two messages each to two people, both of whom would have replied; it was impossible that nothing had gone through unless it was the ID forgery. The ship's comm system was working okay; he had clear Net access.

What he saw on the Net was also discouraging. Conditions had worsened on Earth in the years since he'd last been there. The crowding was worse, the poverty was worse, the crime was worse. He looked out the viewpoint at a blue and white jewel of a world, but the close-up satellite views showed mile after mile of drab, run-down buildings and factory farms, with little if any wild land separating them except in inaccessible mountainous regions. There were, to be sure, enclaves for the wealthy like the one where Kathryn's grandparents had lived, but they weren't noticeable except in commercials designed to inspire avarice. The vast majority of the population had stopped caring about anything beyond the dreary daily existence that had become the norm.

The enterprising people had gone to the colonies, the hope of humankind. But that hope must be kept alive, Terry knew, or sooner or later they'd be just like Earth—would succumb to the stifling bureaucracy the League imposed on all citizens who had no motive to resist conformity. There had to be something beyond the here and now, something to look forward to. He wasn't sure what it was, but advanced mind-powers were a clue to it. The only means of transcending stagnation lay in the human mind.

And so those powers couldn't be suppressed. The enemies of their development couldn't be allowed to intimidate people. How was the Ku Klux Klan getting away with it? he wondered. Surely there must be some uncorrupted police, some who would try to prevent outright attacks. . . .

The more he studied the reports on the Net, the clearer it became why they didn't. Violence by criminal gangs was so routine that a few more incidents were scarcely noticed. It wasn't that people tolerated prejudice, much less physical harassment of the innocent; it was simply that there wasn't enough drama in it to draw attention.

The Klan didn't attack in force; its members didn't gather in groups even as large as the average gang. They came a few at a time and were gone before understaffed police departments knew what was happening. The robes and masks they wore disguised them so that even when people knew who they were, nothing could be proven; all that was left behind was the frightening trail of burned crosses, burned houses, and sometimes dead bodies. Not a lot. Just enough so that when someone received a threatening message, it couldn't be attributed to a mere maniac.

The role of the Captain of *Estel* was to counter the

threats with hope, he saw. To take a few people to safety, so that even those he couldn't take would know that escape might be possible. And to show the public that *somebody* cared even when the bad guys seemed invulnerable.

But how was he going to locate victims to help? He couldn't even try, of course, before finding Jon and Gwen— he could neither keep refugees aboard nor leave his crew behind. Even apart from his concern for Jon, he couldn't manage long without a copilot. He was helpless to proceed; he had no way to contact Zach, and he still saw no safe means of warning the Maclairn Foundation.

That night Terry lay awake while Alison slept beside him, unwilling to drop off through use of his volitional mind skills in case some urgent message from Jon or Gwen arrived. Finally, too restless to remain in bed, he went to the bridge and sat looking out at the sky-filling Moon, despite himself recalling times he'd orbited here in *Promise*. How many times? He'd come every sixty days or so for nearly two years. . . . And suddenly he was struck by a fact he'd overlooked—*Promise* must still be coming! There was no reason to think it hadn't kept right on bringing mentors to Earth, and Laesara had told him that Kathryn was still Maclairn's ambassador to headquarters.

So Kathryn would still be aboard.

Kathryn . . . she might be here now, only a few miles from him in orbit, or at least no more distant than the Moon. He had never expected to be near her again. He had made himself stop thinking about her because he knew that although he no longer grieved over losing her, his love for her would never completely fade. This in no way lessened his love for Alison. On Maclairn it was acknowledged that telepathic bonds were not exclusive and that it was therefore possible to love more than one person at a time. But he wanted to live in the present, not the past, and the thought of confronting his past left him deeply shaken.

Could he and Kathryn touch, telepathically, over this

distance? If she was in orbit close to his, above the same part of the moon's surface, they probably could. He would not do it, of course; it would be devastating to her. She too must have tried to push aside the memories, and the last thing she needed was to believe she was communing with a ghost. Still, he couldn't resist the temptation just to look. . . . Terry reached out, for the first time in years consciously employing the long-distance remote viewing skill in which he'd been trained . . . and the familiar shape of the ship he'd once commanded loomed before him with a clarity that was more than memory.

Promise was there, in an orbit not far from his. Kathryn wasn't, at least he sensed no trace of her mind; probably she was on the surface, at League Headquarters. The captain had no doubt gone down with her and there would be only one or two crew members on board.

Terry began to sweat, torn by the emotions he'd been repressing—and by a new idea that suddenly came to him. *Promise* was a link to the Maclairn Foundation, in fact a direct link to Maclairn itself. If he could get his prepared text message to *Promise* there would be no need to send it through a public comm system. Ship-to-ship comm over dedicated channels was not subject to surveillance. And he remembered what channel *Promise* had used for communication with Earth.

Dared he assume that it still used the same one, or that if it didn't, the channel had not been reassigned? There would have been no reason to change it; dedicated channels were hard to come by. They would wonder how a stranger could possibly have learned its code. Well, let them wonder. The text would be transmitted instantaneously, and before their AI could alert them to it, his would have switched to a different channel. Perhaps he could time it so that he'd be on the other side of the Moon.

He would never know, of course, whether the message had been received. But he wouldn't know if he sent it some other way, either; that had always been true. All he could do was make an effort to warn them. If they did receive it, they might dismiss it as the raving of a crackpot; they might even interpret it as a threat. Yet it still might keep them from taking intruders to Maclairn's surface.

Terry set to work programming the AI to track *Promise* and transmit at the optimum moment for moving out of range. What, he thought in dismay, if Kathryn *was* there? No matter; she'd see it eventually anyway, and would have no grounds to suspect that it had come from him. To her and to everyone else connected with Maclairn, he was dead. And so he was, as far as that world was concerned, for he would never be in a position to make contact with it again.

~ *45* ~

THE NET, TERRY found, was already rife with rumors about *Estel*. Word had already reached Earth that the Captain of *Estel* had been arrested at Stelo Haveno and had escaped; either at least one talkative crew had arrived from there, or someone had thought the news worth transmitting by ansible. As long as neither Fleet nor the bounty hunters knew that his ship was now *Bright Hope*, this was a good thing. It would help to counter the vehement denunciations of psi that were also rife.

These stemmed from various motives. The religious opponents maintained that psi was the work of the devil; many of them apparently believed this literally, as Becka's father had, rather than recognizing it as a metaphor. Terry found this hard to comprehend, though he knew from his reading that some people's minds really did perceive ideas in terms of concrete images rather than in abstract form. What they feared, they projected onto an external entity they felt justified in hating, and while in principle this was better than hating psi-gifted humans, all too many of them used it to excuse abuse of humans they considered "possessed." Because the idea of strange new abilities involved strong emotion, they were easily led into action they would never have taken under normal circumstances—which was why Becka had been beaten and why otherwise-ordinary people joined the Ku Klux Klan.

Sickening as it was, this reaction was at least sincere. The rants of the men who promoted it were much worse. Some of the preachers, he suspected, had had no true religious objections to psi, but merely wanted the power—and sometimes money—that could be acquired by exploiting people's fear of what was different and their natural wish to combat evil. Such exploitation had gone on throughout history; there was nothing new about it. But psi and related mind faculties were new to most people, so there was greater scope for it than in the recent past, and technology enabled it to be spread more widely. Moreover, the conspirators in the government were undoubtedly behind it.

To his dismay, Terry saw that there was more going on than a mere attempt to suppress awareness of individual mind-powers. The conspirators had always been a small minority within the government, working in secret without any wish to gain open support. Now, they appeared to have political ambitions. He suspected that they were aiming to influence the outcome of elections, and perhaps to eventually attain high office—even to take over the actual administration of the League. If the voters could be stirred up enough. . . . Chilled, he realized that it would mean a plunge from bureaucracy into an oppressive regime that would be impossible to overcome without widespread violence, a regime under which Maclairn's plan might not survive.

Not all the rabble-rousers used religion as an excuse; some took the opposite line of attack and maintained that belief in psi was objectionable on scientific grounds. Just as on Ciencia, they claimed that any form of unscientific thinking was not only foolish but harmful. "Centuries of effort have been expended to defeat superstition," declared one orator, speaking live on the Net. "Yet still it infects society. You wonder why civilization is on the verge of collapse? You wonder why no authoritative leadership has succeeded in eliminating sickness and poverty? It is because superstition has been allowed to encroach on reason again, and fools have listened to those who would drag us back into the Dark Ages. This infection must be expunged. We must drive out the purveyors of false notions about mind and spirit before they contaminate young people who know no better than to fall for such nonsense, put an end to these pernicious lies before it's too late. . . . "

Terry forced himself to watch tirades of this sort in the hope of learning how the conspiracy operated. They were familiar, even this man's voice was familiar . . . He had been listening with half his mind and his eyes weren't on the screen, but at the word "contaminate," which rang a bell, he looked up—and saw, with shock, the speaker's face.

It was Quaid.

Quaid, on Earth! He must have escaped retribution on Ciencia by persuading his contacts among the government conspirators to send a charter ship for him, perhaps by threatening to expose their part in the the the plot to destroy Maclairn. No wonder he'd been in a position to induce them to offer a bounty for the man he no doubt suspected was responsible for its failure. Oh, God, Terry thought—Jon had been right. He shouldn't have made that broadcast denouncing Quaid; it had backfired.

Jon . . . Quaid had known very well that Terry was Jon Darrow's friend, that he had allowed himself to be arrested in order to save him from prison. Had he guessed that Jon's presumed death in space had been faked? If so, he might well have offered a bounty for Jon, too, intending to use him as bait. And Jon was missing. . . .

But Jon and Gwen had new names; Quaid could not possibly know them. Even if word had gotten to him that they'd been members of *Estel*'s crew at Stelo Haveno, he couldn't connect them with the identities they had now. Unless . . . unless bounty hunters had connections in Fleet through which they'd learned what ship carried the deportees. They could have monitored its comm, watched its shuttle dock at the transit station to see if anyone of Jon's description disembarked.

Surely that was far-fetched, Terry told himself. But underneath he knew it wasn't. Precognitively—or perhaps through remote sensing—he perceived that it wasn't.

"I'm helpless!" he told Alison in agony. "I can't leave the ship unguarded, and trying to reach Zach through the arcade wouldn't work fast enough anyway. The police on the Moon don't bother with missing person reports any more than they do on Earth, and even if they did—"

"If they did, you'd have to tell them how to contact you," she pointed out, "and if it's true that they've been corrupted by your enemies, you'd be walking into a trap."

"But I can't just do nothing."

Alison, superficially calm as always, said quietly, "There's nothing you can do but wait. If it's true, you'll get a ransom demand, and they won't hurt Jon; he's of no value to them if not there to be ransomed."

"God, Alison. Of course they'll hurt him. They don't know how to reach me and they'll try to make him tell them."

She blanched. "He hasn't had the mind training."

"No." Their eyes met with anguished awareness—Jon was the only one of the crew who didn't know how to stop suffering from pain. He knew Jon wouldn't betray him voluntarily, but anyone without some sort of preparation was vulnerable. . . .

When some hours later the comm announced a hail from an approaching shuttle, Terry was so near panic that he could scarcely respond. It was a free trader's shuttle, as might be expected; any demand made of him wouldn't come through official channels even if the League conspirators were back of it. And it probably wasn't a demand. If bounty hunters already knew where he was, why would they bother to ask for his surrender?

"HS *Bright Hope*, this is HS *Goldfire*," the voice said. "Request permission to dock our shuttle. Over."

How had they known his ship's new name? Had Jon been forced to tell, by a threat to Gwen if other attempts to break him had failed? "*Goldfire*, identify your captain and your business with us," Terry said, steadying his voice. "Over."

He couldn't prevent them from docking, and in any case there was a chance they might have Jon with them. He would have to let them board. He hoped that at least Alison could hide; once they had him at their mercy, they'd have no use for her.

"*Bright Hope*, this is Captain López of *Goldfire*, aboard the shuttle," came the reply. "I'm here to arrange for delivery of your package. Over."

Package? That was an odd way to put it. It was probably just a ruse. "I'm not expecting any package," he replied.

"Captain Ryan, we understood that you had agreed to accept one," the shuttle pilot replied. "It comes from a box belonging to Zach Dyllon."

Oh, my God, Terry thought. Zach must have contacted Jenna and learned the name he was using; the shuttle must be his agent's, bringing refugees. "Permission to dock granted," he said shortly. "Out."

How could he accept refugees now, when he was sick with worry about Jon and in any case couldn't leave the solar system without him? Yet he had promised to take them, and if they'd been brought from Earth, both they and the pilot who'd transported them might be in serious danger.

In frozen silence Terry waited for López to dock, trying to decide what to say. This might be his only chance to make a contact through which he might locate Jon—

Zach had underworld contacts who might know where to look. But would they be willing to, considering that it would be likely to lead to trouble?

When docking was complete and the airlock opened, only one person accompanied López into the ship, a woman with long, blond hair and heavy makeup who was dressed like a cheap hooker. Strange, Terry thought, that they'd send just one—and then in the next instant the woman rushed forward and he saw that it was Gwen.

"We were waiting to board the shuttle for Earth and three men grabbed me," she told him. "Jon tried to fight them off but they forced us into a robocar and then a different shuttle, and took us to the Moon, the lowest underground level, and Jon—" her voice broke and she stumbled into Alison's embrace, at the same time tearing off the disguising wig.

"Where's Jon now?" Terry asked urgently.

"Still in their hideout," Gwen said shakily. "When they saw they couldn't make him talk, they let me go. They said it was so I could take you a ransom demand, but I knew they'd track me—they don't care about ransom, they just want to find you. I couldn't send a message, they'd be able to trace that. So I went up to the main level and bought the wig and these clothes, and dumped everything I'd been wearing they might have tagged with a tracker. And then I went to the arcade like Jenna said, and told the man behind the bar that I'd come to pick up Zach's box. He let me see the manager and after a few hours Captain López came for me."

"We have refugees in hiding who need to get out," López said, "and there's no time to waste. But I figured you'd want to know about your copilot first."

"I'm not leaving without him," Terry declared. "Do you know where the hideout is?"

"From what Gwen told us, I can guess. Guys in the bounty business—and I admit I'm one of them—keep tabs on the competition. There's just one scumbag active at

Moonbase right now who'd have the connections to learn what ship to meet, and I know where he hangs out." He added scornfully, "Me, I go after criminals, and when I turn them over to the law I collect what's due me. I don't try to extort more cash from their friends."

"They're not aiming for ransom," Terry said grimly. "They want *me*, because I'm worth more than Jon—if there's a bounty on him at all, it's just to get at me."

"That fits what Zach said—he put the word out that there's a still bigger bounty on this Captain of *Estel* everyone's talking about, and that you know how to reach the guy. He made damn sure we heard that anyone who wants to stay friends with him had better keep hands off both of you."

Gwen, fighting back tears, said "Jon made me promise not to come to you—he was afraid I'd be watched, and that if I did get through, you'd try to rescue him. He doesn't want that; it's too risky. But oh, God, Terry—"

Terry's heart contracted. It would be not merely risky, but suicidal. Yet he couldn't leave Jon in a bounty hunter's hands. . . .

"At least if he's wanted for bait they won't kill him," said López, "and if they were going to sell him to someone higher up, they'd have done it by now. But as for rescue, it doesn't look good. We'd need more men to have any hope of it, and I'm in no position to call in favors."

"I'll pay all I've got," Terry said, realizing that even if he kept only what was needed for supplies to maintain *Estel*'s life support, it wouldn't be enough

"What do you know about where the bounty's coming from?" López asked. "Is the boss likely to move in fast if he hears someone's holding out on him?"

"If I know Quaid, whoever holds out on him will be made sorry."

"Quaid? My God, that's the guy from nowhere who's muscling his way into the Klan. Is the Klan after you specifically, Ryan? Because if it is, you'd better jump as far as your ship can go while you still have the chance."

"Quaid's interest in me is personal. I wouldn't have thought he'd had time to get any sway over the Klan, though he shares its sick aims—but if he's got influence there, then yes, I've been targeted by it, as well as by his government cronies. If they get us both, they're likely to kill Jon in front of me, slowly." Seeing Gwen's face, Terry tried too late to bite back the words.

"Then you've got to face facts and get out of here. You can't help him by staying and you could do him harm."

López was right, Terry knew. He bowed his head, at a loss for where to turn. Logic told him he should go, yet he couldn't bring himself to do that.

~ *46* ~

SEEING THAT TERRY wouldn't budge, López agreed to ask around and see if he could verify Jon's location and recruit men willing to aid a potential Klan victim. They helped the refugees, Terry thought hopefully, and that involved risk. But not as much risk as an armed confrontation.

Somehow, he got through the rest of the day and the night that followed. Alison persuaded Gwen to use neurofeedback for relaxing tension and he did what he could to refresh their mind training, which momentarily distracted him from his own agony. Jon, he thought— steady, reliable Jon, who had lived for years in peril of arrest on Ciencia yet had gone on defying its corrupt government, who had never wanted anything more than a ship to fly and the freedom to use it as he chose, who had at last been happy when he became copilot of *Estel*, thinking the future was now bright for him . . . and who had offered to take the blame for the crime of helping Becka, to go to prison for it, in order to repay what he unnecessarily perceived as an outstanding debt. Who had begged

Gwen not to report his capture lest the others risk themselves for him . . .

The next morning López returned, again without the refugees, which was a good sign because they had agreed that he would bring them if there was no chance of achieving anything by waiting.

"I lined up some pals of Zach's willing to take on bounty hunters," he said. "We'll show up in force claiming to be Quaid's men and scare the hell out of the losers stupid enough to hold out on him. But there will be a price, Ryan. It's not the kind of job guys do for nothing."

"I don't expect them to," Terry said, "but I haven't got much to offer, short of my ship." Would he give up *Estel* to save Jon? he thought in anguish. It would be worse than dying, yet he couldn't *not* save him. . . .

"They don't want your ship," López said. "What they do want is passage on it for a guy named Nelson. He wants to get to Skyros, which is a long way from here."

"Is that all? Of course I'll take him. It means I can carry one less refugee, that's all."

"Well, you see, Nelson's had some trouble with the law. He's hot."

"So am I," Terry pointed out.

"Not for aiding and abetting the escape of a killer, which is what you'll be guilty of once you let him onto your ship. He's wanted for murder—it was a righteous killing, I think, but that doesn't let you off the hook. If he's caught and goes to trial you'll go with him, and if you've already got other charges against you, you're not likely to be released."

"If I'm caught I won't be released anyway; I've already escaped from custody twice, and Fleet's got enough on me to convict, though they don't yet know about half my so-called crimes." Terry drew a breath of relief; it was like escaping a third time to know that Jon would have a chance.

He wanted to confront Jon's captors personally, but

López vetoed that. "One look at you shows you're not experienced in this kind of work," he said flatly.

"I know how to handle a gun." He hadn't actually used
one in Fleet but he'd had considerable practice and had
proved to be a good shot.

"No doubt, but we're not planning to shoot these
lowlifes and get ourselves charged with homicide. The
idea is to scare them into thinking we're from whoever's
paying the bounty, that he's in a rage and will do worse
things than shoot them if they don't turn the captive over
to us without a fight."

It was true, Terry thought with chagrin, that he didn't
look like a man accustomed to violence and was not likely
to be perceived as a threat apart from any weapon he
might brandish. Latent telepathy would tell them he wasn't
a hireling of someone like Quaid, and in fact it might also
tell them that he wouldn't kill in cold blood. He wondered
for a moment why the same couldn't be said of López, but
decided that he didn't want to know.

"What if something went wrong?" Alison asked. "If
you were killed or captured in freeing him, it would destroy Jon! He was devastated when you went to prison on
Ciencia for his sake, and if the same thing happened again
he'd never get over it."

That too was true. Moreover, López pointed out that
he'd agreed to transport Nelson and had to have *Bright
Hope* ready to move out fast as soon as he and Jon were
on board. So reluctantly he conceded that he couldn't take
part in the rescue.

The refugees, who had been hiding in *Goldfire* since
escaping from Earth, were brought aboard first. There
were two couples with two children each, all past pre-
school age. With the crew and Nelson, that would make
thirteen people, but considering that none of the passengers had transit permits, being over the legal maximum
would make the penalty no worse. Alison got them settled
in the spare staterooms with the young girls sharing their

parents' quarters and the boys assigned to couches in the lounge. Nelson would also have to sleep there; Terry hoped he wasn't really a murderer.

The story of what had happened to these people was horrifying. They had been members of a small church less dogmatic than some in which the congregation had been divided over the issue of whether the use of psi was sinful, and were among those who believed it wasn't. Two of the kids had joined a group of teens who were fascinated by such faculties and were trying to learn about them—a sign, Terry thought, that the possibility was beginning to spread through the collective unconscious of new generations. The defenders of psi had prevailed in the congregation and had dismissed the pastor who'd been preaching against it, but his followers had been unwilling to accept the majority decision. Evidently some had been Klansmen, because one night the Klan had arrived during a meeting of the teen group and burned the church to the ground. One boy had died and others had been hospitalized for burns. The next day, vids of burning crosses had been sent to their parents' Net addresses.

"We'd never have been safe on Earth," said one of the women. "They could have tracked us through our IDs by hacking the Net and tracing our addresses back to them."

They could, Terry knew. With a chill he realized that *he* could, which meant a Klan member with equivalent hacking skills would have the same ability. "But why would they pick on you?" he asked, puzzled. "You didn't do anything spectacular."

"Just as an example to terrorize others," she said. "The burning of the church was reported on the Net; they saw to it that it was. Now all the members who voted against the pastor will be attacked one by one, and the public will know why."

Yes, but there would be no mass surge of indignation, Terry thought, because it would happen slowly, unpre-

dictably, with no visible public event to rouse feeling while
the violence was in progress. If the Klan burned a large
church in the center of a city while observers were present,
decent people would rise in protest even if the police did
nothing. Surreptitious attacks on small ones produced
only apathy or fear.

Somehow it must be made known that the Captain of
Estel had rescued these victims—the symbol he'd created
must be used to counter the impression that people who
used psi were inevitably doomed. But how? He couldn't
reveal his own identity or that of his ship even to the
victims themselves.

But he could publicize the underlying idea. If the burning of the church had been widely reported, there must
be plenty of discussions where he could insert remarks.
Forcing himself to suppress worry about the rescue in
progress, Terry spent the hours waiting for Jon's arrival
on the Net. Rather than post comments in the normal
way—which would have required his ID—he went back to
hacking, programming them to appear after he was gone;
he didn't want them traced to Moon orbit before *Bright
Hope* had departed.

"There is hope for those persecuted by the enemies of
mind-power," he wrote, "for the Captain of *Estel* is not
unaware of their peril. And though he can save only a
few, he comes when least expected, even as a break in
the clouds on a dark night may reveal a sudden glimpse
of the stars. Let it be known that eight victims of the evil
unleashed against this church have been taken to safety
by the Captain of *Estel*, and his thoughts are with the
rest; and let all who share his beliefs trust those who
speak in his name."

Over and over Terry inserted these words into Net
forums, both on Earth and on the Moon. By the time the
shuttle was back, he was fairly sure of wide coverage.

"*Bright Hope*, this is Captain López of *Goldfire*," the
comm announced. "I will be docking in ten minutes and I

have two more packages for you. Please be ready to receive them. Over."

Two! "Oh, thank God," Gwen burst out. No mention of passengers could be made on a public comm channel, of course, but one would be Nelson, and the other had to be Jon.

"López of *Goldfire,* we acknowledge," Terry declared fervently. "We are awaiting our packages with gratitude to you for their safe delivery." He knew López couldn't come aboard; he would have to take *Goldfire* out of orbit fast in case he had been tracked to his shuttle. There would be no chance to thank him.

Everyone crowded around the airlock; the refugees had been told what was happening and were eager to see that Jon was safe. Gwen was closest to the hatch. She rushed forward as it opened and then let out a cry.

Jon was half-carried in by a big man, presumably Nelson, who was supporting most of his weight; obviously he couldn't walk by himself and was in great pain. "Gwen," he whispered with effort. "Terry." Then he slumped, having lost consciousness.

"Get him into bed," said Alison quickly. "He may be in shock."

Terry helped Nelson carry Jon into the stateroom he shared with Gwen, "He's got an injured leg and some burns, and he's badly bruised," Nelson said. "They wanted information he wouldn't give them. López said they wanted you."

"There's a bigger bounty for me than for Jon. I'd have given anything to prevent this, but they wouldn't have let him go if they'd got hold of me—the man behind the bounty would have gone on hurting him and made me watch. And I've got responsibilities I can't ignore."

"According to Zach, you're important. He thinks you're a link to the Captain of *Estel.* Is that true?"

"I'm not free to answer," Terry said. "The Captain of *Estel* is wanted by bounty hunters, by the Klan, and by

Fleet, which would condemn him for a long list of alleged crimes. All I can say is that I act in his name."

He turned to examining Jon. Having had training in emergency medicine as a member of a Fleet explorer team, he knew what to look for, and checked first for symptoms of shock and then for pulse in the ankle before doing anything else. Thank God, there was no impaired circulation. Then Gwen cut away Jon's pants and Terry examined the leg carefully. There were no breaks in the skin and the lower leg seemed okay, but the bone of the knee was displaced, forming a grotesque bulge on one side. He felt it gently. "It's just a dislocated kneecap, not the whole knee and not a fracture," he told them, letting out a sigh of relief. If the entire knee had been dislocated there would have been danger of losing the leg, considering that it would be days before they could get medical care.

"I can fix it," he went on, "but right now I have to get this ship out of here." Telling Gwen to let him know when Jon was fully conscious, he went to the bridge and set course at top speed for the nearest jump point. During the hours of waiting he had programmed the jump to Skyros; he'd be free until time to execute it. In the meantime there were other things to consider.

~ *47* ~

TERRY'S FIRST IMPULSE at the sight of Jon's condition had been to relieve his pain, but he'd lost consciousness before that could be done. Now he wondered. Jon would certainly be better off if he could stop his own suffering, as Alison and Gwen had learned to do in New Afrika. He'd regretted having no opportunity for the training. Might he, Terry, be able to give it to him now that he had the neurofeedback helmets?

Enough of the programming was finished to display basic states of consciousness such as normal vs. pain control. He'd tested it on himself and was confident that it would work. His main barrier to conducting initial mind training sessions had been not the lack of neurofeedback facilities—which were necessary but not sufficient—but the fact that it would involve inflicting severe pain on the trainee. He didn't think he could bring himself to do that. Mentors served a long apprenticeship under the guidance of supportive teachers before having to do it.

But Jon's pain was already severe, and fixing the dislocated kneecap would mean intensifying it. Through telepathy that suffering could be prevented—but should it be? Might it not be more beneficial to use it to prevent future suffering and open the door to training that would increase his lifespan?

He would try, Terry decided, if Jon wanted him to. That people could learn to end their own suffering was one of the things he'd been telling them, one of the beliefs he and his crew were risking themselves to uphold. He was obligated to stand by it.

He called Alison and Gwen to the bridge and asked them to set up the neurofeedback equipment in Jon's stateroom. "You both know what a breakthrough involves," he reminded them. "Can you stay away, avoid any attempt to give him telepathic assistance, if he chooses to go through with it? That won't be easy."

They nodded, but he could see that Gwen's eyes were wet with tears. "He's already been through so much," she said unhappily.

"Yes, and that's why he deserves to gain something from it."

"But the secret part, the deception, after he's been so brave—he won't suspect that when he decides. And we can't encourage him."

"It will be hard, but we needn't worry whether he'll come through because we know he *is* brave. I wouldn't start if I weren't sure of that."

Once Jon was conscious Terry went into his stateroom alone. "I see you've set up for neurofeedback," Jon said. "You helped with the pain when I was recovering from my injuries on Ciencia, and Alison says neurofeedback makes that easier. But I envy her and Gwen their mind training right now. There was a while back there on the Moon when I thought I might not get through without it."

"You would have," Terry said, "but it would be better if you never had to worry about pain again. I can give you the training if you like, now that we've got the helmets."

"You can? I thought you said you weren't qualified."

"I didn't have the nerve to inflict the pain needed for a breakthrough on someone who wasn't already suffering. But your knee already hurts a lot. I have to put it back into position, which will hurt still more. The question is, do you want me to relieve your suffering while I do it, or would you rather learn to relieve it for yourself from now on?"

Surprised, Jon said, "I think you know the answer to that. But I'm not sure I'm up to it right now."

"It works better when your normal responses are weakened. Just trust me, and the bad part won't last long. Okay?"

Jon nodded, and Terry put one of the helmets on him, setting the neurofeedback computer to record brain patterns but not display them. "All right then, here goes," he said resolutely, suppressing his own hesitancy. To teach the skill of ending suffering demanded telepathic contact, just as relieving pain did, and if he failed to project total confidence Jon would be unable to absorb that skill. He grasped the leg and pulled it straight, not trying to be gentle.

For a moment Jon turned white, gritting his teeth, and then he screamed.

Withholding telepathic communication of pain relief was the hardest thing Terry had ever done. How did the mentors endure it? he thought hazily. He'd always wondered, but what he'd imagined was nothing compared to the real thing. He had relieved so many people's pain on Ciencia and on Toliman, experiencing it in his own body and carrying them along with his shift into a state of not minding it—*not* shifting was almost unendurable.

The worst of it lasted only seconds; he let go of the leg, seeing that the kneecap was now properly in place, and the pain faded. But Jon's thoughts were dark with despair. "So much for that," he said miserably. "I knew, with the bounty hunters, that I couldn't take much more—your rescue team got there just in time. But underneath ... well, I didn't really believe I was going to lose control, certainly not with *you*. I thought I could learn to do what the rest of you did. I guess I can't . . ."

He'd been mistaken in thinking that withholding telepathic aid was the hardest, Terry thought in anguish as he left the stateroom in silence. It was much harder to go without telling Jon that he hadn't failed.

Everyone else was in the lounge; the scream had shocked them. "Haven't you got any painkillers aboard?" said one of the refugee women reproachfully.

"We don't need them," Terry said steadily. "Jon's going to be okay. Have you read what the Captain of *Estel* says about pain? Well, he's right; it's possible to end suffering from it, and I'm going to teach Jon how."

Nelson stared at him in awe. "You said you act in his name," he said. "Can others do that, too? Because if so, I want to enlist—not for teaching esoteric stuff, of course, but to support him any way I can. That man is waking people up. He might even get them to vote against the bastards trying to take over the government."

Terry considered it. He'd mentioned acting in his name in the Net posting because he expected Zach's contacts to send him more refugees. Recruits needn't be limited to them; after all, on Ciencia his followers had created an Estelan party. An accused murderer, though. . . .

"It depends on whether their actions are things he'd

approve of," he replied slowly. "He's not a killer, even when he sees someone who ought to be eliminated—not unless it's to save himself or others."

"I killed a Klansman," Nelson admitted. "A bunch of masked ones had a woman tied to a tree and were about to set fire to it—they called her a witch. I shot the one with the torch and the rest ran off like the cowards they are. But they saw me, and the next day I was arrested for murder, because the one I hit turned out to be the police chief of that town."

Terry, struggling for composure, declared, "I think the Captain of *Estel* would be happy to have you act in his name."

He waited only an hour before returning to Jon, sure that he was by then past resuming the fight demanded by his ingrained assumptions about how to manage pain. This was the crucial step; he had to get Jon's consent to face it without hope of fighting. The psychology required was different for different people. In this case not much subterfuge would be required.

"I know what you're feeling," he said. "Finding that you've got limits is worse than the pain itself, isn't it?"

Jon looked away, not answering, but Terry winced at what he sensed of his emotions. Keeping his voice expressionless he said, "Your leg needs to be stretched a little more and I could do it without letting you suffer, but I don't think you want that. If you tell me to, you'll never be sure you won't chicken out any time there's a chance of being humiliated."

"You're right," Jon said, "but of course you would be— you're telepathic. I've spent the last three days telling myself I'd never crack. Actually it's a relief to know that it's useless to fight."

"Then don't try. It will be better if you do scream, because then you'll know you can bounce back from whatever happens." Terry put the helmet back on him, this time setting the computer to display live neurofeedback and showed Jon the earlier recording, cruder than what mentors used because the level of pain from an injury could not be measured precisely. Then with live brain output he pulled on the leg again, knowing that because Jon had stopped struggling for control, it wouldn't feel nearly as painful.

"Go ahead, do what you did before," Jon said. "If I'm going to prove I'm willing to reach the screaming stage, we can't stop now."

"You're never going to reach it," Terry said. "This is as bad as it gets when you don't fight, which is something nobody can learn without having tried both strategies. That's the big secret that has to be kept about this training."

"God, Terry! You mean you knew I'd scream the first time, and then resign myself to letting it happen?"

"The resignation part is the worst, and we've all been through it," Terry agreed. "But it's necessary, because the instinct of anyone with courage is to stiffen and show no weakness. You have to reach the point where you've no hope of that before you can relax enough to turn off suffering."

He put on the second helmet and began demonstrating, with neurofeedback from both Jon and himself, how altering brain patterns eliminated suffering from the sensation of pain, elated at the discovery that he himself was able to pass on such skills—that people other than Maclairnans, and those taught by Maclairnans, could develop them. He'd felt uneasy about promising that someday people in pain would no longer have to suffer. The proof that it was true, thrilling them both at the moment of Jon's breakthrough, was worth the risk he had taken to get hold of the helmets.

It took several more sessions after the jump before Jon was able to stop suffering from his burns and bruises by himself, after which Terry speeded their healing to the best of his limited ability, wishing that he possessed

the gift with which the crowd at Centauri had mistakenly credited him. He then turned to wondering what
awaited them at Skyros, the backwater world to which
he'd agreed to take Nelson. He knew no more of it than
that like many colonies, it had been named after an
island in Greece; and he'd had time to look up only its
star's coordinates. "Can the refugees stay there?" he
asked.

"I expect so," Nelson said. "The residents aren't particular about who they accept."

Including alleged murderers, Terry thought. "What I
mean is, what kind of world is it? Will they be able to
earn a living?" He couldn't abandon them some place where
they'd be destitute, yet if he had to take them elsewhere
it would be costly and would delay rescuing more people
from Earth.

"All I know is that Zach has contacts there with ansible
access, apparently private access they don't pay for," said
Nelson. "He uses it as a clearinghouse—I'm supposed to
tell you to check for messages addressed to you."

Thank God, Terry thought. He needed to stay in touch
with Zach and, barring perilous visits to the transit station arcade, he didn't know how to reach his underground
friends on Earth.

He was not eager to go back to the vicinity of Earth.
He knew the more he saw of it, the more depressing it
would become, and the more he would worry about the
increasing power of the men conspiring to take control of
the League government. But he was committed now—
committed not merely to spreading hopeful ideas, but
to taking the direct action rumor would attribute to
the Captain of *Estel*. He'd started something bigger than
he'd intended, and he had no choice but to carry it
through.

~ *48* ~

DURING THE NEXT two years Terry and his crew made many trips to Skyros, taking refugees there from Earth. It proved to be a pleasant colony, not rich enough to attract much commerce but able to support a growing population employed in agriculture and local trades. The people had liberty, the government wasn't corrupt, and the planet's gravity and climate were comfortable. The only reason it was not more crowded was the cost of passage, which wasn't subsidized as it was in the case of worlds producing goods the League had widespread need for. The lack of frequent traffic meant Fleet didn't pay much attention to it, which from the standpoint of fugitives was a good thing.

Another good thing for Terry was his ability to communicate with Zach from Skyros. Nelson introduced him to the ansible owner and found that he did indeed have a message waiting—Zach promised that the expense of servicing and refueling *Bright Hope*'s hyperdrive engine at Moonbase, required after every three round trips, would be prepaid. Provisioning proved to be no problem; the refugees on Skyros collected money to buy his consumables, in many cases from supporters appalled by what they heard of conditions on Earth. Before long other ships were also bringing refugees, less frequently than Terry because for them it was still undercover activity secondary to smuggling cargo. They too carried passengers who'd been rescued in the name of the Captain of *Estel*, a phrase that on Earth was being used as a password for making contact with a willing captain.

There was little cargo to be had on Skyros and no opportunity to sell it at Moonbase or on Earth, so Terry was out of the free trading business. He didn't need it; he was now fully occupied with smuggling people. He wondered if Fleet would attempt to keep count if they knew;

if so, there would be hundreds of charges against him. That would make no difference to his fate if he was caught; just a few, combined with the crimes of which he was already accused, would be enough to condemn him.

In theory, since the refugees didn't have transit permits, they had to be smuggled onto Skyros as well as off Earth. They couldn't be landed in broad daylight despite the forged IDs they'd been given. Since there was a community ready to aid them, this was rarely a problem. On occasions when there was a Fleet merchant ship in orbit, Terry had to be careful, and on the remote chance that his face might be recognized from "wanted" transmissions, he let Jon or Gwen, for whom he obtained a legal Class C license, fly the shuttle. But there were no serious incidents.

All of them liked Skyros. They stayed a night or two each time they came, taking turns remaining with *Bright Hope*, and they found good friends, good food, and comfortable beds waiting for them. Usually there was a party. And there was always a gathering where he spoke of Estelan ideas, referring to the Captain of *Estel* in third person, but inspiring listeners through his own growing ability to establish telepathic rapport.

He didn't have to worry about having no time to visit other colonies. Visitors who arrived from them were familiar with Net rumors about *Estel*; there was no world that had not heard of its Captain and the actions taken in his name. The fact that no one had ever seen him magnified his influence. The officers at Stelo Haveno, who alone *had* seen him, kept quiet about it, mistakenly assuming that interest in him would increase if it were acknowledged that he was real. Presumably they had sent a report to Headquarters about his escape, but Fleet, Terry knew, was a ponderous bureaucracy, and he did not expect them to pursue his case. If they had done a full biometric search on every captain who orbited the Moon they would have him by now, but he wasn't considered important enough for that.

The visits to Skyros were happy and the transit time in normal space was productive. On outbound trips the crew socialized with the refugees and Alison, as an experienced psychotherapist, counseled those who had suffered trauma. When by themselves, inbound to Earth, Terry used neurofeedback to teach her and the others how to preserve their health by controlling their heart rate and inner biochemistry. Probably neither he nor they would live as long as the Maclairnans did, not having developed such skills in adolescence, but at least they wouldn't die of an illness produced by stress.

Good as life was on Skyros and in space, the time in Earth orbit was another matter. Terry dreaded it. They weren't constantly in danger; there were only a few hours each trip when refugees were being brought aboard, after which he departed at maximum speed. It took a day or two to make contact with Zach's agents, however, and sometimes longer for them to get the refugees off the ground. Occasionally Jon or Gwen had to take *Bright Hope*'s shuttle down to pick them up, and that was perilous. Terry would have preferred to go himself, but as Alison pointed out, if one of the others was arrested *Bright Hope* could go on saving people, whereas if he was, it couldn't. More importantly, he felt he must stick to his vow not to land on Earth; orbiting was okay, but on the surface he might meet mentors.

This had become a more worrisome consideration, for mentors were now seeking him. When he first got a message through Zach's friends that the Captain of *Estel* should be told that he had followers at Earth's Bramfield Clubs, Terry was dismayed; he assumed they had somehow connected him with the warning he'd sent to the Maclairn Foundation. But that was impossible. There was nothing in it that could suggest a link either to *Estel* or to him. He soon realized that they must simply have decided that since the Captain of *Estel*'s ideas were so similar to theirs, it might be good to join forces. That was natural enough. They wouldn't be planning to tell him about Maclairn—they just wanted to give him mind training and offer their support of his mission. It was ironic, since his goal had always been to support *them*.

It would be disastrous, of course, if Maclairnans found out that he knew what went on at the Bramfield Clubs. From the beginning he'd been careful to avoid saying anything that might imply that he did. Now he became more wary than ever. Yet the mentors didn't stop trying to contact him. Perhaps they feared that someone who'd received training from them had given them away, and were trying to trace the leak. The more he thought about it, the more Terry felt that this was likely. It was indeed odd that a man without any connection could have come up with the same convictions about mind faculties; why had that never occurred to him? It didn't matter, since he wouldn't have acted differently if it had. But he was sorry they had to be kept in the dark.

The situation became critical when one day at Moonbase, waiting to enter the space dock for service on *Bright Hope*, Terry received a direct comm call from a woman who identified herself as a devotee of *Estel*. She would like to know more about it, she said. She had heard he knew how to get in touch with its Captain. Could she come over in a shuttle to talk about him?

The call came from *Promise*.

Oh God, Terry thought. It must be a member of its crew. That would mean a Fleet officer, but she wouldn't necessarily know about the Captain's crimes; they wouldn't have been mentioned in official dispatches to Maclairn. Rumors about *Estel* might have reached there, and in any case would have been heard by the crew while on shore leave at Moonbase or on Earth. Or she could have been asked specifically by mentors to investigate. She could even have been asked by Kathryn!

Kathryn. She undoubtedly knew of the rumors. As Maclairn's ambassador, she might be behind the entire effort to find the Captain of *Estel*, might even be hoping to meet him.

It would be so simple. He had been made physically unrecognizable; he could see her, ask about her son, and she would not guess. He didn't want to reopen that chapter of his life, and yet . . . all he'd have to do was tell this officer that he'd be willing to visit *Promise*. . . .

But no. His face wasn't recognizable, but his mind-touch would be. Even if Kathryn didn't grasp who he was, she would sense that he knew about Maclairn. And because their bond had been close, she would probably sense his knowledge of the Elders just as a mentor would.

"I'm sorry," he told the woman who had called, "but there's really no more I can tell you than what's already on the Net, and right now I'm on my way into the space dock." When the work on *Bright Hope* was finished he moved quickly to Earth orbit and, once his passengers were aboard, headed with relief out to Skyros.

After that he was nervous when near Earth or the Moon, adding to the discomfort he always felt when watching the news from there. The Klan was becoming bolder. This, Terry felt, was related to the ever more offensive diatribes of Quaid, whose Net show was quite popular. As López had said, Quaid had become a leader within the Klan and although this was not publicly acknowledged, everyone with leanings in that direction knew it.

And an increasing number of people did have such leanings. It wasn't just that they feared psi. The government conspirators had succeeded in making it a scapegoat for all the ills of Earth's depressing, decaying civilization. Quaid had imported from Ciencia the notion that unscientific thinking was responsible for the failure to eliminate pollution, poverty and squalor, and the enemies of Maclairn had seized that notion with zeal. As on pre-reformation Ciencia, the concept of the "supernatural" was extended beyond psi and volitional control of the body to everything spiritual or imaginative—although promoters of this fallacy were not above simultaneously condemning "witchcraft" in the name of religion.

More and more, they were exploiting the growing aversion to the so-called paranormal for political ends—overtly political, not just in recognizing that suppression of personal mind-power weakens resistance to authority. To Terry's horror, he arrived at Earth near the end of his second year of refugee rescue to discover that Commissioner Hiller was running for the position of League Premier.

Hiller was one of the original undercover enemies of Maclairn. Terry remembered him as a rather pompous bureaucrat who had once subtly threatened him with a suggestion that pirates might attack *Promise,* "pirates" he had undoubtedly hired. More ominously, he had very likely been among those who conspired with Quaid to attack the colony with bioweapons. He certainly wasn't competent to assume leadership of the entire League, so no doubt he was slated to be a figurehead; and the thought of what might be behind his candidacy was frightening. It meant that the conspirators at League Headquarters would no longer be mere conspirators, but would have full control of the government.

Terry clenched his fists in anger and frustration. His deepest fear was about to be realized: if the rabid opponents of psi got complete control of Fleet, they would withdraw the cruiser *Shepard* from Maclairn. Then Maclairn would be at the mercy of whoever might land on it, and there was little doubt as to who that would be.

The Klan. The Klan would move in on Maclairn, secretly of course because attacks on one planet by another were prohibited by the League charter and Fleet was sworn to enforce it—but officers loyal to the charter could not enforce it when the planet being attacked was isolated and unknown to exist. They would not even be told what was happening.

The mentors on Earth could do nothing. They could read the handwriting on the wall as well as he could, and would guess that *Shepard* was gone even before *Promise* arrived to say so. They would wait helplessly, knowing their loved ones on Maclairn were in danger but unable to take any action. It wouldn't be the danger of which he'd warned them; a government in power, unlike a small group of conspirators, could not sanction genocide, for if word got out it would be held responsible. Instead, it would let the Klan do the dirty work through its usual tactics— not bothering with white robes or a low profile, but simply unleashing violent hate. If the ruin came to light and the Klan was blamed, so be it—it had always been a tool and was expendable.

Would the Elders step in? They were guarding Maclairn, would know when the cruiser left, and would see the intruders arrive. But there would be too many intruders to deal with secretly, which was something they hadn't anticipated. It would be self-defeating for them to take action resulting in the revelation they believed would harm humankind. They would grieve for Maclairn and for the loss of its influence on Earth, but they would not intervene.

Cold with horror at this thought, Terry knew that he had to *do* something—he didn't know what, but *something*. He had saved Maclairn from destruction before, and it was now up to him to save it again.

~ *49* ~

THROUGHOUT THE NEXT trip to Skyros, Terry could think of little else but the dilemma he was facing. He had, of course, made plenty of comments on Earth's Net opposing Hiller, both in public forums and, via hacking, in various other places. But that was not enough. Somehow, he decided, the Ku Klux Klan must be exposed.

He had known all along that the Klan would not be tolerated if it acted openly, in force. In ancient times like the early twentieth century it had held demonstrations and parades, but most people today abhorred hate groups—at least in public. Its strength lay in pretending it didn't exist while letting vulnerable individuals know, through Net rumors and small-scale acts of terrorism, that it did. The police ignored such acts. They could not ignore a major public incident involving violence.

And if that incident occurred just before the election, and Hiller was known to have instigated it, he would lose.

But how could Hiller be induced to instigate it? And if he could, how could violence occur without actually endangering anyone?

Hiller might be dealing with the Klan behind closed doors, just as he had dealt with the thugs he'd hired to pose as pirates. But he wasn't compelling enough to be among its leaders. Quaid, on the other hand—Quaid was known to be one of them, and he had a large Net following. He was actively campaigning for Hiller, which might well be payback for the commissioner's surreptitious support of Klan activity. He was motivated by fanaticism rather than politics, he had no scruples, and if he was confronted with accusations he would not hesitate to shift the blame.

Quaid, to be sure, was too smart to instigate a major public incident. He surely knew that it would arouse opposition to the Klan. But his antipathy to all things "unscientific" was so great that it overwhelmed the dictates of reason. In his tirades, he got carried away by repressed fear and hatred. And what, or who, was he likely to hate most of all?

The Captain of *Estel*.

Terry, calling himself Captain of *Estel* before there was such a ship, had bested Quaid during interrogation in prison, had frightened him by his mysterious ability to resist torture, had thwarted his plan for a biochemical attack on Maclairn—and later, had denounced him to the colleagues he had cheated, necessitating his escape from Ciencia. Since then the Captain of *Estel* had become a public symbol of all that he most despised. Quaid had put a price on his head yet he'd managed to elude all the bounty hunters. To say the man hated him was a colossal understatement. And he would therefore be easily provoked.

A plan began to form in Terry's mind. It was a desperate plan, a horrifyingly dangerous plan, one he dared not confide to Alison or even to Jon. It might well require sacrificing more than he had in defeating the two terrorists, for now he had more to lose. And it would mean breaking his vow not to land on Earth. But it was the only way he could see to save Maclairn from the Klan.

He would need help and money, and these could come only from Zach. His idea was too complicated to be discussed through ansible messages, so he would have to go to Centauri. The Fleet officers at Centauri's spaceport might recognize him; if they did, they would arrest him. And what excuse could he give to his crew for going there?

No excuse was possible. He would have to tell them part of the truth.

He waited until they'd left Skyros and were near the end of the normal-space transit to jump distance. Then he called them together in the lounge. "Look," he said, "there's something I've got to do, and I can't say much about it. All I can tell you is why I have to act."

They looked at him in bewilderment, and Alison said, "I know there's something wrong, Terry—I've known since before we left Earth. You haven't been yourself, even when we're alone together."

That was true; he hadn't made love because he couldn't let their minds merge, which during sex was inevitable. "I told you all at the beginning that there'd be things I had to hide," he reminded them. "Well, this is connected to Maclairn, and you do know how I feel about that, how much I care what happens to it—"

"Of course. You found a way to send the warning; it wasn't—too late, was it?" Oh, God, Terry, don't say more terrorists got there!"

"No, but the Klan will if Hiller wins the election. He'll recall the cruiser that's protecting Maclairn. It's a small colony with no defenses and no police; they'll burn everything in sight, and kill, too, because Hiller and his friends want it neutralized."

"Then he mustn't win," Jon declared. "The colonies won't vote for him, but from what I've heard, he's got Earth sewed up, at least among people who bother to vote at all."

"That's what I've got to change," Terry said. "I know it sounds impossible and maybe it is, but I have to try."

"To fix an election? That does seem dicey, even given your hacking skills," Gwen said.

"Hacking alone can't do it," Terry agreed, "though that will be involved. The first step is to go to Centauri and talk to Zach, so that's where we're going to jump now."

They didn't contest it, and during the days of approach in normal space after the jump, they respected his evident unwillingness to talk about his plan. At night in bed Alison lay silent in his arms, understanding why he went no further, and the worry Terry sensed in her tore at his heart. She had a right to be worried. Without knowing any of the facts, she perceived that they might soon be separated.

The landing on Centauri went smoothly enough; Spaceport Control had no reason to connect *Bright Hope* with *Estel* or with *Coralie*, the name under which they'd known it. The only risky part lay in being recognized by someone on the field, and since he didn't land until well after dark, that was unlikely. It wasn't until he was through the gate and into the city that it dawned on him that people on the street might recognize him. It had been over two years since he'd been mobbed, yet there had been the newscasts, too, which might have made an impression. He pulled a skull cap down over his face and reached Zach's Emporium as fast as could get there.

He'd messaged Zach from orbit that he was coming, which was, naturally, a big surprise to him. "I'm glad to see you, Steward—or is it Ryan, now, for more than just ansible addressing? The report I got from Jenna wasn't too clear."

"In private it's still Steward, or rather, Terry. But Tom Ryan anywhere Fleet or the Klan might hear of me. I've got a long list of felonies on my record."

"You need a place to hide out away from your ship?"

"No. This is something bigger, something that needs to be done if we want to stop the Klan from doing worse things than it already has."

"I'm listening," said Zach, "though it's hard to see what could be worse."

"It's important for Hiller to lose the election," Terry said. "If he wins, the Klan will be in a position to wipe out a whole colony, or most of it—a colony where something that really matters is going on. I can't tell you the details, I'm sworn to secrecy. But no price is too high to keep it from happening."

"I'll take your word for it," Zach said. "I don't like what I've heard of Hiller and his bunch myself. I'll make sure everyone in my network knows not to vote for him. What more can I do?"

"The outcome can't be left to chance," Terry replied slowly. "The Klan has to be discredited to the public at large, and it's got to be made plain that Hiller is backing it. The only way I see to do it will require help from Estelan supporters on Earth. You're in touch with a lot of them, the ones willing to take risks."

Zach gave him a penetrating look. "You know how to reach the Captain of *Estel*. That might be a better source of help. If he spoke out personally—"

"He will, in due course. But it will probably mean being arrested, so the timing has to be right."

"He'd let himself be arrested over this? Has he told you so?"

Terry drew breath; the time had come when Zach had to know. "Zach, I *am* the Captain of *Estel*," he said. "It's always been me. I started the rumors myself, on purpose, to give people hope."

"My God," Zach said, recovering from shock. "I don't know why I didn't guess. I knew when I first saw you that you were something special."

"Not so special. Just lucky enough to own a starship named *Estel*."

"In your mind, you mean? Or have you got another one I don't know about?"

"It's the same ship. It's got two transponders; the one we've been renaming is the fake. I had to use the real one at Stelo Haveno, which is why I changed my name."

Zach frowned. "If you're arrested, they're likely to take it away from you."

"They already did; it's been attached under forfeiture laws. I stole it back, but I don't expect I can do that again." Zach didn't need telepathy, Terry thought, to know how he felt about that. He couldn't bear to dwell on it, so moved on rapidly, "If you're willing to get involved in defeating Hiller, I need a major contribution."

"You've got it, if it's something I can provide."

"I mean a financial contribution—large, but no more than wealthy donors give to political campaigns. I need you to buy me a building, one you can get possession of before the election. In any major city on Earth where you can locate one that's suitable."

"A building? What sort of a building?"

"Something in a public place, big enough to stand out and not too close to others. It should be cheaply constructed, no fireproof synthetics, and it doesn't have to be in good shape; I'm only going to use it for a couple of days."

"For a couple of days, why not rent it?"

"Because the Klan is going to burn it down and I don't want to destroy somebody else's property."

"My God, Terry," Zach said. "I take it you think they'll be discredited if a lot of people see them in action. But they'll realize that, won't they? Anyway, they burn stuff to terrorize weak people—what would they get out of attacking you that way? You already know they've targeted you, and they're aware that you don't scare easily."

"Well," said Terry, "in the first place, it will be labeled "Estelan Party Headquarters," so they'll want to impress potential members. In the second place, the Klansmen who live nearby will get private Net messages telling them they're supposed to burn it, saying when. And in the third place, the man who engineered the bounty on me, a guy named Quaid, hates me so much that he'll lose all sense of caution and be first in line with a torch the minute he sees me."

"Sees you? You're not going to be on the premises when they set fire to this place, are you?"

"Not for long. But I have to put in an appearance because that's how we'll get an audience—there will be rumors all over the Net that the Captain of *Estel* will come to his party's headquarters that night."

Zach stared at him with admiration. "When you decide to do something, you sure as hell don't go half way. But how do you know they won't bomb it instead of just setting it on fire? A lot of people could get hurt that way."

"That's why I don't want a building close to others that might be occupied—though in any case the Klan doesn't use bombs. If they did, all the Bramfield Clubs would be gone by now, and a lot of major public buildings. That's not their kind of terrorism; it would get the police, and maybe Fleet, to come after them. They don't want to stir up public opinion against them when they're trying to create scapegoats. Besides, they use fire as a symbol, at least the twentieth-century ones did."

"I've wondered about that. What's with the cross burn-ing? I thought most of them claim to be Christians."

"The original Klan didn't look at it as destroying crosses—they were lighting them up, illuminating them. I don't suppose they know or care what they're doing now. Quaid, for one, despises all religions and attacks them all equally except when he's encouraging them to oppose psi."

"Quaid?" Suddenly recollecting something, Zach said, "I got a message a couple days ago from López about him. Said you'd be interested to know that he's now top dog in the Klan, their Imperial Wizard, whatever that is."

"It's the title used by the head of the historical Ku Klux Klan." This was good news, Terry thought. If Quaid was the official top leader, the discrediting of the Klan would be all the more complete.

Zach grinned. "The Klan's Imperial Wizard versus the Captain of *Estel*—that should make some new history."

~ *50* ~

THEY TALKED UNTIL late in the night, and then suddenly Zach said, "If you don't mind, I think I'll come along to see the show. I've been planning to retire from the forgery business, and this is as good a time as any. I don't want to push my luck too far; the last agent I had in the box acted like he might be onto something. It stands to reason I can't fool them forever, and besides, since I got involved in this refugee stuff I've kind of lost interest in just out-witting bureaucrats."

"It would be great to have you with me," Terry said, "though hopefully there won't be many more refugees af-ter the Klan loses its power." Zach had plenty of friends on Earth, he knew, and evidently plenty of money stashed away since he hadn't balked at buying the building. If he ever ran short, there would be a demand for skilled ID forgers anywhere.

So after a day spent sealing up the famous box and closing the emporium for future sale, Terry and Zach, carrying four duffels of Zach's gear between them, boarded the shuttle and returned to *Bright Hope*. Terry warned Zach not to talk about their upcoming enterprise in front of the crew. He knew all three of them would oppose it.

"Will you promise that if I'm arrested you'll take care of them till they find work?" he asked him. "I've been handling all the money but what they may want to spend on Skyros, and if I transfer it to them now they'll be suspicious."

"Sure," said Zach. "You can count on that."

After a moment's thought Terry added, "You once asked about the mind training I've had. Well, at a Bramfield Club on Earth you can get it. Alison had it at the one on New Afrika and she can recommend you. But don't ever, under any circumstances, let on that the Captain of *Estel* knows where it's offered."

Terry picked up more refugees and made two trips to Skyros and back while Zach scouted Earth for a suitable building to buy and, with the aid of López and other friends, cleaned up its front. It was in Greater Los Angeles, an ancient, empty big-box store of the cheap sort that should have been torn down but hadn't been, isolated in the middle of a huge parking lot that served a busy strip mall. Trash and discarded packing materials had been left inside, along with scattered items of unsold merchandise. Zach put up a banner reading "Estelan Party Headquarters, Opening Soon," but obtained no permits to open; he did not arrange for the utilities to be turned on and thus the sprinkler system would be inoperative.

Then, with the election only a week away, Terry began planting rumors on the Net about the coming appearance of the Captain of *Estel*. They included the date and time, which would be in the evening, before the strip mall stores closed. And he made sure that they would reach the news media.

The rumors soon went viral. There was no way to keep *Bright Hope*'s crew from seeing them.

"What does it mean?" Alison asked him. "Who would start such a rumor when you've never revealed your identity? People are going to be furious when you don't show up."

"I have to show up," Terry said reluctantly.

"But you can't. You can't land on Earth."

"Just this once, I have to. There won't be any mentors near there." Privately he wondered; the mentors had been trying to contact him, and they would see the notices.

"Is there really an Estelan Party, like there was on Ciencia?" Gwen asked.

"Not yet, but there should be. The Estelans on Ciencia won."

"Even if you could start a party, it wouldn't help defeat Hiller," Alison said. "It's too close to the election. Besides, I thought you aim to influence only colony worlds."

"Terry, I don't see how you can go to this meeting," Jon declared. "The bounty hunters are still looking for you, and they'll have seen the publicity. It would be better to disappoint your followers than for you to get caught."

"I don't have a choice," Terry said. "Don't ask me why."

"Well, I'll find out when we get there, won't I?"

"You can't come with me, Jon. The bounty hunters are still looking for you, too, and there's no point in our both being at risk. Zach will be there if I need help." At this, Terry sensed sadness in Jon, and realized that he had hurt him by implying that despite his long loyalty, Zach was being preferred over him. Quickly he said, "Don't think I wouldn't rather have you, but I may be there awhile and I don't like to leave Gwen in charge of the ship in Earth orbit. There's too much traffic here."

The ship he might never see again once he left it, Terry thought miserably. What if his crazy scheme didn't work, and Hiller won anyway?

The next day he spent hacking, sending messages to local Klansmen whose Net addresses he found in a database he had cracked. Purporting to come from Klan headquarters, they said that they were to come robed and masked to the address given at the hour stated and were to bring torches. Believers in *Estel,* they were told, could not be allowed to form a political party.

Quaid would see some of these messages, of course, and would wonder who had taken the initiative that rightly belonged to him. But he wouldn't disclaim them. As he would also see rumors that the Captain of *Estel* was coming, he would certainly show up, as would numerous bounty hunters.

And so, of course, would Fleet. Although normally Fleet had no jurisdiction outside the bounds of the spaceport, recapturing someone who'd escaped from them was an exception. If they could get their hands on him, they would.

That night with Alison was agony. It might be years before he would see her again, and Terry could not suppress that awareness—they were too close telepathically now for her not to guess. Yet he could not speak of it. If he did, neither of them could get through the hours until his departure. He held her close and felt her tears wet against his skin, and he wondered why he had ever taken on a role that demanded giving up the freedom to live like other people. He had thought he was free when he received *Estel,* but it had bound him just as surely as had his confinement to Ciencia. As its now-legendary Captain, he had obligations that overrode all other choices he might ever make.

"Alison," he whispered. "We've had two good years—a little more than two—and if anything happens to me, they're what I want you to remember. We knew from the beginning that there might not be many. Don't grieve for the time we didn't have, look back on what we did, and be glad that fate allowed us this much."

In the morning, alone on the bridge, Terry got together the few things he would need on Earth, wondering if he should take a gun from the captain's locker.

The Klan did not use guns. Guns were illegal and only criminals had them, whereas Klan members were otherwise-respectable citizens in disguise. Their aim was not to slaughter people in a way that might be mistaken for a gang killing, but to terrorize; thus their weapon was fire. They burned crosses, buildings, and occasionally victims they'd captured; they sometimes hanged them; but they would not shoot into a crowd. In his two years of talking to refugees he had never heard of anyone being shot by the Klan. Yet it seemed rash to go unarmed into a riot, and it wasn't as if he hadn't been trained to defend himself. He decided to take one.

He avoided saying goodbye to the crew. All that could be said to Alison had been said last night, and Jon would try to talk him out of going alone. So he went to the shuttle bay when the coast was clear, assuming they were in their staterooms.

When he boarded the shuttle Jon was already in the copilot's seat.

"I don't know what you're up to," Jon said, "but whatever it is, you're not going without me. Gwen is perfectly capable of maintaining the ship in orbit, and you know it."

Terry protested, "You can't do anything to help—your being there wouldn't make any difference to the outcome. It's something I have to take on alone."

"Terry," said Jon, "the Estelan movement on Ciencia gave me something to believe in, and I want a part in whatever you're doing to spread it. On top of that, you've done more for me than I can ever repay, and if you got into trouble while I wasn't beside you, I'd never forgive myself. Give me a chance to keep my self-respect."

Reluctantly, Terry gave in. If by any chance he did escape he would need to make a fast getaway, and Jon might help with that.

They landed at the Los Angeles spaceport after considerable red tape and delay; he hadn't dealt with so much orbital traffic since his Fleet days. He was tempted to order Jon to remain with the shuttle, which really ought not to be left unguarded, but in the end he decided it would be cruel to deprive him of the chance to see the action, however painful watching the probable arrest turned out to be.

By the time they neared "Estelan Party Headquarters" in a rented groundcar, the streets were already clogged with traffic and local cops were turning cars away from the parking lot. Terry had known he'd attract an audience, but nothing like the mass of people gathered there, filling the aisles, some sitting on the tops of cars. Belatedly it dawned on him that the Klan members would also have to park. Most residents of Los Angeles, however, were well accustomed to gridlock and had sense enough to leave their groundcars at malls up to a mile away. Presumably the Klansmen had arranged for some closer meeting place where they could put on their robes.

Zach was waiting at the building, accompanied by the friends he'd recruited for crowd control, who wore security guard uniforms. Terry took him aside and assured himself that the building had been thoroughly checked and the entrances guarded to make sure that no enthusiasts hoping for a close look at the celebrity got inside. The closest parking spaces had been cordoned off, not only to make room for spectators but to prevent cars from being trapped too near the fire.

"We haven't got an assembly permit," Zach said, "but by the time the traffic cops realize that, it will be too late for it to matter. The backup force is too busy with gang shootouts to bother about spontaneous gatherings."

Terry had not been recognized by anyone in the crowd, of course, and though he could see news crews and several Fleet officers, they were too far off to compare his face with a picture. Not until he made himself known would he be in danger from them. He didn't intend to do that until the Klan appeared. The confrontation, if it was to be effective, had to happen fast. He waited on tenterhooks, just inside the building's entrance. What if they didn't come?

Then, in a massive wave of white robes and pointed white hats, they did.

"Oh, my God." Jon looked at Terry, appalled. "You're aware of how much the Klan hates you. How could you not know they'd find out that you'd be here?"

"I did know," Terry said. "I set it up."

"But they'll kill you!"

"No, they won't." They might try to toss him into the flames, Terry thought nervously, but they wouldn't get to him; the security guards were here for his protection. "They won't kill me," he repeated. "They'll burn the building, though. That's what Zach bought it for."

The Klansmen advanced. It didn't matter that the crowd was already filling all the space between parked groundcars; they simply pushed their way through, shoving people aside, and the people shrank back in terror. Many fled the lot entirely, though most didn't go far enough to avoid watching, with morbid fascination, what was going to happen. Terry could sense the surge of emotion from the crowd and he became aware to his distress that because the onlookers were ardent followers of the Captain of *Estel*, they believed he had some supernatural power against the Klan. They thought his presence would protect them. And he supposed that in a sense, it would; the Klan's venom would be focused not on them, but on him.

He threw open the doors and stepped forward and when he spoke, using the wireless mike Zach handed him, the crowd hushed. Tonight above all, he must evoke a mass telepathic response. "I am the Captain of *Estel*," he said, "and I have come to say in my own person something so vital that I can no longer afford to hide. In the coming election you must vote against Hiller! Tell your friends and anyone you meet to vote against him! He must not be elected, for he is the enemy of all that I stand for, and he is a friend of the Ku Klux Klan."

A murmur rose from the crowd, and then suddenly, as if by prearranged signal, the unlighted torches of the Klansmen burst into flame. For a moment Terry was thrown off balance by the memory of torches on Maclairn . . . torches by the river, on the terraces at Corwin's memorial, at his own Ritual . . . this travesty of those things sickened him, and he was jarred back to reality only by the voice of the nearest Klansman. The white robe and mask hid his identity but the voice was unforgettable. It was Quaid.

"This is not the Captain of *Estel*," the man shouted. "Do not listen to his lies! This is a fool I once knew, a braggart and a swindler, who was sentenced long ago to life in prison on Ciencia. He claimed even then to own a ship named *Estel,* though there was no such ship. There were no starships at all there. He was, and is, a megalomaniac."

"Do you deny, Quaid, that you wish to destroy all traces of belief in the human mind and spirit, wiping out everything that does not serve your own distorted view of reality?" Terry demanded. "Do you deny that while ridiculing the whole idea of symbolism, you have duped your Klan followers into letting themselves be roused by symbols of hatred to do things they would never do without those symbols?"

Confused, Quaid was at a loss for words, and Terry, hoping that the news cameras were on him, went on, "Do you deny that you have gained your own power by agreeing to place the Klan at the disposal of Commissioner Hiller and that he has been backing you in secret ever since you arrived on Earth? Do you deny that you once plotted the destruction of a world at his behest and that he or his friends paid you a large sum for your role in that failed attempt, which you hid from the other evildoers involved?"

"Don't listen to this fraud!" cried Quaid. "He has fantastic delusions about supernatural powers, with which he seeks to divert honest citizens from the real issues in the coming election and to defame a candidate he knows will take strong action to stamp out such nonsense! He is now attempting to set up a base from which to spread his absurdities even on Earth! This nest of pernicious notions must be wiped out—Klansmen, now is the time to destroy it!"

The robed figures, shouting, rushed forward to surround the windowless building, tossing their torches onto its roof. As many as could reach the doors surged inside, setting fire to any combustibles they saw and quickly retreating before the flames. Terry anticipating the crush, had moved to one side; his eyes were on a cluster of men aiming to grab him, who were being held back by the guards. He'd lost sight of Quaid—and then suddenly he turned and Quaid was only a few feet away, with a gun pointed straight at him.

Instantly Terry drew his own gun, but it had been years since he'd practiced and he was not quite fast enough; before he could pull the trigger he felt himself shoved aside. He heard the shot, assuming it had gone wild. But it hadn't. New horror struck him like a blow as he realized that Jon had seen Quaid before he did and had moved to shield him—and had now slumped to the pavement between them.

He didn't give himself time to absorb the sight. Quaid raised his gun to fire again; without hesitation Terry aimed and shot him through the heart.

~ *51* ~

FROM THEN ON it was all a blur. Terry was aware that the building was ablaze and that the crowd had moved out of the cordoned area, as had he himself, flanked by Zach and the security guards. He was conscious of cops rounding up the Klansmen, whose blatantly public acts of arson and murder they could not ignore. He smelled the acrid smoke and felt, even from a safe distance, the heat of the flames.

And he knew when the Fleet officers clamped handcuffs on him, having won an argument with the local police about who should have custody. He too was charged with murder, of course, although those who'd been watching declared that he'd killed Quaid in self-defense. But since he was already a fugitive, Fleet claimed priority.

None of this mattered to Terry. The only thing that penetrated his numbness was the knowledge that Jon had taken a bullet for him, and Jon was dead.

Later, in the Fleet lockup to which he was transported, he revived enough to worry about Alison and Gwen. Had the shootings been shown live on the news? If not, who would tell them what happened? When Fleet took over the ship, where would they go? Zach had promised to take care of them; he would explain why the building had been burned and would see that their immediate needs were met. But who would help them deal with the shock and grief?

He knew that Fleet would confiscate *Bright Hope* and would no doubt discover that it was the same ship they had seized as *Estel*. From his admission to be its captain they had booked him under his most recent true name despite the fact that his ID identified him as Tom Ryan. Mainly for the legal record, they had taken a DNA sample and would compare it with his Stelo Haveno arrest record. He was not sure whether they could find concrete proof that he had been carrying passengers without transit permits, though it was public knowledge that the Captain of *Estel* did so. Proof was unlikely to make much difference; there were plenty of charges against him without that.

It was the next day before he could bring himself to watch replays of the newscast. The reporters had got it all, his speech and Quaid's as well as the action.

Commentators were taking them seriously and League spokesmen had promised a full investigation. The open killing of Jon had created outrage that secret violence had never aroused. There were already calls for action against the Klan, and, at the moment leaderless, it was offering no organized response. Hiller's campaign manager had no comment. Hiller himself could not be reached.

The satisfaction he would otherwise have felt over these developments roused no emotion in Terry. He could think of nothing beyond his grief for Jon and the prospect of what lay ahead of him.

He had never expected that lives would be lost through his manipulation—not even Quaid's. And there wouldn't have been, from the fire alone. Should he have predicted that Quaid would have a gun when the Klan didn't ordinarily carry them? As an interrogator in the Ciencian prison Quaid always had one, so perhaps he should have realized that such a man would be used to relying on it. So was Jon's death his fault?

He couldn't stop dwelling on that question. Even if the answer was no, he could never feel reconciled to the turn events had taken. No matter that Jon's martyrdom had mobilized the public against the Klan. It should have been *him*! He had always been willing to die for Maclairn. But not to have Jon die for him.

The following day a lawyer sent by Zach came to see him. "We can get the murder charge dismissed," he said. "It was clearly self-defense and there are witnesses to testify to that. But you are also charged with inciting a riot."

Since he had in fact incited it, Terry intended to plead guilty; still, he hesitated. If he pleaded guilty there would be no trial, which would be fine if Hiller was defeated—but if he won, a trial would be the only opportunity for speaking out against him. "I'll let you know how I want to plead after the election," he told the lawyer. "I set up that riot and if it served to reveal Hiller's connection with the Klan, it accomplished its purpose. If not, I need to go public with more details."

He was allowed to attend Jon's funeral under guard. Zach had arranged it on behalf of Gwen, and apart from her and Alison, only he and López were present; but though held at the transit station in Moon orbit, it was telecast to Earth and a simultaneous memorial in Los Angeles was attended by hundreds of irate mourners. As Jon's ashes were committed to space, Terry exchanged anguished glances with Alison and Gwen, his heart aching for them, but they were permitted no private time together. Afterward he was taken to the brig at Fleet Headquarters on the Moon.

There, he was more thoroughly searched than in the temporary lockup and was given prison clothing; the small flame pin that meant so much was for the second time taken from him—to be returned with his other belongings, he was told, upon his release. He did not expect that would be soon.

When election day arrived Terry watched the news with trepidation. If Hiller lost, he could accept Jon's death as the price of saving Maclairn, plus a great many other people on Earth and elsewhere. But if he won, if the incident had no permanent effect, Jon had died for nothing, and the Klan's terrorist acts would continue—and Maclairn would be doomed.

The balloting from the colony worlds, transmitted by ansible, had already been tabulated; as expected, Hiller's opponent won there by a landslide. But Earth leaned the other way, not as heavily as in the polls, but the early returns showed that it was going to be close. Throughout the day Terry remained glued to the read-only Net monitor in his cell, unable to eat the food brought to him or to focus on the mind skills that ordinarily relaxed his body. All over the world, people desperate for better living conditions had believed Hiller's claim that he could improve them and his hypocritical promise to suppress the Klan.

The opponent, with whose record Terry wasn't familiar but who was known for honesty, had made no unrealistic promises and was therefore at a disadvantage. He had neither charisma nor secret backing from shady politicians, and the outcome would thus depend not on support for him, but on desire to defeat Hiller. Followers of *Estel* would vote against Hiller—but would enough others?

In the end, the California vote decided it. The burning building in Los Angeles with the sea of white-robed Klansmen in the foreground had been widely shown on the local news, and like the killing of Jon, it had made its mark. Quaid had not denied receiving backing from Hiller, he had sidestepped with invective against Terry and had made an obvious attempt to silence him permanently. The public hadn't been blind.

Terry, overcome with released emotion, at last gave way to tears—tears of relief at Maclairn's salvation that turned, once his icy calm was broken, into anguished weeping for Jon, for his separation from Alison, and finally for the loss of *Estel*. It took him a long time to regain his balance.

After that, life in the brig settled into a routine. He was given a cellmate, a Fleet officer accused of accepting bribes with whom he had nothing in common. He ate in the mess hall with other prisoners and worked out daily in the gym. Alison was allowed to visit once a week, but there was no privacy and their conversation was therefore restricted to mundane matters. She and Gwen were sharing an apartment at Moonbase, for which Zach was paying. Gwen thought she might get work as an engineer there; if not, they would go to Earth together as soon as he was sentenced; Alison would go in any case, since there was no demand for psychotherapists or neurofeedback technicians on the Moon. She would try to get a job at a Bramfield Club. They avoided telepathic communication, unwilling to express feelings too deep for words out of fear that their composure would crack.

It took many days of red tape and several court appearances before Terry's shooting of Quaid was ruled self-defense and his plea of guilty with respect to the riot was duly recorded. There remained the original charges against him—instigating a revolution on Ciencia, fraudulently claiming to having supernatural powers, hacking, operating a starship under a false name, ID tampering, and escape from custody—plus many counts of unauthorized transportation of passengers, of which they had managed to find hard evidence, and the so-called kidnapping of Becka, whose father identified him from a police vid.

Some of these Terry was determined to fight. There had been no revolution on Ciencia, and his lawyer was able to obtain affidavits from several officials there stating that the Estelan party had won a legitimate election. He produced expert witnesses willing to state that psi was not supernatural and that Terry had never said that he could heal, as distinguished from providing pain relief. As to the rest, there was nothing to be said and Terry pleaded no contest. Six weeks after his final flight from *Estel*, he stood in a League court on the Moon and received a sentence of twenty years at hard labor in the penal colony on Sigma Draconis Two.

He had known it was coming, and had hardened himself to the blow; but it was nevertheless painful. Twice in his life he had lost everything—his loved ones, his work, the home he cared about—and twice he had been sentenced to prison. He did not expect fate to restore his freedom this time.

His one solace was what he read on the Net. The incumbent administration was still in power, as the new one would not be inaugurated for some time; but Commissioner Hiller was keeping a low profile and the Klan was no longer immune from police surveillance. Officially-sanctioned persecution of people with psi had stopped, as the premier-elect had called it unacceptable. That much, at least, Terry had achieved. And because of his ill-fated personal appearance, comments about *Estel* were increasing. He had succeeded in starting something lasting with that symbol—people who wrote about it did have hope for the future. There was even talk of forming a real Estelan Party on Earth.

The Captain of *Estel*, Terry read, was considered a hero. No one knew exactly what had become of him— Fleet, hoping to quash a movement they considered threatening, had allowed no news coverage of his case. There were rumors that he had gone back to anonymity, that he had escaped from the law, even that he had died in the fire. But his invisibility only added to the admiration accorded him. Everything he'd said was being taken seriously, enhanced by an air of mystery.

Two days before he was to board a transport for the penal colony, Terry was informed that Alison was there to see him. To his surprise, he was led to a private visiting room—he hadn't expected they'd be permitted an unguarded farewell. He resolved to close his mind to telepathic contact, knowing that otherwise they couldn't get through it without tears.

Alison, to his amazement, was animated and smiling. "It's all set," she said. "They're letting me go with you."

"Go with me to Sigma Draconis? That can't be," he said, bewildered. "There's nothing on the planet except the penal colony."

"But families are permitted in penal colonies. Many prisoners have them."

"Oh, God, Alison. You can't go there—it's a terrible place! I won't let you do it." He couldn't bear the thought; it would be as if she herself were imprisoned. "Anyway," he pointed out, "we're not legally a family. They only accept marriage partners."

"I know. That's why we're going to be married here and now."

"Married? Alison, I—" Terry broke off. She would be hurt if he said he didn't want to marry her. And it would be a lie, of course. They had not married sooner because they'd seen no need; they had never been on the surface of a planet long enough for it to matter. Marriage meant a home and children, and they'd known they could never have that if he kept *Estel*. But now. . . .

Now it would mean committing herself to twenty years under miserable living conditions, where she would undoubtedly be required to work at some job far beneath her level of competence, where though not a convict, she'd be treated little better than if she were one. Much as he longed to have her with him, he couldn't let her make such a sacrifice.

"No," he said gently. "It would be bigamy; I'm still married to Kathryn."

"That's not true. You were declared dead, and even if you hadn't been, divorce is automatic after six years of separation."

He was silent. He'd known she wouldn't believe the excuse, but he'd hoped she would pretend to and spare him the ordeal of flatly refusing.

"Please, Terry," Alison begged, "don't leave me behind. I can't bear not to go with you. Don't you see what it would do to me to be here alone, thinking of you in that place? If you care about me, about what we've had together, you can't want that."

She meant it—despite himself, he allowed their thoughts to merge and sensed the desperation underlying her words. Her desire was as intense as his own, and he knew that to insist on protecting her would be no protection at all.

The marriage formalities had already been arranged, he found. They went together to the brig office and signed the papers, and in the presence of two guards the warden pronounced them husband and wife.

But after they kissed, Terry was taken back to his cell. They would not live as husband and wife until they reached Sigma Draconis.

Part Six: Wayfaring

~ 52 ~

THE FIRST HALF-YEAR was the hardest. From the moment
the shuttle settled onto the sterile surface of Sigma
Draconis Two, it was apparent to Terry and Alison that
the term "penal colony" was a mere euphemism. This was
not a colony in any normal sense of the word. It was a
prison, and a high-security one at that, since there was
no conceivable means of escape from it. The convicts were
confined not by bars but by the poisonous atmosphere
that surrounded its domes—not to mention the fact that
there were no ships to get away in. *Twenty years*, Terry
thought in despair. Twenty years grounded on the drea-
riest planet he had ever seen, never even permitted to go
outdoors. . . .

The latter assumption proved mistaken; convicts were
taken out daily to work in the salt mines. On first hearing
this, he assumed it was merely a figurative expression,
labor in salt mines having been a form of punishment used
on ancient Earth. To his surprise and dismay he found it
was literally true. Earth had run out of accessible minerals long ago and its salt was recovered from seawater.
But colony worlds also needed salt to sustain life, and
some of them did not have any—it existed only on planets where there had once been significant amounts of
water. Draconis had been wet in the distant past and salt

was plentiful underground, though by now the surface supply had been exhausted. Since the world had no other resources of value, Fleet had taken it over for the dual purpose of housing prisoners and providing salt for export aboard its merchant ships.

Terry wasn't used to manual labor, and the days in the mines were long and hard. While most of the heavy work was done by robotic machines, men were nevertheless needed underground to control them. Moreover, they frequently broke down, so that workers had to take over some functions to avoid bottlenecks. Considering Terry's knowledge of AI, which had been his secondary field of expertise as a Fleet officer, fixing some of the problems would have been faster and less frustrating than waiting for the arrival of technicians; but of course his experience was not on record and in any case prisoners were not permitted to usurp the technicians' privileges. Moreover, he was encumbered by a pressure suit and helmet not designed for doing skilled work.

Alison was assigned to the kitchen, not because she was female—women worked in the mines alongside men—but because she wasn't a convict and was therefore given a less arduous job. She nevertheless found it trying; though she never said so, she and Terry were too close telepathically for her to hide feelings from him. And for both of them, the worst part was not the work but the lack of control over the conduct of their daily lives.

Sigma Draconis Two was not a hospitable planet, which was why it was used only as a penal colony. Since its atmosphere was unbreathable the living accommodations were domed; the mines and salt processing facilities, however, were not sealed. Workers not accustomed to pressure suits underwent a difficult period of adjustment that Terry, being an experienced spacer, was spared. It was nonetheless unpleasant; wearing a suit and helmet in space was one thing, but being stuck in it all day under 1.3 g's was something else. At least his mind training gave him control over his temperature, so that he didn't suffer from the heat as most of the others did. Sigma Draconis was a relatively dim star compared to Earth's, which created an illusion of perpetual smog weakening its light; this did not keep the air inside a suit from getting hot.

The living quarters consisted of domed barracks, each containing small double sleeping rooms surrounding a central recreation area that was connected by enclosed passages to the mess hall and the gym. The rooms weren't called cells, but apart from absence of bars the distinction was merely one of terminology. They were cramped and windowless. Here again, however, Terry and Alison were at an advantage since they were used to living on a ship with staterooms no larger and in the physical sense, equally claustrophobic. And of course, married couples shared rooms whereas singles had to bunk with strangers who might or might not be congenial. Actually the colony was not very different from the Fleet training base on Titan where Terry had lived during two separate tours of duty. Nevertheless, the psychological impact was in no way comparable.

On Titan he had been young. An exciting future had lain ahead of him, and he hadn't minded the restrictions imposed by paramilitary life. He'd been where he wanted to be, and had known he was free to resign his commission if and when he so wished. Now he was over forty and no longer used to taking orders from anyone. He'd been captain of his own ship too long to find subservience tolerable, particularly since the guards were Fleet officers of lower rank than he had once held. To be sure, he had not been free to leave during the years on Ciencia, but except for those last weeks in prison, he'd been able to act as he chose there. And he hadn't had to watch Alison struggle to adjust to a lifestyle unlike any she had ever experienced.

Fortunately, convicts were segregated according to

the nature of their offenses; he and Alison were not housed with violent criminals, and he knew she was safe from the kind of thing usually encountered in prisons on Earth. Neither of them had to worry about being attacked or raped. Still, with very few exceptions their fellow-prisoners were not people they'd have picked as friends. Many were of a low sort, with very little on their minds beyond bodily appetites and crude conversation. Activity in the rec room consisted mainly of gambling. Terry did not like to think what went on in the singles' communal washrooms; married couples lived in a different section of the dome. In the mess hall and gym, at least, behavior was no worse than what could be seen anywhere.

In theory, the population of the colony included people like Zach, those who'd tampered with League databases or who, like himself, had engaged in smuggling. But apparently the smart ones did not get caught, at least Terry didn't meet any—to his regret, as he would have liked their company. He didn't have much in common with men sentenced for theft or fraud. To be sure, the long hours of mine labor left him too tired to care about what he did with the rest of his time, and what little of it was free he spent with Alison. They found themselves withdrawing from social interaction, retreating to their room and their bed, clinging together for comfort more than for the sex they were often too exhausted to enjoy.

Sometimes, on days when Alison had to get up before dawn for the early kitchen shift, Terry lay alone in the dark thinking about the Elders. They had given him *Estel*; how would they feel if they knew he had lost it? Would they see his defeat of the Klan as confirmation of their hopes for the human race, or had the mere existence of the Klan been a setback that brought it perilously near the danger point? He wished, suddenly, that he could know. He would never know their reaction to what was happening, good or bad; he would never know whether humans were accepted into the alien Federation. For the first time in his life, this aspect of mortality struck him as tragic. People never knew what would happen to their descendants, but having been given an extraordinary glimpse of what *might* be, he began to feel that as time went on the frustration of not knowing might prove unbearable.

He also, in those dark hours, found himself recalling his life on Maclairn. Perhaps because thinking of *Estel* was so painful, he retreated to the earlier time when he'd been happy and secure in the belief that however far he might travel, he would always have a base, a loved home—one specific place in the universe to which his heart was anchored. Despite all that had happened since he was exiled, the good and the bad, he still missed that world. He still longed to see it once more, though he would never be free to go there; and the fact that he had again saved it from destruction was ample consolation for the deprivations he was now forced to endure.

Prisoners were allowed no personal communication with Earth or any other world except for rare messages to and from their immediate families. Since neither Terry nor Alison had close relatives, the exception didn't apply to them. They were cut off from the wider universe. They could not even get a look at it; just as on Ciencia, Terry never saw the stars, for though stars were visible from Draconis, miners were taken into the domes before dark.

Yet the colony was not quite as isolated as Ciencia; League news received via ansible was posted periodically by the authorities. Thus he knew that the Ku Klux Klan had been put down—some of its members were here on Draconis, he supposed, though being classed as violent, they were not in his dome. And he knew that there had been upheaval in the League government. After Hiller's defeat the voters on Earth, mobilized by awareness of government collusion with the Klan, had forced a thorough investigation and in the next election had thrown out the rest of the administration. Although equally bureaucratic and regimentary, the new one was at least more

liberal with respect to human rights; the incoming premier had announced that freedom of belief concerning
human nature would from now on have equal status with
freedom of religion, and no persecution of psi capability
would be tolerated.

He had brought that about, Terry thought with wonder. He had set in motion events that not only saved
Maclairn but would free it to work toward its goal. Lying
in the dark beside Alison, he grieved for the misery she
was experiencing, for Jon's death, and for the loss of *Estel*.
At times he nearly wept. But he could not regret the action he'd taken, nor could he curse fate for its consequences. What he'd accomplished was worth the price.

~ *53* ~

NEAR THE END of his third year of imprisonment, Terry
was unexpectedly called in from the mines one day and
told to report to the warden's office. What now? he wondered, struggling out of his pressure suit and into clean
clothes. He had by this time encountered fellow-prisoners who had heard the *Estel* rumors—even several who
knew Zach—and had talked with them at length about
new mind-powers, inspiring enthusiastic response when
he explained that such powers would make people less
vulnerable to government control. Had the prison officials found out about his proselytizing, and disapproved?
He hadn't done anything else he might be disciplined for.
Yet since freedom of thought about human abilities was
now specifically protected under the law, they had no right
to prevent him from discussing such ideas.

"In there, Steward," said the sublieutenant on duty,
motioning him to a door on his left. "Your attorney's here
to consult with you."

Astonished, Terry entered the adjacent room. Attorney? He knew no attorneys except the one who'd handled

his case, who would hardly have come all the way to Draconis to talk to him. Occasionally legal advisers did arrive on the weekly supply ship to see prisoners who were appealing their conviction. But no supporter could have initiated an appeal on his behalf when he had pleaded guilty.

"Hello, Terry," said the tall, vibrant man seated at the desk in front of him. "My name is Gabriel Travis, and I was sent here by an employer who chooses to remain anonymous. Sit down—I have quite a lot to tell you."

Terry sat, feeling more bewildered than ever. This man looked younger than was consistent with his calm self-assurance. Except for that, he didn't seem the sort of person who would be sent halfway across the galaxy on an errand, as he was obviously highly intelligent and accustomed to being in charge.

"This will come as a shock to you," Travis went on, "but I'm happy to say that my employer has arranged your pardon. You and your wife will be returning with me on the supply ship tonight."

For a moment Terry thought he couldn't have heard right. It was too improbable to be anything but an illusion. Finally he managed to blurt out, "How is that possible? Fleet would never endorse a move to pardon me— or did someone intervene?" Perhaps, he thought, the Premier knew that he'd helped to get him elected.

"The League administration took action," Travis said, "but only after long effort on the part of my employer, who has wealth and influence. You weren't told because he didn't want to raise your hopes before being sure it could be managed."

"I–I don't know what to say. I don't see how I can ever repay—"

"No repayment is necessary. But if you want to please him, you'll continue to offer your message of hope to the colonies. He is a very strong advocate of the ideas you're known to have been spreading."

"It goes without saying that I'll do that to the best of my ability. Does he have a preference as to what colony I go to?"

"It's his wish that you travel to as many as possible."

"How can I? I'll have no money to pay for passage, and I no longer have a ship."

"You do have a ship," said Travis, smiling. "You have *Estel*."

"Not anymore," Terry said sadly. "As your employer must know, it was confiscated. I suppose it was sold long ago, hopefully as a charter ship rather than as scrap." It still pained him to think about it.

"It was sold by Fleet at auction," Travis agreed. "My employer was the high bidder, through me as his agent."

Stunned, Terry was suddenly aware of what he had not grasped at first—the man had said *Estel*. Not *Bright Hope*, but *Estel*. Surely they wouldn't have auctioned it under that name when they wanted to end its influence. "How did you know it was mine?" he asked.

"We found the hidden transponder; it is still registered in your name."

Terry was speechless; no words seemed adequate, so he remained silent.

"You'll be given possession of the ship," Travis continued, "but there are several conditions to which you must agree. I need your word that you'll honor them."

"Of course. Anything I can do in good conscience, I will." This was all too good to be true, Terry thought. There must be a catch; perhaps, since he was already classed as a criminal, they planned to use him in some illegal underground operation.

"First," said Travis, "you must promise never to make any attempt to learn my employer's identity."

Terry nodded. "If that's what he wants, I'll respect it. But whatever secrets he has would be safe with me in any case."

"I'm sure they would, but he insists on total anonymity.

Second, you must never, under any circumstances, go to Earth."

"I pledged to stay away from Earth long ago, for reasons I'm not free to tell you. I broke that pledge once to confront the Klan, but you can be sure I won't break it again."

Travis went on, "Third, you must agree not to violate any laws. After getting you pardoned we don't want to have to bail you out a second time."

Frowning, Terry asked, "Does that include smuggling? I don't see any other way to earn a living if I'm to travel instead of staying put where I could get a job."

"You will be offered legal charter work. My employer has many connections; he'll have no trouble locating clients to send you."

A limited amount of charter flying did occur, Terry knew—cases where some company that could afford it wanted to expedite transport of a few people or items instead of booking space on a scheduled Fleet liner. He had never considered such work, except the illegal refugee transport Zach had paid for, because no free trader would have the contacts to get charter jobs on his own.

"Finally," Travis told him, "you must engage a copilot of my employer's choosing."

Why not? Terry thought. He hadn't any other means of finding a copilot, and no one he might get could ever replace Jon. But he supposed this meant that his mysterious benefactor wanted to check up on him. . . .

"No, he won't be there to spy," Travis said hastily, and abruptly Terry realized that the man was a trained telepath. His mind was closed to probing, yet he'd picked up the thought and responded. That put a whole new face on the situation. These people weren't just supporters of what he believed. At least some of them had mind training, which meant they were in contact with mentors.

Were the mentors behind this? Had the Maclairn Foundation put up the money? It had connections and influence, certainly. It kept its actions secret. And the mentors had been seeking the Captain of *Estel* for a long time.

He would have to be very careful.

He shouldn't get involved at all. He shouldn't agree to take on a copilot who was undoubtedly also telepathic; he would have to guard his thoughts constantly for the rest of his life. Yet he had no choice. He couldn't turn down release from prison, nor could he reject this miraculous chance to regain *Estel*.

"Okay," he said, hoping his reservations weren't being perceived. "Is he qualified to handle jumps?"

"Certainly. He is an excellent pilot, and has in fact been in command of *Estel* since we purchased it."

"Then why would he want to be merely copilot?"

"That's not a problem for him; he is dedicated to your cause. You will be captain, and he won't question your orders," Travis assured him.

"Is he going to be reporting to you?"

"It's true that he may be in touch with my employer from time to time; he has his own reasons for that, connected to his own background. You must not ask him to explain. But you can rely on his discretion—as long as you don't violate the conditions to which you have agreed, he will not report anything that you wish to conceal."

And if he did violate them, the copilot no doubt had the authority to take the ship back, Terry thought. Well, that was all right; there weren't any he objected to. In any case, if he couldn't go to Earth they couldn't be planning to put him in touch with mentors, so the secret of the Elders would be safe.

The secret of Maclairn, if by any chance the "employer" was not the Maclairn Foundation, might be harder to keep to himself. The probability that Travis and his associates had been trained by mentors didn't mean they'd been let in on that secret, and he would not have the justification for revealing it that he'd had with his former crew. But he would deal with that problem when it arose. For now, all he wanted was to see Alison and share with her the joy of their release.

"She's waiting in the outer office for you," Travis said, confirming his telepathic awareness. "Go to her, and then collect your things."

~ *54* ~

THE SUPPLY SHIP left Draconis that night and departed from the Sigma Draconis system within a few hours. Never before in his years of star travel had Terry been so happy to emerge from a jump.

They headed for the Fleet base on the Moon. During the days of approach in normal space, Terry and Alison spent most of the time in their stateroom catching up on sleep; it had been nearly three years since they'd been able to truly rest. At first he could hardly believe that mine labor was behind him—he kept waking with the thought that in the next moment the bell would ring to rouse him for another shift. But eventually the daze wore off and he was infused by the elation of being free.

"I never stopped believing that fate would free you," Alison told him. "It favored you so often in the past, there had to be some meaning in it—some future role that you were destined to fill."

"I doubt that I'll be called on to do anything dramatic again," Terry said, fingering the priceless flame pin that had been given back to him. "Saving Maclairn twice in one lifetime is more than enough to account for Aldren's precognitive dream about my having some extraordinary destiny. But I will devote the rest of my life to living up to what's expected of the Captain of *Estel*, Alison. You're right that there's got to be meaning in our escape, even if it's just that someone with power is willing to back me."

During meals they sat with Gabriel Travis and talked

about their plans. "There's a lot of persuasion yet to be done," Travis said. "The fact that belief in psi is now protected doesn't mean that most people share it. It has to be absorbed into the collective unconscious of humankind."

"It will take a long time for that to happen," Terry agreed.

"It's already begun to happen on Earth, at least among small groups."

"Has there been much progress? I've been—out of touch." He had been out of touch with Maclairn for nearly twenty years now, and nowhere else had success been described in those terms. He rather hoped that Travis might elaborate and thereby provide some hint as to whether he had contacts there. But remembering that he'd promised to make no effort to learn his benefactor's identity, Terry didn't pursue the issue.

"As you know, enough people accept the possibility of psi to have stirred up violent opposition to it," Travis said. "Are you aware that a conspiracy within the former government, and not just Hiller, was behind the Klan?"

"Yes," said Terry. "I've assumed so for a long time. Am I right in assuming now that the new administration has succeeded in getting rid of that faction?"

Travis nodded. "The credit for that belongs to you. 'In the name of the Captain of *Estel*' has become a catchphrase, and recently an Estelan Party has sprung up, small but growing. There will still be opponents of change, but from now on they'll have no real clout. All the same, winning people over will be a slow process. Symbolism will help, which is why my employer feels it's vital to keep the idea of *Estel* alive."

"It was the symbol that attracted converts, more than anything we actually did," Alison said. "So I wonder if it's going to work as well now that Terry's identity is known."

"It's not known to the public," Travis said. "Just to my employer and a few of his friends, aside from Fleet, which is keeping it quiet."

"Then I think we should keep it that way," Terry declared, thinking not only of the symbolic value but of his desire to avoid adulation. "Go on traveling as *Bright Hope* so that *Estel* will be seen only when I purposely reveal it to someone, even though I don't have to worry about Quaid's bounty hunters anymore."

"That's been our intention. We've kept it hidden since we bought it, and its real transponder has not been used. The ship's had a thorough overhaul, by the way. It's fueled, provisioned, and ready to go."

"How do I get to it?" Terry asked, hoping there wouldn't be much delay.

"When we reach Moon orbit its shuttle will meet this starship."

"Really? I'm surprised that was authorized." Fleet ships didn't dock with private ones; Captain Garick had done so only because Undine was too isolated for it to be observed. Near Moonbase there was plenty of Fleet traffic.

"It wasn't," Travis admitted. "We'll be a long way out and the pilot is cooperative; as I told you, my employer is wealthy."

Another night passed before the rendezvous. Now completely rested, Terry was unable to sleep; his mind was too full of wonder. The future stretched ahead of him, unknowable yet full of hope. At forty-three, he might be Captain of *Estel* for at least another half-century. Surely in that time he'd be able to make a real impact on thought in the colonies—an impact that would bring humankind closer to the destiny of which the Elders had told him long ago.

As in the dark days on Draconis, his thoughts turned to the Elders; but now with a resurgence of faith. "I suspect your influence will be wide," Laesara had said to him. She was psi-gifted; perhaps it had been precognition. Why else would fate have intervened in his life so often?

When the ship's comm announced the completion of docking, Terry and Alison picked up their duffels and waited by the airlock, hearts pounding with anticipation. "Good luck, Terry," Gabriel Travis said. "We won't be seeing each other again, but I'll watch for news of what you're achieving."

"Thanks for everything," Terry said, feeling the words were inadequate. "I don't know how to express my gratitude to the employer you can't name—"

"Don't worry about that," Travis said. "Just do what you'd do if you'd never been imprisoned, and our expectations will be fulfilled."

The lock cycled, and they walked through the open passage to the shuttle—the familiar shuttle belonging to *Estel*.

A slender, sandy-haired man was waiting by the hatch. "Welcome, Captain Steward," he said with warmth. "I'm Liam Holden, your copilot."

Terry stared at him in shocked recognition. Holden, the commander who had helped him escape from Stelo Haveno! Young as he had seemed then, he now looked no older than he had on that day. Most certainly he wasn't old enough to have retired from flight status. "My God!" he exclaimed. "Did they catch you after I left? If you were forced out of Fleet because of what you did for me—"

"I was never in Fleet. I was no more a commander than you were a warrant officer."

That was even worse; impersonating a senior officer was a felony. "Tell me you didn't serve time," he said, thinking unhappily that if Holden had escaped from custody, that could well explain his willingness to accept a subordinate role like this where he would remain obscure.

"Don't worry, sir," the pilot said. "I usually manage to avoid trouble."

"But then how—why—did you end up here? You were the best pilot I've ever flown with. If you're not evading the law you could have your own command. And how did you make connections with the man who bought *Estel*?"

"Our mutual benefactor has wealth and connections, as you were told," Holden said, "and he has eyes and ears in many places. He has kept track of the whereabouts of *Estel* for a very long time."

"Are you saying he *sent* you to Stelo Haveno?" That would explain a lot he'd wondered about, Terry realized, but it would also raise new questions.

"That's one way to look at it," said the pilot. "I'm not free to say more, and you've promised to make no attempt to learn about him."

"I can never thank you enough for what you did—and I understand that you've been taking care of *Estel* since it was auctioned, so I have even more reason to be grateful to you."

"It was my privilege, sir. It's a beautiful ship." He meant this, Terry perceived; Holden's feelings came through clearly although his mind was closed to deeper probing. As had been evident at Stelo Haveno, he was a strong telepath, naturally gifted as well as trained; if he chose to pry it would be very hard to keep secrets from him.

"You needn't call me 'sir'—this isn't Fleet," he said. "I'm Terry."

"And I'm Liam," the man replied, smiling again. "I hope we'll be friends, Terry, but I won't forget that you're captain. To serve under the Captain of *Estel* is a high honor, and I'm happy to have been given the opportunity."

After reintroducing Alison, Terry went to the cockpit. Liam held back, motioning him to the command pilot's seat.

"You take it this time," Terry said. "I'm rusty; I haven't flown for nearly three years." He didn't really think he'd lost his edge, but if he had, he didn't want to find out with Liam beside him. The young man had far greater skill than a copilot's job required; if he'd never been in Fleet, where had he learned to handle a fast, high-powered Fleet shuttle like the one he'd escaped in?

As they approached *Estel*, Terry's heart swelled with happiness. To be back aboard in real life when for so long he'd been there only in dreams . . . he had never imagined such a turn of events. Excitement rose in him until he felt it would overflow and release the secrets he must keep hidden.

The rendezvous and docking went smoothly. As they entered the ship he paused for a moment, thinking of Jon. Then, leaving Alison to make herself at home, he proceeded to the bridge and settled into the place where he had always known he belonged.

"What are your orders, Captain?" Liam asked, with the air not of a subordinate but of a friend and equal.

"We'll head out to jump distance," Terry said. "I'm not sure yet where I'll go first. But I'm going to visit all the worlds in the League before I'm through."

~ 55 ~

FROM THE BEGINNING, Terry liked Liam. He was a good companion despite his reticence about his own background, of which he revealed nothing; his wholehearted belief in spreading acceptance of advanced mind-powers drew them together. More importantly, Terry's telepathic sensitivity told him that this was a man who was not only a congenial friend who shared his goals, but wise for his age and absolutely trustworthy.

Though it was apparent that Liam had had mind training, he never said where or when he'd received it. He'd shown when they met at Stelo Haveno that he was aware of Maclairn's existence, of course, and had heard of the Stewards of the Flame. So if he was not a former member of *Shepard*'s crew, as Terry had then assumed, what was he? He knew about the Bramfield Clubs and the work of the mentors there, but could not be pinned down as to any specific personal experience; and since Terry had to steer clear of the subject of his own training he made no attempt to draw him out. With one exception, they were limited to discussing generalities.

The exception was the matter of Alison's training. This first arose when, soon after they boarded *Estel*, Liam took something from the secure storage cabinet on the bridge and handed it to him. "I imagine you'll be glad to have these back," he said.

The neurofeedback helmets! Terry had not dared to hope that they had been retained when the ship was sold. His personal possessions hadn't been; Alison had been able to take only her own clothes, most of which she'd had to discard when they embarked for Draconis. They both would have to buy new ones at the first world they visited, and he'd have to replace his lost tablet computer as well as the rest of the neurofeedback gear. But somehow, the helmets had escaped confiscation.

"They were hidden with the true transponder," Liam explained. But that was no real explanation, because Terry had not put them there and Alison said she hadn't done so either. And he'd been wondering why Fleet hadn't found that transponder. When pressed, Liam told him that Gabriel Travis had inspected the ship with an eye to buying it before Fleet had a chance to search it thoroughly. It seemed strange, however, that Travis had known what to look for.

In any case, it was necessary to tell Liam how the helmets had been used, and this led to the revelation that Alison had gone to the Bramfield Club in New Afrika and met mentors there. That couldn't be concealed, for she wanted to continue with neurofeedback and refresh abilities she'd had no opportunity to practice in the past three years. "How did you get hold of the helmets?" Liam inquired.

Terry told him. "I did the programming for processing

their output myself," he added, realizing that this must make him sound like a genius since he couldn't mention having studied the original source code on Titan. Liam didn't question it. Nor did he ask why, if he was aware there were mentors in New Afrika, he hadn't made contact with them instead of sending Alison and Gwen to the Bramfield Club alone. But he didn't let the subject of New Afrika drop.

"If I may make a suggestion, Captain," he said, "there's charter work to be had in that colony. I heard about it only yesterday and there are no private ships there right now, so we might be in time to get the job. There would be no passengers, just data too sensitive to send by ansible."

Terry froze. Travis had promised that he'd be offered charter jobs and he certainly needed to earn some money; they had only Alison's credits—which unlike his own had not been confiscated—to cover immediate expenses. But New Afrika, the one place apart from Earth and Maclairn that he could not go. . . .

He couldn't avoid saying so; even if he were able to make a plausible excuse to turn down the job, sooner or later the issue would arise again. Best to make plain from the outset that as captain, he didn't have to account for his decisions. "Unfortunately, I'll have to pass on it," he said. "I have reasons to avoid New Afrika."

"You wouldn't have to go to the surface," Liam pointed out. "I can make all the arrangements if you authorize me to do so on your behalf."

That was true enough; since he trusted Liam implicitly with the ship, there was no reason not to trust him with business dealings. And he'd surely like to find out what was now being said about *Estel* on New Afrika's Net. So it was to that world they went first, and Terry, logging on from orbit as he had in the past, found that discussion was very much alive. The story of how the Captain of *Estel* had faced down the Ku Klux Klan had been endlessly repeated and, not surprisingly, exaggerated. No one knew what had happened to him afterward, but people suspected that he had escaped somehow and gone undercover, and that should persecution of psi arise again, he would appear out of space to save its victims.

"They expect too much of me," he said to Alison in dismay. "I can't work miracles. And I can't be everywhere, even if I help a few people as we did before."

"Yes, you can," she assured him. "You are a symbol, and the symbol *can* be everywhere—isn't that what we're aiming for?"

It was. And from that time forward, Terry carried the symbol to countless worlds.

He lost track of where he'd been after awhile, relying on *Estel*'s log for the details. They followed a routine: a jump, days in normal space learning about the next colony from the knowledgebase, then more days connecting with its Net. Sometimes they contacted Port Control as *Bright Hope* and went to the surface; other times, if there was no charter work, they stayed in high orbit and made their presence known as the mysterious, unseen *Estel*. Charter work was plentiful; Liam had contacts on many worlds, presumably through Gabriel Travis, with whom he admitted he communicated via ansible from the larger colonies. Occasionally they carried passengers, but in most cases they merely served as couriers.

Once in a while they returned to Skyros, where they had many friends; and from there Terry was able to contact Zach, who had remained on Earth and—after forging his own ID to remove all traces of his past—had become involved in politics. He'd decided that the support of freedom-loving candidates was where his wealth would do the most good. He was, of course, still in touch with his network, and had by no means given up illegal activities he considered harmless. But he no longer took money for such work.

As time wore on, Terry's liking for Liam grew and he

came to rely on him more and more. He was as skilled at everything else as at flying, including engineering; they had no need to enlarge the crew. His quiet efficiency also extended to business arrangements with clients, but he refused the partnership in charter proceeds that Terry offered him and would take no more than his agreed-upon salary as copilot. It became obvious that despite his youth he was well qualified to be captain of his own ship, yet he never questioned Terry's authority or made him feel his command decisions were superfluous. How, Terry wondered, could anyone so competent be so lacking in ambition?

One clue was that Liam was a loner who seemed to have no need for contact with people. Though he was friendly when with them and was well-liked by everyone he met, he never sought company by choice. He didn't mind staying with the ship while Terry and Alison spent time on the surface of a world, and in fact he didn't seem to be lonely while they were in their stateroom aboard ship, something that had initially worried Terry. He often spent free time in his own stateroom, reading, so that they had the lounge to themselves—he was an even more voracious reader than Terry and despite wide knowledge of science seemed especially fascinated by the history of civilization.

After awhile, when it seemed unnatural for Liam to be content so long without an intimate relationship, Terry broached the subject. "If there's anyone you'd like to have aboard, I'll be glad to take on another crew member," he said.

"Thanks, but it's not necessary," Liam replied. "I'm comfortable with the way things are." And telepathically, Terry perceived that this was true; yet there was nothing unhealthy about it. Sometime in Liam's hidden past, he decided, there must have been tragedy. He must have lost a loved one for whom he was still grieving.

Or perhaps he met someone on the rare occasions

when he took leave. He did disappear periodically on the surface of one planet or another, sometimes for several days—especially when they stopped at Stelo Haveno for hyperdrive maintenance. He never said where he went or what he did, nor did he permit it to be sensed telepathically; but he invariably returned on schedule.

They had traveled together for nearly a year before Liam admitted how much he knew about Maclairn. Terry and Alison had been extremely careful not to mention it in his presence, since though he was surely aware that they shared the secret, he apparently didn't want to discuss it. Then one day when Terry was pondering the Maclairnans' long-range plan, he was suddenly aware that Liam had far greater knowledge of it than he'd supposed, more than merely hearing about the colony could account for. At first, fearing that he'd slipped and projected telepathically, he clamped his mind tight against sensing, but in the next moment he realized that it was Liam who had slipped—or that perhaps he had deliberately leaked the extent of his involvement. He certainly wasn't feeling any surprise.

"There's no need for us to hide it from each other anymore," Liam said. "What you're doing is what the Maclairnans aim to do on Earth. That's why it's so important."

A startling suspicion flooded into Terry's mind, one that would explain a lot that had puzzled him. "Liam—are you . . . Maclairnan? Born on Maclairn, though not a mentor?"

"No," Liam told him. "I've never been there, though I've met people who have. To visit as an observer one must be invited, and few are, as I'm sure you know."

"Has Gabriel Travis been there?"

"No, though he too has been informed."

That left the mysterious employer. There could be no doubt now that it was the Maclairn Foundation; who else could have revealed so much to Liam and Travis?

Evidently the implication of an individual benefactor was a smokescreen; perhaps the Foundation's leaders wished to judge his success in continuing what he'd started before filling him in on the details. What irony, he thought, that they'd hidden them from someone who was already far more familiar with Maclairn than even the invited observers!

But as weeks and then years passed, he wondered why they still kept him in the dark. Once in a while charter work took him to New Afrika again, and from there to Earth's moon and back; it occurred to him that he might be handling communication between the mentors there and those on Earth—or even, via *Promise*, those on Maclairn itself, where no ansible existed. Yet he couldn't think of any reason why they'd want to conceal this from him.

From year to year the colonies' interest in new mind faculties increased. Terry no longer had to hack the Nets to insert references to *Estel*; it had become a legend known and discussed everywhere, and his comments were welcomed. Among people who believed it was more than a legend, it was generally believed that he, Terry Steward—a name he now used openly, but had not been made public at the time of his arrest—was in contact with *Estel's* captain and was authorized to act in his name. He didn't deny this, but he offered no hints as to where or when they met.

Once, after learning that its current regime welcomed interstellar visitors, he returned to Ciencia. Because people there knew him by sight as the Captain of *Estel* under the name Terry Rivera, he was able to communicate with them only via the Net, from orbit, so that they wouldn't connect that persona with his current identity. And Alison couldn't reveal her presence. Neither of them minded not visiting the planet's dreary, cloud-enshrouded surface again. But it was good to be in touch with former friends and hear details about the successful establishment of a new government.

With one person only was their reunion complete.

Shortly after reporting *Bright Hope*'s presence in orbit, Terry was startled by a familiar voice requesting permission to rendezvous. It was Gwen. She'd taken a job as a maintenance engineer on Earth, too absorbed in her grief for Jon to care how little she liked it there; but after several years she'd gone back to Ciencia. Eventually she had married and was now working as an engineer and shuttle pilot in her husband's charter business. Not having known of Terry's release from Draconis, she was elated to find that he was indeed behind the widespread rumors that the Captain of *Estel* still roamed the galaxy; she'd been afraid they were merely legends.

Terry and Alison now had many friends on various worlds into whose homes they were invited; and he began to speak more formally to small groups. In this he was spectacularly successful, for his telepathic rapport with his listeners was as strong as it had been on Toliman. People came away utterly convinced that in the future humans would have mind-powers greatly to be desired.

The biggest problem, Terry felt, was that unlike residents of Earth and New Afrika, most of these people had no opportunity for mind training themselves. Having found himself capable of providing breakthrough sessions as he had for Jon, he and Alison did train a few special individuals aboard *Estel*, people they trusted with the secret of his identity. But no mentors had come to other colonies—to his great relief, as he would have had to avoid them—and that seemed rather unfair. Liam apparently didn't know why the Maclairn Foundation failed to extend its secret outreach, but he speculated that focusing all its effort on Earth was considered the most effective way to influence humanity's collective unconscious. Remembering that he'd been told the collective unconscious didn't extend from planet to planet, Terry had to agree. And perhaps, he thought with awe, they were relying on *him* to prepare the other worlds, so that mentors would be welcomed when they arrived.

~ *56* ~

THE YEARS TURNED into decades. Gradually, the concept of psi passed into the mainstream on Earth; while only a small minority of the population was psi-gifted, these people were now not merely accepted, but admired. Opponents, though vehement, now had no public support and little influence. Mind training for preservation of health, too, became common; Bramfield Clubs were to be found in every major city and the existence of instructors called mentors was no longer hidden, although their origin was still carefully concealed. The Estelan Party grew into a major one, and Ciencia was not the only colony where it won elections. Terry found it hard to believe that the name he had chosen long ago for an imaginary ship was now universally applied to a philosophy he hadn't originated and a political movement his illegal actions had inspired.

In his youth, Terry's deepest wish had been to explore new planets, those not yet settled, perhaps so far undiscovered. That was the work he'd chosen in Fleet, and when he acquired *Estel* he'd planned to go back to it. Responsibilities had intervened, but as the need to spread now-common ideas decreased, he began to think about it again. He had earned enough through charter work to last for awhile, and Liam had no objections although he didn't share Terry's enthusiasm. It seemed justifiable to take what amounted to a vacation.

They bought prospecting equipment, Jon's having been lost when the ship was confiscated, and hired a small crew. Then Terry set out to do what he'd always longed to do, and traveled far off the beaten track. He made no startling discoveries—unopened worlds were, after all, very much like colonized ones if not less well-endowed. Wryly, he recalled having once wished he might discover aliens if he flew far enough; fate, he thought, fulfilled wishes in ironic ways. Nevertheless he enjoyed the sense of not knowing what each new landfall would reveal, and they came back with enough rare minerals to pay for the trip. So over the course of time he made more such trips, even after he passed eighty.

Neither Terry nor Alison showed much aging; their mind training, consistently practiced, had protected them from the physiological effects of stress that produce bodily deterioration. Silver-haired now, they were otherwise still in their prime, with the strong, lean bodies they had possessed since youth. Maclairnans lived in good health to be a hundred and twenty or more; Terry didn't think he would last quite that long since he'd had less ongoing training, but he was happy that Alison seemed likely to keep her health as long as he did.

Liam, once past his prolonged youthful appearance, never seemed to age at all. He couldn't be more than twenty years younger than Terry, yet his face was unlined and his hair was still blond when Terry reached ninety. Then, abruptly, it turned white overnight, as if he'd decided it might otherwise be too noticeable. Terry had never heard that mind training extended to control over hair color, but then, Liam was far more psi-gifted than he was—that had been evident for a long time. No wonder he'd been shy about mingling with people, born so unlike the rest.

It was shortly after this that a new colony named Futuro was established by emigrants from Earth, all of whom had received mind training from mentors. News of it spread among the other worlds and was greeted with elation by the Estelans there. To them, it was the first world ever to be populated entirely by people with new mind faculties who would pass them on to their children. Terry, Alison, and Liam, who knew it was not the first, were equally thrilled. At last it was happening! The human race was starting to evolve.

Much as he wanted to see Futuro, Terry dared not go

there, for he assumed mentors would be included among the settlers. Liam, however, heard through Gabriel Travis that there were none. Maclairnans couldn't handle all training forever, and mind skills could be learned more easily by adolescents than by adults, so less skill on the part of the instructor was required. The essential initial ordeal wasn't as demanding when presented as a rite through which kids attained adulthood; that was how it worked on Maclairn, where young mentors learned to conduct it. Now Earthborn instructors had evidently been taught to do so.

When *Estel* arrived at Futuro it was barely past the camp stage; the world had been terraformed by Fleet but the colonists themselves were responsible for all building. It wasn't as harsh an environment as some, and unlike Maclairn's founders they were receiving regular shipments of supplies. Everyone was happy to be there, working together as a team—they had, of course, been individually chosen for ability and enthusiasm. Terry was struck by the telepathic accord among them, which though unconscious on the part of most, was immediately apparent to him. He had almost forgotten what it was like to be in such company.

Though the colony admitted no tourists he and Alison were welcomed as special guests, for the Futurans knew his reputation for promoting Estelan beliefs and wanted to hear what he had to say. "Whether or not there's really a Captain of *Estel*," they told him, "he'll go down in history as the herald of the new way. Our kids have been fans of him since they were small—*Estel* toys and vids are their favorites."

Toys? Vids? Terry needed no words to convey his astonishment. "No one knows what *Estel* looks like, let alone its captain," he managed to say.

"Everyone knows, just as they know Superman, or King Arthur, or any other figure cast in the role of a hero. It doesn't matter if the image is literally accurate. What counts is what people think it means."

And Terry realized, with awe and thankfulness, that this was true.

The founding of Futuro was a turning point. Now, when they visited other worlds, Terry spoke not just in friends' homes but to crowds. They turned out to meet him, listening with awe to his description of their hope's fulfillment in the new colony. He had been repeating the same words about the human mind over and over for more than fifty years, yet he never tired of it, since the current of conviction went both ways; the telepathic link with his audience was as inspiring each time as it had been long ago at his trial on Ciencia. He had had a strange life, Terry thought, yet the second half of it had brought him happiness—more than he'd ever expected to find.

"You earned it," said Liam. "Twelve years of exile on Ciencia, the near-loss of your life more than once to save Maclairn, nearly three years' imprisonment on Draconis—"

Terry stared at him. Liam had known about Draconis, of course—but how had he known about Ciencia? Though he was well aware of what he'd accomplished there, how could he have known he'd been exiled from somewhere else? No human alive knew that except Alison and Gwen— nor did anyone else know about the first time he'd nearly lost his life. Had he in fact leaked more telepathically than he'd realized?

Perhaps it didn't matter. Liam certainly hadn't picked up anything about the Elders, and if he hadn't done so in all these years, it wasn't likely to happen now. They went on as before, and Terry scarcely noticed when his hundredth birthday passed.

But happiness can't last forever. When he was a hundred sixteen, Alison died. She had shown no signs of decline, and though somewhat less energetic than usual during her last weeks, she seemed healthy. Then one night, as they cuddled close in bed as always, she told him silently, *It's been a good life, Terry. What we've had together is all I ever wanted. I love you—don't ever forget how much I love you....* In the morning she was gone.

Terry, at first unbelieving, was so stricken that he felt unable to move; he lay beside her still form for half an hour before stumbling out of the stateroom to call Liam. All his mind training ebbed away and he could not control his tears, let alone his inner physical reactions.

With Liam's help he shrouded Alison's body and committed it to space, where they had spent their years together. That was the kind of burial he himself wished to have. "When my time comes," he told Liam. "I'm counting on you to remember."

"Your time isn't coming for many years yet," Liam declared with confidence.

"Don't insult me with platitudes. I've already far exceeded a normal lifespan." Though it was true that physically he was still vigorous, it didn't seem likely that he would reach the age people did on Maclairn—they received advanced mind training in midlife for a reason, and he hadn't had that training.

It was miraculous that Alison had lived as long as she had with only the training he'd been able to give her. He should be thankful for that, Terry knew—for her life to be shorter than his was what he'd most feared, his reason for taking the risks he had to get the neurofeedback helmets. But having gotten them, he hadn't expected her to die while he still felt perfectly normal.

Alison had been his lover and constant companion for nearly eighty years. She had given up the comforts of living on a planet's surface to stay with him. She'd accepted the necessity of forgoing a home and children. She had supported his mission wholeheartedly and never questioned any of the difficulties it entailed. Now Terry did not see how he was going to survive without her. He had never felt such overwhelming pain . . . not since he was torn away from Kathryn. It all came rushing back; he hadn't thought about Kathryn while he was with Alison, except for those few days on the Moon, but now the grief was doubled, and he was crushed by it.

He could commission no tangible memorial for Alison; they hadn't spent enough time on any particular world for there to be an appropriate site. He would get a portrait to hang in his stateroom when he next visited a city equipped to make hard copies of images, but there was no permanence in that. Their only home had been *Estel*, and what would happen to *Estel* when he was gone?

Liam was supportive. They resumed their normal routine, revisiting all the worlds where Terry had friends. But he went to the surface alone. Liam refused to take part in discussions with colonists, and since one of them had to stay with the ship anyway, Terry didn't urge him. Liam's shyness about being with people seemed no less inhibiting in old age than it had been when he was young. "Spreading the word is your role," Liam said. "Mine is simply to be here when I'm needed." And there he remained, self-sufficient, even when Terry was onworld for weeks at a time, though he continued to take leave when *Estel* was in port for maintenance.

Presumably, when on leave, he still had contact with some agent of the Maclairn Foundation. But evidently they'd never seen fit to let him acknowledge their aid, and he'd never even hinted at it, though surely he must suspect that Terry had figured it out. In the beginning they'd no doubt wanted to be sure Terry's actions would further their aims, but that had been proven a long way back. So why go on pretending it was a mystery? Perhaps, Terry thought, like many anonymous donors to worthy causes they simply didn't want gratitude.

~ *57* ~

DURING THE NEXT decade two more new colonies were founded by people with mind training, one of them including emigrants from New Afrika. Moreover, Earthborn instructors equipped with neurofeedback helmets were sent to some of the older colonies—at last people there had the chance to learn the mind skills in which they'd come to believe. On Earth, Liam reported, both such skills and psi capability were widespread. The Estelans were the majority party almost everywhere.

Elated though Terry was by these developments, eventually his energy began to wane. Jumping from world to world required more effort than it once had, not in terms of bodily strength, but emotionally. Realizing this, he was dismayed. He had come to terms with Alison's death long ago. He enjoyed Liam's company and that of his many friends. But he found himself turning more and more to thoughts of his youth, and Maclairn, as he supposed old men did; and that frightened him. Was there nothing left for him to look forward to?

And then one day the cause of his depressed mood suddenly became clear to him. *He wasn't needed anymore.* He had succeeded in what he set out to do, and there was no longer any essential role for him to play. To the kids of many worlds the Captain of *Estel* was a hero, revered throughout the galaxy—but a figure from history with nothing new to offer. Whatever might be said of him now would make no difference.

That night Terry dreamed, and the dream was so vivid, so real, that as he woke the years fell away and he was a young man again, torn by the agony of exile as he had been on Ciencia. A hundred years—could it really have been a hundred years since the morning he had left Maclairn forever?

He was now one hundred twenty-six years old, so yes, it had been a century. And it had been a fulfilling life after the first. He had accomplished a lot more than he'd ever expected he could. He had not only furthered belief in the human mind's power; he had saved Maclairn twice from disaster. And he'd visited enough new worlds to satisfy the longing to explore that had been so strong in youth. So why did he now feel unsatisfied, restless, as if something beyond reach must be still ahead?

Long ago, when he'd first heard about the lengthened lives of the Maclairnans, he'd been told that they were in good health until near the end and then died quickly, as Alison had, simply because they had gotten all they could out of life and had begun to crave something beyond. Was that what was happening to him? He was not ready to die. Whatever unnamed thing he now longed for was not purely of the spirit. Nor was it simply a matter of the nostalgia for the past said to be common in old age. He could not define what it was. But he knew, suddenly, that he must search for it. *Estel* must make one more voyage into the unknown, and if it took him to his death, then the time for that had indeed come, though he felt deeply, unreasonably, that he was about to find something revitalizing.

Precognition? Terry wondered. That had happened to him a number of times before. Whether or not this was such a time, the feeling was compelling.

"Another vacation will be good for you," Liam agreed. "Do you want me to hire a prospecting crew?"

"No," said Terry. "It'll be just the two of us." And he sensed that Liam was relieved, as if for some reason he didn't think prospecting would be wise.

The trip took little planning; they went first to Stelo Haveno to provision the ship and replenish the antimatter, then jumped to one of the farthest unexplored stars on the charts. The thrill Terry had always felt during such jumps came back; it made him feel young again.

When they found, fortuitously, a planet with a breathable atmosphere, they camped there for a few days, glorying in the sight of the stars from a vantage point offering a better view than the narrow one from the ship's bridge. The vast panorama of sparkling lights stretched from horizon to horizon, unobstructed; and Terry knew that space was where he was meant to be, had always been meant to be, aware that beyond what he could see lay an infinity of stars, so that there need never be an end to exploring. And humankind would keep on exploring long after he was gone.

At dawn of the third day Liam said, "We'd better go, if you're ready. I'll program the jump for you if you like." Terry shook his head; since they had only six days of consumables left, this would be their last jump into the unknown. He might never have the chance to make another. "You can program our next one, when we return to civilization," he said.

Once aboard *Estel*, he chose the most distant star they could safely reach, marked on the charts but unnamed. He entered its coordinates carefully and double-checked the AI's calculations as he always did, then showered and joined Liam for breakfast. They returned to the bridge together; it was almost time. When the countdown paused for the captain's authorization, Terry drew a deep breath and gave the command to execute.

The familiar sense of disorientation came over him briefly, then faded into a sense of completion. They had jumped.

But they had not emerged near a star.

He could see no light in any direction, nor was there any detectable by the instruments. The space around them was black, and the constellations visible through the viewport were unknown to him. Terry could not believe it had happened. A miscalculated jump was what every pilot feared, and it was not unusual for ships to be lost that way. But he'd jumped so many times in the hundred-odd years he'd been flying. . . . surely he couldn't have miscalculated now. . . .

Perhaps the AI had malfunctioned. Or perhaps fate had, for the last time, intervened.

It took a few moments for him to absorb the implications. With no knowledge of where they were, there was no way he could program a jump to a charted location;

the charts were useless. They could jump from star to star forever without happening on one with a settled planet. And they did not have forever. They had life support for only six days.

Terry turned to Liam, knowing that these facts didn't have to be stated. "Liam," he said, "I've sensed all along that something was going to happen on this trip, though it didn't feel like danger. Now I see that was because death *isn't* danger when the time comes for it. I've had a long life, and this is the way I've always wanted to go—in space, out among the stars, not tied to the surface of some planet. My only regret is that I didn't recognize the premonition and come alone."

Liam, as he expected, was calm; he showed no signs of having received a death sentence, and in fact seemed unwilling to acknowledge the inevitable. "You've still got plenty of life ahead of you," he said.

"I wouldn't have, even if we weren't in this fix. I'm not immortal, Liam. You may not realize it, but I'm already older than anyone else not born on Maclairn—"

"You are one hundred twenty-six years old."

Astonished, Terry said, "I guess you picked that up telepathically, because I never told anyone except Alison. And if you're in that close rapport with me, you know I meant what I said. I don't mind dying, just so I don't have to watch you die, too.'

"Neither of us is going to die, not now."

Terry ignored this and went on, "There's a chance, a small chance, that you can eventually find your way back to a known region of space. We've got power for more jumps and life support to last one person for twelve days. I won't be using any—I'm going to put on a spacesuit and go out the airlock right now."

"You know I won't let you do that, Captain."

"You can't stop me."

Liam looked at him for a long moment. Then, slowly, he said, "There'll be no need to. In a few minutes you'll see the light of the star we jumped to shining on a beautiful new planet."

"That's crazy," Terry protested, wondering whether the shock of their situation had driven the normally-imperturbable Liam out of his mind or whether he was pretending it had in the hope of seeming too far gone to save. "Why say something I'm not going to believe?"

"Because it's time you knew the truth about me. I am not what you think, Terry. I'm what you would call an Elder, an agent of the interstellar Federation."

Terry recoiled, stunned. Oh, God—he had failed, then, after all he'd gone through the past hundred years to stay away from anyone who might draw the secret from his unconscious mind. There was nowhere else Liam could have found out about the Elders.

"I knew you were psi-gifted, but I didn't think you had the power to breach private thoughts," he said bitterly. "And now you taunt me with the evidence, when you know in your heart I've got only a few minutes left to live—"

"I didn't steal anything from your mind," Liam assured him. "You hid your knowledge of us well, and I know what that cost you. But the need for total secrecy is past. What I just told you is true—I am an alien Elder. You are on the threshold of your destiny, and I'm here to help you reach it."

Part Seven: Ydoril

~ *58* ~

LIAM AN ALIEN Elder? At first it seemed too incredible to take seriously. And yet, Terry realized, it would surely explain many of the mysteries that had surrounded him: his agelessness, his self-containment, his superb skill at everything he did. . . .

"Why now?" he asked after a pause to get his bearings. "Why, when I was led to believe I must pretend not to know about the Elders for the rest of my life . . . or are we about to die after all? I suppose it's okay to enlighten me further if I won't be seeing any more humans."

"You've got many more years to live," Liam declared. "But the situation has changed. You were told long ago, weren't you, that your human race would soon be ready to join us?"

"Not as we reckon time—Laesara said several generations—" He broke off, suddenly grasping what had never before occurred to him. He had assumed it wouldn't be within his lifetime. But generations were short compared to the century since he'd first met Laesara. His son was nearly a hundred years old and quite probably had great-grandchildren, even great-great-grandchildren by now.

Terry drew breath. "You said we'll see a planet—you mean *your* planet? But there are no worlds out here, we're not even near a star."

Liam smiled. "There are worlds. As you know, our solar systems are shielded from the sight of immature civilizations. The AI didn't fail during the jump—I reprogrammed it while you were in the shower. If you choose to accept the role we hope you will, a shield will be lowered for *Estel*."

"Oh, my God—I'm to be the first official contactee after all? But then why didn't you just say so when you did the programming?"

"You wouldn't have believed me if we hadn't been in a seemingly-desperate situation. You wouldn't have been ready for the shock. Accepting the end of your former life is good preparation for being born into a new one."

Terry's head was spinning. To see the Elders' worlds, to meet them not as a captive but as an equal. . . . He had known, in principle, that it would happen to humans someday; it was what he had striven for. He had not expected to be among the lucky ones.

Frowning, he asked, "Is this compensation for what was taken from me, or a reward for my silence all these years?" He wasn't sure he liked that. He hadn't resigned himself to their decree for a reward. The idea made him feel manipulated, somehow, as if his decisions hadn't been wholly his own.

"If you feel that way," said Liam, sensing his thought, "then you understand why silence was necessary. We do not manipulate; that's the point of concealing our existence."

"Then is it because of what I did to further Maclairn's goal?"

"What's ahead is far more than a matter of what's behind you," Liam replied. "It is a recognition of your fitness to confront the experience. We have not manipulated you, but we have watched you. Since the day you took command of *Estel*, we've wanted it to turn out this way."

"I might not have lived long enough. I never had the

advanced mind training the Maclairnans receive, so I don't know how I managed to stay healthy."

"You did receive the training, Terry—unconsciously, hypnotically, at the time you were healed from your crash injuries. And there were subtle changes made to your body. Laesara couldn't be sure that Maclairn's goal would be achieved within your potential lifespan, but she saw to it that you wouldn't die prematurely of old age."

"I might have been killed, though. I nearly was, on Earth."

"It's true that Quaid might have killed you—we're not omnipotent, though in most situations we could have intervened to save you if it had been necessary. It wasn't; you managed just fine on your own."

"But you did save me from losing *Estel* on Stelo Haveno," Terry said. "All these years I've wondered how someone with your talents had been stuck there, and how you escaped from Fleet after you'd defied them—"

"One of our ships was waiting for me in high orbit, and I simply abandoned the Fleet shuttle. They probably never knew what happened to it."

"How did you find out that I was in trouble there? Were you watching me all the time, way back then?"

"Even further back. I guarded *Estel* while you returned to Ciencia to get Alison; I was chosen then to be your protector, though I was forbidden to take action except in case of desperate necessity. I put a tracker on the ship, undetectable by your technology, so that I'd always know your location."

Suddenly outraged, Terry protested, "Are you saying Laesara didn't trust me after all, that if it had looked as if I might give away the secret I'd have been stopped?"

"No!" Liam assured him. "She trusted you implicitly. But you were too important to be lost in some risky enterprise or worse, some senseless accident."

"I don't understand," Terry said in bewilderment. "I thought you never intervened in human affairs, yet somehow you got the Maclairn Foundation to require that I take you as copilot."

"The Maclairn Foundation had nothing to do with your release from Draconis. I know you've been assuming it was your mysterious benefactor, which was a convenient cover for us. But actually the Elders arranged your pardon. As you've long known, we have agents at League Headquarters."

"Was Gabriel Travis an Elder, too?"

"He was, and still is, the head of our team for liaison with your people."

"But then why did he make me promise not to go to Earth when he must have known that I'd already pledged to stay away from it?"

"So that if you did assume he represented the Maclairn Foundation, you wouldn't fear that it might put you in touch with mentors."

Slowly, Terry took this in. "You're telling me it's been planned for me to visit your world all along."

"Only since fate brought you back from exile. When that happened, Laesara began to believe that this is your destiny, the one Aldren foresaw. You could have rejected it—you could have stopped working for Maclairn's cause and retired to a comfortable old age on some backwater colony world. But everything we knew from the probing of your mind indicated that you wouldn't. That you'd keep trying to move humankind forward, and would gain enough wisdom along the way to adjust to contact with an alien society."

Terry's head spun. "I'm honored by your opinion of me."

"The honor is mine to have been given this assignment, and to have gained your friendship. But Terry, we are asking a great deal of you. The role we're offering you will not be easy to fill. You are free to decide whether to accept it—I can get *Estel* to Stelo Haveno if you'd rather not go on."

"You know I won't turn down a chance like this," Terry said indignantly.

"I do, but you're entitled to fair warning." Liam paused, then said seriously, "Someone must be first, any time a human race is brought into the Federation, and you are far better qualified than is usual because you've had time to get used to knowing about our existence. Still, you should understand that there will be many challenges, not all of them pleasant. And you must decide now, because once you've been in contact with our culture there will be no going back."

"I can never go back to the League worlds?"

"Physically you can, but you will be changed past your friends' understanding. Interacting with us will be more overwhelming than you anticipate. To know that other species, other civilizations exist—even to read about them, see vids, and meet their representatives—is one thing, and it's the closest contact most citizens of the League will ever have. But to visit alien worlds is something else. Few of your people are ready to cope with it, though we believe you are."

"You're underestimating us," Terry protested. "A lot of us have psi capabilities now, and I'm hardly the only one who's not prejudiced against new mind-powers."

"It's not a matter of prejudice. And psi sensitivity, important as it is, lies at the heart of the problem. You're familiar with the concept of the collective unconscious, and know it doesn't extend from world to world—"

"That's why Maclairnans are born able to use abilities people in other colonies can't," Terry agreed.

"That's right. Well, the collective unconscious of the worlds of different species contains a great deal that is foreign to you. Not only are their cultures based on it, but it's inherent in the minds of those worlds' inhabitants. And because you are telepathic, your mind will be constantly bombarded with input arising from that foundation, a core of concepts different from the one you're

used to. Unlike people born among us, you don't know
how to shut it out, and until you learn to do so, you'll be
uncomfortable and confused. The average Earthborn human would be crushed by it, but you are stronger and
better prepared than most."

Terry pondered this. "Liam . . . will I be going to your
world as a guinea pig?"

"In a sense, though we have no doubts about you."

"I mean if I proved unable to adjust to your society,
would that change your decision about Earth being ready
for contact?"

"No. We'd recruit one of the mentors, as we would
have if you'd died. But your having known about us for
the past century gives you an advantage."

"If contact with alien minds is so upsetting," Terry
demanded, "why haven't I been uncomfortable being with
you all these years? Why didn't I suspect you weren't one
of us?"

"Because I've been trained to close part of my mind
to telepathic sensing—not just for secrecy, but to prevent perception of content that's alien to you. That won't
be the case with everyone you meet on our worlds."

Thoughtfully, Terry said, "You must also have been
trained to cope with *our* collective unconscious, and to
understand our culture well enough to pass as Earthborn.
That's why you've devoted so much time to reading."

"Yes, from the time I entered the Anthropological
Service, which is the organization responsible for observing younger species. Most members travel from one young
world to another, but in an era when contact with a newly-
mature civilization is close, some are selected to devote
themselves wholly to preparation for it. I was privileged
to be among them—and especially privileged to be your
companion and ultimately, your guide."

He would need a guide, Terry realized, and he was
glad it would be someone he already trusted. Their
thoughts touched without words, and for the first time in

their decades together, the barriers in Liam's mind fell. Gasping, Terry became aware that what lay ahead of him might indeed be overwhelming.

~ *59* ~

SILENTLY, TERRY GAZED out at the stars while Liam spoke over the comm in a language strange to him. Then in the center of the viewport those stars shimmered, faded— and the dark patch was abruptly filled by a planet—a spectacular blue-and-green planet that looked as Earth must have before its forests were gone. He had approached hundreds of worlds during the past century, but not since his first sight of golden Maclairn had he been so awe-stricken.

"All your life you've wanted to discover something no human has seen before," Liam reminded him. "Well, this is your chance."

The sun, too, was now unshielded; they were no longer in total darkness. Sunlight illuminated the alien world so that it seemed to sparkle. As they came closer, he could see that there were indeed large circles of reflected light amid the green areas. "Those are domes," Liam told him. "They're much larger than any on your League worlds, created by a technology you have yet to develop."

"But why are domes needed?" Terry asked. "Surely that planet has a thick atmosphere, with so much vegetation there."

"Think," Liam said. "When you were aboard Laesara's ship, weren't there airlocks between compartments?"

Yes, of course there had been; she'd said the starship was crewed by members of various races who'd evolved on different planets. He'd been warned that the air outside her sealed quarters would be poisonous to him.

"You mean not all this world's people are native to it," he said, surprised.

"None of them are native to it; it's a special-purpose colony and was created by a process you would call terraforming. Its atmosphere is breathable by only about half the inhabitants—and not, incidentally, by you and me."

"It's not your birthworld, then."

"No, just my adopted one. Its name is Ydoril and it's the headquarters of the Service I told you about, where all agents are trained and where they work between field assignments. No one else lives here but children, which not many of us have."

Aware that his thought would need no elaboration, Terry ventured, "Liam, I've always wondered—"

"Why I've always seemed to get along without sex?" Liam smiled. "Actually I have returned here a number of times during my leaves—jumps are instantaneous, after all, and our ships are faster than yours in normal space. We're forbidden to have intimate relationships with people on young worlds, which would exploit them and endanger our secret; but I do have women friends among fellow agents."

"But not a lifemate."

"I've never been so fortunate. You see, Terry, the Service is composed of different races, relatively few of which find each other sexually attractive. When a pairing does occur, there are no offspring because cross-breeding between species is genetically impossible. Even couples of the same species don't often stay in one place long enough to raise children, any more than you and Alison did. So families are the exception among us."

Terry thought with sadness of how hard it must have been for Liam through the years, watching him retire with Alison to their stateroom every night, perhaps with envy. But apparently he would have been just as lonely if he'd had some other assignment on Earth. His choice of career had been made long ago, in youth; had he ever had any regrets?

"I've brought you to this particular colony for two reasons," Liam went on. "First, it will give you a chance to meet people of various species, which is essential to comprehension of our culture. And second, because Service field agents are used to interacting with members of immature civilizations. They'll shield their minds to some extent so you can get used to new concepts gradually before you go to worlds where you'll be immersed in ours."

It was an awesome prospect. Would he be able to meet beings different from humankind without revealing any revulsion he might feel at their appearance? Terry wondered. Laesara had said he wouldn't want to meet the rest of her crew, and the more he thought about it, the more obvious it became that the average human wouldn't be ready for such contact.

"You won't find them as physically grotesque as you're expecting," Liam assured him. "Most fictional ideas about aliens are rather silly. There aren't any reptiles, much less giant insects, among us, and none of us have tentacles. Evolution produces pretty much the same kind of people everywhere, because it's the form best equipped to become highly intelligent and develop culture. There are variations in size, skin color, and amount of hair, and in placement of internal organs—plus differences in the shapes of faces, which will probably be the thing most noticeable to you. But they're not going to look like something out of a monster vid."

Embarrassed, Terry realized that his biggest problem was going to be hiding such foolish concerns from Liam. Now that their minds were more closely linked, he could have no private thoughts about the Elders unless he shut him out entirely; and he didn't want to do that. Even if it weren't that he needed his guidance, he wouldn't want to hurt Liam's feelings. He would have to accept the fact that as a newcomer here, he might seem naive.

They descended to low orbit, the planet seeming more and more beautiful the closer he came to it. It was a garden world, designed to be everything its inhabitants admired in nature. "They're not all so ideal," Liam said. "This one is special because everyone here belongs to a closely-bonded group and faces similar stresses when elsewhere. We need an inspiring base to return to."

Again Liam conversed by comm in his own language, which, Terry supposed, he'd need to learn before he could interact with people. "Not really," Liam said, answering the unspoken thought, "though you'll probably pick some of it up. You'll rely mostly on telepathy, which you do anyway without being aware of it—for anyone with your degree of ability, spoken words are merely a means of focusing thought." He switched to silent communication: *My teammates know Anglo because they've studied Earth's civilization through vids. So you'll have time to adjust.*

"If we can't breathe the atmosphere will we have to suit up to land?" Terry asked. "Or do you have breathing apparatus of some kind?"

"We have apparatus to use outside our own domes. But not for landing—we'll be met by a shuttle equipped for the port facilities."

This proved to be a small spherical ship with four seats quite a bit larger than normal—or rather, indicative of a different norm. Seatbelts weren't necessary; there was gravity but no feeling of deceleration as they dropped into a port that opened in one of the domes. The shuttle had no pilot other than its AI, which had evidently been remotely commanded to rendezvous.

Will Estel *be safe alone in orbit?* Terry wondered. He would probably be away for days, and he had never before left it unattended longer than an hour. For the first time since Liam's revelation he felt a tinge of panic. He wanted desperately to see the Elders' worlds—but was his presence here permanent? Might he never get back to *Estel* at all?

Take one step at a time, Liam advised him. But he did not answer the unspoken question.

The dome they had entered was a hub; they went from the shuttle directly into a tunnel leading to the residential dome they were headed for, evidently containing the same air since the automated car that took them there wasn't sealed. As they disembarked Terry drew a deep breath. He was on the verge of the most thrilling experience of his life, beyond anything he had ever hoped for. It was hard to believe that such a thing was really happening.

A small group of people stood waiting at the gate to the tunnel. They were indeed alien.

"Welcome, Terry Steward," said the first to come forward, a tall man—at least he supposed it was a man—with reddish skin. From facial features it was impossible to determine the person's sex. And in that instant Terry fully understood the goal Laesara had stated to him long ago, the key factor in the crusade for development of psi powers to which he'd devoted his life. Alien faces revealed nothing to a human about feelings, and no doubt the same was true in reverse. The "normal" means of judging people did not apply. Their sincerity, their goodwill, could be perceived *only* by telepathy.

This man, and the others around him, were offering a genuinely warm welcome. But if he were not a telepath he would not know that. To the average human they would seem strange and perhaps hostile, and nothing they might say in his language could be trusted. No wonder the Elders didn't reveal themselves to civilizations in which psi wasn't yet widespread.

He had expected to be at a loss for words—but words weren't needed. Terry found that nothing he wanted to say had to be expressed. It was simply understood, and he was aware that they got the gist of it, just as he himself understood that they had been awaiting his coming for years and were truly happy to meet him. It was a big occasion in their lives, a cause for celebration. Startled by their essential humanity, he scarcely noticed their physical variation at first.

But as they walked through a wide high-ceilinged corridor toward a meeting with a larger assembly, he began to take it in. They were of various heights, ranging from that of a human child to a couple of feet taller than himself. Skin colors included everything from purplish red to pale gold like Laesara's—in fact one member of the group was obviously of Laesara's race, with sparse fuzzy white hair and a face with flat nose and receding chin. He realized that he had not heard many voices; hers had been synthesized and their natural ones would likely be unintelligible to him even in a language he understood. He was indeed grasping what was said aloud via telepathy.

He suspected that some people's features were even less like his own than those he could see, since some were covered by full-face breathing apparatus—it was natural that the most dissimilar species would be the most likely to need different air. They all wore clothes of the same style, loose unisex tunics and trousers, so that he couldn't tell much about bodily shape apart from the fact that everyone had two arms and two legs. Some of the arms were hair-covered, almost furred. Again, there was no indication of sex since size wasn't relevant. He wondered if it even mattered among members of different species not physically attracted to each other. Culturally, they might make no distinction. Perhaps that was one of the things about this society that he was expected to find confusing.

They entered a large circular room directly beneath the center of the dome, through which light poured. A crowd gathered silently around him, and Terry became aware that *he* was the oddity, the strange person at whom everyone wanted a look. Yet somehow they managed to look without making him feel inferior. They viewed him not as a specimen in a zoo, but as a celebrity, an honored guest.

He was offered food, and to his surprise it was

delicious despite being unidentifiable. *It's a form of fruit*, Liam told him. *A rare fruit that comes from offworld, since this is a special occasion.* There were also small, sweet cakes. Everyone was obviously enjoying the repast, to which wine was soon added. The room was, however, much quieter than a human gathering would have been anywhere but on Maclairn. As telepaths, they didn't equate noise with conviviality.

At last, when the gathering dispersed and Liam took him down another corridor to what proved to be his sleeping quarters, Terry collapsed on the bed, shaking with the strain of the momentous day. He'd reached turning points often in his life, but this one topped them all.

"I'm bushed," Liam said. "I've looked forward to today for nearly eighty-eight Earth-years, and now that it's come, there's bound to be a letdown. But it's been a joyous day for me, and for you too, I hope."

There were no words strong enough for what Terry felt; the emotion brought him near tears. It didn't need to be expressed aloud; just as telepathy was sufficient with the newly-met aliens, so was it now with Liam. Released from the tension of a century of unacknowledged longing, he slept.

~ *60* ~

TERRY WOKE TO diffused light seeping through the entire outer wall beside the bed. Sitting up, he reached for the control buttons that Liam had showed him before retiring to an adjacent room. As he pressed first one and then another, the light brightened until he had a clear view of the sunlit landscape beyond the wall. The bedrooms were at the outer edge of the translucent dome, giving their occupants the feeling of being outdoors. There was a meadow patched with low-growing yellow flowers, bordered by trees whose glistening leaves shimmered in the wind. Beyond them, he caught a glimpse of another dome's reflective surface.

The bed itself was huge, at least a meter longer than necessary, and Terry realized that the guest rooms had been designed to accommodate the tallest of the species for whom this dome's air was breathable. It was soft compared to those aboard human starships, perhaps to allow for bodies of differing shapes. He rose and went into the small private lavatory, which had fixtures of unfamiliar design though obvious in their purpose. Water was evidently not scarce on this planet; after a lifetime of meager shipboard showers, he reveled in a continuous drenching spray from jets adjustable to the height of his shoulders. When ready to dress he found that suitable clothes had been provided, loose grey pants and a green tunic of some soft but sturdy material; his pilot's apparel had disappeared.

Terry sat down on the bed again, unsure as what to do next. He was torn by conflicting feelings: eagerness for the experiences ahead, mixed with uneasiness he couldn't put a name to. He had not slept soundly. Weird dreams had intruded—dreams he didn't remember, yet knew had been disturbing. Not nightmares, not even frightening, but just . . . different. Things for which there were no words.

Liam, when he appeared, didn't have to be told this. "Bear with it, Terry," he advised. "Remember what I said about the collective unconscious—you're not going to adjust to an alien one overnight. Telepathically you're absorbing much more than what you see and hear, and it's bound to be upsetting because you lack the context in which the people here perceive it."

"It—feels like precognition, almost," Terry reflected. "Is any of that real?"

"Perhaps. Your psi faculties are being stimulated by use, so you're probably more sensitive to precognition as well as telepathy. You may be aware of future impressions as well those you're picking up now.

Then did it mean problems ahead? he wondered. He wanted to embrace this world wholly. He'd seen nothing about it that he didn't like. But he felt out of place here, somehow, and that was a feeling he'd never had on any of the countless planets he had visited in the past.

They ate breakfast served buffet-style in a dining room one level higher than their bedrooms, also with a gorgeous view. Liam led the way to a table where a woman was waiting for them. "This is Rowyn," he said, and though she didn't speak aloud, Terry had no difficulty exchanging pleasantries with her. She welcomed him warmly and was instantly likeable.

It was clear that to Liam she was more than likeable.

There was no doubt about Rowyn's gender, for she was of a species quite close to human. She was about the same height as Liam, and might almost have been of his race if it weren't that her skin had a purplish tinge, as if it were bruised, and she had extra fingers. Her facial features were odd, but not startlingly alien. Her body, what he could see of it, matched the human ideal; it was enough to rouse any man's desire.

But it didn't stir Terry. Though she was attractive by all reasonable standards, she left him cold. That was unusual. His advanced age had not diminished his virility; while he would never want anyone but Alison, on League worlds his inner reaction to the sight of desirable women had been normal. Why then did Rowyn seem totally lacking in sex appeal, when in Liam's eyes she evidently had plenty of it?

After they left the dining room and could talk privately, he asked, "Why didn't she seem female to me? _Am_ I just not able to connect with other species as people?" It was a disappointment; he had assumed he was broadminded enough not to let small physical differences affect him.

"Of course you can connect. But not always in a sexual

way—unless two species are genetically attracted to each other, which may or may not be the case when they look similar, the physical triggers simply aren't there."

"But you . . . I sensed that something triggered a response in *you*. Even more than when we met human women, to whom I've never felt you react."

Liam said slowly, "Terry, it's time you knew. Rowyn and I are of the same species. When I first came to this world, my body was the male equivalent of hers."

Terry stared at him. "That's impossible. I know you Elders can change people's identifying physical characteristics, as you did mine when I was sent to Ciencia. My voice was changed and my skin tone was altered—but not so drastically as from Rowyn's skin to yours! The alterations to my face were minor, nothing like transformation into a different *species*."

"Much larger changes can be, and are, made," Liam told him. "It's rare for it not to be necessary. There are one or two other races that can pass as Earthborn, but only a very few members of them happen to be in the Service. When the contact team was chosen, long ago when I was barely past adolescence, most of us were surgically altered. Facial reconstruction was only part of it. For instance, my heart was moved from the right side of my body to the left. Some of my fingers were amputated, just as your missing ones were restored. I was given permanent contact lenses to change my eye color."

It struck Terry as appalling. For a person to be transformed into something unlike the race he'd been born into . . . to be cut off from his own people in such a way, so that he was neither one thing nor another. . . . "Why?" he asked in dismay. "Why did you allow it, I mean?"

"Bringing Earth into the Federation is important," Liam said. "When we join the Service, we make a binding choice to devote our lives to observing and protecting younger species—we swear a formal oath to put their welfare above all other considerations. But mostly, this means observing passively without any chance of taking action. Not every generation has the opportunity to help the people of a new world gain their rightful place among us. We who were students here when the team was selected vied for that opportunity. Physical alteration was a small price to pay."

"Laesara wasn't altered," Terry protested. "She said the others on her starship weren't."

"No, because they'll have no direct contact with your people. Laesara was a mission coordinator and ultimately fleet commander; she had no reason to go to the surface. Only a small number of us have been prepared for that."

"It's so . . . permanent. You can never go back to what you were born to be."

"We couldn't go back to our birthworlds anyway, except for brief visits; the Service is a lifelong commitment. Besides, it didn't change anything essential about us. The Maclairnans founded their culture on the principle that minds are more significant than bodies, didn't they? You have spent your own life promoting the importance of the mind. To be consistent, you must admit that a person's physical form *doesn't matter*."

Chagrined, Terry agreed. Yet as the day wore on, he found to his dismay that it did matter. He had lived with Liam aboard *Estel* for more than eighty years believing him to be human; finding out that he was an Elder had been a shock, but the difference had seemed a mere technicality. Now he couldn't help thinking of him as an impostor, someone who underneath was not what he appeared to be. He told himself that it didn't affect their friendship. But he shrank from telepathic contact, knowing that Liam would sense his horror and be hurt.

They toured the interior of the dome with its conference rooms, libraries, and immense central knowledgebase—a copy of which, Liam said, existed on every Federation world. Its size and complexity was almost incomprehensible, despite Terry's extensive experience with information technology and skill in programming. Hundreds of worlds, each with an independently-developed civilization. . . . "And here at Service headquarters," Liam added, "we also have data about all the young worlds not ready for Federation membership. We spend years in study before being allowed to visit them—and people not in the Service aren't permitted to visit young inhabited worlds at all. It's a strictly-enforced policy because any premature contact with such a world would interfere with its evolution."

Laesara had told him that, and he'd found it hard to understand, though he'd come to terms with it over the years. Now he perceived that Service people—all the people he met on this world—saw it as a sacred obligation. They were literally committed to die rather than reveal the Elders' existence to a developing civilization and, Liam told him, that sometimes happened. Sometimes it was the only way to hide their alien origin.

Yet the Service was an adventurous life; they saw much that other Federation citizens had no chance to see. There was never any shortage of recruits, despite formidable admission standards. "I grew up wanting to be a Service agent, just as you wanted to be a pilot," Liam said. "I was born in a backwater colony of my species' original homeworld that didn't have much to offer, and most of us aren't free to travel on our own, you know—passage is expensive, just as it between League colonies."

The Service's special knowledgebase was off-limits to Terry, but he was free to explore the Federation knowledgebase whenever he wished. The difficulty was that it wasn't written in Anglo or any other language of Earth, so he would be limited to viewing holographic representations. Terry found, however, that if he watched a holo in the company of some other person—and there were plenty of volunteers—he could pick up enough telepathically to grasp what it was about. In this way he was flooded with information about the look of diverse Federation worlds. By nightfall his head was swimming; he fell into bed scarcely able to remember where he was.

Again, there were disturbing dreams, and this time they were haunted by images of Liam with an alien, purplish face, like some figure out of a fantasy vid, yet more evocative of emotion. He woke in the dark trembling with it. *What's happening to me?* he thought in desperation. *Why does it bother me so? Meeting aliens was what I always longed for. . . .*

For the next few days nothing changed. Terry spent them communicating with people of various races, enjoying their company and watching holos about their home worlds with enthusiasm. It was an experience beyond anything he had ever imagined; he was alternately overcome by gratitude to fate and an inner tumult he tried his best to shut out of his mind. The nights were less happy. Innumerable images crowded into his thoughts and overflowed, until he was unsure which he had been shown and which had merely risen from dreams. And always, the dreams included Liam, Liam in alien form, arousing a deep sense of loss, a feeling that everything had changed and that he himself could never go back to what he once had been.

~ *61* ~

ON THE FIFTH morning Liam announced, "Laesara wants to see you, Terry."

"Laesara's *here?*" Terry was astonished; why had this not been mentioned?

"She retired here many years ago, as all Service agents do in old age. She's near death now, yet has hung on, which is unusual—most people die quickly, as Alison did. She has been too weak to leave her room and we weren't sure she was up to seeing anyone. But when she perceived by remote viewing that you're here now, she said that's what she's been waiting for."

They rose several levels in one of the controlled-gravity shafts spaced around the dome's perimeter. Terry entered Laesara's room alone. It was larger than his, but otherwise similar except for being furnished with personal belongings. A slight figure in the huge bed, she sat back against a pile of cushions, looking no older than she had a century ago during their first meeting. Her hair had been white even then, of course; that was its natural color. Her golden skin glowed against the white pillow covers, and she was smiling.

Terry, she said silently. *I knew that if I could live long enough, you'd come.*

He realized that she didn't have the voice synthesizer with which she'd spoken to him before. Though there was no need for him to speak aloud either, he did so, because his mind was too full of confused ideas and images to convey a clear thought otherwise. "I'm honored by your belief in my fitness to come," he said. "I wasn't aware of all you did for me until a few days ago. I don't know how to express my thanks."

It is I who am thankful that you are what you are. I knew a century ago that fate had sent you to us, but not until it brought you back from the exile we imposed did I see your true destiny. Can you forgive us, Terry?

"For Ciencia? I forgave you long ago, even before I knew how it would turn out."

And for the years on Draconis. We tried our best to secure your release sooner.

"I've been amply repaid for my misfortunes—you gave me *Estel* not just once, but twice. I've had a good life all in all, Laesara. And being here is a bigger climax to it than I ever imagined."

She beckoned and reached for his hand, clasping it with her seven-fingered one. *Will you allow me to probe your mind?*

Terry nodded assent; from her he could hold nothing back, nor did he want to. She had probed him a century ago, as had the Council head Jessica on Maclairn and later, another Elder at the time of his rescue from the crash. It had been overwhelming, and now he was already feeling overwhelmed. But it was her right to judge him, and he trusted her completely. He knelt by the side of the bed, his hand still in hers.

He felt her powerful mind touch his, and then he was spinning back through the years, reliving all that had passed since their farewell after the rescue, experiencing again the dangers and triumphs, the joy and the sadness. It took only a few moments, but he was as stirred emotionally as he would have been if they'd talked for hours.

Releasing his hand, Laesara told him, *As I expected, you have proved worthy of what we're demanding of you. But they are heavy demands. You are not entirely happy here.*

"To be entirely happy while plunging into a whole new universe unknown to humankind isn't possible, I guess. But I'd rather be here than anywhere else, especially since your people seem to think I'm achieving some greater good by it."

Some greater good? Terry, you are the key—the person on whom the future of Earth's civilization depends! Fate has been preparing you for this responsibility since long before you and I first met.

"Well, I hardly think being first contactee is as significant as that," Terry said, embarrassed by her intensity.

Laesara seemed startled. *They have not told you, then . . . no, I suppose not. It's too soon.*

"Told me what?"

Never mind. You will learn in due course why you are so important to us. But in the meantime, don't be discouraged by your doubts about Liam. They will pass.

Oh, God. He'd hoped she hadn't picked that up. "I haven't lost any respect for Liam, if that's what you mean," he declared. "I'll be forever grateful to him. I

don't know why I can't feel as close to him as I did before
I knew—"

*Before you knew the extent of the difference between
you. That is a natural reaction, Terry. It is one thing to
accept beings of other species as equals, but much harder
to identify with them in the way one does with an intimate friend. You have had very few close relationships in
your life—Kathryn, whom you lost a century ago; your
friend Jon, who died defending you from the Klan; Alison,
whose death left you alone and grieving after nearly eighty
years of a stable marriage; and finally Liam. At present
Liam is your only anchor to the past. When your conception of him changed, you were set adrift; you cannot help
feeling that perhaps you, too, are changing.*

As always, Laesara understood more than he could
have expressed. It occurred to Terry that she must have
served not only as a mission coordinator and fleet commander, but as a mentor among her people; perhaps in
the Service they were one and the same. Absorbing her
advice—which he was perceiving telepathically in the form
of concepts rather than words—he suddenly knew that
the brief barrier to closeness with Liam had fallen. It
would never trouble him again.

But it was true that he feared he himself was changing. He didn't know his own mind anymore; there was too
much in it that had come unbidden—he'd seen too much
in too short a time that was unlike any human norm. And
no doubt he had, as Liam predicted, drawn much from
this world's collective unconscious. . . .

You will adjust to it, Laesara assured him. *You are
capable of that, which is why you were chosen. I can move
on now, happy in the knowledge that I chose wisely.*

Move on? She meant death, Terry realized. Liam had
said she was dying. Grief struck him, though he knew she
was far older than he was and that it was past time for
her to die.

I have looked forward to your coming for eighty-seven

of Earth's years, Laesara declared, *and although I will not be here to see the culmination of our mission, I have been given the privilege of seeing you pick up the torch. Godspeed, Terry. Never forget that I have faith in you. . . .*

Her thought drifted, and he saw that she was exhausted. He did not know how to take leave of her, but it became apparent that he didn't have to, for she had lost consciousness. Hoping that she nevertheless sensed the depth of his feeling for her, he quietly left the room.

Liam was waiting just outside. "What did she mean?" Terry asked in bewilderment. "She told me I'm the key to Earth's future. She said something about a torch. But surely there will be plenty of other contactees before long. Being first is an honor, still it can't make a difference to anyone but me."

"It made a difference to *her* because she chose you personally," Liam pointed out. "And she knew there are challenges ahead for you. Don't worry about them. Just take one step at a time."

That was what he'd advised before. Terry didn't pursue the subject, but he went on wondering. Why a torch? The torch, on Maclairn, was the symbol of mind-power, the power to be passed on to all humankind. Her use of the metaphor revived his vivid memory of the Ritual, and again, as so many times in dreams, he thrust his hand into the flame and knew he was one with his fellow Stewards, a part of Maclairn forever, no matter how far he might travel from it. . . .

Laesara had known about the Ritual; she had drawn it from his mind the first time she probed him, to his dismay in view of the fact that he had sworn to keep it secret. And of course, it was she who had preserved and returned his flame pin, which he wore openly on his new tunic since from the Elders it need not be hidden. Perhaps that symbol was what she'd been referring to. She had made it possible for him to spread belief in new mind-powers throughout the League colonies. Yet that was the

past; his work was done. From now on people would believe because of Earth's contact with the Elders.

Late that night Laesara died. Many in the dome, and
in the other domes on the planet, knew instantly; a collective wave of grief magnified the telepathic perception
of her passing. Terry, too, sensed it, and alone in his room
he wept for her. She, more than any other individual, had
influenced the course of his life, though during most of it
he hadn't known that.

The next evening people of all races gathered for the
funeral, which was holographically transmitted to the
other domes. Laesara had been loved by everyone in the
Service, and few had dry eyes—but only because she would
be sorely missed. To them, as to the Maclairnans, death
in old age was cause not for sadness but for celebrating
the fulfillment of a life. The ceremony was formal; Liam
and most of the others wore the white uniforms of Service agents, which, he said, were used only on special
occasions and never on other worlds. They were symbols
of unity. Terry envied them; he liked and admired these
people but could never be part of their fellowship, nor
could he ever again feel the unity he'd experienced on
Maclairn.

Terry, because Laesara had sponsored him, stood in
the front row of the circle surrounding the flower-decked
catafalque, along with Liam and the few other members
of her team not presently observing Earth. It was a beautiful rite, including music with a tonality strange to him,
yet pleasing—electronic rather than vocal, since the different voices of the various species present precluded
singing. There was little speech, and it was of course unintelligible to him; but the gist of it was shared telepathically by the gathering in any case—an outpouring of admiration and love for a person who would never be lost to
memory.

The dome overhead had been set to full transparency
so that the stars shone through with awesome clarity as

if seen from a ship. The sight of them was dimmed only by the light of the torches that encircled the room. Torches again . . . was that a universal symbol of solemnity? Terry wondered. He recalled Corwin's memorial on Maclairn, with rows of torches lining the terraces above the lake. Corwin's death had been tragically premature; there had been no consoling awareness of a full life's completion, as was shared among assembled mourners here. Had it been like this for the other mentors he'd admired, who must all be gone by now: Aldren . . . Tristan . . . Jessica?

When it was over he said to Liam, "It brought back memories of Maclairn—the older I get, the more vivid they are, sometimes. The mentors I knew would have liked so much to know the truth I had to keep from them. And to know Laesara—would she have met those alive now, if she'd lived a little longer? Would she have visited the world her team has guarded in secret for more than a century?"

"Perhaps. If it had been possible for her, she might have. Maclairn's safety meant a lot to her, and she spoke of it often after she retired."

Liam had never mentioned the timetable for contact with humankind, Terry realized. He'd been told only that he was first; how soon would there be others, perhaps a public revelation? He didn't ask aloud, for he could sense that Liam perceived the question and was unwilling to answer it.

"It isn't quite time yet," Liam said, smiling. "I can't say any more now, but when I'm free to discuss it, you'll be the first to know."

~ *62* ~

THEY SPENT SEVERAL more weeks on Ydoril, with excursions to the planet's surface and to the other domes—which required breathing masks—as well as ongoing study of other worlds. It was a happy time. Terry became comfortable with the variety of people he met and their physical differences were soon scarcely noticeable. The underlying barrage of input from alien minds also became less overwhelming, and his disturbing dreams ceased.

As for his feeling toward Liam, it was as if there had never been any worry. Liam was his friend, as always, and the thought of his body's alterations became less intrusive. He was aware that Liam and Rowyn had indeed been lovers, and still were on occasion; but the images this brought to mind no longer troubled him.

Terry wondered, at times, what the future held for him. He was enjoying his stay and felt there were enough new experiences ahead to outlast a lifetime, and he'd made many good friends. Often he woke with a sense that his presence among aliens was too incredibly wondrous to be real. Still, there were other days when he felt restless, on edge, waiting for something he could not name, just as he had before starting out on his last trip in *Estel*. And though he had no desire to turn back time, he missed *Estel*. It had been the center of his life for too many years to be easily abandoned.

So when Liam suggested that it was time to move on, to see other Federation planets, Terry was glad. Holos were fascinating but no substitute for the real thing. He looked forward to traveling from world to world again.

As before, they went alone, just the two of them. They didn't go in *Estel*, however. It would be better, Liam said, not to spend unnecessary days on the approach to each planet. So they chose a small Service ship like the landers in which the Elders had taken him to Ciencia. It could jump as well as land, and was fast enough in normal space to reach the destination world within a few hours after emergence near a star.

"This is going to be challenging," Liam warned. "On Ydoril, people of many species live together as a single culture, and all of them are used to dealing with younger species, through study even if not on previous missions. But most Federation worlds are populated by the species native to them. They welcome delegates and tourists, but their own cultures dominate, just as Earth will retain its own culture despite contact with alien ones. You will be immersed, telepathically, in that culture—you'll feel the effect of a different collective unconscious much more strongly than in a mixed one."

They went first to Liam's birthworld, a sparsely settled planet of a small bluish star. It being a colony world, his species hadn't evolved there and its ecology revealed nothing about their origins, though they seemed to fit in well enough. The people, of course, looked like Rowan; Terry was glad that he'd had some time to prepare himself for the striking difference between Liam and his parents. The change must have been hard for them to accept, he thought—but they greeted their son with the same warmth and love any family would feel toward a returning member, apparently untroubled. To be sure, they'd had many years to get used to it.

Although they were cordial to Terry, Liam's parents and sister didn't connect with him as well as the people on Ydoril had, nor did he feel at ease in their company. They seemed somewhat in awe of him, and attempts at communication were a bit awkward. "They're not used to strangers," Liam explained, "not even those from well-established Federation societies; and they're not as telepathic as the others you've met—Service members are selected for psi-giftedness, among other things. You'll need to adjust to being viewed as an outsider."

This proved to be the case on the other planets they visited. In the large cities where visitors from other worlds were common, he attracted little notice, though a few people went out of their way to be friendly. In less cosmopolitan areas he and Liam were stared at. Everywhere they were treated with courtesy; that was a basic rule of

Federation society. But it was generally formal courtesy rather than hospitality.

Only once was their reception really cold. While admiring the architecture of the towering cathedrals on a low-gravity world obviously steeped in tradition, they were pointedly avoided by passers-by, almost as if they were suspected of carrying some plague. Terry's skin crawled; his telepathic sensitivity told him that they were not welcome here, regardless of the outward tolerance its inhabitants had displayed. Was there some unusual distaste for their physical features? he wondered. Since Liam looked Earthborn, they appeared to be of the same species. Perhaps these people hadn't seen anyone like them before.

They haven't, Liam told him silently. *What's more, they notice the Service insignia on my jacket. Most know that means you're new among us, and the reaction spreads.*

Later, Liam explained, "Not everyone in the Federation agrees with Service policy. Some believe we shouldn't admit species that haven't outgrown the barbarisms that still exist on worlds at the level of those we bring in."

"Barbarisms? I thought Earth *had* outgrown them."

"If you mean full-scale wars, prejudice on the basis of skin color, widespread starvation, yes. But there is still crime and poverty and squalor on Earth. Heavy industry is still on the surface instead of in orbit where it wouldn't mar the planet's beauty. Worst of all, people are still under the thumb of a controlling government. And you certainly can't say the revival of the Ku Klux Klan wasn't barbaric."

"You're saying such things don't exist on every world?"

"They don't on Maclairn, do they?

"It's a small new colony. We don't expect Earth can ever get rid of its problems, even after the majority of citizens gain mind-powers."

"Not soon. But the Federation worlds have had many more centuries of progress than Earth has had. There are always a few evildoers on any world—no culture is a utopia. Where the collective unconscious rules out imma- ture behavior, though, the small minority of deviants don't affect the overall condition of a civilization."

"I suppose Federation citizens won't think much of ours," Terry said unhappily.

"It will be off-limits except to official delegates for some time. The hardest part of a Service agent's training is learning to accept the things he or she will see in young civilizations—especially those too young for admission, where there's a lot of bloodshed and cruelty, but also those at the level of Earth. It takes a while for us to reconcile ourselves to the fact that evolution can't be hurried."

Most Federation species had indeed moved heavy in- dustry from planetary surfaces into orbit, Terry discov- ered, and in many cases a large share of the population had moved into artificial orbiting colonies—little habitats, complete with diverse ecologies, within outer shells that provided life support facilities. He knew from his reading of history that this had been proposed as far back as the twentieth century on Earth, but people had never fol- lowed through. As a result Earth had become the dreary, crowded, polluted world he knew, whereas the worlds where advanced Federation species had evolved were park-like. Was it too late, he wondered to change course and restore its former beauty?

"It's not," Liam assured him, "but it won't happen in your lifetime. Most species focus on moving outward first, as is necessary as a hedge against disaster. Only later can they afford to move enough of their industry into orbit to clean up their home worlds."

During the next few weeks they traveled to many of those worlds, seeing wonders beyond anything Terry had envisioned—buildings strangely shaped, yet graceful; pas- toral lands where countless homes blended unobtrusively with the natural growth; once a whole city rising out of the sea. And animals, an incredible array of separately evolved animals, different on each world, not caged but running free in areas set apart for them and observed from bordering stations or through satellite vid closeups. He and Liam visited historic sites, attended concerts of incredibly complex music, experienced the impact of technologies unimaginable by the science known to the League. They met Elders with psi powers far more advanced than their own, Elders who depended almost entirely on silent communication and who, to Terry's well-concealed unease, used psychokinesis in their daily lives as well as in creation of their habitations. Through it all, he felt the strangeness of the psychic ambience, of contact with people whose thoughts were inexpressible in his own language; and at night, his dreams blended reality with metaphor so that he could not tell how much of the whole he had really seen.

At last one morning he woke shaky, feeling that though he wanted desperately to grasp more of this new universe, he hadn't the energy to take it in. With reluctance he said, "I think maybe we should just relax for a few days."

Liam nodded. "You're on the edge of burnout," he agreed. "We'll go back to Ydoril for some rest. One more world before we do, though—the most important one for you to visit."

Wearily Terry protested, "Can't it wait?"

"No, I'm afraid this one can't. It's the Federation's headquarters, and you are expected there."

~ *63* ~

THEY EMERGED NEAR a yellow sun somewhat smaller than Earth's; the planet was closer to it. It was a brilliant green jewel of a world with few oceans. "This was where the Federation was formed, millennia ago," Liam said. "It's a less rigid organization than the League—as you know, each member world runs its own affairs. But delegates do meet here to exchange ideas, and there's a ceremonial head of state whose role is to represent their collective ideals."

"A premier?"

"No, he has no executive power and like the sovereigns of modern monarchies on Earth, he's not involved in politics. His position is purely symbolic. When you meet him, though, you'll find that as a person he's worthy of honor."

"I'm going to meet him?" Terry exclaimed, surprised. "Out of all the billions of citizens of countless worlds, why would I rate his notice?"

"Because you are the first of your species to visit us, and through you, he will formally welcome Earth into the Federation."

"Oh, my God. Is this why Laesara said I'm important?"

"Not only this. But it's a significant occasion. He will probe you, which won't feel the same as when she did because he knows nothing of your background or culture. He'll merely judge your humanity."

"What if he doesn't like what he finds?" Terry inquired. "I'm hardly the pinnacle of the human race, I'm not even as psi-gifted as a lot of the mentors—"

"He will approve of you. Laesara wouldn't have chosen you if there were any question about it."

Nevertheless Terry felt nervous when the time arrived. He felt uncomfortably conspicuous in the close-fitting white tunic and tights with which he had been provided, styled so unlike the Fleet dress uniform he'd worn on formal occasions long ago. It reminded him of something out of a costume drama, yet was similar enough to the Service uniform Liam wore to convince him that it was appropriate. People from different worlds favored various colors, and on Ydoril bright ones had been predominant. Had white been chosen for him because it was the Service's ceremonial color, he wondered, or because

Liam knew that on Maclairn it was the color worn for the Ritual?

The building to which Liam took him appeared to be made of crystal, not just its windows, like those on Ciencia, but the entire structure. In the center of its vast rotunda was a moving staircase wide enough for six average-sized people to ascend abreast, evidently designed for its dramatic effect since the more common controlled-gravity lifts would have carried them between levels more efficiently. Light from an immense skylight poured through a shaft that extended all the way to the ground floor.

Like most of the others present, he and Liam wore their indispensable breathing apparatus. "But the meeting rooms have sections sealed off by invisible force fields to provide different air for different species," Liam told him. "That's the reason why delegates don't greet each other by handshakes or any other form of physical contact. You won't notice the barrier unless you touch it."

He led the way into an anteroom on the top level where their masks could be removed. "Have you been here before?" Terry asked.

"No, I haven't been invited till now. I've seen holos, though, so I know what to expect."

"Must I talk to the head man? What's his title—how should I address him?"

"He doesn't know your language, of course. You can speak aloud if you wish, as I will for your benefit; but the communication between you will be entirely telepathic. You can refer to him simply as "Eldest." He's that to all of us, for he's one of the oldest living members of the Federation's oldest race."

As on Maclairn, age was admired over youth here, Terry realized; he'd been told that Earth's glorification of youth was the reverse not only of most other cultures' custom but of common sense. Through long life one developed wisdom, he supposed, though he personally didn't feel very wise.

They proceeded into what appeared to be a comfortable office with soft foam-covered furniture styled to accommodate people of various sizes and holos of diverse worlds' landscapes artistically placed within its translucent walls. The air on their side of the invisible force field must have been adjusted for them, since the room was too small to have more than one section for guests. On the other side there was only an immense desk, cleared of everything but the recessed controls for its vid screen. No obstruction hid their sight of the person seated behind it.

He was of a race Terry hadn't seen before, smaller than most, with skin so dark that it was almost literally black and huge orange eyes. They were penetrating eyes, yet kind, and the magnetic personality of an inspired leader shone through them. Terry knew instantly that anything good said of this man would be an understatement.

"Venerable Eldest, I present to you Terry Steward, our first representative from the planet known to its people as Earth," said Liam aloud. "I ask you in the name of the Service to acknowledge that world and all its colonies, through him, as a member of the Federation."

Though the Eldest's alien features were unreadable, telepathic perception told Terry that he was smiling. *Sit down, Terry,* he said silently. *I cannot invite you to approach closer because of the force field, but that barrier will in no way diminish the touch of our minds.*

There was a curved couch facing the Eldest's chair; Terry and Liam sat down on it. "Venerable Eldest, I am honored to be in your presence," he said. The spoken words were superfluous, but he needed the focus they provided.

Have I your permission to probe you?

"Yes, Eldest. I welcome it." He leaned back, gathering himself, hoping that the probe would not cause him to lose his poise.

When the Eldest's mind touched his he felt nothing, for all sense of space and time slipped away. With Laesara his memories had been drawn into consciousness and passed to her, but now the past lay beyond recall. He had no words or even thoughts; he was simply one with the Eldest, not judging or being judged, yet aware that their perspective was in accord. Whether time passed or their union was instantaneous, he neither knew nor cared. But when he was wholly himself again, it was with the knowledge that there were no aliens—that all peoples in the universe were alike underneath, and that the mind-powers he'd spent his life advocating, whether conscious or unconscious, were the essence of what made them human.

You are a worthy representative of your people, the Eldest told him, *and it will be my joy to welcome them into the fellowship of all human worlds. Go with my blessing, Terry Steward. I have no doubt that you will meet the challenge to come with dignity and courage.*

Terry bowed his head briefly, uncertain as to how to respond. Courage? He didn't know of any coming challenge that would demand it. To be sure, this man was more psi-gifted than any Earthborn person; perhaps his precognition had revealed a future of which he himself as yet had no idea.

He realized that no further speech was needed; polite phrases would have been anticlimactic after the deep communication they had experienced. Silently, he and Liam left the room.

They went immediately back to the ship, and then to Ydoril. More weeks passed, with Terry resuming his former routine. But holos were less absorbing than they had been before he had seen real alien worlds. He recovered from burnout only to find his earlier restlessness stronger than ever. He had everything—good friends, a pleasant place to live, access to a knowledgebase more vast than he had ever imagined in his hacking days—but something was missing. It was a while before it struck him what it was.

He was homesick. He missed the sight of Earthborn humans with bodies like his own, a cultural heritage like his own. He was with people he liked and admired, but they were not *his* people.

At first he was ashamed of these feelings, which seemed like prejudice though he could honestly say that he had none. As time wore on he was torn by them. He had been given an opportunity no member of humankind had been offered before; how could he admit, even to himself, that he was less than totally content with it? How could he ever tell Liam that he longed for his former life? And supposing that he could bring himself to do that, how could he abandon the exciting new universe he had yet to fully explore? He did not want to go back . . . yet a part of him did want to. He wanted to have it both ways, yet he could hardly expect to be transported back and forth between League territory and the hidden realm of the Federation. He would have to choose.

It would be better, perhaps, once Earth was aware of the Elders. Liam still hadn't told him how soon that would be. And it might *not* be better . . . he'd been told initially that he could never go back to being what he'd been before. If he kept silent about his experiences he would burst with the immensity of them, and if he went public, he would be looked upon as a curiosity—pursued, perhaps, in the way he would have been if exposed as the Captain of *Estel*. What role could the Captain of *Estel* play in the new era, when his work was done and he was no more than an aged spacer traveling from world to world to relive the past?

And yet more and more, he felt drawn back to the civilization into which he had been born.

This, Terry realized, must be what the Eldest had meant by his reference to a challenge requiring courage. Perhaps it hadn't been based on precognition, but simply on understanding of the human heart. In his wisdom he must have known that anyone brought from an isolated young world would have to make this choice, a choice in which there would be pain either way.

Finally, on a bright afternoon with the light of the alien sun pouring through the translucent walls of the sunroom he'd come to love, he spoke. "Liam," he said slowly, "I don't know just how to put this. I'm honored by what the Service has done for me and I'll always be grateful for the welcome I've received. But . . . Ydoril's not my world. I admire what I've seen of the Federation and I'm happy about humankind being accepted into it, yet I don't belong here—not forever. I don't know what I want, only that I can't be just an observer. I need to be with my own people during our transition."

"Yes," Liam agreed. "I've been wondering if you'd realize that without my having to bring it up."

"You knew?" Terry burst out in astonishment. "You're not hurt that I want to leave?"

"It was never intended for you to spend the rest of your life with us, Terry. This is only a stopover on your way home."

"Home? I don't have one—not unless you count *Estel*. I don't really know where I'll go now."

"To Maclairn, of course," Liam said. "Isn't that where you've always wanted to be?"

Part Eight: Homecoming

~ 64 ~

"*MACLAIRN*? STUNNED, TERRY felt his heart swell within him. Laesara had told him he could never go there again ... he had lived with that sorrow for a whole century. And yet once the Elders revealed themselves to humankind, the reason for the prohibition would be gone. He had not considered that; he was so used to suppressing his longing for Maclairn that he hadn't stopped to think that he might soon be free to return.

"When?" he asked, his excitement rising. "When will it be okay for me to go?"

"Tomorrow, if you like," Liam said, smiling.

"You mean you've already made contact with the League?" Somewhat indignant, Terry protested, "You promised I'd be the first to know—"

"You are the first. Did you think we would land on Earth and announce ourselves, like aliens from some ancient UFO tale? It will be a long, slow process that won't involve the League for many years. At first we'll have contact only with the Maclairnans, who are far better qualified to deal with it than Earth's citizens."

It made sense. The Elders hadn't put Maclairn under their protection just for its importance in spreading acceptance of human mind-powers, Terry perceived suddenly. They had always intended to make their first

contact there. It would become part of the secret Maclairn was already keeping, and not until that secret
was disclosed would the aliens' existence be generally
known.

"You're inviting me go with your ambassadors, then.
But *tomorrow*? I suppose I sensed something, it can't be
coincidence that I spoke out on the very day—"

"The day is of your choosing, Terry. *You* are the ambassador," Liam announced. "The shock to a newly-ad-
mitted world's people is lessened if the initial disclosure
comes from one of their own kind. It is for this that we've
been preparing you all these years—it's what Laesara chose
you for."

"Oh, my God."

"Your whole life has been preparation," Liam continued, "though that wasn't known until your second meeting with Laesara, when she learned how fate had posi-
tioned you to save Maclairn at the moment of its greatest
peril. It was decided then that if you fulfilled your potential, and if the mentors achieved their goal while you were
alive, you would be given this responsibility."

Terry drew breath. "All the years you've flown with
me, you were judging my fitness for it?"

Liam nodded. "The final step was bringing you here
to make sure you could adapt and that your impressions
of us would be favorable. The mentors will draw them
from you telepathically, you see. It's too vast a revelation
to be made in words alone."

"That's ironic," Terry declared, "considering that I've
spent the past hundred years in isolation from them to
prevent their sensing what I knew of you."

"Yes. And the mission isn't an easy one," Liam said
soberly. "We believe it's your destiny, but you are of course
free to refuse."

"God, Liam, you surely don't think I will." It was an
awesome prospect to be sent as ambassador, Terry realized. He had never imagined such a role as this. He was

not sure he wanted it. And yet to go back to Maclairn not merely as a repatriate, but as the herald of a future beyond anything its pioneers had ever dreamed of. . . .

"Of course not, which is why I feel guilty about sending you off knowing that you expect to gain your heart's desire," Liam admitted. "I don't want to spoil your pleasure in the prospect of homecoming, so I won't offer specific warnings right now—some of the potential problems may never arise. But unless you're willing to risk being hurt, you must not take this on."

No risk could keep him away, Terry thought with elation. The people he'd known and loved would be gone, of course. He'd had few friends near his own age except for Fleet officers. Even Kathryn had been several years older. Dared he hope . . ?

"Kathryn may be still alive," Liam told him. "She no longer travels with *Promise* to League Headquarters so we've had no recent news of her, though we do know that her second lifemate died long ago, and that your son became a mentor."

His son! The son he had never seen, who was now just half a year short of his hundredth birthday and must have many descendants. He might be reunited not only with his wife, but with a whole new family. . . .

It was too much happiness to take in.

For a few minutes they were silent, while Terry absorbed the reality of it. Then Liam said, "There are going to be difficulties. In the first place, you can reveal our existence to the Maclairnans but not to Fleet. There's no way Fleet could keep such a secret from the League; their duty would be to report it. And Fleet doesn't let unauthorized ships approach Maclairn."

Of course it didn't. He himself had set up the surveillance system, all those years ago. "But," Terry said, "when I reveal my identity—" he broke off, dismayed. He could not prove his identity. They had made sure that he couldn't; his voice, his face, his fingerprints, even his DNA had been changed along with his ID chip. An old man's claim to be Terry Radnor would be thought preposterous.

Can't you change me back to what I was? he pleaded silently.

No, unfortunately. We could restore your coloring, but not your facial features or your voice. We don't have a record of your original voice, or of your fingerprints.

And even if they did have, the Fleet cruiser now guarding Maclairn probably wouldn't. Not after a hundred years. Possibly Fleet Headquarters, which couldn't be contacted, would still have files containing his retinal pattern, but when combined with contrary evidence a match would be viewed as coincidence.

For there would be pictures of him. And it would be known that in defending *Promise* from pirates he had lost two fingers of his left hand. No League technology could have restored his natural fingers. Perhaps, he thought grimly, he should ask Liam to cut them off again.

Once, it wouldn't have mattered if he wasn't recognized. The original plan had been for any intruders to be kept permanently on Maclairn, a measure designed only to prevent the secret from getting out. But he had changed that. He had sent the message warning them never to allow a landing, never to make it possible for suicidal terrorists to destroy their world.

What would they do with an intruder now? Did they have some sort of orbital prison?

"Your best bet," Liam said, "will be to identify yourself as the Captain of *Estel.*"

"Fleet wasn't pleased by the Captain of *Estel*'s pardon. They can't touch me as long as I obey the law, but if I ignore their order to leave Maclairn's star, they'll be only too happy to arrest me."

"Yes. We'll have to play it by ear."

"You'll be with me? Maybe you can do something with psi—"

"I'll be along as your copilot and friend, but I can't

take any action a man of your own people couldn't. It will be up to you to find a way to get to the surface."

He would get there somehow, Terry told himself firmly. It was impossible to think he might approach Maclairn a second time without being able to land. And once there, Kathryn would know him . . . wouldn't she? Despite lack of physical resemblance, she would surely recognize the touch of his mind. But what if they didn't let him see Kathryn? What if they denied him any contact with Maclairnans?

Terry slept very little that night. Each time he wakened from a doze, he had to remind himself that what was happening wasn't just one of the recurrent dreams he'd had so often, dreams in which he walked again on the surface of Maclairn, the only planet he had ever cared about. And held Kathryn in his arms again. . . . That he might be given a chance to relive his youth was beyond anything he had ever wished for, strong though his trust in fate had been since his once-futile exile had proved meaningful. There had to be a catch, he told himself—he mustn't believe too strongly, because once he did, he would find it past bearing if it didn't come true after all. He knew deep down that such a blow would put an end to his long-extended life.

He was sure Liam wouldn't tantalize him. The Elders were too wise to have made unworkable plans—if they sent him to Maclairn, there could be no doubt that he would get there. And yet in the midst of elation a feeling of unease swept over him, something just beneath the surface, something he feared but could not put a finger on. Despite his wholehearted desire to go, a part of him was hesitant.

Was he perhaps afraid it wouldn't be as good as he remembered? No, that couldn't be it—he knew Maclairn wasn't perfect; he didn't expect that returning there would bring him undiluted joy in life. He knew he would not really be young again. He even knew that Kathryn might not love him as he still loved her, and that his son would consider him a stranger. But there was something else. . . . Not just the fear that Fleet would turn him away—a deeper and more subtle fear he dared not acknowledge consciously. . . .

No matter. He was going home. Past all hope, he was going to see Maclairn again before he died. Whatever trouble he might face was insignificant compared to that.

~ *65* ~

THEY LEFT YDORIL early the next morning. Surprisingly, Liam urged him to depart without saying goodbye to anyone. Perhaps that was wise, Terry thought. There would have been sadness in farewells.

It was good to be back aboard *Estel;* he eased into the familiar captain's seat with gladness. Yet he felt a pang of regret, too, as shining Ydoril receded into the distance. He'd experienced wonders there to which nothing could ever compare. If it were possible to go home without leaving the Elders' universe behind . . .

He would miss it. Yet he felt no doubt at all about preferring Maclairn. Why then did he still have a sense of repressed unease? What could he possibly fear beyond the acknowledged problems?

He shut that puzzle out of his mind while preparing to jump, programming the AI with the coordinates he had learned when he was captain of *Promise*. The coordinates the terrorists had later provided when he'd taken *Venture* there, only to turn away. . . . He had never expected to use them again. To be entering them once more seemed unreal. Dizzy with the excitement of it, he jumped.

But when they emerged in Maclairn's star system and settled in *Estel*'s lounge for the long trip through normal space, the nagging worry swept over him again.

And looking across at Liam, he became aware that Liam knew its cause.

There's no use hiding from it, Liam said silently. *It has to be faced by the time you're on Maclairn, so it's best to come to terms with it now, while you're under less stress.*

I don't understand—

It would have been cruel for me to bring it up last night. You deserved some hours of undiluted happiness. But as I warned you, Terry, this is a very difficult mission. Even assuming that you reach Maclairn's surface, its success is not guaranteed.

Terry frowned. Aloud he said, "What potential is there for failure—of the mission, I mean? Whatever disappointments there may be for me personally, the Maclairnans will learn what I'm there to reveal—"

He broke off, sensing Liam's uncertainty, and in horror grasped the thought beneath it—the thought he himself had not dared to let rise to the surface. "My God . . . are you saying they *might not believe me?*"

"Humans have been claiming to have met aliens for hundreds of years," Liam pointed out, "and listeners are used to assuming that it isn't true. There's an old fable on Earth that applies, I believe—something about crying wolf."

"But—Laesara said—" She had said the mentors would draw it from his mind whether they were trying to probe or not. That was why he hadn't been allowed to return to Maclairn. If they didn't believe even when he told them the secret outright, the century of exile *hadn't been necessary.*

His parting from Kathryn hadn't been necessary. The years of confinement to Ciencia had been pointless. The loss of his identity had served no purpose. . . .

"You know better, Terry," Liam said. "If you had not been on Ciencia for that precise length of time, you couldn't have saved Maclairn from the terrorists—not to mention all you've achieved since. You couldn't have gotten the

colonies to believe in mind-powers. You couldn't have defeated the Klan."

"Laesara didn't know about any of that when she
barred me from Maclairn," Terry said bitterly.

"No. That was why she grieved for you, and took joy
in the fate that brought you back to us."

"When she was dying she asked my forgiveness," he
recalled. "Did she know then what might be in store for
me as your ambassador?"

"Of course. If you hadn't been chosen for that role,
you'd never have guessed that our revelation of truth will
be resisted. So it might have been kinder not to have
burdened you with it; but we judged you'd want to go
back at any price."

He did want to, of course—but how could he face
Kathryn if they didn't believe?

"Your exile *was* necessary," Liam said. "It was virtually certain that at least a few of the mentors who knew
you, who had contacted your mind before, would have
realized that what they sensed in it was authentic; and
they would have vouched for your sanity to any mentor
you might have encountered. Only since the last of them
died has that danger ceased to exist. And think, Terry—
would you have wanted to go back later and be thought
insane? Would you have been happy these past years on
Maclairn, tolerated but not fully accepted as normal?"

"That's a loaded question," Terry declared, "and don't
think I don't see what you're getting at."

"I'm sure I don't need to spell it out." Liam said sadly.

"But why, if I may not be believed, are you sending
me instead of an Elder who could offer proof?"

"Because some human has to do it, and you are better
qualified than anyone else. An Elder's mind, if opened to
probing, would contain too much that's alien to be grasped
without preparation—our culture needs to be seen
through the lens of a human one. We could have taken a
mentor to Ydoril, someone known to the others and there-

fore more likely than you to be believed—but that person, having just been stunned by the fact that we exist, would be in shock for a long time. In too much shock to absorb what you have absorbed about the essence of humanity common to all species."

"I suppose that's true," Terry admitted.

"Besides," Liam continued, "the stakes would not be as high for such a person. As you know, emotion plays a large part in psi. You will be desperate to inspire belief, which will give you a better chance to succeed than someone who doesn't care as much."

"And if I fail, they'll at least start thinking about the possibility, so that the next ambassador won't meet so much resistance. I'm expendable."

"Perhaps. If so, it's for the cause to which you've devoted your life."

That too was true, Terry realized. He had nothing to complain about even if things went badly, and much to gain if they went well.

"The stakes are high not just for you, but for humankind," Liam went on. "Ever since your first meeting with Laesara you've known that Earth's civilization is on the verge of collapse. Only progression to Federation level can save it, which is why the success of Maclairn's plan was so important. But the transition won't begin until the Maclairnans choose to join us, and if they can't be persuaded to believe now, it will mean they're not ready. No other ambassador will be sent for many years, and perhaps that will be too late."

"It's asking a lot to expect them to believe without proof."

"There could be no proof short of contact with another species—remember that you didn't believe Laesara until she showed you her physical form. And for that to occur prematurely would destroy the sense of equality a new member race must feel. It would undo what has been gained by our keeping the secret this long."

"How can so much depend on me?" Terry protested. "I'm just one ordinary person out of billions."

"Hardly that. The fate of the world has depended on you several times before, after all. And the Eldest judged you a worthy representative. It's not just a matter of your virtues—not your integrity or your courage, important though they are. It's the content of your mind, Terry. What needs to be known about us is there for the mentors to draw on, whether or not they interpret it accurately. That's not the case with anyone else."

"Suppose I don't know how to make them do it?"

"You will know. You've had enough past success in conveying your message to let yourself be guided by unconscious instinct."

Terry gazed at his surroundings, at the interior of *Estel* where he had lived so long with the goal of spreading belief in coming change. *This is where it all led*, he acknowledged silently. *I pledged long ago in the Ritual to serve Maclairn's cause, no matter what the cost, and I reaffirmed that choice when I took command of* Estel. *And being the envoy of the Elders is part of the same thing. It'll just be what I've been doing all along—believing in something, and persuading people to share my belief because I know the future hinges on it.*

"You've accomplished a lot in the past hundred years," Liam agreed, "and you've always come through. This is your last and greatest challenge. Whatever happens, you'll be honored throughout the Federation, and ultimately by the people of Earth. But to me, what matters most is that I've had the privilege of being your friend."

~ *66* ~

TERRY PROGRAMMED *ESTEL*'S course so that they wouldn't pass near the outer planets or major asteroids on the approach to Maclairn, knowing the sensor stations he had placed on them a century ago were probably still there. Had Fleet spent a century watching for signals that never came? he wondered. Had there been any intruders besides the close call with the terrorists he himself had brought in? The cruiser *Shepard* was still in place, Liam had told him. It had never left, though personnel had been taken back and forth in small passenger vessels.

"Is there a Service ship on guard now?" he asked Liam as they neared the orbit of Corwin.

"Yes, as always, but we won't see it," Liam said. "I'm not permitted any contact before representatives of the Elders are invited to Maclairn—until then I'm here only as a member of your crew."

Their relationship had reverted to what it was before he knew Liam's true identity, Terry realized. He would receive no more advice from him. From now on, for better or for worse, he was on his own.

Because he'd successfully avoided all the outlying sensors, they weren't detected until they reached Maclairn's satellite ring. "Unidentified ship, this is Fleet Patroller Alpha from FHS *Shepard*. This entire system has been placed off-limits, as maneuvers are underway here," the comm announced, echoing the words with which he'd challenged the Elders' ship in *Skywalker* long ago. "You are required to jump at your earliest opportunity. Over."

"Fleet Patroller, this is HS *Estel*, the captain speaking," Terry responded. "The secret you are guarding is known to me. I come in peace to confer with the Council of Maclairn. Over."

He could imagine the shock with which this declaration was being met, not only by the patroller pilot but by the officers aboard *Shepard* who must have heard it. By the time a reply came he was surrounded by more patrollers, small fast ships based on the cruiser, not the ground. "HS *Estel*, if that's indeed your identity, you are not welcome here," a new voice said. "You are ordered to leave this system immediately. Acknowledge, please."

"*Shepard*, if you are listening, know that I have cause to believe the Council will welcome me. Maclairn's representatives have tried to contact me in the past. Over."

"*Estel*, they may have wished to contact your original captain, but we are aware that you are not he. If the Captain of *Estel* who was sentenced to prison were alive now, he would be well over a hundred years old."

If they knew the truth they would be even more incredulous, Terry realized. When the Elders had forged a new ID for him after the crash, they had subtracted ten years from his age, in anticipation, he now saw, of the unbelievable longevity they had given him. According to Fleet's records he was therefore a hundred sixteen. Although since there was no ansible on Maclairn these officers couldn't know that, anything over a hundred was unreasonably old for starship command.

"All who've heard of the Captain of *Estel*," he replied, "know that I have often spoken about new powers of the mind. Long life is among the results of using those powers. I am Terry Steward, the man who was imprisoned."

"That may be so, though I doubt it; but if it is, then you are risking another prison term by remaining here. For the last time, I order you to abort your approach."

"Negative, *Shepard*," Terry declared. "I will wait in high orbit until you have contacted the Council."

"*Estel,* this is Captain Aaronson of *Shepard* speaking, You are not permitted to orbit. Turn back now, or you will be fired on."

Terry held his course, uncomfortably aware that *Estel* was visibly armed. They wouldn't fire to kill; he knew, as most pirates did not, that it was against Fleet policy unless the target fired first. But they would hit harder than they would hit an unarmed ship. "Brace yourself," he told Liam, opaquing the viewport. "They'll aim to take out the laser cannon."

There was a blinding burst of light dead ahead and the force of the hit threw him hard against the straps of his seat. A warning light flashed on his console, confirming that the laser cannon was no longer operational.

"Why do you persist, Steward?" Aaronson's voice was cold. "You can't reach us, and you've nothing to gain by incurring more damage."

For first time real fear struck Terry. Fleet could rescue the crew easily enough if they damaged the ship past possibility of repair, so they might well decide to do it. He hadn't bargained on having to sacrifice *Estel*. Since the Elders' existence couldn't be revealed to Fleet, they wouldn't be able to restore it this time. . . .

"I can't leave without speaking with the Council," he declared. "But I will surrender my ship to your custody."

There was a long pause. Finally Aaronson replied, "Very well. Come no closer; we will send a shuttle to dock with you. How many have you in your crew?"

"Just myself and my copilot."

"Stand by, then, and prepare to be boarded."

"Affirmative, *Shepard*. We will establish orbit at this distance. Out."

The wait was not long; they must have deployed the shuttle earlier with the expectation of picking up personnel from a crippled ship. The patrollers remained in position until it docked and the airlock opened to admit four lieutenants. The first to come through the hatch stared at Terry and Liam, exclaiming, "My God, you *are* old men. Is this the real *Estel*, the one no one's ever seen?"

"You're seeing it now," Terry replied. They evidently weren't aware that it had been seized twice in the past; Fleet had kept that quiet. He was using its real transponder, the one for *Bright Hope* having been disconnected; but without access to an ansible *Shepard* could not verify it.

"How did you locate this planet? Its sun's coordinates aren't public knowledge."

"The Captain of *Estel* is not the public," Liam pointed out. "He knows much that he has never revealed."

The lieutenant nodded. "I don't doubt it, but he won't

be allowed to go down to the surface, you know. We have a strict policy against permitting any landings."

"Then what do you intend to do with us?" Terry demanded. "You can hardly keep us aboard your ship for the rest of our lives." It was like déjà vu, he thought; he'd asked Laesara the same thing when *Skywalker* was captured by the Elders. . . .

"The captain will decide that after you've been debriefed," the lieutenant said coldly. "Get your gear and go through to our shuttle."

Terry and Liam complied. They had packed duffels ahead of time, knowing they'd be leaving *Estel* one way or another. They were immediately shut out of the bridge, which one of the officers took over; Terry couldn't help feeling dismay at the possibility that the ship might be confiscated by Fleet again. But surely it wouldn't be for long—the Council would request its return, and the wishes of Maclairn's leaders were always respected.

As they neared Maclairn in Fleet's shuttle, Terry looked out at the glorious golden sphere, the years since he'd last seen it slipping away. It was still beautiful in his eyes, even after the sight of the Federation worlds. This was what he'd dreamed of, both in conscious contemplation and literally; this was the one place in the universe that tugged at his heart. No matter that it was a dry, rocky planet, gold only because of those rocks and its sparse alien vegetation; that the blue jewels with which it was spattered were drying lakes bordered by salt flats; that the green oases of the settlements, which they were still too far out to see, were small. No other world could ever evoke his allegiance.

So many times he'd made this approach in *Promise*, coming home after a trip to polluted, depressing Earth. Home . . . now it would be that again, if his mission succeeded, and perhaps even if it didn't; he had not asked Liam whether he would be taken back to Ydoril in that case.

The choice will be up to you, Liam told him silently,

sensing the question. *You will have to balance the joy and sorrow; no one can do that for you.*

At the moment, Terry felt sure that it would be all joy.

Aboard *Shepard*, they were taken at once to Captain Aaronson by routes through the maze of passageways that he well remembered, realizing just in time that he must pretend not to know how to reach the bridge. It had not changed. In all this time Fleet must have acquired new cruisers, but guarding Maclairn was not a high priority mission and evidently this one had not been refurbished.

Aaronson, too, expressed surprise at the sight of two aged pilots, though neither of them looked anywhere near as old as they actually were. "It's true," he conceded, "that there's some affinity between the ideals of the Captain of *Estel* and those of the Maclairnans. But you must realize that even if I were positive that you are not an imposter, which I'm not, I don't have the authority to let you land. This ship has orbited the colony for over a century with the express purpose of keeping intruders away. Only once did one come near enough for us to scramble patrollers, and though that was before my time, I have been well informed about its pilot's attempt to deceive us. If anyone not authorized ever does get down there, it won't be on my watch."

"Call in the mentors," Terry declared. "Let them judge me." He was certain of this; no secrets needed to be revealed for psi-gifted people to perceive that he and Liam were harmless.

"There are no mentors aboard at present," Aaronson said.

"Well, call Petersville and request that the Council send someone up."

"I'm not about to involve the Council in the job I'm stationed here to do," declared the captain decisively. "My orders are to detain intruders. I'm not expected to ask for advice on whether to follow them."

"The Council won't thank you when they hear you're denying them contact with the Captain of *Estel*," Liam warned.

"They won't hear. I don't bother them with such matters."

"Sooner or later it will get back to them," Terry said. "The rumor is already spreading among your crew; those lieutenants aren't going to keep quiet about it. And during shore leave some will tell friends among the Maclairnans."

"Perhaps. But by that time you'll be gone."

"Haven't I made plain that I'm not going to be coerced into leaving? Not unless you make me a prisoner on my own ship and crew it with your officers, who I don't think you can afford to spare for such a job."

"Fortunately, that won't be necessary," Aaronson informed him. "There's a Fleet transport in orbit for crew rotation. It's leaving for headquarters tomorrow and you two are going to be aboard it."

Terry, struck by vertigo, barely managed to hide his dismay. There were not supposed to be any Fleet transports at Maclairn; in his era it had been visited only by *Promise*. He hadn't stopped to think about crew rotation. *Oh, God, Liam!* he cried silently. *We can't let this happen, it would be impossible for me to get back! You couldn't get anyone else in, either, if they won't consult the Council. . . .*

They would confiscate *Estel* and neither he nor Liam could regain possession of it. Liam would be free to find some other way to contact the Maclairnans, perhaps through the mentors on Earth. But he himself would have no part in it. He would be arrested for resisting the patrollers, and would be sent back to Draconis. He might be there for what little remained of his life.

Liam, for the first time since Terry had known him, was disconcerted; he had spent his entire career preparing for this mission and had not expected that it could be thwarted. *Don't panic,* he responded. *I can't believe fate won't provide some way out..*

Can't you contact the Service ship?

I would, despite my instructions, but there's nothing they could do.

They could turn the transport back, maybe—not let it jump.

It would be self-defeating, Liam pointed out, *to reveal the presence of aliens that way when our aim is to do it peacefully, through you.*

"You'll stay here under guard overnight," Aaronson stated, and motioned to the lieutenants to take them away.

"Wait," Terry said desperately. He couldn't leave without at least finding out about Kathryn. "There was a woman, Kathryn, who used to be Maclairn's ambassador to the League—do you know if she's still living?"

"Kathryn of Maclairn is a respected member of the Council; of course I know her. But it's unlikely that you do, considering that you don't know whether or not she's alive."

Terry's heart leaped. "I have news I'm sure she would wish to be given," he persisted. But Aaronson did not reply.

They were taken to a small stateroom identical to the one he had shared with his engineer Drew Larssen before his marriage. The guards departed, locking the hatch behind them. Terry, in despair, sat down on a bunk and bowed his head, feeling his courage ebb away. This *couldn't* be happening again, not twice! For the second time since his exile he'd come close to Maclairn, only to find himself unable to reach it. He would be torn away, having failed to live up to the Elders' expectations. . . .

Liam wasn't blaming him, of course. Terry was buoyed by his silent sympathy. But he was aware that underneath Liam, too, was appalled by their helplessness.

At noon by ship's time food was brought by one of the lieutenants who'd boarded *Estel,* a young one who'd observed it with interest but said nothing. He set down the tray and started to leave, then hesitated and turned back. "Captain," he said to Terry, "I think I might be able to get a message to the councilor Kathryn, if you wish."

"God, yes!" Terry burst out. "Do you mean tonight?"

"Possibly, if I can reach my friend in Petersville by phone—she's acquainted with Kathryn. I'll try."

"You'll be well rewarded even for trying," said Terry, realizing that his credits could be transferred for future use even though League money couldn't be spent here.

"I don't want pay," the young lieutenant declared. "I believe you *are* the Captain of *Estel*, and I've followed you online ever since I was in grade school. Is there something I can say to let her know the message is important?"

"Yes," said Terry, with rising hope. "Tell her that I can provide facts she does not know about the fate of her first husband, Terry Radnor."

~ 67 ~

THE DAY WORE on interminably, with no word. But early in the evening a guard appeared, saying "Come along, Steward. The Captain says a member of the Council has come to question you."

Terry trembled with relief and excitement. Kathryn! Within a few minutes now he'd be with Kathryn. . . .

"Go, Terry," Liam said, "and good luck." Silently he added, *We may not see each other again—I can't come down if your efforts fail, and you may choose to stay there permanently. Whatever happens, I'll always cherish the memory of our years together.*

Liam, I'm not going to fail! Before long I'll be introducing you to the Council.

I trust you will—I believe it's your destiny to accomplish this mission. Godspeed, my friend. I wish you joy in your homecoming. Liam's eyes were wet with emotion; shaken, Terry realized what this parting meant to them both. But he was too full of the thought of Kathryn to dwell on it.

He was taken to the mess deck, now deserted after the evening meal. "The wardroom is in use," the officer said, "so since the Maclairnan has requested privacy, you will be interviewed here. There are guards outside the exits, so don't try to cause trouble." The man departed, and Terry was left alone.

He waited, his heart pounding. Kathryn entered from behind the dais as she had for their wedding, held in this room long ago. For a moment he thought he had moved back in time. In essence she had not changed. Her hair was white now, of course, but still short and wavy, and her figure was as slim and straight as a young girl's. Aging had had as little effect on her as it had on him, though their faces were marked by maturity.

"I understand that you have information for me," Kathryn said. "I couldn't authorize a stranger's transport to the surface, but since I wished to hear it in person, the captain sent a shuttle as I asked. Are you really the Captain of *Estel*, the original one?"

Terry came forward, unsure how to break the news. His own white hair and age disguised his physical alterations somewhat; still the Elders had purposely made his face unidentifiable. "I am," he said. "I'm sorry it was not possible for us to meet sooner."

"So am I. I tried to arrange it, but was told you refused."

"Like much else I regret, it was necessary."

"Yet somehow you obtained information about what happened to my husband Terry, and did not give it to me until now? Or has it just come to light? If so, and you've come expressly to tell me, I apologize for the treatment you've received by Fleet."

"Kathryn." He realized that he could not say aloud

what must be said; if she didn't recognize his mind-touch, she would never believe any of the rest of it. *Oh, Kathryn, you know who I am, if you still love me as I love you. . . .*

Stunned, she stood motionless, unable to speak. *Terry . . . Terry? You can't be, your voice isn't his, you don't even look like him. It's an illusion. . . .*

It's not an illusion. I'm here, after all the years I was forced to stay away. He stepped forward, wanting to embrace her but afraid she would shrink from him.

They told me old age on Maclairn doesn't bring dementia, she said silently, *but I've lost touch with reality now.*

"No, you haven't, Terry replied aloud. "I'm real—the man you remember."

"Terry died a hundred years ago. If he hadn't, he would have come back to me!"

He'd known this issue would bring pain to her, but there was no way around it. "I couldn't come back," he said forthrightly. "I was confined for many years to a planet from which there was no escape. I thought I *would* die without you, Kathryn. I paid a smuggler to carry a message to your grandfather, but was informed that he was dead. After that I lost hope of ever seeing you again."

"But you did escape. The Captain of *Estel* has been traveling around the galaxy for more than eighty years! And, I've heard, a wife traveled with him."

"You had a new lifemate, too."

"Yes, when I thought you were dead. You knew you were still married to me."

"Not legally. After six years of separation a marriage is dissolved, and it was twice that before I loved Alison. Yes, I escaped from my prison world, but there were restrictions on my freedom—I was barred both from Maclairn and from Earth."

"Barred even from communication? I was at League Headquarters on the Moon from time to time, you knew that. Why didn't you contact me?"

"That's a long story, Kathryn, the one I've come here to tell."

He reached out to touch her, only to see her retreat in horror. "You're not Terry!" she exclaimed. "My mind is deceiving me. Terry had lost two fingers of his left hand."

For the moment he had forgotten about that; he should have kept the hand hidden until she was sure. "There are technologies unknown on Earth," he said, "and healing powers greater than are known on Maclairn."

"And yet you know them? You have psi gifts greater than any of the mentors?" Bewildered, she turned away, saying, "That's harder to believe than that my own can no longer be trusted."

"Telepathy can't lie, Kathryn," he said gravely. "I have spent the last century persuading people to believe in the capabilities of the mind. You have spent it on Maclairn, which was founded on that belief. If we can't trust our own perceptions, all that has gone for nothing—all the first Stewards endured, all the effort put into the plan to spread mind-powers to humankind. The hope we've had for the future is meaningless if what those powers reveal isn't true."

For a few moments she stood silent, staring at him with a kind of awe. Then her mind met his in full communion, as it had when they were in love. *Terry . . . Terry, you're alive . . . what is this miracle that has brought you back to me alive? Hold me, show me that you're here in the flesh and not just in spirit. . . .*

He took her in his arms and held her close. She was crying, and he could barely keep back his own tears. *Dearest, I've lived so long thinking I'd lost you, lost so much I could never regain. . . . Fate has favored me in many ways, saved my life more than once and given me a chance to serve the cause we share; but never has there been so great a blessing as this.*

When he could speak again, he said, "Tell me about our son. For a hundred years I've been longing to know—

I once heard he was well, and psi-gifted, but nothing more. How soon can I see him?"

"You can't, unless you go to Earth—he's a mentor there now. At the original Bramfield Club—he's heir to what remains of the Bramfield fortune. I donated most of it to the Maclairn Foundation, but he heads that, too."

Terry was glad, as it was fitting; yet at the same time deeply disappointed. Still, since he was no longer forbidden to contact mentors he was now free to visit Earth, so a trip there might eventually be arranged.

For now, there were more pressing responsibilities. Kathryn would find it harder to believe in the Elders than in his own presence, and he didn't look forward to making the revelation—but she would have to be told before he met with the Council. And it would have to be done soon.

"Will I be allowed to go down to the surface with you?" he asked, smiling.

"Of course. The shuttle's waiting for me, and I'll set Captain Aaronson straight. He doesn't think you're dangerous, he's just careful to keep clear of Maclairnan politics."

"Politics? What kind of politics?" There had been no political conflicts on Maclairn when he left; it was a happy, unified society.

"Well, it's complicated—I'll fill you in later. But he knew asking the Council to let an unauthorized person land, especially one as well known as the Captain of *Estel*, could cause friction."

"Does *Promise* still bring observers?"

"Yes, but they're chosen by the Foundation, of course. Some people here think its policies are too conservative."

Obviously there was a lot to catch up on, Terry thought. "What will be done with my copilot?" he asked. "He's locked in his stateroom."

"I'll see that he's released, but as for taking him with us, I don't know—I think it might be better to wait till you've met the Council."

"I agree," Terry said. "He normally guards *Estel* when I'm on the ground."

It was dark by the time the shuttle reached the surface of Maclairn. The pilot—the same young officer who had gotten the message to Kathryn—accompanied them from the Fleet landing area in the historic Old Settlement down to the lake and the boat that would take them to the dam. From there, the main colony was reached by funicular. So many times he'd followed this route, in the flesh and since, in dreams. . . .

The night of their wedding had been like tonight, leaving *Shepard* after the ceremony, the trip down the lake, cuddling together in the chill wind while laughing and singing from other boats echoed across the water; and then, in Petersville, the wedding feast. Now they were alone except for the boatman, and the lake was silent . . . silent and calm, as it had been at dawn on the morning he'd left Maclairn forever. . . .

They didn't talk. What he had to tell Kathryn was too momentous to be said during the journey, and she sensed that for now he wanted to remain absorbed in his memories.

Kathryn's house in Petersville was one of the old ones, large enough for several generations and built mainly of stone instead of brick like the more modest dwellings. She had bought it after inheriting her grandfather's fortune, leaving the room she'd occupied in the house of Jessica, then head of the Council. "I hated to," she told him, "because that was the room where you and I lived together. But when Radnor was born, I knew I'd need more space while he was growing up."

She told him about her second lifemate, a widowed mentor quite a bit older than she was. "Radnor worshiped him," she said, "but he always knew you were his father. He loved to hear me talk about you, and about how I'd searched for word of you. For years I tracked down every speculation anyone came up with, at League headquarters and on Earth. Aldren couldn't believe you'd died in space, you see. He'd had that vision about your strange destiny. He said that if you had been killed it must have been while doing something significant for Maclairn's cause."

"You saw Aldren?"

"Yes, first when *Promise* stopped at Titan and often later, after he came back here to retire. To the end of his life he insisted that there must have been truth in the dream he'd believed was precognitive."

"He was right," Terry said, thankful that she'd given him an opening. "Fate led me to several strange destinies, and this last one, my mission here, is the strangest of all."

They settled on the cushions before the fireplace in her great room, in which as was customary in Maclairnan homes, all seating was on the floor. The firelight illuminated Kathryn's familiar face, now raised expectantly. He wanted only to caress her, love her, and not spoil the joy he knew she was sharing. But she was eager to know the details, and reluctantly he went on.

"You know that the morning I left, I'd sensed something strange through psi, by remote viewing—a ship of some kind that didn't belong in this system. Well, there was a ship and I was captured by it. And because I'd learned its crew's secret, they couldn't set me free. They told me I could never return to Maclairn because the mentors would perceive what I knew, even if I tried to conceal it. I refused to accept that, but they gave me no choice—they changed my body so I couldn't be recognized, and forged a new ID, and took me to the planet I told you about, a world where no starships were allowed to come."

"Changed your body? Were they the ones who restored your natural fingers?"

"Yes, and altered my face, and voice, and skin color— even my DNA."

"How could they do such things, things medical science can't do on Earth?"

Terry drew a deep breath. "Because they were not human in the sense that we are, Kathryn. Their species did not evolve on Earth. They were aliens."

"Don't joke with me—I need to know what happened to you."

"I'm telling you. It's not a joke; there are inhabited planets elsewhere in the universe, and I encountered one of their ships."

He felt the shock in her mind like a blow. "My God, Terry—I think you *believe* that! I know you do, if telepathy can't lie, but that doesn't mean what you believe is true. Something did happen, something so traumatic that it affected your memory. That's why you didn't come back to me."

~ 68 ~

OH, GOD, TERRY thought. He'd known she would be incredulous, but hadn't anticipated the interpretation she'd put on his revelation. "It *is* true," he assured her. "How could I have gotten my fingers back if I hadn't met people with superior technology? How could I have been taken, as I have been since then, to dozens of worlds concealed from the League?"

"I know you think you went there," Kathryn said sorrowfully. "But that's a delusion, Terry. You've been wandering, confused as to who you are—amnesia can work that way. You built a whole new life as the Captain of *Estel*, and you've done a lot of good with that persona. You didn't remember where you belong till now, so I can't blame you for not coming sooner. But you need to realize that some of what you recall is false memory. We'll go to see Devan tomorrow, he's been my mentor since Jessica died, and I'm sure he can help you clear it up."

Terry steadied himself, knowing he must not protest, must not be angry at her for coming to a conclusion that was actually quite logical. "I'll be happy to see him," he told her. "That's what I'm here for, to tell the mentors about the Elders—the aliens. They couldn't let their presence be known until Earth accepted the reality of psi because that's the only way they can communicate with us, for one thing. Now that we're ready to join their Federation, they've appointed me to be the first go-between."

He was aware, sensing her dismay, that it did sound like a crazy story, the sort of thing mental patients on Earth had been saying for centuries. Liam had warned that he might be thought insane . . . but he hadn't expected to be doubted even by Kathryn. All the anguish of the separation, the years during which he'd been exiled under the assumption that she and others would learn what he knew, swept over him—despite what Liam had said, he might have come back long ago without endangering the secret. . . .

He left it for the moment and went on to tell Kathryn what had happened to him on Ciencia—how bad it had been at first, his work in the underground, his initially-platonic relationship with Alison. She listened, obviously trying to sort fantasy from reality. "You always wanted to believe in aliens, she reminded him. "You talked about how exciting it would be if there were some. So when you got stuck in a situation you couldn't escape from, couldn't account for as a result of anything you'd done, it was natural to let yourself think aliens had put you there."

Yes, he'd wished there were aliens—they had talked about it more than once. And Kathryn had not shared his interest in the idea. He recalled a day when she'd told him that aboard the Foundation ship that discovered Maclairn, at her first sight from space of an unknown colony she and the others had half-thought it might be alien. And she had been scared, she'd said. She had thought it would have a devastating effect on Earth's civilization.

Which of course was exactly why the Elders had said

it would be damaging for them to be discovered too soon.

Encouraged, he told her so. She had been right all along, he said, as far as premature contact was concerned. The Elders wanted to protect Earth's civilization. Their goal, and his while he stayed away from mentors, had been to conceal their existence until humankind could meet them as equals. In Kathryn's eyes, however, he had simply imagined aliens as he felt they ought to be.

Maybe it would go better in the morning, Terry thought. They were both tired now and it was time for bed. That was awkward; he did not dare ask if he could share hers. Perhaps she did not know if he would want to.

They were still married, even if not under the law, for neither of them had intentionally broken the vow they'd made to love forever. But he could not be sure that she still felt desire for him. Age wasn't a barrier; the mind training that prevented decline in old age applied to more than just health and appearance. Looking at Kathryn, he wanted her as much as when they both were young.

He took her in his arms and kissed her, restraining himself, being careful not to let her think he expected more than she wished to offer. They'd both closed their minds to probing; perhaps she was repelled by his supposed mental illness.

The room she led him to was next to her own. "This was Radnor's room," she told him. "No one else has slept here; I have other guest rooms, and I like to think he may be back someday."

Alone in the bed of the son he had never seen, he gave way to tears of frustration. If Kathryn didn't believe him despite telepathic evidence that he was sincere, who would? He had been given an impossible task. Looking back, he saw that Liam must have known the chances were slim. His mission was a calculated sacrifice, one he'd been deemed willing to make because of his longing to go home. The first man to tell the Maclairnans that contact with aliens had finally occurred wouldn't be taken seriously. But he would be remembered, especially if he stayed and persisted despite being viewed as crazy. The next man to make exactly the same claim, describing the aliens in the same way after passage of time, would be believed. The Elders took a long view of history.

He didn't regret having returned here; there had never been a time when he wouldn't have chosen to do so under any terms whatsoever. The Elders had given him more wondrous experiences than any human before him had encountered. He couldn't complain about being asked to repay through a role that was not exactly the sort of homecoming he would have wished.

He was free to refuse it, Terry thought suddenly. He could say nothing to the mentors, tell Kathryn that seeing her had cleared his mind, and live out his life happily with her, honored by the Maclairnans as a returning hero. The Elders, unable to land here, could do nothing about it. Yet he knew he couldn't bring himself to let them down—to let humankind down, when he'd worked for so long to hasten its readiness for contact. The Eldest had trusted him; Laesara had trusted him . . . and so had Liam. Whatever else might tempt him to back out, he could not betray Liam's trust.

And yet, Terry wondered suddenly, what was it all *for*? He had spent decades spreading hope to the colonies, and there had been more to it than his commitment to further Maclairn's cause, for he and he alone had known that acquiring mind-powers was essential to contact with the Elders. He'd been told that time was running out, that Earth's civilization might die before it became eligible for contact, and he had never stopped to wonder what difference the contact would make. He'd never doubted that reaching that point would produce a brighter future. But *why*?

The Elders didn't interfere with developing worlds— he'd known that. They weren't going to step in and solve Earth's problems. And it still had many, even though belief in volitional health control and in psi was now an accepted view. Eventually, telepathy would enable people to live in greater harmony, but that was a long way off for most. So how was membership in the Federation going to help? Dismayed, he realized that he'd never asked Liam about that. It had just been understood between them that revealing the Elders' existence to Maclairn was essential. That it would matter in some significant way. . . .

Terry lay wakeful, not using the mind training that would let him sleep. Liam had said he would know what to tell the Council, that he'd had enough past success in conveying beliefs to let himself be guided by unconscious instinct. But so far instinct wasn't offering any answers . . . or was it? A glimmer of an idea came to him, but he could not capture it. Finally he stopped trying and turned to reliving in reverse his memories of the years when he and Kathryn were young.

Kathryn—she shone through them all, illuminating the events of those short years. The Ritual, falling on the day she'd told him she was pregnant . . . the trips to Earth and back in *Promise*, with layovers in New Tahiti where they'd lain on white beaches by a blue sea . . . their wedding . . . his captaincy of *Picard* and near death on the icy moon of Planet Five, not letting himself picture her grief . . . the raising of the ancient *Picard* from Maclairn, at dawn following their first night together. . . . He wondered if he would have a chance to see the stone hut in the Old Settlement where they'd spent it, the night after which he'd been forever changed.

It had been his first experience with the full mind merge of telepathic lovers. Terry's heart ached for that; he wished he could experience it just one more time. With Alison it had never been quite complete, deep though his love for her had been, for she was neither psi-gifted nor sufficiently trained in telepathy. Only with Kathryn had all barriers to total union come down. He'd hoped . . . but she would be unlikely to want it now, at least not after the mentors confirmed her suspicion that he was mentally unbalanced.

Abruptly he realized that this was his only chance. He loved her, longed for her, all the more after hours of recalling their life together while knowing she was no further away than the next room. If he made no move now, there might never be another opportunity; she would treat him courteously as a guest, but would have no wish for intimacy. It might already be too late; still he would always regret not having tried.

The sky outside the window was already brightening; it was almost dawn. Terry rose. Without putting on a shirt he left his room and quietly opened the door to hers, telling himself that the invasion of privacy was forgivable because in his heart, at least, they were still married. Again he felt that he'd traveled through time, for she looked just as she had on that distant morning when he'd left without waking her, thinking they would be separated no more than a day or two. Her face was hidden by the pillow but the outline of her slim body showed clearly through the light coverlet under which she slept; for a moment he felt impelled to pull it away and embrace her without asking.

Kathryn? he called silently. In the past, unconscious perception would have wakened her, and he did not want to make any noise by which she might be startled.

She turned over and opened her eyes. *Terry! I was afraid you wouldn't come. . . .*

Did you want me to? I thought that maybe because—

Because some of your memories aren't real? That doesn't matter! It doesn't change love—you do remember now that you loved me.

I have never for an instant forgotten that I loved you.

She smiled and threw back the coverlet. *Then come and show me. Pretend that you never went away.*

Terry undressed and lay down beside her, stirred not only by their mutual response to each other's bodies but by the forging of the telepathic bond. It strengthened along with mounting passion, not as rapidly as it had in their youth, yet with the same intensity. Her breasts were less firm than he remembered but just as sensitive; as always, he felt her sensations as well as his own. But the physical ones were unimportant compared to the union of their minds.

At first it was only an overpowering sense of love; he experienced her love for him along with his for her, as well as her awareness of his pleasure. He rolled over and seized her, sensing that despite age she was not fragile and there was no need to hold himself back. Then, with full arousal, came the total merging—he felt the pain of her past grief as his own, and her joy at their reunion. He saw fleeting images of places she'd been, people she'd known—and their son! He held their baby in his own arms, saw him grow, saw him reach manhood and become a mentor. All the things he'd imagined about him were now true memories, transferred directly from her mind into his. . . .

And he was aware that the flashes of recall went both ways. Through her eyes, he saw his own history, Ciencia, Alison, *Estel,* New Afrika . . . and, at the moment of their climax, the Elders.

He had tried not to envision them, fearing she would recoil from what she viewed as fantasy; but he'd forgotten that mind merging, except with regard to deep secrets purposely concealed, was not subject to control. She drew on his subconscious store of impressions as he drew on hers, randomly, as if from background awareness of her own past. Liam, whom she did not recognize as alien . . . Laesara, whom she did . . . and others, more alien still. . . .

Oh, God, Kathryn cried out silently, *it's true! And I don't want it to be true!* She recoiled, gasping. "I'm—scared, Terry!" she murmured. "Not of them—I could tell from your memories that they mean us no harm. But knowing they exist changes so much! The universe seems so much stranger than before!"

All at once Terry understood. She had not believed him because she didn't want to believe. Just as people on Earth had refused to believe in psi because underneath they feared changing their view of reality, she feared a new conception of what it meant to belong to the human race. And he knew with foreboding that it was a fear other Maclairnans might share.

~ *69* ~

THEY LAY IN bed and talked for a long time. Terry told her the details of his capture and exile, skipping over his work on Ciencia but explaining how he'd created the legend of *Estel* to inspire belief in mind-powers. "After my escape from prison, when I met the Elders again and was given the real *Estel*, Laesara made me see I'd been doing the same work as the mentors," he said. "It was then, well over eighty years ago, that she chose me to be the first to visit alien worlds, though I didn't know that till I was on the way there."

"And you were happy about it? You didn't hate them for what they'd done to you?"

"Yes, I was happy. I'd stopped hating them a long way back. All those years I'd longed to know more about their civilization—but I understood that they didn't want to have any effect on humankind until we could meet them as equals."

Was simply meeting them as equals going to bring Earth's civilization to their level? he asked himself. His sleepless night hadn't given him an answer.

There was so much more to tell Kathryn about his own past, and about the Elders' culture, that he knew it would take many days; she could absorb only a little of it at a time. For now, he needed to get on with his mission, sacrificial though it might prove to be. "The morning's half over," he said, "and I'd like to see the Council today, if that's possible. Can you arrange it?"

"I think so—any member can call a meeting. They'll be stunned, and so excited, to know that you're alive. Did you know they named planet Four after you?"

"I heard that, yes."

"Corwin was the first to die for Maclairn's cause, and we thought you were the second, so since you'd named Three after him, it seemed fitting."

"Well, it's embarrassing now, though I hope ultimately I'll have a place in our history as the Elders' ambassador."

Kathryn frowned. "Do you have to tell the others about the Elders? They'll think what I thought, and it could be awkward—I'm not sure they'll take my word that you're not crazy. Let's just keep it our secret."

Terry stared at her in dismay. "Telling them is what I was sent back for," he said. "I'm the official envoy to humankind; they can't come here till I've prepared the Council to receive them. I thought you knew."

She paled. "I didn't. Oh, God, Terry, are they going to come *here*? Isn't there some way you can talk them out of it?"

"Yes," he said grimly, "there's a way. I can fail to convince the Council that they're real and should be welcomed. That would set Earth's admission to the Federation back by many years, because they won't force themselves on a civilization that isn't ready. I'd be betraying their trust in me, and betraying all I worked for as Captain of *Estel*."

Bewildered, she protested, "But why must you bring them here, when this world's secret even from most humans?

"Secrecy is the point! Don't you see, Kathryn—they can't appear on Earth till long after contact with humans has been established. The public would think they were alien invaders, like in an ancient UFO vid. Maclairnans are better qualified than anyone else to learn about them, so the plan is not to reveal the Elders' existence until Maclairn's is made known."

She was silent, trying to absorb an idea she clearly found disturbing. "I've come as ambassador," he went on, "just as you were ambassador from Maclairn to the League when this world was discovered. Remember what a hard time you had convincing League officials that powers greater than what they thought "normal" were real, and setting up the terms for contact with us? I've got to do the same thing, so that Elders can serve here the way mentors have served on Earth."

"Did they know about Maclairn before you told them?"

"Of course. What do you think they were doing in this solar system when I was captured? They have guarded Maclairn in secret for many years, knowing how important it is to Earth's progress."

"Then we've been their pawns—"

"No. It was to avoid influencing us that they wouldn't risk letting the mentors learn prematurely from me that they exist."

"And you're their pawn! They've set you up to be thought mentally ill when you may not be able to convince anyone that you're not."

"I know that," Terry said seriously. "But I consented to it. Not just because I longed to come home, or because of what I owe them for what they've given me, but because this is the fulfillment of the commitment I made to Maclairn in the Ritual."

Kathryn sighed. "If it's a matter of the Ritual then I know I can't talk you out of it. But I don't see the connection, Terry. As Stewards of the Flame we've pledged to pass mind-powers on to others, and to future generations—"

"And to move past our fears," he reminded her.

She reddened. "That's true. I guess it means we can't let ourselves be afraid of aliens. But there's nothing in the pledge about learning everything there is to know in the universe. We're succeeding in the plan to get acceptance of psi into Earth's collective unconscious—some think we've already reached the tipping point. What more are we obliged to do?"

Terry pondered it, trying to think of a way to express what he felt. And all at once it became clear. His glimmer of understanding blazed into the answer he'd spent the night searching for.

"Why are mind-powers important?" he asked.

"Because they're the next step in evolution. And because having personal power frees people from tyranny, and telepathy leads to harmony between them."

"Yes, but there's got to be more than that. There's got to be challenge ahead. Suppose we eventually do teach everyone in the world to use their whole minds—what then? A civilization can't stay static; if it doesn't look forward, it dies."

"Maclairn's culture hasn't changed in three hundred years. People are content."

"Maclairn has a goal, something yet to be achieved. People in the League colonies aren't content—they're depressed, in spite of having better living conditions than Earth's, because founding more colonies is no longer a challenge. And people on Earth have given up looking for one; they're just surviving with nothing ahead to live for. You know that, Kathryn."

"Yes," she said sadly. "It was that way when I was growing up there, and it's even more true now."

"A civilization can't survive without challenge," Terry declared. "Individual people are challenged by acquiring new mind-powers, which is why they were excited by what I said about *Estel*. But I also made them feel there was more, a bright future of some sort. Even though I didn't reason it out, I knew inside that there'd be a time when humankind would enter a vast universe of new ideas and new experiences."

"I–I never thought of it that way," Kathryn said. "We looked at gaining mind-powers as the *end,* after which people could get rid of the League's dictatorial government and concentrate on cleaning up the slums and putting an end to hate and violence. What about that, Terry? Isn't it a challenge?"

"It doesn't work like that," Terry declared. "I've read Earth's history—"

"I remember you always liked to."

"Well, after more than eighty years on a ship with a full knowledgebase and time to kill in normal space between jumps, I've read a lot more. For centuries people thought they could do away with Earth's problems if only everybody would make enough effort, and it never happened. There were always troublemakers, just as there still are—the Klan, for instance—and when they defeated some, others rose in their place; and the people not busy fighting them were nearly as bad off because the majority of them stopped trying to achieve anything at all. And that left them prey to autocratic governments like the League that create worse problems than the ones they claim to be solving."

"But surely there were *some* challenges, or there would never have been any progress."

"Sure there were—creating things, making discoveries—but those challenged just a few individuals. The only one that did have widespread impact was exploration, first of different areas on Earth and then of space. And the settling of new lands and new worlds. That's why the colonies are less run-down than Earth, but they won't be for long because the challenge is over for them now, and already they're sinking into lethargy. People there have stopped thinking about the future."

"Oh . . . you're saying that just contact with something new and different, without the aliens taking any action to change us—"

"Yes—that's what I didn't see at first, because they

said time was short for Earth's civilization and yet I knew they wouldn't interfere. Besides, despite all I'd thought about the Elders, I didn't imagine how much there was to learn and think about till I went to their worlds. It will be like the Renaissance in ancient times, only far more exciting."

Kathryn sat up and reached for her robe. "You may be right," she said. "Only I don't want you to be hurt, Terry—and you will be, if the Council doesn't buy it. It's a good theory, you see, but if they don't believe there really are aliens, it will be *just* theory. Something you've convinced yourself could save Earth from decline."

"I know. But do you understand now why I have to try?"

She nodded. "When I think about what Aldren would say, I realize you haven't got a choice. You never did have, even when you left me to hunt for the intruding ship— you are what you are, and I guess I wouldn't have loved you if you were less."

~ 70 ~

THE COUNCIL MEETING was scheduled for late afternoon. Terry wanted to spend the day renewing his acquaintance with Petersville, revisiting the places he'd envisioned with longing during the past century; but Kathryn pointed out that they'd meet people she knew and the presence of an unrecognized old man couldn't be explained. She could hardly introduce him as her long-lost husband to one person at a time, and certainly not before she'd told their grandchildren.

"We have three," she told him. "Bram and Arthur, named after my grandfather, and Mikaela, named after your shipmate Mikaela Orlov, who became copilot and later captain of *Promise*—she was one of my best friends until she and her husband Drew Larssen were promoted and transferred to Fleet headquarters. The kids live in other towns on Maclairn now with their own families— our great-grandkids and great-great grandkids—but they gather here often. I'll call them tonight after you've talked to the Council and we can set a time for them to come."

After lunch Terry and Kathryn sat under the trees in her garden, admiring her patch of the sunflowers that were grown in profusion on the planet, until it was time for the meeting. She had called the Council members individually but had said nothing about its purpose except that it was important. Only to the Council Head, Kenard, had she confessed that she'd brought the Captain of *Estel* down from *Shepard* on her own authority. He was surprised, she said, and not happy; but since the situation would have to be considered by the Council, there was nothing he could do to prevent Terry's appearance.

"There's something you need to know," Kathryn told Terry. "There are two factions on Maclairn now. Most people believe we should go on as we always have, allowing contact with the League only through *Promise*, with the mentors and former observers on Earth maintaining strict secrecy. But there are some who think that since there's little prejudice against psi remaining on Earth, we should start making ourselves known to everyone the mentors train. Kenard and most of the Council members are conservatives—that's why he doesn't like the idea of having the Captain of *Estel* here. He's afraid it will lead to a push for more communication with the outside."

Terry frowned. He was going to have enough trouble winning the Council over without being opposed on political grounds.

Just before sunset, they walked over to the house where the Council met—the house that had once been Jessica's, where he had lived with Kathryn during his leaves from *Shepard*. It was a beautiful old structure of wood and stone with a great room patterned after the lodge on Undine where Maclairn's founders had formed their group. Should he mention that he'd been to Undine? Terry wondered. The Maclairnans had probably received no news of what was happening there; would the thought of the Isle of Sleep be disturbing, or would they be comforted by knowing that their ancestors had at last been laid to rest?

As he entered the great room, memories swept over him. Here he had met Jessica and his mentor Tristan; here he and Kathryn had spent their wedding night beside the huge central fireplace; here the Ritual had been held. . . .

The Council had already gathered; Kathryn had timed their arrival so that Terry could be introduced to everyone at once. Her ten fellow-members were settled on the floor cushions by the fireplace and looked up, startled by the appearance of a stranger. Kenard rose and greeted Kathryn with a nod to Terry, saying "I suppose this is the mysterious Captain of *Estel*. It's a pleasure to meet you, Captain."

Terry took his hand and smiled, telepathically projecting friendliness but closing his mind to sensing of his thoughts. "Call me Terry," he said. Since Maclairnans didn't have surnames he didn't offer his current one.

"Terry? That's an honored name among us, one of our historical heroes." Kenard looked troubled; he evidently regretted the presence of an outsider. Like all Maclairn's top leaders he was well over a hundred—he had led the Council for forty years, Kathryn had said, following Arnam, who had taken over when Jessica died at the age of one hundred thirty-three. He was, of course, a highly gifted mentor, as were several of the other Council members. Most of the rest were younger people in charge of practical affairs such as engineering and agriculture. It was an administrative rather than a legislative body; Maclairn had never needed formal laws.

They joined the others on the floor cushions and Kathryn introduced the members to Terry. "The Captain has come to us with momentous things to tell," she announced, "so last night I brought him down from *Shepard* with me."

"He is welcome, of course," said Klarysa, a distinguished-looking woman with silver hair. "But I'm surprised, Kathryn, that you took it upon yourself to let an offworlder land without consulting us. We usually vote on exceptions to normal policies."

"The Foundation has been trying to get in touch with the Captain of *Estel* for decades," one of the younger members, Niall, protested. "Surely none of us would have turned him away, though I suppose Captain Aaronson tried to."

"That was why I had to act last night," Kathryn agreed. "Aaronson was all set to send him back on today's crew transport. And you see, I was informed through another officer that he bore news about Terry Radnor."

"Terry Radnor? But he died a hundred years ago!" exclaimed another of the women, Sumiko.

"No, we only thought he did," said Kathryn, her voice strong with emotion. "*This* Terry is he, my first husband, who was taken from us by a strange turn of fate and is only now free to return. I hope you'll all share my joy and listen to what he has to say."

There was a stunned silence. Finally Kenard said, "Kathryn, we all respect you and the service you've given to Maclairn over the years. But sometimes remembered grief can do strange things to people our age. If this man has told you he is Terry Radnor it's understandable that you want to believe it—but we've seen pictures of him uncolored by old memories, and there are differences that can't be accounted for by age. For one, he seems to have regained two missing fingers."

"Kenard," Kathryn said, "surely you're aware that a loved one is recognized by mind-touch, not by physical characteristics! I could hardly be mistaken about the mind-touch of my former husband."

"There were deep bonds between you, of course," said her mentor Devan. "But when a century has passed, isn't possible that you might be feeling what you remember instead of what's coming to your mind from outside? You have no real evidence—"

Kathryn looked him in the eye. "I have evidence," she declared. "Last night Terry and I were intimate, and you know very well that the merging of minds during intimacy involves shared knowledge too vivid to be denied."

"We'll take your word then, Kathryn," Kenard said. "But there's a great deal that needs explaining."

Terry stood. He drew a deep breath and declared, "What I'm about to tell you will be hard to believe. I swear by the flame I have worn in secret through most of the past century that it is true." He opened his shirt and withdrew the lapel pin that, except during the years on Ciencia and on Draconis, had always been with him.

The Council members gasped. This, more than anything else, convinced them, for no one on Earth possessed those pins except the mentors, and if one had ever been lost or stolen, they would have been informed.

As they listened, fascinated, he recounted the events that had led to his confinement to Ciencia just as he had to Jon and Alison, not revealing the identity of his captors, and briefly summarized what had happened since. When he got to the part about the terrorists, they were overcome by astonishment and dismay—the approach of his ship had been recorded in Maclairn's history, but no one had known why it had turned back and crashed on an asteroid in a collision that was improbable, to say the least. They had not known about the colony's close escape from destruction, or why Fleet had later decided that no intruder must ever be brought to the surface.

Kathryn turned pale; he had not mentioned this incident to her before. "God, Terry," she burst out. "You might have been killed!"

"I almost was," he admitted, "but I was able to get

away in the damaged ship." Silently he added, *Don't ask why I didn't bring it here after the terrorists were dead. The Elders saved me, but I can't say so to the Council yet.*

"Now of course you're wondering what kept me from coming back to Kathryn during the years since then," he said. "Bear with me—I'm getting to that."

They had grasped enough telepathically as he talked to know that he was being honest with them, but he'd kept his mind closed to deeper probing. When there was nothing left to tell except the most important thing, Terry paused. At last it was time to take the plunge, and he did not know how to begin. They would be too incredulous if he stated the whole truth directly. He would have to ease into it somehow.

An idea came to him. He recalled that when he'd first encountered the Elders and found them telepathic, he'd assumed they must have come from another human group that had discovered the same powers as the Maclairnans. Implying this would undoubtedly make his account easier to swallow.

"It was because I didn't want to discourage your effort to teach mind-powers by revealing that I knew of greater ones of which you're not aware," he continued. "Aboard the ship that captured me I learned that there is another world where psi capability is universal, a world far in advance of Maclairn, and that for this secret to be revealed too soon would do great harm. Its people said the mentors would draw it from my unconscious mind, and later I came to see that they were right. So I swore never again to have any contact with a mentor; and only now am I free to break that oath."

"Another hidden world?" exclaimed Niall. "A world aware of ours?"

"Yes, they had a ship in this system observing Maclairn," Terry said. "That was what I sensed, and as I've said, its technology was superior to the League's; it would have gone undetected if I'd hadn't been trained in remote viewing. They were guarding us, in case something slipped past Fleet, you see. Though they prevented me from returning here, they convinced me that they mean us no harm."

"But why do they keep their presence secret from us?" Sumiko asked. "Are you sure they're not a danger?"

"Absolutely. They want Maclairn's mission to succeed—they said it is vitally important that humankind gain mind-powers, but they can't openly encourage it themselves, or even reveal their existence."

"That doesn't make sense," Kenard protested. "I suppose it's reasonable that if psi is the next step in human evolution, it might develop independently on several worlds, perhaps one advanced in technology from which the psi-gifted didn't have to escape. And they might keep it secret for the same reason we did—to avoid opposition on Earth before our ideas were too firmly established to be suppressed. But they'd have no cause to hide from *us*. If they wanted the same thing we do, they would help."

This was the key point, Terry knew. Neither his own actions or the Elders' would be comprehensible if the Council could not be made to understand the harm that would have come from premature contact.

"Suppose you had known that we were *behind* others instead of ahead, that whatever we might accomplish would be just reinventing the wheel, so to speak. Suppose you'd thought it was pointless to do what someone else could do better. Would you have made the effort, taken the risks—sacrificed lives, as at least one mentor did?"

"More than one," Devan said grimly. "You have a point, Terry. We wouldn't have made such a great effort. But we wouldn't have needed to, after all, if these others could have done it instead. The effect on humankind would have been the same."

"Really? Or would there now be two classes of people, the supermen and the rest of us who would know underneath that at the time of first meeting we were not their equals? That we had to be helped along as if we were retarded?"

"The mentors have never made *anyone* feel that way!" declared Klarysa indignantly.

"No. But Maclairn wasn't nearly as far ahead of Earth as these others are. Now that the majority of humans are open to the idea of psi, and many can communicate that way, the gap has narrowed. We can meet on equal terms, without the misunderstanding that would have come between us earlier. It had to wait until the time was ripe."

"I fail to see how our meeting the inhabitants of one small colony world could ever have had any major impact," said Kenard skeptically.

It could be put off no longer; this was the point of no return, Terry thought wryly, though he had never seriously considered backing out. "It's not a matter of a small colony world," he declared. "The people I've spoken of represent a federation of more worlds than can be counted. My life since the day I left Maclairn has been informed by one overwhelming fact: humankind is not alone in the universe. My captors, who are now my friends, are extraterrestrials; and I'm here as their ambassador because Maclairn was long ago selected as the first world to have contact with them."

~ *71* ~

EVERYONE STARED AT him, speechless. Finally Kenard said, "I assume you're not serious. You've told us a long, fascinating story, and you almost had us believing it was all true. But it's obvious that in what you just said, at least, you were speaking as the Captain of *Estel*—figuratively, as you have often done in the past. I'm not sure just what you're trying to tell us, since we're already aware of the importance of mind-powers."

"I'm telling you the facts," said Terry. "I don't expect you to believe from words alone—probe my mind now, all of you, and you'll find that I'm sincere." Letting feelings flood him, he opened his mind fully to the others' sensing, willing them to absorb the knowledge he was projecting.

To his relief he sensed, in turn, that they were responding. They were too experienced with telepathy to think he was fabricating; his conviction came through to them clearly.

"He's seen them, extraterrestrials!" Niall exclaimed. "They want contact with humankind—"

"I'm afraid not," said Devan with a tinge of regret. "The fact that Terry believes what he's saying proves nothing. I've studied the records of such things quite extensively. Throughout history there have been strange memories—of past lives, of communication with departed spirits, of channeling, and so forth—that some human minds, though pronounced sane by psychiatrists, have perceived as absolutely real when they were in fact illusions. Contact with aliens, and especially abduction by aliens, has been a common manifestation of that phenomenon. When a man who has lived apart for a hundred years suddenly returns and claims to have experienced it, it's not unreasonable to assume that he may have been subject to whatever mysterious influence caused all the other cases."

Oh God, Terry thought. He'd known that such an interpretation was likely, but hearing it stated still hurt.

"There are holes in the story," Klarysa pointed out. "He says his captors prevented him from coming back to Maclairn because they believed the mentors would learn about them from his unconscious mind. But we see that what's in his mind is mere illusion—which if such a phenomenon is common, these advanced beings would surely have predicted."

"The mentors who lived at that time, at least those

who knew me, would have known my memories are authentic because they'd linked with my mind before," Terry said. "And as long as they were alive, they'd have said so to any other mentors I might have encountered." He suspected, but did not say, that some mentors might have been more open to new ideas than Kenard and his contemporaries.

"Naturally you believe they're authentic, because it's impossible for a person to tell whether his own memories are true or false," Devan said. "We have no way of getting any objective evidence."

"You're all forgetting what I told you a little while ago," Kathryn protested. "Terry and I made love, and I have evidence from the union of our minds."

"That's valid as far as his identity is concerned," Devan agreed, "because you share remembrance of the same past events. But as to other things, lovers can know only what the partner believes, not whether it really happened."

"Listen to yourself, Kathryn!" Klarysa said. "The shock of learning your husband didn't die after all has made you believe that if he deserted you for a hundred years, it could only be because he was abducted by aliens! What would you think if someone else made such a claim?"

"I think we're being too quick to judge Terry," declared Niall. "We have no proof that his story isn't true. People have always believed there must be other civilizations elsewhere in the universe. Sooner or later we were bound to encounter them."

"We would have encountered them long before this is there were any," Klarysa argued. "We've explored the whole galaxy—they'd have found us even if we missed finding them first."

"They did," Terry pointed out. "I've told you why they didn't contact us till now. As to us finding them, their solar systems are shielded from our sight. When I was first taken to one, I thought I was lost in empty space until the shield was lowered for me."

"No doubt you have answers for any objection raised," Sumiko said, "but they get more and more fantastic! How could a star be shielded from sight?"

"As I said, their technology is superior to ours."

"Why are we arguing? Niall persisted. "Terry says the aliens want contact with Maclairn. So why don't we just see if he can produce these people, perhaps take some of us to the world he's described?"

There were several nods of agreement, but the majority shrank from the thought; Terry could sense their dismay. Like Kathryn, they didn't want his story to be true. Underneath, they feared a fundamental alteration of their conception of the world, and despite their long-standing awareness that such fear had been the cause of the opposition to acceptance of psi, they were not immune.

"To go off on a wild goose chase wouldn't be smart," declared Sumiko. "Who knows where a madman might take us? We might end up lost in deep space ourselves."

"I think we can assume that the Captain of *Estel* knows how to astrogate," said Niall dryly.

"No doubt," agreed Kenard, "but that's not the main objection. Any attempt to follow through on a proposal like this encourages the idea that we should have more dealings with other worlds. We couldn't keep it from other Maclairnans; even if it weren't that some would sense it telepathically, secrecy within our own society is not our way. Whether or not there are aliens, people would interpret our search for them as a sign that we're reaching out. And as I've said many times, to let our existence become known to offworlders would be premature—mind-powers aren't yet widely enough spread among Earth's population."

"The Elders think so, too," Terry said. "That's why they want contact with Maclairn alone, to cushion the shock it will be to the rest of humankind."

"Elders? Why do you call them that?" Sumiko inquired.

"Because their civilizations have existed much longer than ours. The species that make up their Federation are all biologically older, and further evolved." He went on, "They aren't inviting Maclairnans to their worlds yet. They'll come here first to get acquainted and evaluate individuals' readiness to become observers, the way the Foundation and the mentors on Earth select observers to come here."

"We certainly aren't going to let strangers land on Maclairn," Klarysa said. "That's against basic policy, Fleet's as well as ours."

"Well, can some of us visit their ship?" Niall suggested. "We need to settle this one way or the other, because I for one will go on wanting to know, even if the rest of you don't."

"A few believers aren't enough," Terry said. "The Elders won't show themselves unless Maclairn officially welcomes them, because if we're unwilling to do so, that would mean humankind isn't ready to explore new ways of looking at our place in the universe. To turn them away now would be tragic—you all know Earth's civilization is on the verge of collapse."

"Are these Elders going to save it, then?" Devan asked skeptically. "That strikes me as just as bad as what you say would have happened if they'd been discovered a hundred years ago."

"They won't intervene. But just knowing about them, now that we're on their level—well, it's complicated—"

"I think the issue is already settled," Kenard interrupted. "To pursue it any further is pointless since we have no reason to think it's anything more than wild speculation. But out of respect for you, Terry, we will vote here and now on whether to welcome aliens to this world."

Desperately, Terry made a final attempt to project the truth, wondering why he sensed none of the telepathic rapport he'd always felt with people he'd spoken to about

Estel. And suddenly it struck him. Psi power was enhanced by emotion—and these people's emotions were
leading them in the wrong direction. They didn't want to
believe there were aliens, and fear that there might be
made them unconsciously avoid the deep psychic probing
that would enable them to find out. The same had been
true of Kathryn until love and sexual arousal overrode
that barrier. . . .

Yet fear and love weren't the only emotions that intensified psi. Risk could do it, and dedication to a cause,
and so could strong group bonding. The Council members
had all experienced this during the Ritual, in which they
risked being burned and explicitly committed themselves
to overcoming not only the fear of it, but fear in general.
The most skilled mentors among them could probe deeply
enough under those circumstances to have full knowledge
of a willing subject's unconscious mind. He recalled the
long-ago moment when Jessica probed him, and was sure
that she, like Laesara, would have known positively that
his memories were genuine.

"Wait," he said, seeing that the vote was about to be
taken. "Don't decide something this important at an informal meeting, as if it were nothing more than approv-
ing the appointment of a new mentor! Judge me in the
Ritual, so you can see more deeply into my mind."

"The Ritual?" Kenard burst out in surprise. He hesitated, frowning. "You haven't participated for over a century and then only once, I believe. It would be dangerous
for you and for the others in the inner circle."

"If I fail, then so be it. I can prove myself only under
that stress," Terry declared. "I'm a Steward of the Flame,
and it's my right."

"He has a point," said Devan. "It's the only way we
can be sure, and in any case it *is* his right, as it would be
for any Steward."

"That's true," Kenard said reluctantly. "I can't refuse
such a request, but I'm afraid the consequences may be

unfortunate." It wasn't clear whether he meant unfortunate for Terry, or for his own well-established view of Maclairn's future.

~ 72 ~

THE RITUAL WAS set for the following evening. It was described to those invited as a celebration of Terry's return from presumed death with no comment about any additional purpose. Kenard would have preferred only Council members to be present, but the telepathic support of at least fifty people was needed for safety, as well as to give Terry a chance to be evaluated by other mentors. So as many Stewards of the Flame as would fit into the great room were asked to come.

Since the day was free, Terry wanted to revisit the places he had loved on Maclairn. There might not be another chance. "I'm not sure what will happen if the judgment goes against me," he said to Kathryn. "I may not be welcome here."

"You'll always be welcome in my home," she declared, "and considering my position and the fact that you're my ex-husband, not to mention your own status as one of Maclairn's heroes, nobody could possibly disapprove."

"Of course I want us to be together," Terry said, "yet to live out my life here, honored for my past achievements yet pitied, perhaps patronized, as an old man whose mind has betrayed him—"

Kathryn was silent. There really wasn't anything she could say, though he sensed her sorrow.

"I always thought I would give anything to be back on Maclairn to stay," he continued. "But not like that. And not without possibility of flying again, which is how it will be, since Fleet surely won't release *Estel*. They won't let a man judged unstable leave the solar system with knowledge of Maclairn's secret."

"Well, they won't know how you were judged."

"They'll find out unless I leave right away; crew members on shore leave will hear things. Besides, I've disobeyed Fleet's orders to depart. The Council can give me sanctuary, but unless it officially charters *Estel*, I'll be subject to arrest anywhere but here."

"Not on Earth; Fleet has no jurisdiction except in space." Thoughtfully, Kathryn said, "We're worrying too soon; in the Ritual you may be vindicated. But if things go wrong, I think we should go to Earth in *Promise*, which is legally under Maclairn's control. We could live with Radnor, you know. He and his lifemate would love to have us."

"That would be great for a little while," Terry agreed. "But you hate Earth, Kathryn! If you wanted to live on it you'd be there with him now. I couldn't let you leave Maclairn for my sake. Besides, I don't like Earth either, and it's going to get worse year by year if the Elders are turned away. We'll be better off here, no matter what people think of me. If I'm allowed to stay, I will, and be thankful that fate granted me one last favor by letting me regain what I lost a century ago."

He did not tell her that he had another option. Liam had said that if he failed in his mission he could choose between staying on Maclairn and going back to Ydoril . . . and he knew that no matter what human planet he was grounded on, he would never be content without contact with the Elders and their worlds. What had happened to him there could not be undone; his horizons were now wider than the universe known to humankind. If Elders came to Maclairn and took human observers to Ydoril, he would no doubt be invited to visit. Otherwise he would never see them again.

Yet the choice was really no choice, for having been reunited with Kathryn he could not endure another parting—and he knew she wouldn't consider going to an alien world with him even if it was permitted.

Word had gotten around about Terry's presence and people crowded up to him wherever he went in Petersville, knowing nothing of the circumstances of his return and eager to hear why he wasn't dead. So before long, he and Kathryn went back to the lake and hired a boat to take them to the beach at the Old Settlement, which he'd seen little of on arrival after dark. Now, early on a weekday, few people were there; no noisy crowd intruded on his memories.

This was the place he'd come to so often in dreams, the place where he'd met Kathryn at the cookout held his first evening on Maclairn . . . where two days later he'd watched her as she stood on the dock, for the first time aware that he loved her . . . where they'd come to swim many times during their life together, both with friends and alone. And where Corwin's memorial had been held by torchlight, the night he'd decided to commit himself fully to Maclairn.

He had not been here since that night, except to reach the shuttle pads on the day he left this world. Now he looked up at the stepped terraces, green with crops in contrast to the bare yellowish rock of the narrow canyon in which the lake had been created, and thought of that last time he climbed them. After a century of longing, he couldn't quite believe that he was actually here.

It wasn't the same as he remembered. It lacked the brilliance that had shone through the dark hours of his exile. And yet he knew it had not changed; it was just that the eager young Fleet officer he'd been in those days no longer existed. What was that phrase he'd seen somewhere in reading, "You can't go home again?" He still loved Maclairn, but whether or not he gained its people's respect he could never again look at it quite the same way as before. He had traveled too far and seen too much.

They walked along the waterfront to the stone monument where the names of those consigned to the depths were listed—only a fraction of Maclairn's dead after so many years, of course; now lake burial was reserved for those distinguished in some way. The entire first generation: Hari, for whom the lake was named; Anne; Kira; Jesse; Peter; Nadia . . . and later generations' leaders: Kel; Ivana; Jessica; Arnam. . . . Corwin's name, like Anne's, was there though his remains were not—and so was Terry's. When they thought he'd died they had placed it beneath the others. Long ago while on this beach, he'd had a precognitive flash in which he'd seen it, and now, though its inclusion was premature, he knew that this was where he would someday rest.

They sat on the pebbly ground beneath the trees and Terry put his arm around Kathryn's shoulder, silently communicating his love for her. After a while he saw that she was crying. *Kathryn, don't grieve!* he told her. *No matter what happens, this is where I belong. My life here may not be perfect, nothing ever is—but I have you, and being back on the one world I care about is worth whatever price I have to pay . . . .*

I'm not grieving, she told him. *Well, I am, for the pain you may face, but mostly I'm crying because I'm happy— happy that we're together again after I'd believed so long that you were gone.*

They remained on the beach until the sun dropped below the steep cliffs on the opposite shore, then headed home to bathe and dress for the Ritual. White shirts— white was reserved for the Ritual on Maclairn—with one that had been Radnor's provided for Terry by Kathryn. It was a strange feeling to be wearing his son's shirt after the years of imagining him as a young boy, which awareness of time passing had never quite overcome.

The great room of Kenard's house was crowded by the time they got there. The guests were mostly mentors, the only exceptions being the few spouses who weren't mentors themselves. Terry thought of how he'd fled from the mentor Deion on New Afrika, fearing his memory of the Elders would be drawn from him—how ironic, when he now feared that out of fifty mentors, few if any would perceive its truth.

The lights and the music were turned down and people took their customary places, standing in a semicircle around the central fireplace. Kathryn was to fully participate, as she'd been unable to do at his first Ritual because she was pregnant with their son—such stress might endanger an unborn child. She and Terry joined Kenard, Devan, and two mentors he didn't know on the opposite side of the fire. It was contrary to the normal makeup of a circle for any of the full participants to be strangers to each other, but Kathryn assured him they were among the most experienced and psychically adept of the current Maclairnans. Kenard had not cheated by bringing in someone who was less.

Terry swallowed; he knew he was taking a big risk, and not only with regard to being seen as deluded. It had been a hundred years since he'd placed his hand in fire. If he were to panic, he would be burned, and though the mentors could heal him quickly, all possibility of their probing his mind deeply would be lost. Participants in rapport too could be burned if a novice faltered; he felt troubled about exposing Kathryn to that possibility. Still, technically he was not a novice. He had been initiated as a Steward, and what he'd done once, he surely could do again.

Standing before the fire, anticipating the formal words that had echoed in his mind for the past century, Terry was aware that his entire life had been leading to this moment. This was the culmination of all he had hoped and striven for. Everything that had happened to him— his mind training, his commitment to Maclairn, his meeting with the Elders, his years of promoting belief in their mutual goal—had prepared him to serve as the herald of a new era in human history. Now that the hour had arrived, all worry ebbed away. Fate had been with him so far. If it was humankind's destiny to join a larger fellowship, it surely wouldn't permit him to fail.

"We are gathered tonight to celebrate Terry's return to us," Kenard began. "But there is a more pressing reason for the Ritual we are about to hold. You are all eager to hear the reason for his long absence, and there won't be time to tell the details here and now. The essence of it, however, is something very hard to believe. There is no doubt that Terry's account of what happened to him is an honest one, yet we of the Council feel his memory may have been clouded by some overwhelming experience he does not remember. He has asked that we probe his mind ritually, under conditions that preclude self-deception either on his part or on ours; this is his right as a Steward of the Flame. You must judge for yourselves, at the moment of full rapport, whether his recollections reflect truth."

~ 73 ~

AT KENARD'S NOD, Terry stepped forward and said, "What I'm about to tell you will be astonishing, and it may sound like a fantastic delusion. I ask you to consider not just whether it happened, but what it means for the future. I have been away from Maclairn for a whole century, and I've always, through many kinds of experiences, been focused on our goal—the goal of moving humankind forward. When my life was spared after I'd nearly lost it, I took it as a sign that I had an obligation to spread belief in mind-powers throughout the colony worlds, and I became known as the Captain of *Estel*—"

This part of the story was undisputed; the Council members' telepathic reassurance made that plain. Most of the listeners had not been told before and were awed to hear that the legendary Captain of *Estel* was not only real, but one of their own—they were well aware, from messages brought from Earth, of what *Estel* had accomplished.

"People believed in the rumors about *Estel*," Terry continued, "because it gave them hope—hope that there's more to life than just repeating what has gone before. More than the depressing routine of one day after another with nothing new to look forward to, the inertia that has robbed Earth and even the colonies of will to do more than simply exist. Isn't that what the mentors have aimed for, too? Why you, and all before you on Maclairn, have believed developing new mind-powers is important to the future?"

They were responding to him now—and it was like the speeches he'd made before, first at his trial on Ciencia and later to countless groups on one world after another. Terry felt their minds draw on his and his words came from its depths, so that he did not know what he was going to say until he heard it.

"I've read a lot about Earth's ancient history," he went on, "so I know that there have been dark times before— times when the lack of exciting challenge led some to apathy and others to producing their own excitement through violence and destruction. The twenty-first century was like that. For awhile it looked as if there was nothing ahead but doom. In parts of the world there was suffering from oppression and poverty and war, and in more fortunate regions people were in despair because they were aware not only of those evils, but of the destruction of Earth's environment and the depletion of the resources on which civilization depends. The majority were afraid underneath to see that the only answer lay in expansion into space, for space was unknown, different from everything humans had met before and perhaps full of terrors—just as people in our time have been afraid to accept the reality of psi.

"Well, eventually they woke up and did colonize space— if they hadn't, we wouldn't be here because humankind wouldn't have survived. And the League eliminated war, and the collective unconscious absorbed the conception of the universe we have today. But after awhile there was no challenge left in it. You all know what happened; conditions on Earth began to decline again. Bureaucracy took over and people stopped bothering to demand freedom, just as they no longer bothered to improve their dreary surroundings. That's less true in the colonies, but they're headed for the same end, or at least they were until the challenging idea of mind-powers came along.

"We've nearly reached our goal now—those powers are being developed, and Earth's collective unconscious has accepted them as real. That's the step in human evolution Ian Maclairn envisioned. There'll be new life in people, new desire to be free of government control, new impetus for pressing forward. Still, how long is that going to last? Have you ever asked yourselves *what comes next*?"

Terry paused and reached out silently to strengthen his rapport with his listeners; then he pushed on, preparing them for shock. "Our work has become routine—it's not touch and go anymore, not dangerous. Some of you think we should soon go public, and others want to maintain our isolation; either way, it's no longer an exciting challenge. So what now? The possession of mind-powers will help people stay healthy and live in harmony, but will that alone save civilization? And what have *we* to look forward to, except more of the same?"

They were jolted less by his words than by the underlying thought, which spread instantly among them. It had not occurred to them before. They had assumed the same goal, the one they had repeatedly affirmed in the Ritual, would always lie ahead.

"I never thought about this either," Terry said. "I was focused on the original goal. But underneath I had a greater goal, for I *knew* what comes next. I knew because I was informed by the people in the strange ship I encountered the day I left Maclairn—people not of our human race."

There were audible gasps, and the telepathic ambience shifted from dismay to incredulity. But with Terry's next words, that faded. He was offering them a way out of the black hole into which they'd briefly fallen.

"My captors spoke of a universe larger than the one we've been living in, a universe full of alien worlds with their own people, their own civilizations, a multitude of worlds that will take centuries to learn about and explore. A challenge that will last virtually forever. At the time I didn't recognize the implications, and I wasn't permitted to reveal my knowledge because it was too soon. I was told that only after humankind possessed the ability to communicate telepathically could there be contact with those worlds and their inhabitants.

He drew a deep breath and declared, "But now I have seen them. I have been there, and I've come back to tell you that the time for contact is approaching—and that for Maclairn alone, it is already here."

Shock rippled through the gathering, but the listeners' rapport with Terry held steady. They had not yet grasped enough to feel apprehensive. He knew that it would be better to deal with underlying feelings frankly than to let them be repressed, so he said quickly, "New views of reality are always frightening. People of the twenty-first century feared moving out into space; people of ours feared gaining mind-powers; and we ourselves may not want to know that there are aliens. I've met them and they're my friends, but some of you who haven't may hesitate to believe in them. But are we not about to hold the Ritual, in which we pledge to go past fear? That's one reason I chose to be judged at the Ritual—I don't want anyone's fears to cloud their perception."

He sensed Kathryn's acknowledgement and the chagrin of several Council members who had abruptly recognized their own reaction. Kenard's mind was closed to sensing.

"One more thing," Terry added. "The Flame we touch,

the Flame we all wear, is a symbol of our commitment to the use of mind-powers, but in a larger sense it symbolizes the ongoing evolution of humankind. That is what we mean when we say it will illuminate future generations. That's what it has always meant, what it meant to Ian Maclairn when he chose those words.

"Whether you judge my own experience true or illusory, keep in mind that worlds and peoples different from those we know *must* exist, for if they don't, there is nowhere to go from here—no hope to inspire future generations. Someday if not now, humankind must encounter a new universe to explore, or civilization can only slide further downhill. Don't let doubt about one man's sanity rob you of that hope."

After a few moments of quiet, Kenard came forward and pronounced the customary invocation: "In silence, let us commend ourselves to whatever Power we hold highest, each of us in our own way."

Then Niall, the torchbearer, took his place among the full participants and lifted his unlit torch high. It burst into flame, seemingly of its own accord but lit by Kenard through the same psi power that Terry had used on Undine. The small candles of the onlookers, too, suddenly blossomed into a half-circle of glowing light that illumined their holders' rapt faces.

At this point formal questions would normally be asked either of a candidate for initiation or of the assembly to be answered in unison. They had been modified, however, for this occasion.

To the group Kenard said, "Do you pledge to judge Terry honestly, determining to the best of your ability whether what you sense in his mind reflects truth or illusion?"

We do. Though a few spoke aloud, the strength of the response was telepathic.

"Will you honor your pledge to support fellow Stewards by offering him whatever aid is appropriate in the light of what you determine?"

We will. Would they decide he needed psychotherapy? Terry wondered. They wouldn't force it on him; that would be contrary to the principles on which Maclairn had been founded. But they might try to persuade him.

"Bearing in mind the precepts of the Stewards of Flame, do you pledge not to let fear of what he has told us interfere with your judgment?"

We do. They meant it, insofar as their fear was conscious; but in some it might be deeply buried.

Turning to Terry, Kenard continued, "Terry, do you affirm that what you have said about your experiences is, to the best of your knowledge, literally true?"

"I do." He spoke out firmly, at the same time projecting his sincerity.

"Do you consent to deep telepathic probing of your mind, by me and by others, for the purpose of judging the validity of your memories?"

"I do so gladly."

"Are you willing to confirm your conviction by trusting the power of your mind to protect you from physical harm?"

"I am." The mind of a person who was deluded would be conflicted, Terry realized, and might therefore be unable to focus on achieving immunity to fire. He hadn't thought of it that way; he'd expected only that both his psi capability and theirs would be intensified by the stress of risk. Perhaps not being burned would in itself prove him sane.

Kenard's probe, when it came, shook him to the core. As with Jessica, with Laesara, and with the Eldest, he sensed that all he had been or ever would be had risen to the surface, timeless and accessible; and he knew that Kenard was not the tradition-bound old man he had seemed, but a vital, psi-gifted leader whose outward show of caution belied the power and wisdom within him. Terry sensed, too, that the people assembled were drawing on that power and absorbing the knowledge Kenard channeled to them; through him, they were experiencing the memories raised by the probe and were finding them to be real.

The intense rapport faded; then as the music surged and Niall lowered the torch, thrusting it horizontally within their reach, Kenard began the traditional declarations:

"Unfaced fear is the destroyer. We will acknowledge fear and accept it, we will go past it and live free.

"We will trust the power of the mind over all restrictions, whether imposed from within or by the world outside.

"We will act always through volition, allowing neither internal nor external pressures to enslave us.

"We will support one another unfailingly in fulfilling this pledge.

"We believe that we are stewards of a flame that will illuminate future generations.

"And we now seal our commitment with the symbol of the mind's power, which is fire."

At these last words, he plunged his hand into the flame and without hesitation Terry thrust out his own to touch it, scarcely noticing when Kathryn and the three other full participants followed. Across the circle all the onlookers touched the flames of their candles, transmitting their own psi power to magnify the psi that was sustaining him. And in that moment, he perceived that no doubt remained in any of them. They had shared his memory of the Elders and knew that it was a true one, and that for them, as soon for everyone on Maclairn, nothing would ever be the same.

Mere seconds passed before the torch was lowered and he was staring dazedly at his unburned hand, overcome by the magnitude of what had happened to him—the climax of all that had happened during the century since he'd first touched fire. He was again one with Maclairn, as he had been on that night long ago, and in spirit at least, he felt no older than he had then—so much that mattered to him was yet to come.

One by one, Kathryn and his fellow-Stewards embraced him. "Your friends will be welcome here, Terry," said Kenard. "We'll be honored to have them among us."

So throughout the rest of the evening, during the customary post-Ritual feast, the mentors drew knowledge of Ydoril from Terry's mind. A day later, at the Council's invitation, Liam took *Estel* to rendezvous with the Service ship that waited nearby; and he brought Gabriel Travis and several other Elders back with him. And Captain Aaronson was told that from now on *Estel* was under Maclairn's jurisdiction and its shuttle must be allowed to land without inspection, for the presence of alien visitors must be hidden from Fleet.

Kenard sent word aboard *Promise* to the Maclairn Foundation, revealing the secret to be shared with the mentors on Earth. But the private message Kathryn and Terry enclosed for Radnor was longer and more detailed, containing the astonishing news that his father was alive and hoped that someday it would be possible for them to meet.

Terry, along with the whole Council, was at the Old Settlement to greet Liam and the Federation delegates when they landed. They were members of the team that had been observing Earth and therefore looked human; an introduction to species alien in appearance would come later. Though there was no language barrier in their case, communication was largely telepathic from the beginning, and sensing their common aims put the Council at ease.

It was a happy day that heralded an exciting new future for Maclairn and ultimately for Earth. Terry's own future, too, was bright, for Liam informed him that the work of the Captain of *Estel* was by no means finished. His ongoing job would be to travel back and forth between Maclairn and Ydoril, just he had traveled between Earth and Maclairn as captain of *Promise*, taking observers from the old world to the new and bringing its representatives to spread knowledge among all who wished to learn.

Thus he would spend his remaining years carrying delegates of both civilizations to and fro aboard *Estel*; but he would be based on Maclairn with Kathryn, and he was awed by the winding route that had brought him back to where he belonged. His century of exile was now behind him. He was home.

About the Author

SYLVIA ENGDAHL is the author of eleven science fiction novels. Six of them are Young Adult books that are also enjoyed by adults, all of which were originally published by Atheneum and have been republished, in both hardcover and paperback, by different publishers in the twenty-first century. The one for which she is best known, *Enchantress from the Stars*, was a Newbery Honor book in 1971, winner of the 1990 Phoenix Award of the Children's Literature Association, and a finalist for the 2002 Book Sense Book of the Year in the Rediscovery category. Her trilogy *Children of the Star* was reissued in a single volume as adult science fiction.

Her five most recent novels, a duology and a trilogy, are not YA books and are not appropriate for middle-school readers, but will be enjoyed by the many adult fans of her work. In addition, she has issued an updated and expanded edition of her nonfiction book *The Planet-Girded Suns: Our Forebears' Firm Belief in Inhabited Exoplanets* (first published by Atheneum in 1974 with a different subtitle) as well as three ebooks of collected essays.

Between 1957 and 1967 Engdahl was a computer programmer and Computer Systems Specialist for the SAGE Air Defense System. Most recently she has worked as a freelance editor of nonfiction anthologies for high schools. Now retired, she lives in Eugene, Oregon, and welcomes visitors to her website www.sylviaengdahl.com, which contains many of her essays, including those dealing with her long-term advocacy of space colonization.

ALSO AVAILABLE FROM SYLVIA ENGDAHL

Other Books in this Trilogy

Book One: *Defender of the Flame*

Starship pilot Terry Radnor is committed to defending the secret colony Maclairn against enemies who pose a threat to the spread of paranormal human mind powers, not guessing how far his effort to protect it will take him from everything else he cares about—his promising career as a Fleet officer, contact with people who share his newly-discovered psi capability, his wife and unborn child.. Torn away against his will after learning a secret too deep for its disclosure to be risked, he is forced to build a new life far from Maclairn. Yet a mysterious and extraordinary destiny has been predicted for Terry, and fate puts him in place to confront the colony's greatest peril.

Book Three: *Envoy of the Flame*

Ardith Moran is elated by the prospect of contact with extraterrestrial civilizations, elated enough to stake her life on her conviction that they exist after the exploratory expedition's leaders turn back. The last thing she expects is to fall in love with an alien, much less for their love to play a key role in saving Earth from tyranny and eventual ruin. As a member of the Anthropological Service, he is willing to make sacrifices and expects her to do the same. Can she, influenced by the legacy of the now-legendary Captain of *Estel*, convince Earthborn people that they can't retreat from the universe? Or will Earth's authorities succeed in killing her to suppress the evidence only she and her fellow envoys can provide?

The Founders of Maclairn Duology

Book One: *Stewards of the Flame*

When burned-out starship captain Jesse Sanders is seized by a dictatorial medical regime and detained on the colony planet Undine, he has no idea that he is about to be plunged into a bewildering new life that will involve ordeals and joys beyond anything he has ever imagined, as well as the love of a woman with powers that seem superhuman .This controversial novel deals with government-imposed health care, with end-of-life issues, and with the so-called paranormal powers of the human mind.

Book Two: *Promise of the Flame.*

Three hundred people, isolated by choice on a raw new planet in the hope of fulfilling a dream, the dream that their psi powers will become the foundation of a culture that can someday shape the future of humankind. If they don't starve first. And if they don't lose heart in the face of hardships beyond any they imagined. Starship captain Jesse Sanders hasn't expected to be responsible for the settlement, but Peter, the visionary leader, has his hands full; so the job of ensuring its survival falls on Jesse. And in the end, he must stake his life in a desperate attempt to prevent the loss of all they have gained.

Children of the Star Trilogy

An omnibus edition containing the complete trilogy *This Star Shall Abide* (known in the UK as *Heritage of the Star*), *Beyond the Tomorrow Mountains*, and *The Doors of the Universe*. Noren knows that his world is not as it should be—it is wrong that only the Scholars and

Technicians can use metal tools and Machines. It's wrong that only those few have access to the mysterious City, which he has always longed to enter. Above all, it is wrong for the Scholars to have sole power over the distribution of knowledge. Unable to believe in the Prophecy that promises these restrictions will someday end, he declares it to be a fraud and defies the High Lew under which they are enforced. His family and the girl to whom he is betrothed reject him. Yet he cannot turn back from the path that leads him to the mysterious fate awaiting heretics.

YOUNG ADULT NOVELS FROM SYLVIA ENGDAHL
THAT ARE ALSO ENJOYED BY ADULTS

The Far Side of Evil

Assigned merely to observe a young world whose people may soon destroy their civilization, Anthropological Service agent Elana finds that only she—at great cost—can prevent a war of annihilation.

Journey Between Worlds

When she reluctantly visits the thriving colony on Mars, Melinda Ashley finds love and a new way of life.

Enchantress from the Stars

A Newbery Honor book that can be enjoyed by younger readers than Engdahl's other novels, but was intended for teens and is also read by many adults. It is of interest to readers of the Rising Flame trilogy because it is where the interstellar Anthropological Service first appeared.